STORM SURGE

*To Bob
All the Best!*

JOHN F. BANAS

Copyright © 2021 John F. Banas
All rights reserved
First Edition

PAGE PUBLISHING, INC.
Conneaut Lake, PA

First originally published by Page Publishing 2021

ISBN 978-1-6624-1612-5 (pbk)
ISBN 978-1-6624-1613-2 (digital)

Printed in the United States of America

To Susan, Victoria and Megan for their patience, encouragement, and reality checks.

To Ernie for his guidance and friendship.

Sunday, August 28, 2005

"For the *last* time, *I'm not evacuating!*"

Ashley Meyers stopped packing, sighed, and spun around to face her great-aunt.

"Aunt May, you *do* realize this is a Category 5 hurricane bearing down on us?"

May shifted her weight and pulled herself upright in her favorite La-Z-Boy across the living room.

"Beau and I lived through Betsy in '65 an' Camille in '69. We took a direct hit from Betsy, an' we made it through all right. This is a sturdy building your mama sent me to. We're on the second floor. I'll be *just fine*."

Ashley shook her head in desperation. It was true that this assisted-living center seemed fairly solid; it was four stories high, and while no expert, Ashley thought it was built out of concrete.

But her ten-year-old Plymouth wasn't in great shape, and the only place she could park it was on the deserted street next to this building. But this building was only a few blocks away from that big industrial canal. If the levees failed, Ashley was sure this block would flood, meaning the end for the old Plymouth.

She really didn't trust the old car at all, but it was their only way out of ground zero.

"May, back then you guys didn't take into account storm surge. And we're below sea level here! Mom and Dad gave me your old car. It's seen better days, and I don't want to get caught in it during the storm. We *have* to leave now *please*!"

"*Oo ye yi, beb!* Dis *possede'* makin' you the *misere*?"

Ashley jumped as a big man strutted into May's suite. Despite being dressed like an orderly or male nurse, he looked unprofessionally annoyed.

Angry even.

"Who are *you*?" she asked.

The big man didn't answer but stared at her and squinted.

"This is Bruno Badeaux, and he takes care of us here," May said in a steady voice as if there was nothing to be afraid of.

Before Ashley could say anything, Bruno looked her up and down, and with an expression that Ashley could only define as distaste bordering on hate, he asked, "An' who might *you* be?"

"I'm Ashley Meyers," but before she could finish the self-introduction, May chimed in.

"This is Ashley, my niece's daughter. She attends Tulane, and she's trying to persuade me to leave before the storm."

Another once-over from Bruno, then, "Not allowed."

It was more like a growl than a spoken phrase. Ashley unconsciously took a step back.

"Ashley may have to stay with me tonight, Bruno," May offered.

"Not allowed, Miss May. You ought to know that by now."

This time, Ashley felt brave enough to answer. "Well, I'm calling my parents then. I'm *sure* they're going to be angry that this place didn't evacuate *anyone*!"

"Well, *pischouette*, you do just that. Then you best be getting up the bayou before you *mal pris*."

"Huh?"

May sighed as if everyone should understand Cajon. "He thinks you're a little girl, and he suggests you call Brenda and…Don. Then he says you better go north before you're caught in a bad spot."

STORM SURGE

By the stance Bruno was taking, full height and fists clenched with a mean-looking frown, Ashley was sure that the bad spot threat might just come from *him*.

1

"WELL, IF YOU really feel that way Brenda, I can *easily* have your husband killed."

Wait, what?

I shook my head back to reality and stared in disbelief at the man sitting on my couch. You had to really watch what you said to John Katsarus and I had just broken that safety rule.

He scooched to the edge of the cushion and sighed as if he were trying to be patient with a child who wasn't paying attention. I instinctively took a half step backward.

"Your heard me, Brenda."

"John," I said, crossing my arms, "you of all people should know me better than that! What I said was just a knee-jerk reaction, nothing more."

John shrugged and allowed that annoying little smirk to grace his face as he leaned back in the couch and cleared his throat.

"Yeah, well, you were jerking your knee very loudly."

I remained standing. If I sat down, he would have taken it as an invitation to continue with this line of discussion. I knew John only too well. I wasn't going to let him control the conversation.

"Let me be absolutely clear about this. I do *not* want Don killed. Period. Understand? For Christ's sake, John, how else would you expect me to react after what you just said?"

"Well, it's true. I can prove it."

My heart skipped a beat. Normally he wouldn't have said that unless he *did* have proof.

My mind grasped for a comeback, something, *anything* to say. I couldn't break down, not in front of John. He would swoop in for the kill and close the deal.

I tried to hide it, but I'm sure my voice broke as I reached for the armchair behind me and allowed gravity to deposit me in it.

"Oh? Let's see it."

"Okay," he said. "It's locked up in my safe in the office. Come with me and I'll show you."

John crossed his arms and smirked. He had successfully challenged my challenge. He knew damn well I'd never go anywhere with him. It would look bad to any of my neighbors peering out their heavily draped windows, wondering why John's massive pickup truck was in my driveway while Don was out. It's why I left the window shades open for all to see that nothing was going on here.

Everyone knew John and I had a history. John had seen to that at every homeowners' association meeting, every block party, and probably every time he was let into a neighbor's house to talk about insurance, annuities, or refinancing their mortgage.

But I had an excuse, a change the topic card I could play; and now was the best time for it.

"John, we haven't heard from Ashley in over twenty-four hours. I'm not going anywhere. Why don't you bring it here while I wait for her call?"

It was true. Earlier, I was popping Tums like candy because the suspense was killing me. But I had to deal with John first. Then I could focus on Ashley.

It's just that my plan was starting to backfire.

He sat up straight on the couch. "What do you mean you haven't heard from her? Wasn't she evacuating? Isn't the school evacuating?"

Great, now he was feigning concern. I could always tell when he was disingenuous and lying. That talent prevented me from making a huge mistake years ago.

"She went to check on my aunt and try to convince May to evacuate with her."

John's face morphed into what looked like a passible frown of deep concern. He stood up and started pacing.

"That car of hers, the one we insured three years back for just liability, it's not in great shape, is it?"

I bit my lip. He wasn't earning points for trying to keep me calm.

"It still runs," I said, voice notably shaky.

He stopped and looked around. "Frankly, I'm even more upset now that Don isn't here."

I stood up and made my way toward the front door, hoping the meaning of the motion wasn't lost on John.

"He went out to the store. He'll be right back," I said as convincingly as I could.

"Guess what? Amy went shopping too. Hmm."

I shook my head. This unbelievable jerk! My daughter is missing, and he pulls the conversation back to his situation!

"John, Don went to get some supplies and batteries. We're going to drive down there and get Ashley and May."

"You'll never make it before the storm. Why don't you wait? I can help you then."

I moved closer to the door and put my hand on the doorknob. "I appreciate the offer, John, but Don and I will be just fine."

Instead of taking the hint, he started pacing again.

"You just said that you'd *kill* that son of a bitch a moment ago. Now you're telling me that you and he are going to go down to a city that is probably going to flood and in the midst of the rubble, you're going to pick out Ashley and May and then get them out of there? I'm sorry, Brenda, but a lot can happen to a person in a disaster area! I believe Don wants to get you down there and get rid of you so he can continue to dance the 'Horizontal Bop' with my wife!"

I closed my eyes so hard I saw stars.

"Do you even hear yourself, John? You have money. Don's going to be unemployed when this merger is finished. Why would Amy want to have *anything* to do with him?"

He turned and, in two steps, was right in front of me, both of his hands on my shoulders.

"Consider how much either of you are worth dead, Brenda. No, I insist on driving down there with you! I have a fishing boat, damn it, and if that city *does* flood…"

"No! I couldn't survive both you and Don in the car on the way down!"

"I'll be good, I promise," he said, taking his left hand off my shoulder and raising it as if he were being sworn in as a witness.

I was about to kick him out when my cell phone rang, and when I read the display, I caught my breath. It was Ashley's cell phone number!

I ripped it open.

"Are you all right? Where are you?" I barked into the phone.

"Mom! There's a problem at the assisted-living center here—"

And that's when the connection went dead.

2

Don Meyers slammed the flip phone shut and dropped it into the Jeep Cherokee's center console.

He could feel the anger rising. It hadn't been a very productive week. The critical executive project status he was trying to prepare lacked needed input from key players on his team—none of whom were available this last week. Managing this team was like herding cats.

And his new boss's attitude was an unquestionable and obvious indication his job was going away, and soon.

Just this last Friday, he had foolishly checked his work e-mail before going home. His boss had invited him to a private meeting Monday morning, first thing, and it was earlier than Don normally arrived at the office.

Being on the *acquired* end of a merger was never comfortable. He'd been in this spot several times in his life, and with Brenda not bringing in an income right now, the bills were mounting and their savings diminishing. If he were laid off from this job, well, it was going to be a rough ride. And being in his mid-forties, it would be awhile before he would find a permanent position in another firm. If he could find one at all.

It seemed as though you were finished at forty in the information technology business these days.

He would most likely end up in contracting. But there were never any guarantees about longevity in that position; once funding was lost, the contractors were always the first to go.

Plus, you usually received no benefits like insurance. Brenda would be forced to buy their insurance from that former lover of hers, and the last thing he wanted to do right now was push them together.

He took a breath, picked up his cell phone, and dialed the number for his work voice mail. He had only one message, and it was from his boss.

"Don, I need to see you in my office at eight o'clock Monday morning. Thanks."

It was never a good thing when your boss wants to see you in his office and doesn't mention why. Unfortunately, Don knew what he was talking about. In fact, he was sort of an expert on what to look for when things went south with an employer.

That awful feeling in the pit of his stomach returned.

Logically, there was nothing more than circumstantial evidence that he would be laid off tomorrow. Nothing solid, at least. So why was he so worried? Because he'd been down this path before, of course. The phone call or the unexplained invitation to a meeting and he was the only invited attendee.

Don repositioned his hands on the steering wheel, and he noticed that he had been gripping it so hard that he had left indentations. He was too tense. But the action broke his attention from his tail-spinning career, and he switched back to the news channel on the radio.

The announcer said that the huge storm had moved even closer to land. It seemed like it was headed straight for New Orleans.

He reached for the cell phone and hit the speed dial button assigned to Ashley's mobile phone once more.

The call quality was bad, and it went to voice mail. Either she'd turned her phone off or the system was down already.

Damn it! He closed the phone and set it down again.

Suddenly, the air was split by the phone's ringtone, and the tone was unique to Ashley.

"Ashley! Where the hell have you been?" he nearly yelled into the phone, not even trying to hide his emotion.

"Dad?"

"Ashley, where are you?" he asked. It was hard to hear her over the static and road noise. He looked for a place to pull over.

"Dad, I have a problem. I can't reach Mom. I went to check on her Aunt May. The assisted-living center didn't evacuate any of the residents, and there's hardly any staff left here!"

"Well, hold on, where are you exactly? Didn't you go with the school evacuation?"

"Like I said, I drove over to check on Aunt May. May's okay, but they didn't evacuate her or anyone else. And she isn't budging either!"

"Look, Ashley, I don't care how much May protests. You need to load her up and get outta there!"

"Uh, that's the other thing, Dad. Remember I told you my car was acting funny? Well…um, when I got back in to repark it, it sort of started smoking and the check-engine light came on, then the temperature gauge went off the scale. I checked the oil and it's really low. I'm afraid to start it again. I'm going to get a ticket or towed, and all my stuff is in it!"

Don took a deep breath. Brenda had wanted to go down there and find Ashley. New Orleans was a good thirteen- to eighteen-hour drive. He did the math; there was no way they could safely make it before the storm.

"Okay, look. Hunker down with Aunt May. That building, if I remember correctly, is made of concrete. Stay in an inner room, fill the bathtub with water for drinking, and wait it out. You don't know how many days you're going to have to stay there until someone comes for you."

"Dad, it won't be safe. They say the city's going to flood!"

"Stay focused, Ashley. Get everything out of your car and up to May's room, then sit tight. Stay away from any windows. You'll be all right. Just don't panic, okay?"

He paused, waiting for the inevitable objection, but it never came. When he glanced down at the phone, he found he was no longer connected.

3

"C'mon, damn it," I said, realizing too late that John was listening intently.

There was just no reconnecting the call. I was starting to fear the worst, and John was right. Don should have been back by now.

While I had been stabbing at the phone, John had remained silent, and it finally dawned on me that, for now, he didn't seem to be trying to barge back into my life like he had for the last two decades. For now, anyway.

After the fourth or fifth time I tried to call Ashley, I realized that I wasn't going to be able to talk to her anytime soon.

I honestly don't remember if I started shaking then or after I looked up at John. I had my mouth open, wanting to say something or scream or just throw the phone against the wall.

John was oddly silent. He said nothing. He just shoved his hands in his pockets and stood there, looking at me and seemingly at a loss for words. But I knew better. At least I thought I did.

"I can't reach her," I mumbled, holding out the phone and pointing to it as if he had no clue what I'd just been trying to do.

He bit his lower lip and allowed a hand to sweep through that thick black mane of his. He nodded slowly and turned toward the door.

"That settles it then. I'll go get my boat."

Dear God in heaven, I couldn't let that happen! The strategy shifted to polite mode with unholy frazzled woman in reserve. I could be very good at that.

"No, John, I can't let you do that."

He turned abruptly, as if angry. "Why?"

Why? Don't get me started.

"This is *my* daughter, John, and she's *my* responsibility. I can't ask you to take time out of your businesses and risk your boat and your health to help us."

He was nodding, but he seemed upset. Perhaps even angry. I felt like he was just about to lose it but hadn't a clue as to why.

"Okay, look, if this has anything to do with…us, you an' me, we have to put that past us. Doesn't Ashley deserve the best assets on this…I don't know what you'd call it…*rescue* mission?"

I honestly had no idea how to answer that. So I stumbled forward, winging it.

"Look, not *everything* is about you or us or our *history*. I appreciate it, but to be honest, do you *really* think that it's wise to have you and Don locked up in a car all the way down to New Orleans? One of you wouldn't survive!"

He nodded. Good, at least he agreed with me on one thing.

"Have you tried the police? The school?" he asked.

"All day long. The school plays a recorded message, and it's Sunday, John. Even the police won't answer. I'm not even sure I have the right number."

He nodded again, looked away with a really serious expression, then he turned back to me.

"You're running out of options, Brenda. I can control myself even if Don can't, or won't. You're going to need help on this. Think about it for Christ's sake, Brenda!"

"Don't think I haven't, John. But really…"

"You likely will need a boat. I have one uniquely suited for this mission. You need to be prepared for anything. Plus, I really owe it to you."

"You don't owe me anything, John." I was heading back to the door. I knew where this was going, and I just couldn't deal with it now.

"Why do you think I've kept up with you all these years? I've… I'm…I feel guilty. It's all my fault, and I've been trying to figure out how to make it up to you. Why won't you let me?"

"Oh pa-leeze, John! You made your choice, and we've both moved on. I am *not* going to discuss this now! I have to pack and find out where Don is."

I was about to twist the knob and show him out. I never should have agreed to this meeting without Don in the first place. All our financial decisions should be made together, and prepping for unemployment by refinancing and reducing our insurance wasn't my decision to make alone.

Plus, I now knew why John really wanted to meet with me. I found it hard to believe, but there was always that doubt. Amy Katsarus and Don, it just didn't make sense!

So it had to be some sort of scheme on John's part. It *had* to be.

And I had to push it out of my mind because I had to focus, Don and I, on Ashley and May. This trip wasn't going to be easy.

I *had* to.

Just as I started to twist the doorknob, my cell phone rang again.

"Ashley?" I said, not looking at the display as I opened it.

"No, but I heard from her."

Don's voice jumped out of the little speaker, entered my ear, and hit my brain like a freight train. I forgot all about John, Amy, and Amy and Don.

"Is she all right?" I nearly blurted out.

"We got cut off. She's at that assisted-living center you dumped May in."

"What did she say?" Yes, the ding Don tossed out wasn't lost on me; I just had other priorities than another fight about money.

"She's trapped. That Acclaim finally packed it in. I think you're right. We're going to have to go down there and get her."

I glanced at my watch, completely forgetting about John.

"If we leave now, we might beat the storm," I said, but in my peripheral vision, I caught John shaking his head violently.

"Better to leave *after* the storm hits, Brenda. We could get caught out in the open on the way down there. And let's face it, neither of our Jeeps are in mint condition," Don said.

"They say the city might flood, Don. We need to get there as soon as possible." I looked over at John to make sure he heard this so he'd leave. When he didn't and actually stepped forward, asking for the phone, I just panicked.

"And you know I was meeting with John Katsarus today about the refinance. He heard about Ashley and offered his boat to us," I said carefully, knowing that I had just lit the fuse.

"What the—"

I didn't let him finish. "But I couldn't concentrate on business, Don. I was too worried about Ashley. So rush home and we can pack."

I thumbed the End button quickly and shut the phone as an afterthought, as if that would ensure I had locked out Don's looming explosion.

John walked past me to the front door. "I'll tell Amy and then I'll be back with the boat. I'm not taking no for an answer, Brenda. You two aren't exactly outdoor types."

Damn it! He *was* right. Don could hardly change a flat tire.

"John, I—"

"You know in your heart I'm right. I take back everything I said today, Brenda. You're right, you moved on. But you need help. Even Don would admit that. So I'll be back soon."

And he was out the door before I could even say anything. Oh god, what did I just get myself into?

But he was right, and that's the irritating part. We were going to need his help no matter what it cost me. So I went upstairs to start getting ready.

And to try to figure out how to keep Don and John from killing each other on the way down.

4

Ashley caught a glimpse of her reflection in the huge glass doors that separated the outside world from the assisted-living center's lobby. And in that transparent, ghostlike image staring back at her, she saw the strain she was experiencing.

Her cell phone's battery just reached 10 percent charge, and that was the end of her link to the outside world until she could recharge it. Of course, recharging would take awhile, and that was time she may not have.

That fact was causing deep lines across her forehead, and she turned away from the reflection.

The Claude Avenue Assisted-Living Center was billed by its owners and operators as an oasis for the *life experienced*. Some oasis. More like a desert island, with her and her great-aunt as a part of the castaways, and the real shipwreck was yet to come.

Taking a deep breath, she put her now-useless cell phone in her hip pocket and pushed on the door. The hot humid air immediately rushed in to envelop her and that only increased her anxiety level.

Her Plymouth was parallel parked at the west end of the block. Claude Avenue should have been jammed with traffic at this time of day with people coming home from their weekend excursions, bemoaning the fact that their playtime was ending and another forty hours of hard labor lay ahead of them.

But the street was empty. This part of New Orleans looked like a ghost town, and that was a good sign to Ashley.

It wasn't the best of neighborhoods. Gang graffiti dotted the side of the very building in which she was going to have to ride out the storm, and just walking down the block made it clear that the neighborhood had seen better days.

Slowly, cautiously, she made her way down the sidewalk toward the car which happened to be the same color as her great-aunt's hair. In fact, the car had been Aunt May's until she had to move into this place. May had given it to her parents to use, and they had given it to her.

Some gift. It had only lasted a year. Now it was nothing more than an expensive and somewhat large boat anchor. Ten years old and useless.

Ashley dug her key out and brandished it like a weapon. Moving faster now, she wanted to grab her bags and get back to the relative safety of the May's building.

Relative was correct. That Bruno Cajun dude wasn't apt to let her stay, but it would be virtually murder to kick her to the curb. Somehow, she didn't think that would bother Bruno at all.

On top of that worry, with only one or two staff members present, the next few days were going to be rough on the residents.

They were basically all left on their own. There were bound to be lawsuits in the aftermath of the storm. She just hoped she and her great-aunt wouldn't be the reason for one of them.

Ashley focused on her car as she walked quickly from the center's front entrance steps. Outside, the air was still, and an uncanny silence fell over the area; in fact, it seemed like the whole city had bugged out.

But as she drew near the trunk of her car, she noticed several figures across the street. They were too far away and in the shade of the storefronts for her to get a good look at them, but it was obvious when they had seen her.

They stopped short and pointed.

Ashley at once tried to put the key in the lock, but her hand was shaking a bit. Finally, after another attempt, she got it in and turned it. The trunk clicked open and she raised it to grab her backpack and duffel bag with the Tulane name and emblem on it.

What made her nervous was the fact that the raised trunk lid blocked her view of the people across the street.

At this point, she didn't care if she forgot something; she just wanted to get back to the relative safety of the center. And lock the damn doors.

She slid the backpack on and put the duffel's shoulder strap over her head. Then she slammed the trunk lid and got the shock of her life.

There were four of them, and they had crossed the street. Even though they were on the far side of the intersection just to the west of her, they looked menacing. And they were pointing and staring at her.

Ashley wasted no time. She broke out in a run toward the steps, hoping to hell that no one had locked her out. That would be the end of everything.

She felt like she had forgotten something. That deep-down nagging feeling in the back of her mind and the pit of her stomach plagued her as she ran. But the sound of their footsteps, clearly running too, lit a fire under her, and she must have set some sort of record in getting back to the steps.

She took them two at a time despite the extra baggage. As she reached out to the door and pulled, she could hear them shouting to her.

"Hey! Where you goin' so fast, *beb*?"

The door opened and she slid in easily, pulling it shut. As the four young men bounded up the steps, she found the Allen wrench key hanging by a string from a nearby fire alarm box and quickly slid it in the hole made for the locking mechanism.

The handle popped out. Mission accomplished. The door was locked.

But that didn't stop the gang from rattling it. Heart pounding, Ashley quickly moved past the threshold into the lobby and started heading for the stairs. Behind her, she could hear the shouts and catcalling and the occasional rattling of the doors.

She'd made it, for now. She'd beaten one danger, but the worst, she figured, was yet to come.

5

John Katsarus guided his Ford F-150 swiftly through the streets of Brenda's neighborhood development. He lived on the other side of town, but it would take him less than fifteen minutes to get to his house. When he came to a traffic light, he finally reached for his cell phone.

He glanced down at the devise as the light remained red and dialed the number he hated to dial most. It was answered after a full four rings.

"This better be good."

"Every opportunity is *good*, and that's what I want to speak to VT about," Katsarus said.

"That's Mr. Taccone to you."

"Yes, yes, that's what I meant. I have a plan that needs Mr. Taccone's approval, and he's gonna love it," Katsarus said.

"About what?"

"It's rather *personal*," Katsarus said, trying not to let his contempt for the person on the other side of the connection come through in his tone.

He knew full well who he was speaking to—Tony Zanetti, lieutenant to Vincent "VT" Taccone. Zanetti was said to have been personally assigned to his position by Taccone's father.

Katsarus was convinced that Zanetti's job description was simple: stay attached to VT at the hip and fix whatever gets broken by the prodigal son. Word was that Zanetti was the real reason for the success of VT's businesses. And that meant that speaking directly to the overprotective Zanetti would likely mean Katsarus's offer would never be heard and the chances of getting out from under his debt would be nil.

Katsarus disliked having VT as a major investor in his businesses. But when business went south six months ago, Katsarus was forced to make one of his famous deals, and now VT was a full partner in Katsarus Financial Corp., a holding company for a mortgage brokerage, insurance sales, and smaller annuity offerings.

This further investment by VT did not receive Zanetti's blessing; Katsarus had successfully performed an end run around the formidable wall of projection, so naturally Zanetti had it in for him.

In short, the only reason he was still breathing was because VT was in too deep.

"Mr. Taccone is in a meeting. I'll give him the message."

Katsarus squeezed the steering wheel hard. He knew he was being lied to, but what could he do? These weren't the kind of people you started an argument with; ultimately, they settled the argument—their way.

"Is that you, Mr. Zanetti? I almost didn't recognize your voice. We must have a bad connection. I have a proposal for Mr. Taccone that will resolve a lot of problems."

"He's tired of hearing your proposals, especially since the last one isn't working out so well."

"What if I had a foolproof way to pay off the interest on the loans that are underperforming?"

"Those loans you asked us to finance aren't just underperforming. They're not paying no matter what we do. This is a problem, Katsarus. And it's about to come down on your head. You have sixty seconds to convince me or I'll kill your wife."

Wouldn't that be just too bad? John thought sarcastically.

"I'll do it in ninety if you promise to make it painful," Katsarus said, gearing up for the sales pitch of his life.

6

AFTER JOHN PULLED out of the driveway, I rushed about the house knowing full well how upset Don was going to be. He was going to come home ready for a fight.

But I didn't have time for an argument now; I wanted to get upstairs, pack quickly, and get back downstairs before John got back with his boat. Of all the people in the world who should not be left alone together without supervision, Don and John topped the list.

If those two were left unsupervised, there was a better than even chance there'd be bloodshed. I paused and considered that last thought.

John wasn't really *serious*, was he? I mean, I knew he was in business with some pretty smarmy people, but would he go that far as to take Don out?

I pushed the thought out of my mind. For about three seconds. No way. There was *no way* John could be serious. This trip was about saving Ashley and Aunt May. It would take all our energy to find and rescue them.

Still, the uneasiness I felt only got stronger the more I thought about it. The next forty-eight hours were going to be hell. The two men that will be prominent in my life during that period of time hated each other, and we will all be trapped together in a rolling metal cage for up to eighteen hours.

Suddenly, I heard the garage-door opener rumble to life. Game on.

I sprinted to the service door and popped it open. As the outer door rose to reveal the grill of Don's green-and-rust-colored Jeep Cherokee pulling into the garage, I mentally ticked off the pros and cons for bringing John along. I was going to need plenty of ammo.

Pulling up to the tire stop was agonizingly slow. Finally, Don cut the motor, and after a brief moment, his door clicked open.

I took a deep breath.

"I take it that since Katsarus is letting us use his beloved scow that he's coming with," Don said in response.

I sighed. "That's my understanding," I said calmly, trying to look normal while hanging out the service door.

"What *fun* that will be," Don said as he walked over to grab some toolboxes and stuff them in the cargo area of his Cherokee.

"He'll handle the boat, Don. Face it, neither of us are exactly Horatio Hornblower. There is no way John is going to entrust his beloved boat to you or me or anyone, for that matter," I tried to say as calmly as possible, knowing this was on the verge of going to go south quickly just by Don's body language.

"Did you ask him, or did he offer? I thought today was about the refinance options."

"It…it started out to be. Which makes me wonder why you weren't here too."

Don reached into the Jeep and brought out a few of the things he had purchased, and he made a big show of unwrapping the items. He unwrapped ropes and bungee cords and rearranged them in the back of the Jeep. He even walked over to the shelves against the far wall and grabbed two coolers and dumped a bunch of ice from four large bags in them.

"Don't you want to wash those coolers out first?" I asked.

"You still haven't answered my question about how John came to be going with us, Brenda."

Not to be petty, but I snapped out an answer. "And you haven't answered me about not being here."

He sighed and held up the empty bag of ice that he had just emptied into one of the coolers. "We needed supplies."

I nodded.

"He offered when he saw I was distracted and worried about Ashley," I told him, turning toward the service door to the mudroom, hoping that action would end the conversation.

I was wrong.

"That son of a bitch is going to try something. John Katsarus never does anything for anyone else. It's always for *him*. You more than anyone else should know that."

I tried, really tried, to keep walking toward the service door to the mudroom. I really wanted to hurry and pack. But then Don forced the issue.

"Why is he *really* coming, Brenda? Are you *fucking* him again?"

Ever hear words that you could swear physically hit you when they reach your ears? Well, those words kicked me in the stomach. With the remnants of John's words about my husband and John's wife, Amy, still ringing in my head despite the logical side of my brain denying it, I lost it.

I turned slowly, no longer worried about packing in a hurry.

"What did you say?"

Don just frowned and closed the hatch of his Jeep, making tiny rust particles fall from underneath the wheel wells.

"Did you ask if I was having an *affair* with him? John Katsarus, the very person who *cheated* on me and caused *us* to end up together? You should know better, Don," I said as calmly as I could, but I was shaking. "I'm not having an affair!"

And I left it like that. I doubted he was smart enough to read in between the lines for my implication by tone of voice. I watched him carefully though, and when he made no expression or sound, I turned and marched through the service doorway, slamming the door as hard as I could.

Upstairs, I changed into a short-sleeve shirt and some light shorts. Nothing too heavy.

Toiletries were easy to pack, but I made sure I had extra rolls of toilet paper, just in case. We had no idea what we would be facing.

As I opened the door to the walk-in closet, I passed the framed desktop picture of Don's deceased sister, Rene, on his dresser. She died in front of him, and it really messed him up. He'd had a tough upbringing.

For a moment, I felt sorry for him.

But only for a moment. I—*we*—had a daughter to find and save.

I thought about what to take. It would be hot and humid. I remember Aunt May telling me stories of what it was like after Hurricane Camille.

The hottest time is right after the storm passes.

So it will be shorts, cargo pants, two more tank tops, a few Columbia shirts, and four pairs of socks. It should all fit nicely into my Weekender.

I even grabbed my wide-brimmed Tilley hat, made for outdoor adventures. And knowing how Don burns, I grabbed his Tilley as well.

Hurrying downstairs, I opened the door to the garage and got the shock of my life.

John was pulling up in the driveway with his huge "I'm compensating for something" pickup truck towing the tiniest boat I'd ever seen. It was an open boat—no cabin or shelter from the elements. It had an outboard motor and one wooden bench seat in the back behind the steering console.

But I dropped my bags on the garage floor not because the size of the boat was the issue. Oh no, not today. Today was a killer bad day because of all the worries and bad news and now, on top of everything else, this.

Sitting next to John in the front seat was his wife, Amy.

7

Tony "The Torpedo" Zanetti walked through the double doors of Vincent "VT" Taccone's walnut-paneled office. He found his boss sitting on the plush couch, not behind the massive mahogany desk. It was unusual, but his boss was watching preseason football.

It was an important game. He knew VT had a lot of cash riding on the outcome. He didn't give a shit. Zanetti knew what everyone else in the organization knew; the prodigal son was screwing up the businesses, and while Daddy covers for the son, other heads roll.

And Zanetti, like everyone else in the know, was sick of it.

It was starting to cause a revolt among the rank and file. Plans were being made. Leaks to rival organizations developed. Revenue was down 15 percent year over year.

Tony the Torpedo waited in the doorway and cleared his throat softly, not caring if he had sounded impatient.

VT closed his eyes and forced his attention away from the wide screen. Zanetti could almost smell the annoyance, but he knew that his boss was well aware he normally wouldn't bother him with trivial matters.

"What is it?" VT sighed, muting the big screen.

"It has to do with Katsarus. He has an unusual request. Well, for him, that is."

VT narrowed his eyes, and the frown telegraphed extreme displeasure. Usually, some poor bastard would pay for transgressions—real or perceived—when that expression appeared.

Zanetti wasn't worried. He'd tussled with many men a lot tougher than this pampered prick.

VT set the remote down and got up to sit at his desk. Zanetti waited while his boss pulled open a large and ornate grandfather's clock and reached in past the pendulum case, touched the back wall in a certain way, then pulled the back wall open to reveal a safe. A few quick keystrokes and VT was reaching in to pull out a file.

Zanetti respectfully waited while VT examined the file. His boss's expression only got worse.

Finally, VT looked up and rubbed the bridge of his nose.

"It seems Katsarus has a plan to get current, or should I say make up for the bad loans he pawned off on us? He just needs our help," Zanetti said quietly.

"He'd *better* have a plan to get current. The last four loans he fronted for us needed collection activities."

Zanetti knew what that meant. Too many of these collection activities and the loan would be written off with disastrous implications for the borrower and the front man. Katsarus had been on the bubble for far too long.

VT sighed. "What does he want?"

"Seems he has a way to, ah…realize a windfall."

VT leaned back, mildly interested now. "How much?"

"Claims it's about a million two. Maybe a little more."

The eyes narrowed again. "And he's also said that these borrowers he introduced us to were good for the repayment, even at our interest rates," VT reminded him.

"Well, apparently, this deal he has cooked up is the husband of a former girlfriend of his. She's headed for a divorce, and she doesn't want to pay the lawyers."

"So?"

Zanetti ignored the tone. "Well, seems there won't be enough marital assets left after the legal process takes place. The guy is heavily insured, though, and as it turns out, she has a house with about a quarter of a mil in equity."

VT was deep in thought. "Any children?" he asked.

Zanetti nodded. "A daughter attending Tulane University," he said.

"And her place in all this?"

Zanetti shrugged. "Flexible. Depends on her cooperation afterward. Katsarus seems to have set himself up as her financial adviser."

VT kept thinking. After a few moments, he shook his head.

"Big risk. Also, this will only get Katsarus current. There will be a fee for the hit."

"He knows. Katsarus has agreed to our terms. So you want to do this?"

"How did you leave it with him?"

Zanetti shrugged. "Usual noncommittal until I spoke with you."

"Hmm. Well, what do *you* think?"

Zanetti was ready for that question. He was ready because this pimple never made a decision in his life other than to select the blond or the brunette.

"I think the usual fee is too low. This is a hazardous undertaking."

"How so? The target related to or in law enforcement?"

Zanetti shook his head. "No, the hit itself will be easy, and where he wants it to happen will be a natural for eliminating any evidence."

"But you don't leave evidence anyway. So what's so hazardous?"

"The target and his wife, Katsarus's former girlfriend, are leaving tonight for New Orleans."

VT's eyes narrowed again. "Nawr-lens? What the hell? Why there? He does know about that damned hurricane, right?"

"They're going to retrieve the daughter. And they don't know where the hurricane is going to hit just yet, but bets are it will impact New Orleans. It would be a lot easier to cover our tracks in a disaster area."

"Sounds like you've given this some thought."

Zanetti finally referred to his portfolio and his notes.

"JK will bring the target to a place called"—he referred to his notes—"Claude Avenue Assisted-Living Center. That's where the hit should take place. They're traveling by car, bringing down Katsarus's fishing boat. We'll need a boat too, and if we use the corporate jet, we should be down in time to meet them tomorrow about noonish after the hurricane moves on or dissipates. I'll check with the pilot about options."

VT looked stern. "You know what my father always says. *No loose ends.*"

No loose ends. How many times had he heard that? Zanetti wondered. It's what drove the family. It was the mantra of their success.

No loose ends.

VT tapped his fingers on the desk as he looked out toward the pool. Finally, he turned to Zanetti.

"This thing is a Category 5, last time I heard. It's not going to simply fall apart when it makes landfall. Make sure the pilot knows his options. I don't want to die trying to kill someone."

"You're comin' with?" Zanetti asked.

"I wouldn't miss this for the world," VT snorted.

Zanetti instantly changed his mind about this contract. As usual, VT's trail of loose-end tie-ups led a breadcrumb path right to them. If it weren't for the Senior Mr. Taccone's money, lawyers, and connections, VT would be wasting away in prison.

And Zanetti would be keeping Jimmy Hoffa company.

Dying in a plane seemed like an easy way to go compared to what the Senior Taccone would do to him if his son caused problems again.

"So let's get ready," VT said, and the conversation was over.

And probably their lives unless he could talk his boss out of tagging along, Zanetti thought.

8

Ashley was sweating profusely after the trip to her car and then toting her bags up to May's room. May had been watching Ashley from her favorite La-Z-Boy recliner since the TV no longer worked.

"You look frightened, dear," she said to Ashley.

"Yeah, I am. I've never experienced a Category 5 hurricane before. I'm scared to death," she said, dropping her backpack off on the floor next to her other bags.

"Oh, now come on, Beau and I survived the worst Mother Nature could throw at us, in a skimpier building too. I already told you that we're on the second floor and the industrial canal is blocks away. We're not going to have to tread water, dear."

Ashley wasn't convinced. "That's the thing. It's just blocks away and not miles, or whole states away. It's closer than I would like."

Ashley went into the bathroom but kept the door open. "What are you doing?" May called.

"Filling up your tub for drinking water."

"My, my. You really are worried, aren't you? When Beau worked on the oil rigs, they brought him ashore and we just hunkered down. We had a hurricane party with our neighbors. It helped pass the time."

"The *alcohol* helped pass the time, Auntie. Mom told me stories. You were lucky to live through it."

"Oh, you're just overreacting, like your parents. We were tougher back then."

And not as well-informed about storm surge, Ashley thought. "I read that there were a lot of deaths at a hurricane party during Camille and that the water got up to twenty-eight feet in the storm surge," she shouted back over the tub faucet spewing water.

"There weren't no deaths at my building party. We had some flooding, but we were all right."

"But, Auntie," Ashley said, sticking her head out of the bathroom, "this storm is three times as large as Camille. We're bound to get hit harder. Any hurricane pushes a wall of water in front of it, and that storm surge is like a slow-motion tsunami. If we don't get out of the way, we could be caught in it and drown."

"You seriously worry too much, dear."

Ashley shook her head and turned back to filling the tub. All her friends at school weren't concerned either. It was just a big adventure for them. Now on the bus north, they would be having a great time with no studying for a while. She, on the other hand, was stuck with May, who denied the killer nature of this storm. They'd both be lucky to make it through unscathed.

That was seemingly the last word on their conversation for a while. As she watched the tub, she became mesmerized by water swirling around as the tub filled up. Waking up when she nearly fell into the tub, she realized that a she'd lost maybe five or ten minutes and hurried to shut the tap off before the tub over spilled.

When she walked back out to the bedroom, ready to continue her attempt to make May see the danger, she was startled to see Bruno attending to May with an IV.

It seems that he was just as startled to see her as she was to see him.

"I thought I tol' you to get!" he barked in a thick Cajun accent.

"Oh, that's my grandniece," May said proudly. "She came to check up on me before the storm, but her car broke down."

"You already introduced us, May."

Could it be that May was experiencing the onset of Alzheimer's? How was she going to break that news to Mom?

The nurse frowned. "Car broke down, did it? That *make the misere*, for you, eh, *beb*?"

She shrugged. "Yeah, I have no idea what you just said."

"He said, you're having a bad time," May translated.

"Yeah, that's for sure."

"Where you gonna stay at, again?" he asked slowly.

Ashley could have drilled holes in the back of his head with her glare. Challenge accepted!

"Here. There's no other place for me to go."

Bruno's permeant frown seemed to deepen. "I already tol' you, you no gonna stay here. You a *Texian*, an' you can't."

"I'm not from Texas and I can't go anywhere else. Might I remind you just how bad this looks for your center? All these poor people here, and you guys didn't even evacuate them!"

"Well, you stayin', it's against policy," he said.

"Well, you can't throw me out in the storm because my dad will sue this place already for not evacuating my aunt, and I'm stayin' right here."

"What if I give you a room across the hall, all for your own?" Bruno offered.

Ashley hesitated; it sounded like a bad idea. She'd be all alone, and who knows what this guy was capable of.

But Bruno read her mind. "Yeah, I got a master key, but that room has a chain and you can put a chair up against the door if it makes you feel better."

"I'll be right here, across the hall, dear," Aunt May slurred.

"What are you giving her?" Ashley asked Bruno.

"Oh, something to help her sleep."

"What?"

"You wouldn't know what it was."

"I'm majoring in chemistry at Tulane. I damn well would know!"

"Company policy. Are you her guardian?"

Ashley shook her head angrily. She knew where this was going.

"Then I can't tell you. But I can help you with your bags over across the hallway."

"No, thanks, I can move them," she said, still angry. "Why is that room vacant, by the way?"

Ashley was hoping that the person had evacuated.

"He checked out."

Bruno was still frowning when he said that. "Oh," Ashley said. "Where did he go?"

Bruno smiled for the first time since she met him. "Well," he said, "he died."

9

My mouth was suddenly very dry, and I could tell by the look on Amy Katsarus's face that she was at least as uncomfortable as me. When Don noticed her, he immediately busied himself with loading my bags into the back of his Jeep.

His discomfort only seemed to reinforce John's claim about Don and Amy. Suddenly, I wasn't as sure about Don's fidelity. As a consequence, I was beginning to feel very alone.

I stood there at the garage-door opening while John and Amy climbed down out of his truck. Amy nodded to me, and I returned the gesture without a word. Don, on the other hand, just had to open up his mouth in the first volley in what was to become, I was convinced, the new Battle of New Orleans.

"That boat gonna be big enough to hold all of us? Even Ashley and May? Are you going with us, Mrs. Katsarus?"

"My wife needs a car. She's just here to drive the truck back," John said gruffly.

Well, I thought, *we're all off to a jolly start!*

Don wouldn't stop. "But that boat, is it going to big enough?"

"It's a Boston Whaler. It can float completely flooded. It will handle whatever your daughter and relative can stuff into it," John said, dismissing Don's concern.

"Isn't that what they said about the *Titanic*?"

It was obvious that Don's concerns, real or imagined, annoyed John, but I was amazed that he held his tongue. Instead of replying, he reached into the bed of his pickup truck and unloaded a duffel, along with several heavy-looking toolboxes.

As Don opened the rear hatch of the Cherokee, he mumbled that his question was never answered. Thinking this could get nasty and since John was really trying to be cordial, I felt the need to stop Don from continually poking the beast.

"Uh, Amy, would you like some coffee or anything?" It was all I could think to ask at the moment. But John interrupted with, "She's okay."

Amy shook her head and just said, "Um, no, thank you. I'm fine."

I couldn't tell if she was feeling the same thing I did, but she was at least good enough to smile politely. This was obviously as uncomfortable for her as it was for me. Why the two men weren't feeling as uncomfortable as we were, I'll never know. Or maybe they were, and this constant back-and-forth was their way of dealing with it. Either way, all of us were tense.

I was definitely not looking forward to the rest of this trip.

Don shook his head and reached for a yellow toolbox. Immediately, John grabbed if from him with a bit more force than I think he wanted to.

"Uh, sorry, these are my father's tools, sentimental value and all. I get kind of protective of them," he said when we all looked at him strangely.

John walked over to the Cherokee and put the yellow toolbox on the floor just in front of the driver's seat, then went back to tossing the rest of his stuff in the cargo area. Don even got one of his toolboxes and put it in the back.

Then John got in his truck and started the engine, backed it out of the driveway, and parked his truck and boat at the curb on the street.

We all stood around and watched him unhitch the truck and then move it back up the driveway.

When he got out, he asked Don, "I'm guessing you never towed anything by the looks of that hitch. Do you have a ball?"

"What are you talking about?" Don asked.

John closed his eyes, the epitome of patience.

"The ball for your trailer hitch. It fits in there," he said, pointing to the receptacle under the rear bumper of Don's Jeep.

"That? It came with the car when we found it on the lot."

John sighed and headed to his truck and took a part off his hitch, brought it back to the Jeep, and installed it quickly.

"Get in and back your Jeep down in front of my boat. I'll guide you and show you how to hitch this thing up."

Don shrugged, but he started the Jeep and backed it down the driveway. John made sure he went down to the boat, lest Don ram it or something, I guessed.

Amy shook her head. "I don't envy you on this trip. I hope you find your daughter."

I stammered something like, "Uh, thank you."

I thought that would be the end of it. After all, we were standing alone up at the top of the driveway, trying to be polite even though she just might be sleeping with my husband, and for all I knew, she might have suspected me of sleeping with hers.

Finally, she cleared her throat and looked at me as John guided Don in backing up toward the trailer, then going through the motions of hitching it up.

"Look, Mrs. Meyers, you need to be careful down there."

Well, thank you, Mrs. Obvious, for telling me something I already knew. I guess my expression sort of gave away what I was thinking even though I didn't even look at her and kept my focus on the two men, lest they come to fisticuff.

I managed, "We will, of course."

She turned her whole body to face me now, and I couldn't help but to side glance her.

"You don't understand, Brenda."

"What do you mean?" I asked as I saw the two men walking up the driveway.

She saw them too, so she didn't have much time.

"You need to keep your wits about you! All is *not* what it seems," she said.

I just stared at her and blinked. She was frustrated that I wasn't getting the message, but Don and John were within earshot.

"Please be very careful." Then under her breath, she hissed again, "All is *not* what it seems!"

10

In the cramped back seat of the Jeep, I craned my neck to watch Amy Katsarus stare after us as we pulled away. When we turned the corner at the end of the block, Amy finally gave up staring and walked toward the big pickup's driver door.

But the last sight I had of her was the worried look on her face.

She knew more than she had been able to tell me. We should have been so very uncomfortable speaking to each other, but she seemed so...*driven*, and it was really unnerving.

What could possibly be that troubling to her? This was just another thing to worry about, and I had plenty of that—Ashley, May, getting there before the storm, now probably only just getting there before it hit and having to hurry out, and, of course, Don and John forced to share the same small space together for eighteen hours.

And of course, John's casual mentioning he could easily have Don killed.

All this started to wear on me, and my stomach started to ache. It did that when I usually got in over my head at work.

But at least we were on the road now.

John was driving while Don occupied the right front, leaving me in the back. The arrangement was, in John's words, so Don wouldn't wrap John's beloved boat around a street sign. Don, amazingly, said nothing.

As we were negotiating the twists and turns to get out of the neighborhood, John glanced at me in the mirror.

"So what were you and Amy having such a spirited conversation about, Brenda?"

I was caught by surprise at John's question and frankly didn't know how to interpret it. So I gave an answer that I thought would satisfy him and end the conversation.

"She just asked me to be careful." Not a complete lie.

Now Don turned back to face me. Why would *he* be interested?

"So what did you say to her?" he asked.

I caught John's glance in the mirror again. He seemed calm, but you had to be blind not to see that he was concerned about my conversation with Amy.

"I told her that you two were expendable, and if I could, I'd come back alone with May and Ashley so I wouldn't have to deal with your nitpicking each other all the time."

"Not funny, Brenda." Don has no sense of humor. Never had, never will.

But they both dropped it, at least for now. Relieved I wouldn't have to discuss the conversation anymore, I took out my phone and dialed Ashley again.

"Who are you calling?" Don asked.

"Amy. We're best friends now."

"Cut it out. I asked you a question, and I believe I deserve an answer," Don said, more than just a little irritated.

John was smiling. He was enjoying this. A lot.

When I couldn't reach Ashley, I swore and called the assisted-living center again. Again, there was no answer. So I called the police nearest the center.

Again, I got an answering machine!

"Isn't anyone left in New Orleans?" I said out loud, angry and getting more and more worried about Ashley and May. My knuckles were turning white because I was gripping the phone so tightly.

"In case you're interested," Don said without looking at me, "there's a Category 5 hurricane headed toward the city. I doubt that they're going to answer. And Ashley and I got cut off, remember?"

"Thank you for your kind, calming words there, Don. I can understand you're not being worried about May, but do you have to be so flippant when Ashley is concerned?"

I folded my arms as if that would protect me from any further escalation and waited for the inevitable return volley. It came from a surprising source.

John sat up straight in his seat and gripped the wheel with two hands, hard, with a twisting motion as if he were anxious about something.

"Look, you two," he said calmly, "we are in a situation here that could be very dangerous. We don't all get along and we're all stressed to the max because we're stuffed in this situation together. If I have caused any of this, I'm sorry, honest. I hope that the fact I'm taking time out from my businesses and offering the use of my boat, should we need it, can, in some small way, make up for this discomfort I've caused. But let's try to work together, okay? We're going to need all our wits and skills and we all have a different set of them. Okay?"

It was a nice sentiment, but knowing John, I couldn't help but think it was in some way positioning himself as the good guy. It sounds bad, I know, but that's how my defense mechanisms work.

Yours would too if you knew John like *I* knew John.

Don said nothing but sulked and stared out the passenger window.

"See, I'll pay for dinner, okay?" John offered.

No one said anything. I closed my phone and put it in my duffel bag, then sank back into the seat, wondering how this all was going to end.

I was in the middle of World War III. I knew John and didn't trust him. And I knew Don as well, but he had really started to change in the last year. He wasn't the kind, understanding man I had known in college. I knew that Amy Katsarus was concerned, but about what exactly, I didn't know.

I did know that I had find Ashley to save her from the aftermath of a killer storm.

And everything I knew told me that this *thing* between all of us was going to get in the way of rescuing Ashley and May.

It may even kill us.

11

"Can someone turn on the radio?" I asked.

We were bumping our way along the route to I-355 to connect to I-55, which would be a straight shot south to just outside New Orleans.

They both raced to see who could reach the knob first, and since Don wasn't driving the car, he beat John to the radio. He tuned in the premier Chicagoland news radio station.

"And despite Mayor Nagin having made his evacuation order mandatory today, traffic levels have not increased. Mayor Nagin went on to say in that press conference that, 'We're facing the storm most of us have feared,' and the National Weather Service has issued a bulletin predicting, and I quote, 'devastating damage.' Residents have been ordered to evacuate, but just in case, the Superdome has been opened as a refuge of last resort, for those residents who can't obtain safe transport out of the city. The Louisiana National Guard has delivered three truckloads of water and seven truckloads of meals ready to eat to the Superdome, enough to supply fifteen thousand people for three days. Over four thousand Army National Guard and over nine hundred Air National Guard members have been deployed."

"Turn it off," I begged. This was news I didn't need to hear. Don punched the radio.

"Superdome, huh? That's information we can use," Don said smugly.

"Why?" I asked him. "Didn't you tell Ashley to stay put in that old building with May? And how is she going to get May to the Superdome, especially if the city floods like everybody seems to think? The Superdome is on the other side of town from the center and May's in a wheelchair. If that damn *thing* hits the city tonight, they might get caught out in the storm, at night, with no protection and—"

I knew I was building up a head of steam and was actually thankful for Don's interruption. "Ashley's not stupid, Brenda. She got into Tulane. She won't risk getting caught. Plus, with her car dead, she's stuck."

"That doesn't make me feel any better!"

My heart was racing and my temples pounding as each blood cell tried to squeeze its way past my skull.

John spoke softly, "Don, you've been there before, what kind of building is it?"

"It's made of concrete and is four stories tall. Most of the first floor doesn't even have residents' rooms. It has the kitchen, offices and cafeteria stuff. May's room is on the second floor."

"So," John went on as if he were a lawyer proving a point, "May is *above* any potential flood then?"

Don shrugged. "I would think so."

It was painfully obvious that this was all for my benefit. And I was appreciative of their forced teamwork to make me feel better. But I was so exhausted that my mood had not changed.

"What if it floods deeper than that? And what if they lose power, which is practically guaranteed, how will Ashley get May up to higher floors?" I asked no one in particular.

"She'll find a way," John said.

It was supposed to calm me down, but it came out as condescending. John never really knew Ashley, so how could he be so confident?

So John's attempt to calm me down was just another attempt to get me to trust him again. I never would.

After finding John in bed with my roommate, I had a revenge date with Don. Well, from that date, I managed to get pregnant.

At least to Don's credit, he did the right thing and tried to make a life with Ashley and me, but let's face it, it wasn't working anymore.

It was exhausting, getting so worked up. I tried to shut my eyes, but my mind was working on the plan, identifying risks, feeling out backup plans, and trying to even the score in my head.

But the risks were winning.

12

It was late and Zanetti was dead on his feet.

The regular pilots weren't available for this trip, and that was a problem. Too many loose ends.

This is probably what Mr. Taccone Sr. wanted to see him about in person and not over the phone.

This was not how Zanetti wanted to spend his evening. He had too many details to take care of still—the artillery, the boat, the identity badges, and the plan once they got down there.

Now he was going to have to put some of that stuff off for the flight down, and Zanetti hated working aboard airplanes. It made him sick, and he'd rather just nap and not experience the flight at all.

Besides, if he threw up in the plane, VT would never let him live it down.

The mansion in Oak Brook was massive. Zanetti turned down THE HALL and eighty feet away was THE OFFICE. Guarded faithfully by two huge foot soldiers, no one was getting to Mr. Taccone Sr. without his say-so.

He stepped right up to the two guards standing watch and addressed the one of his left.

"He wants to see me."

The guard, who was dressed in an impeccable tailored suit, nodded. "We know."

"What kind of mood is he in?" Zanetti asked.

The guard shrugged. "Who can tell one minute from the next?" he asked.

Zanetti nodded and straightened his collar, ran his fingers through his hair, and waited while the other guard picked up the phone on the table and waited. Finally, he spoke into it, "Mr. Zanetti is here."

They both hit the Enter button on their separate keypads, and after a few clicks, the two massive doors swung open.

It was a great honor for the senior Taccone to immediately get up and come around his desk to greet Zanetti, especially with the walker. Zanetti made sure he bowed and grasped the old man's wrinkled hand with both of his.

"You honor me more than I deserve, sir," Zanetti said, and he meant it.

"Nonsense. You are my right-hand man," the eighty-three-year-old wheezed. "Let's not get gushy. You and I both know your value. Now I have a job for you."

Taccone motioned him to sit, which he obediently did as the old man leaned on his walker with his backside on his desk.

"I hear you're off to New Orleans."

Zanetti nodded.

"And Vinnie is going with you?"

Again, Zanetti nodded.

"Look, who are we kidding here? Vinnie, he has no business going down there. Vinnie will fuck it up. You, on the other hand, are a professional, and I have no doubt in my mind you'll fulfill the contract."

Zanetti suddenly noticed how tight his collar was. In fact, it seemed that the room was heating up too.

"My son, he thinks he's me. A younger me," it was a well-placed pause and smile to which Zanetti dutifully smiled back as if it were actually funny. "And we both know he's *not*. He's a *loose end*, and you know what I always say about loose ends?"

"Yes, Mr. Taccone."

"But he's my *son*."

Zanetti found himself squirming in his chair, and since it was leather, it sounded like he was expelling gas, making him even more uncomfortable.

"So while I don't tolerate loose ends, I need you to prevent that little shit from becoming one and burning down the house with him, *capisce?*"

Zanetti nodded uncomfortably.

"You have all the authority you need, Tony. Understand that. You're in charge. I'll back you."

Zanetti stood up and extended his hands. "Thank you, *Don Taccone*. I won't let you down."

"I know you won't. Now *buon viaggio.*"

Clasping the don's hand with both of his again briefly as a sign of respect and gratitude, Zanetti received his blessing. It didn't make him feel much better about this trip, especially since he had a nasty job to take care of, another loose end, and VT himself had ordered this loose end tied up.

It's just that Zanetti really, really detested resolving loose ends that happened to be women.

13

I WAS MISERABLE in the back seat of the Jeep. The motion was making me nauseous, and the stuffiness because of an aging, ineffective air-conditioning unit, along with the greasy hamburger I wolfed down when we last stopped for food, wasn't helping.

Don was on his phone, probably checking his voice mail. John's phone rang, startling both Don and me.

He picked it up, glanced at it quickly, then said, "I have to take this." He apologized, flipped it open, and growling his last name.

We couldn't help but to hear John's side of the dialogue. "Yes," he said. He was trying hard to speak in generic sentences.

He went on, "Yeah, I know…No, I gave you directions. You could meet us there. No, there won't be any problems…Yeah, I know, no loose ends. So do we have a deal? How long? Well, I need to know as soon as possible. Yeah, okay."

John hung up quickly and glared at his phone. For a moment, I thought he was going to throw it against the dashboard.

When he glanced at me the mirror, he asked, "What?"

I was sitting with my arms crossed and somewhat angry. I've been known to look at things from the pessimistic side; it was one of Don's biggest issues with me, but it really is a defense mechanism. It keeps me from being rudely surprised in life. And if I were wrong about a situation, I'd be pleasantly surprised.

"What do you mean, what?" I asked.

He forced a laugh. "Sorry about that phone call, Brenda. I have three businesses to run, you know? This was just another business deal on a problematic property. There was trouble with the inspection. It's going to be hard to sell the mortgage," he said, trying to reassure me.

I was anything but reassured. Mostly, it was because of John's track record, or lack thereof, with the truth. Something about that call just smelled, but I just couldn't put my finger on it.

As far as John was concerned, however, the conversation was over, and he went back to focusing intently on driving, seemingly wide-awake now.

I wasn't going to get anything more from him. So I turned my attention to Don, who was just hanging up and turning to stare out his side window. He looked kind of pale, and instantly the warning buzzers went off in my head.

"Everything all right, Don?" I asked.

He said nothing for a minute, and for every second of silence, my mood sank deeper.

"Just that I was supposed to be in a meeting tomorrow and my boss is pissed," he said.

"Is there a problem?" I asked cautiously.

"Look, why don't I drive for a while?" Don asked John, and I got the distinct impression he was avoiding answering me.

John nodded, and as luck would have it, we were passing a sign advertising a service area about two miles ahead. It was a convenient way to ignore my question, but I wasn't going to be so easily ignored.

"Don? Is there a *problem*?" I repeated.

He shook his head and resumed his stare out the window.

I knew this behavior. It usually preceded a rant about the world and how it mistreated him. Something was wrong, and it was probably about work and far worse than he was letting on.

Especially in front of John.

As we pulled into the gas station, I had the door open before we even came to a full stop at the pumps and rushed off to the bathroom, Don right behind me.

When I came out of the bathroom, I found Don just a few steps ahead of me.

"Don! What a minute. I need to ask you something," I said.

He paused, but his shoulders slumped, a sure sign he wasn't in a mood to answer me. I wouldn't get anything out of him about work, so I started in on the other problem festering in my head.

"Don, before we left, Amy Katsarus said something to me that concerns me a lot," I started, and immediately I had Don's full, undivided attention.

"What did she say?" he asked carefully.

I looked around to see that we had the bathroom hallway to ourselves. When I was sure we did, I turned back to him. His face was expressionless, but he was definitely tuned in.

"She told me to be careful. All is not what it seems. What the hell does *that* mean?"

He never flinched, but he never took his eyes off mine either. "How the hell am I supposed to know?"

"It doesn't mean *anything* to you?"

"Why would it?"

"Well, what do you make of it?"

He shrugged. "She wants that boat and John back safely. Anyone would say that."

"But," I pressed, "she looked *really* uncomfortable."

"Let's see, her husband is going down with us to a likely disaster area ravaged by a killer hurricane, John being the only source of income, our destination filled with looters, floods, pestilence, Armageddon. Why on earth would she want *us* to be careful when this is going to be such a cakewalk?"

Then he turned to walk away, but I wasn't done.

"Don, really, how is everything at work?"

Now he dramatically stopped and threw his head back, as if rolling his eyes with his whole body. "My boss isn't happy, but he'll get over it because this is a family emergency!"

Then he walked away without even looking at me.

He was obviously hiding something. But I would get nothing more out of him before whatever it was he was hiding hit us like a ton of bricks.

I nearly punched the door open and walked out to the Jeep and trailer. John had taken the several gas cans he carried in the boat and had set them on the ground to fill. I walked up to him, debating whether I should ask him about Amy's comments when he looked up and quickly turned back to filling the cans.

"So what was it you were chatting with Don about in such an animated way?" he asked me without looking away.

I could have brought up Amy's statement, and I could have told him the truth about my concerns that Don was really getting laid off. But that would have given him more power over me because it would have meant I trusted him.

"Nothing of consequence," I said.

John flicked an eyebrow but said nothing.

"You know I was just having a knee-jerk reaction to what you said back home, right?"

He stopped and looked at me, then turned back to his task. "I get it. I was just kidding too."

His unconvincing answer did nothing but start my stomach butterflies up again.

I was about to ask him straight out what his phone conversation was about, but the clatter of a diesel engine broke my train of thought, and even John looked up.

One of those Humvees made popular by the first Gulf War lumbered up to the diesel pump on the other lane, and four soldiers dressed in full camouflage leapt out, the driver going around to the fuel hose.

I glanced at the soldiers, who were checking us out. I sighed and turned away, flicking glances back every now and then while I thought about what I should ask John.

But most of them kept staring at me. Had they never seen a woman before? Then I noticed their expressions. They weren't just checking me out; they were frowning.

I turned, realized what they must be thinking; we were towing a boat, on the southbound side of I-55, loaded with bags and tools, and all of a sudden, I knew why they were staring.

They were not happy about us headed south, and they just might have the power to end our trip, right here and right now!

14

To my absolute horror, John looked up and nodded to them. "How much farther to New Orleans?" he asked.

I froze. Was John out of his mind? Why draw attention to us if going down there was taboo?

The nearest soldier shrugged. "Eight to ten hours, I guess."

John, ever the bombastic bull in the china shop, didn't just stop there. Oh no, he had to push it. "You guys headed down there too?"

"Got called up today. Illinois National Guard. Are you going down there too?"

"CERT, Community Emergency Response Team. We're headed down to help out search and rescue. You think there will be much looting?"

I positioned myself on the other side of John from the soldiers and kicked his feet. *Quit it!*

Another soldier laughed. "There's always looting. We figure it's going to be massive."

"Then we'll be looking for you guys," John said. I was on the verge of punching him.

"I didn't know you guys could self-deploy," the second soldier said.

"We just got trained. We're not that organized yet. But what an opportunity to put the training to good use, huh?"

"If you say so, sir."

"John," I interjected, "your can is nearly full."

He glanced down and made a snide comment. "What are you, a miser? It's only half full," he said.

To my credit, I held my tongue and didn't repeat the mistake I made earlier today about wanting to kill someone. I just wanted to get in the Jeep when another of the soldiers spoke up.

"I got to warn you, guys. It's pretty disorganized down there too. You might have a hard time getting into the city because it's just one big cluster fuck, excuse me, ma'am! No one knows what they're doing."

"How are they controlling the search teams?" I asked.

"They're not, so far. My suggestion is you hook up with a convoy or something," said the first soldier.

"Good to know," John said, looking at me. "Thanks!"

By this time, Don had come out of the store and walked up to us. "What did those Army guys have to say?"

John shook his head as he hoisted the gas cans back in the boat. "They're not Army guys, Don. They're National Guardsmen."

I jumped in before Don could return the volley. "They said to be careful and it's a mess down there. No one knows what they're doing, and that's going to be bad for us CERT people," I said, warning him about the excuse John used.

"They think we're CERT?" Don asked. I rolled my eyes and reached for the Jeep's door.

Everyone climbed back in, with Don behind the wheel and a very nervous John sitting in the right front seat.

As Don started the engine, John went into his wide-turns lecture, and I'm sure Don, like me, tuned him out.

Don put the Jeep in Drive, but before he got his foot off the brake, there was a tap on his window, and all three of us jumped.

Outside, one of the guardsmen was bending down, waiting for Don to roll down the window.

When the window opened, the guardsman leaned on the windowsill.

"Just a word of advice, folks. We've all be given orders to shoot looters, so just be careful, all right?"

None of us said anything, but Don nodded. "Good to know," John managed to stammer.

I couldn't help but look at Amy's warning again in a new light. *All is not what it seems.*

15

Towing a trailer didn't seem to be nearly as hard as I would have thought.

Don was making it look easy, and by now, we were near the Missouri-Arkansas line. I was even feeling comfortable enough to try my hand at driving this rig when Don got tired. But that would require me to be rested, so despite my worries, I needed to try to get some sleep.

I slouched deeply in the seat, with my knees up on the front passenger seat. But it was useless, not because the position wasn't particularly comfy, but I was too worried about Ashley and May.

I tried the center again from my cell phone. It rang and rang and rang. I didn't even bother to leave a message this time. Then I tried the police department where I got a fast busy signal; the circuits were down or busy. It was maddening, but I'd never lived through a hurricane before, so I had no idea what to expect.

John, our resident expert in the outdoors might, but he was sleeping—fitfully anyway. Not that I was overly concerned about his welfare, but we needed him to operate the boat, and he needed his rest, so I wasn't going to bother him with trivial questions now.

So despite my angst, I tried once more to get some sleep. But of course, I was fixating on the sturdiness of the assisted-living center and the integrity of the windows, the levees around the city, and the neighborhood surrounding the center.

None of these thoughts were positive. I spent a few minutes staring out the window at the scenery on I-55 heading south.

That is, what I could see of it.

It had begun to rain, and the sky was fairly dark with no moon and no stars. Being out in the country, the only lights were from the passing and oncoming vehicles on the interstate. Going north, there was a lot of traffic, but not so much heading south with us. Whatever traffic was going our way was passing us.

After a while, I could feel myself drifting off, my head nodding and then me snapping awake, then drifting off again.

That all ended when a semi approached us from the left rear, hell-bent on passing us in the rain.

As the truck approached, the wave of air it was pushing hit the boat and trailer, making them move over to the right side of the interstate, toward the shoulder. This drew the Jeep in to the left, nearly into the lane that the truck was using. As it did so, Don turned the wheel quickly to the right to correct.

But it was an overcorrection, and the wake of the truck, once the cab passed the boat and neared the Jeep, the slipstream seemed to suck the boat and trailer back to the left, away from the shoulder and nearly in to the semitrailer itself. This, of course, pushed the Jeep out to the right, and Don turned the wheel hard to the left.

Fortunately, the semi passed us before we got sucked into his lane completely, but we continued to corkscrew down the interstate with no sign of it stopping as Don made one overcorrection after another.

Finally, a hairy arm flashed across the center console and grabbed the wheel so firmly that Don could not move it.

The Jeep careened toward the center median but corrected itself after a heart-stopping half second flew by. John then made small, very minor adjustments, and the Jeep aligned itself with the trailer in the center lane, one lane over from where we started this roller-coaster ride.

I let out a breath. Then as the sound of a shotgun going off echoed throughout the Jeep's interior, I held my breath once more as a fishtailing, vibrating sensation jarred everyone and everything in our world.

Sitting up now, John had both hands on the wheel. "Ease off the gas! Ease off the gas, damn it!"

Don took his foot off the accelerator completely, and John fought the wheel. Eventually, he got the upper hand and we managed to end up on the left shoulder in the median, and once we stopped, John put the transmission in Park.

"Jesus H…When I said to ease off the gas, I meant to fuckin' ease off the gas," John yelled when everybody was breathing again.

John took a couple of deep breaths before he spoke. I could only guess he was trying to calm himself.

"A semi pushes a lot of air at speed, and it has some fairly expected aerodynamic effects on trailers being towed by cars or light trucks. You can't get too close to them. You need to keep it in the middle of your lane or even give them a wide berth and move away from them," he explained tersely.

Don's hands went to his seat belt. "That's it. I've had enough of Captain Bligh here. God knows this is the first time I've ever driven anything while towing, but I have to perform up to expert level. You want to drive your way? You drive."

Don got out and walked back by the trailer.

"You *could* take it a little easier on him, you know," I prodded John.

"Yeah, well, he *could* have listened to me earlier when I was trying to show him how to drive something like this," he replied.

"Hey, Captain Crunch, you got a flat on the trailer back here," Don yelled.

"Yeah, no shit," John muttered, grabbing door handle violently and opening it. I got out too, following John back to the boat. This had all the earmarks of a fight, and I needed to refocus everyone.

"That's what happens, Don, when you overstress a tire," John started.

Don followed quickly with, "Well, whose fault is that, oh great outdoor sage?"

"Look you two, this is *not* helpful in getting us to New—"

I was interrupted by the flashing of red-and-blue lights behind the boat. We had attracted the attention of some sort of cop, and I held my breath. Could he stop us from going any farther?

16

I watched John glance back at the Jeep, then toward the cop. He was clearly concerned, to put it mildly.

John started walking back toward the patrol car as I wondered why he should be so nervous around a law enforcement officer.

I managed to catch a glimpse of Don. He was watching John walk back to the flashing lights, and then he turned toward me.

I knew that look. He looked just as bewildered as I felt.

It had started raining, and Don walked back to the Jeep. When he got there, he reached for the back door and got in.

I could either stay out there and get soaked or join him in the car. Against my better judgment, I joined him in the Jeep, climbing into the front passenger seat.

I wasn't going to say a thing. I didn't want another fight or to rile him up in front of the police officer.

But his fidgeting in the back seat finally extracted a response from me.

"What's wrong?" I asked.

"He's still talking to the cop," Don said, twisting back in the seat to try and see John through the rain. "He's going to get us thrown in jail with his bombastic lies."

The rain was starting to come down a little heavier now, and Don got out of the Jeep to get in the driver's seat again.

"You sure that's a good idea?" I asked him.

"What makes you think I'm going to drive?" he asked me.

"I…I don't know. You're sitting in the driver's seat maybe?" I said, trying to sound *very* sarcastic. I don't think it worked though.

Don felt around under his legs, immediately finding the yellow toolbox. My heart went up to my throat.

"What do you think you're doing?" I hissed at him, glancing back to see where John was. I couldn't see or hear him talking to the cop. By the time I looked back, Don had the yellow toolbox in his lap between the wheel and his stomach.

He was about to open it when the rear hatch was opened, causing both Don and me to freeze.

"State trooper is going to help me change the tire. You two stay in here nice and dry while I fix this thing. Don't touch anything, okay?" John admonished us.

"Sure," I said.

Don frowned and said nothing.

John grabbed the proper tools and closed the hatch. I immediately turned to Don.

"Put that thing back before we get caught again," I hissed.

Don turned to me and smirked. "John just got his tools out of the rear hatch. Why do you think he left this toolbox here?" he asked me.

"How should I know?" I asked through my teeth, half looking at Don, half back to the boat to see what John was going to do.

"Aren't you the least bit curious?"

"No!"

"C'mon, Brenda! Use logic. He grabbed the tools to work on the tire. He told us this box contained tools. Why didn't he take it?"

"I dunno! Different kind of tools?" I continued to divide my time between Don and the back of the Jeep.

"Well, let's find out." He started to unsnap the latches.

"You can't do that! It's private property!"

"I most certainly can! This is *our* rescue trip. We're in charge here, Brenda. We have a right to know what may prevent us from making it, and thinking about this, I thought it was really suspicious the way he was way too protective of this box," Don said.

Okay, he had me, but I didn't like it one bit. If John came back and found us searching his personal stuff, he could refuse the use of his boat. Don was going to sink us before we started.

"Don, you shouldn't do—"

But it was too late. He had the box open and was staring at the contents. When I looked down, my heart stopped.

17

It took us both a few full seconds to realize just what we were seeing.

Don was the first to recover. "Did you know about this?" he asked, staring me straight in the eyes.

I shook my head slowly. I couldn't take my eyes off the contents of the yellow toolbox. My nerves were on edge already and this, this just made the trip a whole lot darker.

"Just what do you think he was going to do with these?" Don asked.

I could probably guess, but there was no way I was going to tell Don right now, not when he was just about ready to mix it up verbally with John and now this.

Inside the yellow toolbox were two semiautomatic pistols, one a lot larger than the other. They were in leather holsters, and underneath them were neatly piled magazines filled to capacity with ammunition.

Frozen to my seat, my biggest fears had just been confirmed. I could only imagine what Don must be thinking. I gathered all my courage and slowly lifted my eyes to meet his.

"What do *you* think he was going to use them for?" I asked him carefully.

Don looked at me for a few seconds before he answered. "There's only one use for these things. To shoot someone or something," he said deliberately.

"Do you think there are wild animals on the loose down there?" I asked him.

"Of the humankind."

"Well, looting and robbery do occur in a disaster area," I offered, hoping against all odds I was correct. "Maybe he brought them for self-defense. Maybe to defend us."

"Maybe," Don said, hardly convinced.

Then my immediate fears rushed back, and I looked toward the boat again. "Well, if you don't put that away, you may as well ask him when he gets back. But then there's that cop," I warned him.

You could see the lights go on in Don's head, and even he looked back to see where John and the trooper were.

"I just may…later," he said and started to close the box but then stopped.

I looked back for John again and didn't see him. When I looked back at Don, what he was doing scared me even as much as finding the guns.

"What are you *doing*?" I asked.

"I'm taking one. You said that John may have brought these for self-defense. I think that's a pretty good idea," he said, tucking the smaller gun inside the huge pocket on the leg of his cargo pants. He left the holster in the yellow toolbox but grabbed two of the smaller magazines.

"You can't do that!"

"Stop me."

I glanced back again. No sign of John, but I felt the Jeep move. "Shit! He's coming," I nearly screamed.

"Relax," Don said calmly, looking in the mirror. "He's just getting started. He's jacking up the boat. But we don't have gobs of time," he continued as he stated to close the lid of the toolbox.

"Hey, Einstein, it's going to be lighter now that you took a gun and those magazines," I reminded him.

He stopped. "You're right. Look, I need a couple of wrenches from back there. Can you get them?"

"You mean you want *me* to crawl back there and get some of your tools?" I asked incredulously.

"Yes."

Well, I knew he couldn't risk being caught armed with a dangerous weapon if the cop saw him and searched him. "Damnit," I uttered as I crawled painfully back to the rear seat and reached over the back into the cargo area.

"What do you want?" I asked, just as someone outside was making a lot of noise.

"Three or four wrenches. It doesn't matter which ones, just the bigger ones."

I moved a few things around and finally found Don's tools and opened it. I grabbed three heavy wrenches as I felt the Jeep shimmy. *John must be taking the tire off*, I thought.

I needed to hurry.

I handed the wrenches to Don, who put them in the yellow toolbox and shut it, hefting in the air.

"Feels about right," he said as I climbed back over the seat to get in the front.

"Just hurry up and put that damn thing away," I hissed.

Don closed it up and slid it under his legs again. I breathed a sigh of relief, but it only lasted a nanosecond.

"Have you ever handled a gun before?" I asked him.

"How hard can it be?"

"Oh god."

"Relax. These things are easy." He pulled the gun out of his pocket and checked out. It appeared to be loaded as it had a magazine in it already. That made three magazines Don had for this gun.

He pushed a button on the side of the grip, and the magazine fell out of the handle into his hand.

"Oh, Jesus! What are you *doing?*" I demanded, looking back now. The Jeep was moving again. John must be taking the trailer down off the jack.

"It's loaded all right," Don said, snapping the magazine back home and pocketing the gun again. This time, he made sure he buttoned his cargo pocket.

Then he did the unthinkable. He got out and back into the back seat, right in front of the cop and John.

Great. That's all we needed—an overconfident newbie gun handler, an experienced outdoorsman who probably knows his way around guns, and a cop.

Not to mention John had asked me if I had wanted him to kill Don. This exposed a whole new layer to this trip, and I was starting to regret allowing John to come with.

18

THERE WAS NO way Ashley was going to sleep in that bed, not if the elderly gentleman who lived in this room previously had died in it.

It was late. Maybe close to midnight. She was sitting up in the recliner, trying to watch TV, but the cable had stopped working. She thumbed the remote and set it down on the table next to her chair as the TV went blank. She rubbed her eyes, trying not to think about how great some food would be right now.

Maybe May would have a bite to eat if she were awake. But how could anyone sleep with the storm coming?

She moved over to the window that looked out on Claud Avenue. Rain strafed the street, and she found it funny that the traffic lights were working but there was no traffic. She could even see the back end of her broken-down Plymouth weathering the storm nicely as it sat, useless and decaying, next to the curb.

The funny thing was, the rain was coming from the northeast, not from the direction of the storm. Odd, she thought, but then she realized that May's room was on the north side of the building, and it would be taking the full force of the storm when it hit.

If these were just the outer bands, the main event would be intense.

She'd better make sure that May was staying away from the windows. And if she might have something to snack on, well, even better!

Ashley moved her bags over to the bed and set them up on top, just as if it were a table. She dug out her toiletries and put them in the bathroom, then, as an afterthought, filled the tub while she still could.

When the tub was filled, she shut off the faucet, and her stomach growled noisily. It was time to see May, but only if the woman was awake. No sense in disturbing her; Ashley got the impression that the woman could sleep through the worst of hurricanes.

She slid the chair out from under the doorknob and undid the chain. Then grabbing the key from the nightstand where Bruno left it, she checked it in the door. Yes, this was the key to the room.

The hallway lights were dimmed, and it was difficult to see. But she could still hear the storm outside. It was an intermittent type of rain—cats and dogs one minute, then calm the next—but lightning kept flashing outside the two large windows at either end of the hallway.

Her room was down one door and across the hall from May's. She carefully made her way along the carpeted hall with the cheap wallpaper toward May's room, but the door didn't look right.

As she neared it, she realized something was wrong, terribly wrong.

The door was left ajar, and Ashley's first thought was her great-aunt scooting her wheelchair around in the dark and dangerous hallways with the two large plate glass windows at either end. Not to mention, of course, the curved stairway leading down from the open second floor balcony in the middle of the floor, right over the lobby.

Should she check the stairs? The thought weighed heavily on her, but she was so close to May's room that it would be prudent to check there first. At least she wouldn't have to wake May up to get inside, if May were still asleep, that is.

When she got to the door, she listened carefully. Something was going on inside the room, and she didn't want to startle May for want of giving the elderly woman a heart attack.

But this wasn't right. The lights were on, barely, in the hall and no lights coming from May's room.

But May's chest of drawers was getting a workout. Ashley heard what she thought was a drawer being opened and then closed a moment later.

This didn't make sense; if May was looking for something, wouldn't she have turned on the light?

Ashley pushed the door open and poked her head inside.

As lightning strobed May's room, Ashley saw a large figure in front of May's chest of drawers, going through an open drawer.

"May?"

May didn't answer, but the large figure at the dresser jumped and froze. After a few seconds, the figure turned around and pointed a light right into Ashley's eyes.

Now it was her turn to freeze.

19

"Who that?"

Ashley recognized the deep Cajun voice immediately. It belonged to Bruno, and he had been searching inside Aunt May's dresser!

She held up her hand to shield her eyes. "What are you doing in May's room?"

The volume of her voice was meant to wake May up, but the elderly woman only stirred and turned in bed slightly.

"Well?" Ashley demanded.

"I could ask you the same question, *beb*."

"The name's Ashley. Now answer my question!"

There was a slight pause, and it was just long enough to scare Ashley. The guy was clearly looking for an excuse, and he didn't have one. So now what should she do?

And who was available to help her?

"Aunt May, did you know Bruno was going through your things?"

May stirred slightly and, slurring her words, asked, "Is that you, dear?"

Bruno beat Ashley to the punch. "It's me, Miss May. I come to give you your medicine so you can sleep through this ol' storm."

"Oh…"

Ashley went over to May. "Aunt May, it's me, Ashley," she said urgently. "Bruno was going through your chest of drawers. I think he was *stealing* from you!"

Bruno came to the other side of the bed. "My eye, *beb*! Why you gotta make me the *misere*?"

"You can't hide what you're doing by speaking Cajun! You're stealing, in *any* language!"

May said nothing but just lay there. Ashley looked at her to see is she was even coherent. At least May was awake, but really out of it.

By the time she looked up, Bruno had the flashlight in his mouth and was readying an IV.

"What are you giving her?" Ashley demanded.

"Just something to help her sleep. Nothin' more."

"So you can steal from her, is that it?"

"I was lookin' to see where she was hidin' her meds, if you gotta know," Bruno said casually.

It was a great answer, she thought, completely destroying any objections she may have had to giving May more medicine, and a great alibi.

But she didn't believe it. "Who gave you the authority to give her this?"

"*Ya mamma*," Bruno said as he gently injected May with whatever was making her high. When he completed the task, he stood up and turned the flashlight off.

Silhouetted by the lightning strobes, Bruno was a menacing sight.

"Now my little *Texian*, you best *fais do-do* or you gonna be havin' the *misere* tomorrow, for true," he said, moving to the foot of the bed.

Ashley never did understand Cajun. She thought it was loosely based on French, but she didn't speak that either. She did, however, understand body language, and he was waiting for her at the foot of the bed.

"I'm not leaving until you do," she said defiantly.

"Well, you in a *mal pris*," he said. "That means you in a bad place. If you want to wake up tomorrow, you better go to your room."

She couldn't do anything for May since he had injected whatever into her. She couldn't even prevent him from coming back to rob her blind.

She wished she had spent the night with May just to keep this guy from stealing from her.

"I'm going to ask May to take inventory of her things tomorrow, and if anything is missing, I'm reporting you!"

He took a step closer to her, but only a step. It was enough to make her back up.

"If I was you, *beb*, I'd run to your room now before I you make me *en colaire*!"

Ashley didn't have to know what that meant. His low tone and frown, highlighted in the lightning flashes, made it all too clear: he was angry, and she was making him that way.

She immediately ran out of May's room, down the hallway, and dug in her jeans pocket for the key to the room across the hall. Once she got the door open, she glanced back toward May's door to see if Bruno had come after her.

Satisfied he was still in May's room, she pushed through the threshold, and she slammed the heavy door shut.

As an afterthought, she put the chain on the door, then pulled a chair under the doorknob again, then curled up in the recliner in a fetal position.

20

I saw the sign saying that Senatobia, Missouri, was just five miles ahead, only one exit.

The weather was getting worse now, and it was nearly two thirty in the morning. Traffic was virtually nonexistent, and despite the weather, we were making good time.

I said nothing to John as I turned my head to stare out at the darkness embracing the interstate. In the distance, I could make out the lightning of the approaching storm bands that would ultimately lead to the eye of the hurricane.

Ashley was out there somewhere, trapped by a car we can't afford to replace because we were still digging out from Don's last round of unemployment. Don, if he did get laid off, would hunt for months to find his next job. It's just the way his life was.

"We're going to need to fill up soon," John said out of the blue.

"We're coming up to an exit, but I don't see any lights," I said.

"That's not good. They may not have power, and if they don't have power, they can't pump gas. We'd have to wait until they restored power. It could be a major delay."

I looked over at him, exasperated. "You're just a bucket of sunshine tonight."

"Just sayin'," John said.

But he pulled off the interstate anyway at the exit to the small town. There was a huge truck stop near the exit, and thankfully, most of their lights were on.

So I'm guessing their pumps worked. I breathed a grateful sigh of relief.

John pulled in next to the pump, and Don stirred in the back seat.

"Potty break, anyone?" John called out as he turned deliberately to Don.

Don got up and out without a word, much like the rest of us. John started to pump the gas, and it was apparently working, so I hit the ladies' room, and I presumed Don went to the men's room. When I came out, though, the Jeep and boat were parked over beyond the pumps in the RV area.

Don and John were nowhere in sight.

That was troubling enough; if they started arguing, would Don have the willpower not to pull the gun on John? Or maybe shoot him?

Poking around the outside, I finally found John around the corner, on the inside of the garage area. The outside doors were closed, so I wondered what the hell he was doing in there. Since it was starting to rain at that exact moment, precipitated by a pickup in the wind, I ran into the garage area via the single non-vehicular door and walked right up to John.

"Seen Don?" I asked.

John looked at me funny, as if I had lost my mind.

"Right behind you," Don said, and I jumped. He had been just on the other side of me all along. The two of them had been inside this room, in close quarters, and I was surprised that there wasn't any blood.

"I didn't see you, Don. I'm tired," I admitted.

"We're all tired," John said. "You're not going to like this, but I was talking to the manager here a moment ago before you came in. He says he was watching the news, and it seems Katrina's about three or four hours away from landfall somewhere near New Orleans. We're not going to make it before it hits."

It took me a minute to process that. We weren't going to get there before the storm. Even though I knew this was most likely the case, my heart sank.

"Ashley…" I began.

"Will be all right if she stays in the center. But listen, John and I were tossing around an idea. I think you should listen," Don said.

"Wait…You two were discussing a plan? I didn't hear anyone yelling."

John rubbed his nose. "We're all tired, Brenda. We need some rest. We have no idea what we're going to find down there or when we're going to even be able to rest. There's a motel down the road. I think we should leave the tire that blew out here to be fixed, go get some rest, and then pick the fixed tire up in the morning and move on," John suggested.

Shocked, I turned toward Don for support.

"It's the best thing to do. We get caught on the open road with a hundred-and-fifty-mile-an-hour winds, we're toast. We need to hunker down, let this thing pass, and get started early."

I looked at Don and wondered what had gone on between him and John before I got into the service area, but I wasn't so sure they clearly understood what was at stake.

"I know what you're going to say, Brenda," Don said as I opened my mouth. "But a catnap is better than exhausting ourselves with God knows what ahead of us."

And here I was, afraid that Don would be going all Dirty Harry on John and failing miserably with both of them going to jail.

I hated to admit it, but their plan made sense. It was the most sensible thing we could do. John was falling asleep at the wheel, and I was in no condition to drive either. I was far too nervous and tired.

"Go get the tire, John. Leave it here, and let's go to the motel," I said to Don after nodding to John.

The night-service manager came back out from behind a rack of tires. John told him to wait while he got the tire.

"How much farther to New Orleans?" I asked the manager.

He was a typical Southerner, and his accent was thick. "'Bout 'nother five hours, ma'am," he said.

Yeah. We needed a break. But I didn't know which was worse: being cooped up in the Jeep with these two or being cooped up in a motel room with these two.

21

The guilt set in like an avalanche. I was leaving my baby on her own to weather a killer storm with no help from us. If I needed to pray, now was the time for it. But there was something I had to deal with first.

John spun around and headed out to get the tire. I pulled Don aside.

"How are you going to keep that...*thing* a secret?" I asked him.

"You kidding me?" he asked. "You *really* think I'm going to get any sleep at night with Billy the Kid out there, armed? Fat chance," he said.

So much for getting some much-needed rest.

I hit the bathroom again because I felt nauseated, and when I came out, there was John and Don, debating something intensely.

When I walked up, they stopped and turned to me. Don spoke first.

"Well, Brenda, it seems like your former fiancé wants me to pay to get the damned old tire fixed. Says it was my fault."

I closed my eyes. I did not need this now!

The night manager was still standing behind his desk and looking very uncomfortable. I asked him, "How much is it going to be?"

"This tire is pretty old. Looks like it lasted longer than it should have, ma'am. We can fix it, but it's just going to go away again. I suggest that you get a new one. We can use the rim, so the tire will be about twenty bucks with mounting and balancing."

I dug into my pocket and slapped a twenty on the desk. "First thing tomorrow morning," I demanded. "We need to get on the road in a hurry."

John cleared his throat. "Look, Brenda, that's not—"

I cut him off. "I am *tired* of the pettiness. Both of you, *grow up!*" Then I spun around and marched out, heading for the Jeep.

After a few minutes, Don and John joined me, without saying a word. John did, however, take a twenty and put it in the sun visor.

We pulled into the motel's lot. The old neon sign advertised Vacancy, but the looks of the place really made me consider sleeping in the Jeep. The only saving grace was the window air-conditioning units in the one-story structure.

I never liked motels, especially independent ones that didn't belong to a chain. I guess I have a phobia about what may be festering on the sheets. My fears weren't helped by the lobby; it dated back to the 1950s in decor, and it looked like that it hadn't been dusted since the Eisenhower presidency.

Don rang the bell on the desk, and eventually an old woman, heavyset and frowning, ambled up to the desk from behind a heavy curtain.

She gave us a detailed once-over. "I told them that this place would get a reputation," she wheezed.

"What do you mean?" I asked.

"My damned kids. They think they run this place now, they do. More like run it into the ground. I said that if they let them Girls Gone Wild people in here to make them porno movies, well, they'd be linin' up to film here. How many hours you need a room for?"

"No, you don't understand. We're here to get some rest. We're most definitely *not* going to make an adult film," I said. John was trying to hide a laugh, and Don was just shaking his head.

"This is my wife," he said, introducing me.

The old woman just snorted. "That's what they said last time too. Some sick bastards, they were. Wanted to see his wife with a bunch of guys. I spent days cleaning up their filth."

That was it. "I'll sleep in the car, Don."

"No, we both need some rest. We all need some rest," he added as an afterthought.

"So how many hours ya need the room?" she asked again.

I just shook my head and turned away. I heard John tell her about three or four hours.

"That'll be eighty dollars, cash."

"*Cash?*" I nearly shouted.

She pointed to an ATM machine in the corner of the lobby. "Cash," she repeated.

Don sighed heavily and went over to the machine. "Don, that ATM's not in our network," I warned.

"What choice do we have?"

"I'll split it with you two," John offered, and this time, I took him up on it.

After our initial run-in with the desk manager, we all got our bags and met in front of the room. Don put his bags down to unlock the door, and I casually glanced over at John.

To my horror, he was carrying the yellow toolbox.

Immediately, I looked away and tried to act as if it meant nothing to me. Hopefully, John didn't catch me glancing at it for fear of giving us away, but I could always count on Don to put my foot in his mouth.

"Why are you bringing those tools in, John? They mean that much to you?" Don asked as he pushed the door open.

"Like I said, these belonged to my father."

"I need a shower," I said, trying to change the subject.

"Good luck. Never know what you'll find in there," Don said, pointing to the bathroom.

But I couldn't stop thinking about the toolbox. Did John know now? Was it lighter than it should have been? Heavier? Was he going to shoot us while we slept?

Okay, I was building up a head of steam, but that's just my way. I knew he wouldn't shoot me, anyway.

Once we got in and put our things down, John ensuring the yellow toolbox was near his bed on the other side of the room from us, we took stock.

Well, it reeked. The odor of stale cigarettes hung heavily in the room. Mildew and mold seemed to be everywhere.

Don plopped down on the bed and kicked off his shoes, intent on getting some rest. It made my skin crawl.

"You coming to bed?" he asked.

I shook my head and found a chair I could snooze in. "You have no idea what could be in those sheets," I replied, sitting down in the chair and knowing full well it could have been used in a porn movie.

John lay down on his bed too but kept his shoes on, staying outside the covers. The thought of being on those beds were enough to make me vomit, but I put my head in my hand as my arm rested on the table by the window. It wasn't real comfy, but I wouldn't have to be worried about getting a shot of penicillin tomorrow.

Or today rather.

It was Monday, August 29, 2005. I had a hunch that I would remember this day for a long time.

22

Monday, August 29, 2005

As the Cessna Citation lowered its landing gear, the hydraulic pump noise and final clunk made Zanetti jump.

VT seemed to find great amusement in his employee's discomfort. "It's just the landing gear, Tony. You've faced worse enemies than the undercarriage of a plane."

If it was a joke, nobody told Zanetti. His knuckles had turned white long ago, and he had not slept at all on the plane. The fact that they had been routed around the storm in a huge arc by air traffic control, adding a full hour to the flight, just compounded his torture. Because of the storm, Baton Rouge Metropolitan Airport was the closest they could get to New Orleans.

"How much longer till those assholes set this bird down?" he wondered out loud. As soon as the words left his lips, he knew he was going to regret it.

"Depends."

"On *what?*" Zanetti asked tersely.

"Whether they set it down on a runway or we're dashed against the ground by some downdraft," VT said, hardly able to contain his snort.

Someday, Zanetti thought, he was going to take great pleasure in snuffing out the life of one Vincent Taccone.

But the landing soon came, and right as the runway threshold lights darted past his window, Zanetti found he could relax until the reverse thrust threw him against his seat belt.

"*Shit!*"

VT was the very picture of calm. "Just putting on the brakes," he said.

"Why they gotta do it so hard?"

"So we don't burn to death in a huge fireball at the other end of the runway."

"You're an asshole!"

When the plane finally arrived on the ramp and the engines spooled down, the copilot came out of the cockpit, crouching because there wasn't quite enough standing headroom. But he opened the door, and Zanetti finally relaxed.

"C'mon, Mr. Assistant Asshole. That's our queue," VT said, unbuckling his seat belt and moving forward.

Zanetti couldn't follow him fast enough, bumping his head on the ceiling twice in his haste to deplane.

The copilot was waiting for them at the bottom of the stairs incorporated into the door. He held out his hand, but both men refused to take it.

"How are we going to get our luggage?" VT asked.

"We'll get it out of the plane for you and put it on a luggage cart, sir. It will only take just a few moments."

VT and Zanetti waited while the copilot loaded up a cart provided by the local fixed base operator service. Even though it was on the ramp, VT insisted that he take possession of the cart and push it himself through the FBO.

"Limo is waiting for you, sir," the lineman said. VT cast a glance at Zanetti, the meaning obvious.

"You take the limo, and I'll see that the pilots get set up," Zanetti said to VT.

VT nodded and walked through the rain to the automatic doors leading into the private terminal building.

Last thing they needed right now was to make a big scene that would forever sear their faces in the memory of that lineman. Zanetti held back and turned away, back toward the jet where the pilots were closing up the baggage door.

"Mr. Taccone appreciates your willingness and *discretion* regarding this difficult flight," he said, reaching into this suit pocket and withdrawing two stacks of bills worth $5,000 each.

The pilots' eyes bugged out when they saw the money. "What's this for?" the captain asked.

"It's a tip."

Zanetti was beginning to think that VT's belief that he could buy anyone was about to backfire on them.

"Wow, never been tipped that high before," said the copilot. "You're not going to do something, uh, *illegal*, are you?" the captain tried to joke. But the captain's eyes seemed to tell a different tale to Zanetti's attuned senses.

This was about to be become a problem.

"What makes you think that?" Zanetti asked, smiling but deadly serious.

"Oh, uh, nothing, really. Just that, well, that's *a lot* of money," the pilot captain said, glancing quickly between Zanetti, the bills in his own hand, and his copilot.

The captain's actions and tone of voice struck a nerve with Zanetti. It had been a mistake to offer the money to buy the pilot's silence. VT had been wrong. The pilot's interest was captured by the unusual amount of money, and they were going to sing.

Loudly.

"Of course, I can understand that this looks *fishy*," Zanetti said. "It's just that people have certain…opinions about my boss's family. We have *legitimate* business interests down here. We want to protect them, and we just would rather not have anyone know that we came down before a disaster. It may look bad. People often get the wrong idea about us."

Yeah, Zanetti thought, that was the best he could do, but it wasn't making believers out of either of these guys.

"Well, um, ATC knows you flew down here," the captain said. "We can't help that."

Zanetti sighed. Wrong answer, he thought. Just what he didn't need. Another damned loose end.

23

I WAS AWAKE, listening to the two men sleep. It seemed like they were in engaged in a contest to see who could make the loudest biological noise.

How Don could sleep through all this, I'd never know. I found it impossible to drift off to sleep, and I was going to pay for it later. Perhaps I could count on pure adrenaline to keep me going, but I wasn't going to bet on it.

I needed to find something to eat, and at this time of day, that meant vending machines. I was sure even this place would have some. I could just venture out and find a vending machine and get some nuts or pretzels or chips or even a coveted chocolate bar. Even stale food would work.

I unplugged the charger from my cell phone and got up and tiptoed to Don, and careful not to touch the bed, I placed a hand on his shoulder.

"Don? You awake?"

He stirred but turned over away from me. How he could put his *face* on *that* pillow? I shivered.

"I'm going to get something to eat. I'm hungry."

Don didn't even budge.

But John did. He turned over and said softly, "You want me to go with you? This motel is pretty seedy."

Yeah, thanks for telling me something I already knew. "No, I think I'd like to be alone for now."

John shrugged. "Okay, but you should be careful. Never know what drunks might be out there, and let's face it, you'd be the main attraction."

"I'm over forty, John. No redneck is going to be the least bit interested in me."

"You're a woman, a good-looking woman with a great body, and you have all your teeth. You're like a dream come true for these good ol' boys."

What a flatterer. "I'll be back," I said, taking the key and slowly tugging the tight door open.

John didn't roll over, but I could feel his eyes on me as I slipped outside, quickly shutting the door behind me.

The only vending machines I could find were near the office, and since our room was on the end of this particular wing, I had a long way to go. I took my time, listening for any sounds that spelled *impending rape victim*, but I made it to the office all right.

The lone fluorescent bulb buzzed on and off over the ice machine and its soda drink dispensing neighbor.

There was another machine with snacks in it, but the lights were off and even the coin slot was taped over.

It didn't matter. We had snacks in the coolers, and if I could wait, I could get breakfast at the truck stop that was still lit up like a military base.

I had wanted to be alone with Don to tell him what I thought about the guns. Yes, John had spoken about killing Don, but I doubted that he could actually go through with it. I knew his partners were more than shady, but I couldn't believe John would actually take out a hit.

Would he?

Remembering the phone call John had received on the way down, my knees nearly gave way as I put two and two together. Of *course*, John wouldn't kill Don, but his partners might!

I had to lean up against the ice machine for support, not even concerned with the filth and spiderwebs on the top.

That was the plan! John had been on the phone with someone he was going to *meet*! He had asked someone, most likely his partners, to come down and assassinate my husband!

I had to warn Don!

Suddenly, I was no longer afraid about Don taking that gun; it may serve as a deterrent to his demise—*if* he didn't hurt anyone or himself with it.

So I simply *couldn't* confront John. No telling how he would react. He still had the other gun.

My cell phone pushed against me in my pocket. I could *call* Don, and I could still warn him without John knowing about it. It seemed like it could work.

I reached into my pocket and flipped it open, then hit Don's speed-dial button. It rang.

And rang and rang.

Why do men sleep so soundly?

Finally, it was answered before it went to voice mail.

"Don is asleep," John said.

I was dumbfounded. I had no excuse for calling him. But my mind raced.

"The machine needs exact change," was all I could think of to say.

That seemed to work. "You want me to give you some? Hang on," John said, and I could hear the sheets rustling.

"No, come to think of it, the light is out on the machine. It might not be working. I'll just head back."

I hung up before I could do or say anything that would give me away. John was good at reading body language and tone of voice. And I tended to telegraph my feelings.

Damn it! My warning attempt, foiled!

But John was up, and I needed to get back to the room. No telling what he might be doing.

When I got back to the room, John was nodding off again, but he checked to see who was coming in. I nodded to him, then resumed my place in that damned chair.

But there was no way I was going to sleep.

24

Tying to sleep was futile. The room smelled of sex and stale cigarettes, and I had a lot more to worry about now.

Don was out like a light, his breathing coming in long, slow breaths. John, on the other hand, was snoring up a storm. Poor choice of words, I know, but that was my first reaction.

Feeling dirty and itchy, I got up out of the chair to walk around. As I paced at the foot of the two beds, I noticed that I disturbed no one. I couldn't help but feel envious of these two, lying in God knows *what* filth, who could get the rest they needed anywhere and anytime they wanted.

I couldn't.

Look, I was glad Don was recharging, but I didn't want to spend more time than we needed here. Ashley needed me. Us. Don and I.

So while those two slept, I paced and worried.

During my pacing, I neared John's bed and stood between it at the back wall of the room. There was no window on the back wall, so all the light was in front of me, escaping the parking lot into our room through threadbare curtains.

John seemed to be in a deep sleep already, snoring loudly and with long-enough pauses to make me wonder if he had stopped breathing. He was sleeping partially on his side, facing Don's bed near the front window, away from me.

I nearly yelped as my toes came to rest against the side of the yellow toolbox.

Suddenly worried that I'd awakened John, I held my breath until he resumed deep snoring.

Once John resumed snoring, I looked down at the yellow toolbox.

There it was, available and unguarded, so to speak. Why the idea to open it popped in my head, I'll never know, but I had to see if there was something I could do to increase Don's chances of survival.

To open it, though, I'd have to get down on the floor. The idea nauseated me, having seen all the dark stains in the carpet before the lights went out. But I had to do something!

So I held my breath and got down on my knees. As I did so, I nearly lost my balance and had to catch my fall by placing my palm on the carpet.

I nearly vomited.

At first, I wanted to wipe my hand off on the covers, but who knows what I'd be sticking my hand into. I was going to wipe it on my pants but didn't want anything sticking to me. I vowed to wash my hands so hard when I was done that my skin would be raw.

I tried the first latch, and it snapped open with a loud click as it was spring-loaded, and the clasp hit the top of the box. To me, it sounded like a gunshot.

And John stopped snoring.

I froze. My eyes were riveted on the back of John's head, but he didn't move. So I waited until the snoring started again. It took a minute or two, but it started.

Breathing again myself, I put my finger just above the second latch and pulled the tab. The damn piece of metal sprung open, and while it didn't hit the box top, it hit my finger so hard that an uneven edge took some skin.

I nearly cried out in pain. Somehow, I managed to be nonverbal and nearly put my finger in my mouth but then realized that hand had been on the carpet.

Now I was sure to die of some HIV infection or other weird, unholy disease. I had to wash my hands vigorously after I was done!

I opened the top slowly, just in case it made a noise. When it didn't, I sighed almost imperceptibly.

Being dark and in the shadow of the bed, I couldn't see very well into the box. But I could see the huge gun in its holster and a few of Don's wrenches. Underneath the gun were four more magazines loaded with bullets.

I carefully took the gun out, glancing occasionally at John to see if there was any movement. When there wasn't, I proceeded.

Unholstering it made me shake. I was careful not to put my finger inside the trigger guard. It was heavy, and I needed two hands just to hold it. There was a button on the side of the grip, and I pushed it.

Unfortunately, the damn magazine fell out and landed on the soft leather holster with a thump. John stopped snoring and started to turn over toward me!

I ducked down and waited for the inevitable anger and accusations. But as my heart raced and my lungs screamed for air, I vowed that if he did wake up, I could turn any anger back on him and accuse him of bringing a weapon on the trip without our knowledge and then we'd all have it out right there about what he said at the house, and Don would have the only loaded gun.

It seemed fair. Scary as hell, but fair.

John never yelled; he never said anything because, after a minute or so, he started snoring again. He'd never awakened.

But he was now facing me.

After I was sure he was still asleep, I set the gun down and looked for the wayward magazine. When I found it, I lifted it up and tried to pull the bullets out, but they wouldn't budge. Each breath John took paused, and each time I thought I was caught. But when the snoring came again, I started examining the magazine.

It took a minute, but I discovered that if I pushed with my thumb, I could eject the bullet from the magazine. I carefully counted—seven bullets. I scooped them in a pile and pushed the magazine back in the grip.

It clicked loudly and John grunted. I froze. He turned over again, away from me.

Sighing with relief once more, I did the same thing with the rest of the magazines. When I was finished, I had twenty-eight bullets on the floor to hide, but I put everything back and started to close the lid.

That's when I realized I had done the same thing Don had done—made it lighter. I looked around. My eyes landed on the nightstand by the bedside.

Carefully, I pulled on the drawer, and thankfully, it slid open without too much noise. There was nothing inside but a pocket-size Gideon's Bible. I couldn't help but wonder what the hell a Bible was doing on a porn set, but stranger things have happened.

It would have to do.

I reached in, pulled out the Bible, and placed it on top of the other magazines and the gun on top, in its holster. Empty and impotent. Don had a shot at survival.

I locked the box as silently as I could, closing the tabs and making sure the clasps were connected. Then I scooped up the bullets and tiptoed as quickly as I could back to my chair.

My duffel bag was open, and I could hide the bullets under my clothes, but before I could dump them, John sat up!

25

I WAITED FOR the inevitable scream fest. To my shock and great suspicion, it never came.

"What are you still doing up?" John asked softly. "Didn't you get any sleep at all?"

I had been bent over my bag. If I dropped the bullets now, it would be noisy, so I just froze in position and tried to look as if stealing from a potential murderer was an everyday occurrence.

"Too much on my mind," I said as I carefully placed the bullets in the top part of my bag and started to slowly zip it up.

He hadn't seen the bullets. At least I *thought* he hadn't seen them. You never could tell with John. He was many things, and smooth would have been high on the list of adjectives I would have selected.

John nodded, yawned, and stretched. Then to my horror, he swung his legs off the bed and started to get up.

I threw caution to the wind and quickly finished zipping up the bag, then made sure it was near enough to me that I could prevent him from searching it. This also meant I couldn't leave the bag unattended with him in the room.

At least he wasn't naked. He stood up, right over the yellow toolbox, and stretched again. Was this for my benefit? Had he known I was in the toolbox and now just throwing it in my face, like a warning, only to shoot me when I wasn't looking?

He padded off to the bathroom and closed the door, leaving his precious yellow toolbox unattended. I was stunned.

My mind flashed back to Don's poking his nose into the thing. In retrospect, I'm glad he had opened it. Now I was thankful that *I* had, for all intents and purposes, disabled the huge gun.

By the time I heard the toilet flush and faucet run, I was back in my chair, doing my best to look like I was trying to get some shut-eye and not trying to catch my breath.

He came out and flipped off the light in the bedroom.

"How's the weather?"

I looked up at him. "What?"

"Have you at least been making good use of your insomnia? What's the weather report?"

I turned my head and pulled back the curtain, completely forgetting to protect my wounded finger.

It was still dark outside, but the rain was starting to build.

"Looks like the storm is coming through."

He nodded. "You might have to face the fact that we will have to hold up somewhere. Towing a trailer is like holding a sail. The wind really acts on it."

"Don't I know it," I said, thinking about Don's incident with the semitruck.

He nodded. "Look, try and get some rest. You're going to have a very long and emotional day ahead of you."

I nodded, a bit confused. Does that sound like the mentality of a killer? But then again, John was a master manipulator, many of his performances worthy of an Oscar.

Still…

"I'll try."

Before he lay down on the bed, he sat, thinking. My heart stopped. What would he say next? Something about the toolbox? That he saw me fiddling with it earlier?

"You know," he started, and I held my breath, "you're not going to like this."

My heart stopped. I waited for the bombshell.

"But we're going to have to wait until the service guy gets in. Or his mechanic, at least. We should have breakfast there at the truck stop. It will give us the needed shelter from the storm. I'm sorry about this, but we have to be smart."

I was breathing again.

"Yeah, I know. You're right, I don't like it, but I know," I said.

He nodded and lay back down, drifting off to a wonderful place called dreamland. I sat waiting for the snoring to begin to open my duffel bag and hide the bullets on the bottom underneath all my clothes.

Funny how we all had secrets to hide from one another. I looked over at Don, who hadn't moved a muscle throughout the entire night.

I wonder what secrets he had to hide.

26

ASHLEY WOKE UP with a start. Disoriented and uncomfortable, she looked around her dark surroundings, trying to figure out where she was.

It came back to her quickly—dead man's room across from May's, threatened by Bruno, storm.

She got up and flipped the light switch on the table lamp next to her chair. Nothing. She tried it a few more times, then figured the bulb was burned out.

Over by the window, she heard noise that seemed rather violent, so she moved over to investigate, but not too eagerly. Last thing she wanted to see was a street gang stripping her car.

She glanced at her watch. Six-thirty in the morning. What day was it? Monday?

On any normal day, she would be attending orientation as an upperclassman leader for Tulane's incoming freshman class. But not today. Today, she was in hell, for sure, with no clear path to get out.

When she looked out of the window, all she saw was torrential rain, debris flying through the air and tumbling down the street, away from her building. The scene made her wonder how long it would be before her car got hit and trashed.

Turning away, she moved over to the bathroom and tried the light. It wouldn't work either. In fact, she could have sworn she had left it on. Then it hit her; the power was out.

And that meant the storm was upon them. She wanted desperately to see if Aunt May was all right but couldn't quite stir up the courage to go out into the hallway because of big, exposed, and very breakable windows and because she had no idea what Bruno would do to her if he found her wandering around out there.

The sounds the building was making in the storm were unnerving, to say the least. In fact, Ashley could have sworn she heard the building moan.

Back at the window again, she watched as everything blew away from her, to the south, toward the Mississippi River just a few blocks away. That struck her as odd. The storm was coming up from the south; why would the winds be coming from the opposite direction?

Then it hit her. May's window!

It was facing the full force of the storm. Well, maybe a bit of an angle, but something could be blown into it and May might be injured. She had to go and check on May. She'd just have to accept the risk of getting caught by Bruno.

Grabbing her key, she pulled the chair clear of the door and stepped out into the darkened hallway.

The noise was even worse out in the hallway. And lightning flashed occasionally at either end of the wide hall, strobing the space with brilliant flashes of light.

When the lightning flashed particularly brightly, Ashley was startled enough to scream. Right in front of her was an equally startled resident, dressed in bedclothes and limping around.

All the horror movies Ashley had ever seen rushed back into her consciousness, and she nearly ran in the opposite direction, that is, until she saw the elderly man grasping his chest.

Great, she'd given the guy a heart attack and now that would be on her conscience.

"You scared me, young lady! What are you doing here?"

Relieved she hadn't killed the man, Ashley took a breath. "I'm checking on my great-aunt. She's on the other side of this hallway, on the side the wind is coming from."

"Do you work here? Do you know if they are going to dispense medications?"

"No, sir, I don't. I'm sorry. You can ask Bruno when he comes around."

"Aw, he's no good."

Instantly, Ashley took a liking to the old man. But she was in a hurry.

"Yes, I agree. Excuse me," she said and walked the short distance to May's door. She rapped her knuckles softly.

"May? Auntie May?"

She leaned in and put her ear to the door, now closed. Not hearing an answer, she wondered what that meant.

"Do you know when Bruno will be back?"

This was from a woman, who had been wandering the hallway too. A lightning strike nearby created a brilliant flash and a horrendous clasp of thunder. In the flash, Ashley noticed a few more residents milling about.

What the hell? Where was Bruno? Why aren't these people hunkered down in their rooms instead of wandering around the hallway where something could happen to them?

"May?"

She knocked harder and tried the door. Locked. She slapped the door with the palm of her hand. "*May!*"

"Do you know when the storm will end?"

"Where is Bruno?"

"I need my medication. Can you get it for me?"

"May, *damn* it! Wake up!"

The crowd was growing exponentially outside of May's door, and suddenly, Ashley felt trapped.

"Folks, shh! Bruno might come back! He's been stealing from my Aunt May and he's probably stealing from you *too*! Now please go back to your rooms and wait out the storm. Fill up your bathtubs with water so you will have something to drink, and tell your neighbors too! But don't let Bruno into your room! He's a thief! Now please go back to your rooms and watch out for the stairs!"

"Yes, go back to your rooms."

Ashley froze. It was Bruno, and she had no idea how much he had heard.

27

It was a thunderclap, I think, that rattled me awake. Just when I'd started to fall asleep too.

I pulled back the curtains to look outside. Rain was falling horizontally, and lightning constantly flashed across the sky. It was starting to get light out, but the overcast was giving the sun a hard time.

We were starting to see the front edges of Katrina.

Next, my eyes gave it their best shot, but it took me a little longer than usual to focus on my watch. When I did, I was instantly awake. No coffee needed.

It was quarter to seven in the morning!

On my feet instantly, I was shaking Don awake. Don's not a morning person by any stretch of the imagination, especially if he's been up past ten o'clock the night before. I grabbed his shoulder and started shaking.

He twisted around and opened his eyes, blinking heavily and rapidly.

"It's nearly seven in the morning, Don. We have to *go*!"

"Umghp."

"Get up!"

Don angrily sighed and threw the covers off to swing his legs over the side of the bed. He had slept in his pants, no doubt to guard the gun. I stepped back now that he was in motion.

"Where's the great white hunter?"

I hadn't even noticed John wasn't in his bed. But a toilet flush and the sound of the shower starting answered our questions.

I debated whether I should tell Don about my nocturnal activities. I could only imagine what he would accuse me of—up in the middle of the night and near John's bed. Yeah, that would go over well.

As I debated, John's phone rang. That ended my internal debate.

I flew over to the nightstand to answer it, telling Don, "It's probably Amy, and I have a question to ask her. You probably should hear this."

"What do you mean by *that*?"

But I had already scooped up the phone and flipped it open. "Hello?"

I waited, thinking for a moment that we had a bad connection, maybe because of the storm. These were, after all, radios and might be affected by the atmospheric conditions.

So I closed the phone and started to put it back on the nightstand when it rang again.

"Hello!"

When no one spoke again, I looked at the phone's tiny one-line display screen. I didn't recognize the number, and by the time I got it back to my ear, the other party had hung up.

"Who was it?" Don asked, still groggy.

"No one spoke," I said as I placed it back on the nightstand.

"Must be a wrong number."

"Yeah." But as soon as I took my hand off it, it rang again!

I picked it up and tossed it to Don, who fumbled the catch but managed to hold on to the phone. "You should answer it and try to sound like John," I suggested.

He flashed me an annoyed look but flipped it open. "Yeah?" he growled.

As I waited for his reaction, I wondered why a real estate business partner wouldn't speak after the person they called answered the phone.

And I realized I *already knew* why. A wave of horror washed over me, and I could bet my face went pale as the blood drained.

John's partners! They were calling him, maybe to see where he was!

Don had been silent for some time, and I bet he was getting an earful. Maybe I didn't have to warn him anymore; maybe he'd realize that he was in mortal danger.

Yeah, my hopes were dashed when he closed the phone and tossed it back to me. "No one there."

Seriously?

Then an idea flashed through my head, and I opened the phone.

"What are you doing?"

"Star sixty-nine."

"You're calling them back? Does that even work on cell phones?"

Don was rubbing his eyes. Like I said, he's not much of a morning person, and clearly he was in sensory overload.

The phone rang. I had no idea what I was going to say.

"What are you going to ask them?"

I thought it would be obvious.

"I think if someone called me several times in a row like that, they were urgently trying to get ahold of me. So my call is out of legitimate concern about an apparently urgent attempt to get in contact with John."

Someone finally answered the call. But all I heard was someone pick up and very little else.

After a long pause, I finally spoke, "Who's this, and why have you been calling so much?"

Don shook his head and rolled his eyes. I ignored him.

But whoever it was on the other end of the call hung up again.

"What the hell are you doing with my phone?"

Don and I both snapped our heads in the direction of John's voice. He had come out of the bathroom wearing only a towel around his waist.

"Somebody's been trying to get you, but they won't talk to me."

"Why would you answer my phone? It's private, you know! I got customers calling me. It's Monday. This would normally be a working day, you know," he admonished me, walking over and snatching the device from my hands. "They probably thought they misdialed."

"They called three times in a row, and I thought Amy was trying to get hold of you," I said.

He frowned, deeply. "Yeah, well despite what you think, mortgages and insurance sales and questions can be urgent in my business."

"I would have thought they would have asked for you. Why wouldn't they, at least, ask if this was the right number?"

"How should I know?" John asked angrily. "Maybe they're shy, or a female voice caught them off guard. What does it matter?"

"It matters," I said, staring right at him as if he should know I was thinking about his question about killing Don.

He flashed me a really angry expression, then silently turned and headed back to the bathroom where the shower was still on.

"How long are you going to be?" I asked. "It's nearly seven."

"Not long," he said, then pausing with a glance toward Don, John picked up the yellow toolbox, his duffel bag, and his phone, then headed to the bathroom where I heard the door lock.

Loudly.

I turned to Don immediately.

"Don, I have to tell you something," I started to say.

"Save it. I'm not in the mood. Wake me up when he's out, then I'll take my shower."

I watched as he climbed back into bed, pulled the covers over his head, and effectively shut me out of his life.

While the clock ticked.

28

I WAS BRACING for this moment. John came out of the bathroom fully dressed, but no less angry.

Don decided at that precise moment it would be a good time to shower. He grabbed his bag and headed for the bathroom.

"How long are you going to be?" I asked. I was trying to point out that we were delaying our trip unnecessarily.

"Less time than you take."

"Don, please! We need to get on the road!"

"We need to get that tire, we need breakfast, and it should be a big one because we don't know when we're going to eat again." He turned before closing the bathroom door. "And I'm in no hurry to drive through a Category 5 hurricane!"

"It's our *daughter*!"

"Are you saying I don't care about Ashley? She's protected by a huge-ass building, above the waterline. We are currently living in a thin metal box that is older than I'd trust in a hundred-plus-mile-an-hour wind! We can't save Ashley if we die getting there!"

"Yeah, well, when our daughter is in mortal danger, I'd *gladly* risk my life to save her!"

He shook his head, then he slammed the door, leaving me alone with John.

It was suddenly very quiet in the room. I glanced at John, who was staring holes in me.

"*What?*" I snapped.

"You ought to take it easy on him, y'know, Brenda."

Now it was my turn to stare. Not twenty-four hours ago, this man, who was now suggesting to me to take it easy on Don, was sure I wanted to kill him and was going to do it for me.

I turned to face him directly, hands on my hips. "Oh? You think I'm too hard on him, do you?"

He shrugged. "He's here, isn't he?"

"Why the sudden concern about the mark?" I asked him in full sarcasm mode.

He frowned and shook his head, then started to gather some items into his bag. "What the hell are you talking about, Brenda?"

"I'm just surprised how your attitude toward Don has changed, considering our"—I glanced at the bathroom door just in case—"conversation back at the house!"

John said nothing.

"I was just expressing my frustrations with my situation," I said. "I *do not* want to see Don killed, hurt, maimed, or otherwise harmed in *any* way. Do you understand?"

John looked up at me. He set the toolbox and his duffel in front of him on the bed, between us. I tried my best not to even glance at it, but I definitely knew it was there.

I wondered if he had placed it there for a reason. Was he taunting me? Trying to find out if I had, indeed, fiddled with his stuff? Had he opened it?

Was he awake last night when I went through and took his bullets?

Suddenly, the conversation had changed dramatically. I tried to put the thoughts out of my head. If he knew I had taken the bullets, he would have said or done something by now.

I was sure of it.

"Whatever makes you think I'm going to do that, Brenda?"

"It was the damned question you asked me at the house, John. And you didn't let it go for a while. And that phone call. Who called you, John? Tell me, look me in the eyes and tell me it wasn't any of those…oily partners of yours checking in with you."

He couldn't—or wouldn't—do it. John just shook his head and looked down on the floor, picked up his towel, and threw it on the bed.

"It wasn't my partners. I try to avoid them as much as possible," he finally said.

"I *mean* it, John!"

He shook his head again, slowly while looking right at me, boring his gaze right into my head.

Then he reached for the yellow toolbox, and my heart skipped a beat.

I was about to scream for Don, but John moved it over and reached for the zipper on this duffel. My heart started beating again, but my pulse was threatening to set a speed record.

Reaching in to his bag, he pulled out a baseball cap and put it on. Then he looked at me again and folded his arms across his muscular chest.

"You know, I'm going to let all this slide."

"All of *what* slide, John?" I folded my own arms.

"Your accusations about me being a murderer. I came down here to help you because I still have feelings for you, and I'm ashamed of my behavior when we were an item. I may be many things—a cheat, a tax dodger, and I do business with some pretty questionable people who were the only means of me building my companies—but I am *not* a murderer, and you should lighten up on me and Don!"

I said nothing, and I think he was expecting me to. We stood there for another few seconds, just staring at each other. My concentration was finally broken when the toilet flushed and the shower started again.

John turned on the TV and flipped the channels until he found The Weather Channel. What I saw made me feel worse; I'm sick and tired of weathermen standing out in the storm, screaming into their microphones, talking about wind force; it gives me no useful information on the storm, what it's doing, and how people are faring.

As soon as the commercial came on, I turned back to John.

"I want your guarantee that nothing will happen to Don."

He rolled his eyes and sighed. "You know, I can't give that to you. Anything can happen to anyone of us down there!"

"I want your guarantee that you or anyone you know won't try to harm him!"

"I'm not going to do a damn thing to your husband, Mrs. Meyers!"

I nearly asked him about the guns at that point, but I didn't have a chance. Don came out of the shower and asked if we had checked out the weather report.

John pointed to the TV, and we all watched it for a while. Then I noticed that the shower was still on.

"Are you done in there, Don?"

He stood there blinking at me with a towel around his waist. I just shook my head and grabbed my bag, walked in, shut the door, and brushed my teeth. Splashing water on my face didn't help me feel any better, but I came out with my bag, grabbed the keys to the Jeep from the desk, and headed straight for the door.

The shower was still running. Don looked at me if I had lost my mind.

"I'll be waiting in the car when you two finally mosey on out there to rescue Ashley and May."

I didn't believe John for a minute, and I was mad, so mad I slammed the door hard enough to wake everybody up for a mile around, and walked out to the Jeep despite the torrential downpour and nearby lightning strikes.

29

I was soaked to the skin, and I didn't care.

I didn't care about how wet I was getting the back seat; I didn't care what I smelled like.

It felt good, actually, soaking wet like this. The temperature was oppressive despite the rain, and the humidity just added to the misery factor.

But I needed more.

My bags were tossed in the back as soon as I sat down, but the air in the Jeep was unbearable. I endured it for as long as I could, but the heat finally got to me. Not caring about the gas I wasted, I leaned over the center console between the front seats and started the ignition, then reached over and turned the AC on to arctic mode.

After a few more minutes, I glanced at my watch. But since I hadn't noted the time when I walked out, I had no idea how long I had been sitting there. The engine had come up to normal operating temperature, though, so it was a few minutes at least.

Maybe I shouldn't have stormed out. Maybe I should have taken some time to shower and change. Yeah, but maybe that would have been the difference between survival and not for Ashley and May.

So I waited. Impatiently. Another ten minutes went by and I had been counting the times the extra electrically driven fan behind the radiator cycled on and off. Eight times.

What the hell were they *doing* in there?

Was Don still alive? I hadn't heard any gunshots. Of course I was being silly, but I was tired and imagining all sorts of bad things that could have befallen my family members.

Had Don taken precautions and locked the bathroom door so John couldn't snoop? What the hell was taking so long?

So there I sat, all alone, waiting to resume the rescue mission. In my emotional state, which was building to a crescendo, I half imagined John walking out with a gun to blow my brains out.

But wait. I *am* all alone! I could use this time…

I dug out my phone and opened it. What was John's home number again? Turns out, I had it saved in my directory under BANKER, so I selected it and hit Call. Then I put it to my ear and waited while it rang.

My pulse must have been off the charts. I had no idea how I was going to approach the question, but I wanted it answered: what did you mean by "all is not what it seems"? Oh, and by the way, was she aware that John had taken two guns with him? Why?

It rang and rang. I glanced at my watch. It was five after seven in the morning; she should at least be up and out of bed. Hell, I didn't care if I woke her up. I needed answers!

Two more rings. Did she know my number? If she did, was she ignoring me?

It went to voice mail. I hadn't anticipated this. What should I say? Who would be listening? Who would she share this with?

John? Don?

The beep came too quickly, and I hesitated. "Um, Mrs. Katsarus? Amy? This is…um, Brenda Meyers. We're in southern Missouri and waiting while the storm passes. I didn't want you to worry. Please call me when you get a chance. So far, everything is going as well as can be expected, and everyone here is all right. I just wanted to let you know."

I punched End so hard that I nearly broke a nail.

That was a *stupid* idea. She was going to call John and not me. Maybe even let Don know that I called. I'd have to watch his phone and try to see who called either of them. But I doubted that I would ever get access to John's phone again, and he was very good at concealing the real details of his conversations.

But I had to try.

Finally, out of the corner of my eye, I saw some motion. Through the rain-streaked windows, I saw John and Don, lugging their bags and John carrying his yellow toolbox toward the Jeep on a run. As a flash of lightning strobed the parking lot and a clasp of thunder boomed nearly at the same time, Don ducked and even John flinched.

They doubled their speed.

They both went immediately to the back of the Jeep and opened the hatch as far as they could considering the trailer hitch post on the trailer, tossed their bags in unceremoniously, and quickly climbed into the front seats, with John at the wheel, sliding that damned yellow toolbox under his feet.

John took one look at the instrument gauges and asked me, "How long have you been running the engine?"

I was sitting with my arms folded. "Why? Did I use too much gas? You two should have come out earlier then."

"No," he said, shutting off the motor. "We're overheating. We need to let this thing cool down."

"What?"

"Unless you want to end the journey here, we need to let the motor cool down. Do you have any antifreeze in the back?"

Don shook his head. "Never needed it, but then again, I don't usually tow a boat in hot subtropical weather. How bad is it?"

"I shut if off probably right before the warning light came on. Look," he said, pointing down to the gauge.

Don leaned over and sighed.

"Brenda, you can't let this Jeep idle like this. It's an in-line six cylinder, and that's harder on the cooling system," Don chastised me, and it actually sounded like he was trying to impress John.

"If you would have come out instead of powdering your nose, we wouldn't be *in* this mess," I said. "How long do we have to wait?" I asked John.

"Maybe fifteen minutes or so. I'll start it, then and we'll see. Uh, we *may* have to turn the heat on to cycle that hot coolant away from the motor."

Another delay! I was *livid*, but I had no choice in the matter.

But by God, I did have a choice about Don's and my safety. At least I had seen to that last night.

The only question was, what did John know, and what was he going to do about it?

30

It took twenty minutes in hot, sweltering discomfort to get the Jeep cooled down to a normal operating temperature. And then the air-conditioning was kept off, so by the time we pulled into the truck stop and parked, I was a giant sweat gland.

I was really beginning to wish I had showered, even in that filth. It wouldn't have cost us much more time, considering the extra twenty minutes we wasted in the metal sauna.

Before going in, I reached into the back of the Jeep and grabbed my Tilley hat to hide my hair. I'm quite sure I looked like a sticky mess and my body odor would telegraph my whereabouts for a mile.

I headed straight for the ladies' room, taking my bag and sponging off as best I could. I changed into a halter top, new underwear, and shorts. Despite all that, I still felt dirty.

It must have only been six or seven minutes, but by the time I got to the garage area, Don and John were still waiting at the service counter with no one behind it. John had put the keys up on the top of the counter.

"How much longer is this going to take?" Don asked John.

He shrugged, and Don sighed loudly and shook his head.

While those two just stood there wasting time, I reached over and banged the bell on the service desk about twenty times.

Finally, a sloppy young guy with his uniform shirt untucked appeared from the back office. I remember thinking that he looked worse than I felt.

"Can I help you?" he asked, his speech slow and measured.

As John spoke to him about the tire, I turned to Don.

"I need to tell you something," I mouthed, too afraid to even whisper it.

"What?" Don said out loud.

John just side glanced him and turned back to try to explain to this young slob that they were supposed to have already mounted his new tire.

I flashed a very angry expression at Don and mouthed it again, even walking away from John and beckoning Don to follow me.

But he just sighed and shook his head, remaining at the desk.

My eyes must have shot laser beams at him, but he turned his back toward me.

Wow.

I began questioning everything about my philosophy in life. I have tried and tried to warn Don, maybe not hard enough, but then again I'm scared—for him and for myself—if John found out, what would he do?

Of course, what *could* he do now that I effectively disarmed him?

My thought process was interrupted by something I thought I heard from the service-desk redneck.

"Yeah, we're backed up today. Lots of stuff going on out there on the roads, I reckon. We can't get to your tire 'til this afternoon."

"Wait, *what*?" I asked.

"Sorry, lady, we're all backed up today."

"That's *not* what the manager said last night!"

He just shrugged and smiled apologetically.

"Well, that's patently unacceptable!" I said. John turned to me slowly.

"What do you want them to do, Brenda?"

"Well, screw this, and screw the damned tire! Let's get it and get out of here!"

John looked at me like I had just stabbed him in the gut. "Do you have any idea how much a wheel is?"

"Nope, and little did I care, John." I reached over, grabbed the keys, and walked out.

"Hey! Where are you going?" John shouted after me. I never even slowed down or turned around.

The rain was still coming down, but not as hard. Several motorists were gassing up at the pumps, and there was a highway patrol slowly cruising past the large pump awning as I stormed out to the Jeep.

Since John had pulled up to the pumps, I swiped my card and started filling the tank. John came running out of the garage like a man on a mission.

"Brenda! Brenda! Goddamn it! What the *hell* are you doing?"

I wouldn't have been too alarmed in this public place, but everyone at the pumps had turned to see John. I did as well, and what I did see alarmed me.

Don was running after him, hand undoing the button on his cargo pocket. The police car lurched to a stop.

John was nearly beside me now, but he was enraged.

"You can't just leave my wheel in there, damn it! That's expensive to replace! Who do you think you are?"

I glanced back at the squad car. Two officers were starting to climb out of it. I nervously glanced back at Don.

Thankfully, Don had noticed the cops and had slowed to a walk, refastening his pocket.

"Everything all right here?" one of the state policemen asked me behind his open car door.

John had really screwed up. We were going to have to explain ourselves to the officers, and Don had a gun *in his pocket*. I looked back up, and he had changed direction slightly, walking as if he were headed for another car.

"Yes, thank you. We're all tired from the road trip. Been driving too long, I guess, but thank you," I said calmly to the officer.

John stopped, and I turned to him. "Go get your wheel. As soon as I'm done with the tank, I'm leaving."

Frowning, John turned and walked back to the garage. I smiled at the cops, and they asked me again if everything was okay.

"Yes, thank you." I tried to remain as calm as possible, thinking that if I was nervous or showed any sign of distress, they'd investigate and find everything.

They nodded politely and went back to their car. They never moved the car, though, and I could tell they were watching us intently.

Don came back slowly and got in the front seat, but the passenger's side. I completed the transaction and climbed in behind the wheel.

After a minute, John came back, carrying his wounded tire still mounted on the wheel. He tossed it in the boat and walked back to the Jeep. When he saw me in the driver's seat, he looked over to find Don in the passenger's side, huffed, frowned, and got in the rear seat.

The Jeep trembled as he climbed in.

"We'll get your tire fixed on the way back, John, when we have Ashley and May with us," I said to the image in the rearview mirror.

John never said a word but folded his arms and sat back. I cranked the engine and put it in gear, carefully pulling away from the pumps.

As I pulled away from the truck stop and headed for the on ramp, I couldn't help but to glance in the rearview again.

By the look on John's face, I think I just painted a target on *my* back too.

31

WHEN VT WALKED into Zanetti's room at the hotel, he could tell Zanetti needed coffee badly.

"You look like shit. What happened?" he asked, worried something had gone wrong.

"Taking care of some loose ends that I hadn't expected."

"Anything I should know about?"

Zanetti shook his head.

VT nodded slowly and looked around the room as he did so.

"Then no loose ends. Good."

Zanetti stopped pacing and glared at VT. "No loose ends? This whole trip stinks of loose ends."

"You worry too much."

"It's how I stay out of prison."

"See, I have lawyers for that," VT said, sighing as if bored.

Zanetti just shook his head. VT nearly called out the disrespect but caught himself. Why tip his hand? Zanetti was obviously whom his father had in mind to run the family business after he died, and that was a problem.

He finally let his gaze rest on Zanetti, and he raised an eyebrow. Go ahead, disrespect me again.

Zanetti looked away.

VT changed the subject. "Does our contact know where to deliver the boat and supplies we ordered?"

"Yeah. I used the burner phone. But we're leaving a trail. Even if it doesn't tie to us, it's obvious with the plane that there is a definite trail and some detective with a hard-on for you and your father will associate the trip with the target. It's only a matter of time."

VT shook his head. "Circumstantial. Not enough. And the storm seems to be here, so more people are going to be concerned about *that* instead of a missing loser. For Christ's sake, Tony, *you* even said that the storm will cover up a lot."

"I'm taking a shower. We better get dressed for the part before our guy gets here."

"Okay, good."

"Hell of a way to make a living. Constantly looking over your shoulder."

"Go take your shower. I'll change."

VT left for his room and let Zanetti worry. It was a short walk down the hall to his room. He kept his cap low over his face and his head cast downward in case the security cameras were recording him.

Once inside, he realized he really could use a drink. Zanetti was becoming more and more disrespectful, and that was eventually going to lead to some sort of showdown. And since he really didn't know the extent of Zanetti's relationship with dear old dad, it was a huge problem.

Better to see if he could get a take on it.

His father was eighty-three years old, but VT knew he'd be awake at this time, ready for the day. Much to his chagrin, the old man was the real-life Terminator. Time and time again, VT was regaled with stories about how poor his family was in the Depression era and how his father would steal railroad ties from the train tracks they were building through their town of Franklin Park, Illinois, to drag, two at a time, several blocks at night, then chop them up for firewood to heat their small wooden house. That's before the wood was treated chemically.

The old man was tough as nails and would never die.

So he had to get as much intelligence as possible. VT picked up his cell phone.

Right away, by the tone of his father's voice, he could tell the call wasn't welcomed.

"What?"

"Good morning to you too, Father."

"And you're calling me…why?"

VT knew that his father's phone might be tapped. No matter; everyone just needed to calm down. They had businesses here and it was perfectly logical that a caring boss would like to ensure that his employees and his assets were protected in light of the storm.

"Just called to say that we're checking on the employees. They're gonna be safe. We'll make sure nothing is overlooked and ready for the storm," he said as nonchalantly as possible. "Hear anything on your end?"

The old man grunted and hung up.

VT gripped the phone so hard his knuckles turned white, and he could hear the plastic complaining. But he carefully closed the phone and set it down gently on the desk in his room.

He knew what he had to do. He'd better do it to his father before his father could do it to him.

32

I WANTED TO know the time but dared not take my eyes off the road with wind and rain strafing the Jeep. The wiper blades were on high, and I could still barely make out the painted lines designating my lane.

Remembering Don's incident with the wind and the fact that John was in the back seat, I kept the speed down and made darned sure I didn't overcorrect.

"What time is it?" I asked innocently.

"The clock radio is right in front of you," Don said.

"You know, in the time you took to tell me that, you could have looked for me so I don't end up in the ditch or fishtail all over the interstate."

I was losing my patience with Don, but as I quickly glanced in the mirror at John, I knew better than to show it.

"It's nine fifty-one and we're near Jackson, Mississippi. Now how 'bout I drive?" John said from the back seat.

It was only the tenth time he had asked me to relinquish the wheel since he started talking to me again.

"I'm good," I replied as cheerfully as I could, considering everything that was going on.

Traffic was light. Most people had more common sense than we did; we had the road all to ourselves. I silently said a prayer of gratitude that no semitrucks were creeping up on me.

Maybe John was getting sick from all the back-and-forth motion. Maybe that's why he was so anxious to get back in the driver's seat. But there was no way I was going to pull over in this weather. Besides, if we ran over something on the shoulder, I would be blamed for another tire issue and I'd never hear the end of it. Plus, we had no spare.

I shifted my feet around, and my heel hit it. The yellow toolbox was under my feet!

That's what John was so damned concerned with! He was too far away from it, and I was right on top of it. But why would he be so upset? I was hardly going to reach down and open it with the conditions this challenging.

And Don wouldn't reach for it, not while I was driving and not when he already knew what it contained.

I wish I had been able to tell Don that I had disarmed the gun in the yellow toolbox. I wish I had had the guts to reassure him that he wouldn't be shot.

By John, anyway.

Maybe he'd be less likely to reach for his pocket when things got heated. John was going to notice sooner or later, and that would be awkward.

My stomach growled loud enough to be heard over the rain. Don looked at me, and his own stomach growled.

Embarrassed, I asked Don to turn on the radio for some news.

"I got a better idea. Let's stop for some food. Then we can switch drivers," John said.

"I'm good," I repeated for the eleventh time.

"Well, I'm not," Don said. "Look, there's a sign for a Cracker Barrel at this next exit. Weather's getting pretty bad. We should at least stock up on food, and we can get some snacks there to take with us. We'll never know when we're going to eat again."

"Potato chips aren't food," I said, but he was right. So I slowed down and took the exit when we found it.

The restaurant was right at the top of the exit. That was good because I didn't want to waste too much time looking for it. Even with the boat trailer hitched to the Jeep, I managed to park close enough to the porch so we didn't have to run too far in the rain. I shut down the engine and handed the keys to Don.

Springing out of the Jeep, I ran as fast as I dared on the slippery asphalt, and to my surprise, Don was right behind me.

John, on the other hand, wasn't, and Don and I turned around to look for him. John had thumbed the power-lock button, and I could hear all four door locks open. He immediately went to the driver's door, pulled it open, and took out the yellow toolbox, then carried it to the rear hatch. He was going to put it in the back.

This gave me an opportunity to warn Don.

"Don, I need to tell you something," I started to say.

"Look, Brenda, unless you know that John figures I have the gun—"

"Will you just *shut up* and listen to what I have to say?"

Well, my tone was a little angrier than I had wanted it to be; but in my defense, I was frustrated. Don immediately turned and walked away.

"When you can be civil, we can talk," he said.

Stupid bastard! Oh, that stupid, *stupid* bastard!

I didn't wait for John. I turned and headed into the general store and went straight to the bathroom. I went to the sink, splashed water on my face, and looked at myself in the mirror.

Don was going to die. John's partners were going to follow us and hunt him down. Maybe me too. It might be our last few hours on this earth.

I flashed on Ashley and May and what they must be going through. I wondered how Ashley would finish college without us being there. I thought about who was going to walk her down the aisle someday.

I couldn't help it. I was frustrated, angry, and scared. I started sobbing—big, wet, hopeless, angry sobs—and I could not stop.

33

Ashley was running for her life.

She kept hitting the walls in the darkened hallway and nearly fell down the stairs. No matter how fast she tried to get away, Bruno always managed to get ahead of her. Finally catching her, he started tearing at her clothes as she screamed and screamed, but the elderly residents whose faces she could see clearly just watched her being raped without helping.

In fact, a few of them started asking about their meds.

She began to feel overheated and sweaty. When she opened her eyes, what she saw confused the hell out of her.

The sun was shining through the single window by the bed, bathing the room in brilliant and painful light. She was in the recliner, alone, and it was stuffy and hot in the room. The storm had subsided, and it was relatively quiet.

It had been a dream—nightmare really—but she was awake now and all right. It was only a dream.

Not sure if she should be alarmed or relieved, she stiffly got up off the recliner and stumbled to the bathroom, taking care of a few biological needs. She sat down, remembering her nightmare in vivid detail, held her head in her hands, and tried not to shake.

A quick glance at her watch told her it was just two minutes after ten in the morning.

As she was sitting on the commode, she looked over at the tub.

It didn't register at first, but when she looked again, it hit her. The tub was empty!

How the hell could the water drain out? She'd closed the drain plug. Wait, what about May's tub?

She finished as quickly as she could, gathered her toiletry bag, and tried to flush the commode. It wouldn't flush.

Disgusted, she put the lid down and hurried to the door, but she stopped just in front of the chair.

She was going to have to do this. She was just going to have to be strong. Ashley closed her eyes and tried to make peace with the dream; it was only a dream. Only a dream.

Nearly ripping the chair out from under the doorknob, undoing the chain, and opening the door took but a few seconds, then she remembered to check her pockets for the key.

It wasn't there.

There wasn't any time to hunt for it; she had to check on May's tub, and if it was draining, she'd have to find something to put over the drain to save as much water as she could—if it hadn't drained out already like hers.

But the key! Her eyes darted over the room again. They landed on the small desk chair, and she placed it under the doorknob again, but this time to hold the door open. It occurred to her that this might invite curious residents in, looking for information on their damned meds, and her stuff was in the room, in full few of anyone walking by. But she couldn't wait.

Just the same, she pulled the door and chair nearly closed, just open enough to fit the chair between the doorframe and the door, then she hurried across the hall.

But as soon as she got closer, she saw Bruno walking toward May's room from the other direction. He was rubbing his temples and sweating profusely. His dark skin fairly glistened.

It looked like he had had a bad night.

When he looked up and saw her, he didn't even slow down.

"I'm thinkin' you want to see her," he said quietly, but his voice still filled the hallway.

She had slowed to a halt, unsure if she should turn and run or wait and see what would happen; he seemed docile enough. But after what she said about him and knowing he probably heard it, she hesitated.

"Please don' speak loud. That whiskey *made me the misere*," he said.

Whiskey? Had he been drinking last night? Maybe he wouldn't remember what she had said about him to the residents.

So Ashley nodded, silently. Cautiously.

He fished for his key ring and opened May's door. Ashley followed him in, and the door did not swing closed. Actually, she felt more comfortable because of that.

May was lying in bed. Bruno rubbed his temples for a moment while standing at her bedside, and Ashley moved to the bathroom. Fortunately, the tub was still full, and she breathed a sigh of relief.

When she turned around to greet May, she saw Bruno gently shaking her.

"Ms. May? It late in the morning, *beb*."

May did not stir.

Bruno touched her forehead, then reached down to her arm and felt her pulse. Since he made no expression, Ashley asked him, "Is she all right?"

Bruno glanced up at her, still not changing his expression. "I'll be right back. I got more people to check on."

Well, there didn't seem to be any sense of urgency, so she turned back and started brushing her teeth and sponging off. When she was through, she came out and raised her voice.

"Good morning, Auntie May! Time to get up and enjoy the oppressively hot weather!"

May didn't budge; in fact, she was in the exact same position as when Bruno left.

"May?"

Ashley set her bag down on the bed and went up to May's head. She reached out and touched her shoulder.

"May?" she asked, gently shaking her.

But May moved strangely, stiffly.

Concerned, she felt May's forehead. May was cool to the touch, and she wasn't sweating at all.

She grabbed May's wrist and tried to find a pulse. Failing on the first try, Ashley repositioned her hand and tried again.

Still nothing.

Then she put her hand under May's nose. May was not breathing.

May was dead.

34

VT WAS BACK in Zanetti's room, much to Zanetti's annoyance. They had nothing to do but check their inventory again and watch the weather channel.

Finally, there was a soft knock on the hotel room door.

VT grabbed the remote and shut off the TV while Zanetti drew his favorite pistol from its holster behind his back.

He loved this gun—an HK45 Compact Tactical, better known as the HK45CT, a .45 ACP cannon—because he didn't like to shoot twice to get the job done. He also liked it because its barrel was threaded, and since he nearly always used a suppressor, that barrel was a real asset.

Zanetti approached the door and kept the gun at his side, ready for anything. He peered through the peephole and turned to VT.

"It's him."

VT glanced at his watch and frowned.

Zanetti took the chain off the door and opened it, motioning the FEMA agent in. With a quick glance around the hallway and not seeing anyone, he closed the door and put the chain on again.

"Mr. Baxter, you're late," VT said.

Baxter's voice shook. "I'm sorry, really! You have no idea how hard it was to fly under the radar."

"You get everything?" Zanetti asked, hoping to redirect the conversation to where it had to go.

Baxter turned to Zanetti and nodded quickly. "Yes, here, here are your IDs. I even got badges for you. I wouldn't show them around more than you need to. These numbers belonged to people that left the agency. Don't ask how I kept the numbers active."

Zanetti nodded. "Understood, thanks for the heads-up."

"We should have been on our way by now," VT spat. "We're going to lose control of our environment. We were supposed to be someplace before the people we're meeting got there. Fat chance of it now, thanks to you."

Zanetti had had enough. "Give the guy a break, VT," he said, holstering his weapon. "I'd rather him be slow and careful than get noticed and have to answer awkward questions. He's only protecting us."

The statement seemed to ease Baxter's tension a little. VT wasn't happy, but at least he changed the subject.

"Where is it?" VT asked gruffly.

"The boat and truck?"

"No, the tooth fairy," VT said.

"I-It's behind the restaurant across the street, in the back. I figured that it was a bad idea to bring it into the hotel parking lot. Too many people watching, you know."

"Good thinking," Zanetti said.

"Uh, I got you a Suburban to haul it. That's why it took so long. A boat and trailer isn't much good without something to tow it."

"How many people know about this?" VT growled.

"Just me. I forged somebody else's name on checkout. Believe me, no one is going to be able to tie this to you."

VT harrumphed, but Zanetti nodded, saying, "Okay, good job."

"It's a RIBCraft 5.85," Baxter went on, smiling nervously. "It's nineteen feet of nautical badass. Nobody will give you any shit while you're in it."

"Yeah, that means nothing to me," VT said, starting to gather his bags.

"We'll meet you there," Zanetti told Baxter as he ushered him out of the room.

When he closed the door, Zanetti turned to VT. "You ought to lighten up, VT. The guy did spectacular."

"Yeah, well, I never trust a nervous guy."

"What are you saying, VT?"

"Loose end."

This was insane. Zanetti just glared at VT. Too many bodies piling up would leave a trail, leading right to them. VT was being paranoid and stupid. But he nodded.

After giving the two rooms a detailed search and wipe down, the two men gathered their possessions and went down the back stairwell, exiting the hotel from the side, then walked quickly across the street.

It was raining, but neither of them cared. It had a cooling effect, and for once, VT wasn't complaining.

When they got to the vehicle in the back of the closed restaurant, they loaded their bags in the Chevy and Baxter handed them the keys to the Suburban and the boat.

"I paid cash for the gas, and you even have two extra gas cans, just in case. This baby burns more fuel than a runabout," Baxter said.

"Thanks," Zanetti said, motioning Baxter to follow him. When they reached the other side of the building, Zanetti turned to Baxter.

"Here"—handing him several hundred dollars in cash—"take a cab and pay cash. Mr. Taccone and I thank you. We never want to hear from you again, got it? Stay low and keep your mouth shut. You understand what I'm telling you?"

Baxter nodded vigorously.

Zanetti nodded and turned to walk back to the rig, smiling to himself.

35

EVEN THOUGH IT was ten forty-one in the morning, I ordered scrambled eggs and coffee. Lots and lots of coffee.

From the moment we were seated to the last bite, there was dead silence. It was like living in a monastery without the prayers. It should have been uncomfortable, but frankly, I appreciated the forced *me* time. Of course, that allowed my mind to wander to areas I didn't really want it to go just now. But every time it wandered, I managed to force it back to planning out how we were going to convince May to get in the tiny boat to be ripped away from her beloved city.

Finally, Don tossed his napkin and pushed his chair back. "I'm headed for the bathroom," he announced.

This left John and me alone. Now I was feeling uncomfortable.

John barely slowed shoveling grits into his mouth. I cleared my throat.

Nothing.

I wanted to know. I just had to find out if he knew about us moving the guns.

"So I see that you're more comfortable not having that yellow toolbox around you all the time."

He just grunted and kept the conveyer belt running between the plate and his lips.

I would have expected more of a reaction if he suspected his precious yellow toolbox had been violated by the likes of Don.

Okay, so far, so good.

"What do you think we need to stock up on?" I asked.

He barely slowed down. "Whatever you want. Energy bars, drinks. Nuts are good for energy."

Still no indication about what he was thinking. So of course I had to push it.

"What should we do about protection down there?"

John instantly stopped chewing and slowly put his fork down even though it was loaded with food and leaned back, looking directly at me, squinting.

"What do you mean, Brenda?"

Well, I certainly must have struck a nerve *there*. So I went exploring.

"Well, I was thinking about how we would protect ourselves from looters. I mean, you have this boat and all that electronic stuff, and here we are defenseless."

"I guess we'll have to play it by ear," he said. This was his chance to come clean, the one opportunity to earn my trust.

He just lost it forever.

"Maybe we should buy a gun or something," I continued, watching him closely.

He started eating again and shrugged. "Do what you want. But when I buy a gun, in Illinois, anyway, I have to wait three whole days for a pistol. You want to wait that long? Plus, you probably can't buy one in this state. You're not a resident."

Again, he missed a chance to come clean. So either he actually thought that the yellow toolbox contained his father's tools or he was an abject liar.

My money was on the latter.

Suddenly, the eggs weren't sitting very well in my stomach. I got up and pushed the chair back.

"Where are you going?"

I shrugged. "Shouldn't have had the eggs," was all I said.

Obviously underwhelmed, he went back to eating, and I headed for the ladies' room.

Well, if I was the love of his life, I would have thought he'd care about my stomach issues. I was sure that I had painted a target on my own back.

My stomach was complaining, but only a little. It did act up when I bumped into Don in the small corridor leading to the restrooms.

I had to try one more time. I grabbed his elbow and held on.

"Don, you need to *listen* to me."

He sighed. "Really, Brenda, I know you're worried. I know Katsarus has it in for me. Let's just focus on getting there, all right?"

"No, Don, you *don't* understand," I replied, but wouldn't you know it, an elderly man in one of those electric-powered scooters came around the corner and wanted to get to the men's room. Don and I had to separate, and he immediately headed back out to the main room of the store.

As I watched him go, my stomach kicked me. I was going to lose him. Well, I was probably going to lose him in a divorce, but at least he'd be alive that way.

I had to come to grips about living without him, either way. At least with his death, there'd be an insurance benefit.

Immediately, I shook my head and slapped my forehead. That's *not* who I am! I instantly hated myself for trying to rationalize such a horrible thing!

The only way I would ever feel better about myself would be to warn Don and try my best to prevent this horrible thing that I was so afraid of.

I—*we*—would have to prevail against John the sportsman, expert in guns, and an unknown number of potentially professional hitmen.

Piece of cake, right?

Yeah, I didn't think so either. I took a deep breath to calm my nerves as best I could and ran to the bathroom.

36

Ashley gave up trying to stop crying. But it was the stifling heat and stuffiness in May's room that finally broke her focus on the family tragedy.

She glanced at her watch, 10:53 AM, not even the hottest part of the day yet.

Desperate for some air, Ashley got up from her place at May's bedside and moved over to the outside wall and opened one of the large windows in May's room.

But there was no breeze, and the outside was just as hot. With no relief from the heat, she stuck her head out and looked around.

The window was directly over an aluminum awning covering the back porch. She flashed on the memory of sitting with her mother and Aunt May on that back porch when she came down to visit Tulane as a high school senior. The fact that May was so close was a factor in her choice of college, and she remembered thinking how great it was to have a backyard big enough to host family gatherings and how fun it would be to join the home's monthly BBQ.

Unfortunately, Ashley had little time to participate, and she immediately felt the painful grip of guilt.

But now, as she gazed out over the backyard from May's window, she was amazed to see how much water had filled the surrounding area and the backyard itself.

The back fence had been blown over, bending in toward the building itself. But it had managed to hold on tenuously to the post's roots buried underground. Even so, it could not hold back the flood that was creeping up toward the building itself. Even so, the water didn't look too deep—yet.

But the street behind the center was flooded already, and Ashley could see a few cars parked by the curb with water up past the tops of their tires.

She clenched her teeth. That water was coming in fast. When Ashley looked back down at the backyard again, she was startled to see the shore of the water had receded at least a foot closer to the building since she had looked away.

She could feel the panic rising up her throat, and it took all she had to stifle it. Problem was, her mind drifted to Aunt May again.

Eyes welling up once more, she knew she was headed down the depths of a self-pity quagmire, but her process was interrupted by the wump, wump sound echoing among the buildings outside. It sounded like a helicopter, and it was nearby. Lifting her eyes to the sky, she finally caught sight of it—a big red-and-white Coast Guard Rescue Jayhawk helicopter, flying quickly eastward, nearly a hundred feet over the buildings across the street in back of the center.

She wished she were on it, going somewhere safe.

Ashley watched it until it disappeared beyond her view. When she lost sight of it, she sighed; it was like losing hope for escape. She briefly considered whether she should head up to the roof to flag down another helicopter but rejected it. First, she didn't know if there would be any more helicopters, and second, she had no idea how to get on the roof.

To Ashley, it seemed like her hope of rescue was fading with the sound of the retreating coast guard helicopter.

But when that sound faded, another replaced it. It sounded like someone mowing their lawn.

Absurd, it seemed, but that's what it sounded like. She craned her neck to catch a glimpse of the sound's source. It finally floated into view.

A tiny barge-like boat pushed by a small outboard motor sailed slowly past her window. It was traveling westward on the flooded street behind the assisted-living center and was filled to the brim with people of all ages. Ashley counted six people, three of them children and one seemingly very elderly.

There was no room for her in the boat, but she called out anyway.

"Good luck! Be careful," she yelled, waving.

After looking around briefly, the children waved to her in the window. At least she knew that people could hear her over an outboard. That information just might be useful.

Beginning to sweat profusely, she pulled herself in from the window and headed to the bathroom. Sitting down by the tub, she reached in and scooped as much water as she could carry in her cupped hands and splashed it on her face, letting it drip down her neck.

Feeling cooled now, she repeated it until her entire torso had been touched by the precious drops of water.

Now what?

She had no idea if or when another helicopter would be flying overhead, and she had no way of knowing when the next boat would be by. She was going to have to wait until another boat or chopper came by to see if she could flag it down.

It wasn't the best plan, but it's all she had unless she took her chances with the street gangs outside.

Nope, she was now at the mercy of dumb luck.

And since she was convinced that Bruno had overdosed May—on purpose or by accident, not that it mattered—and since he knew she knew about it, she was going to need all the fat dumb luck she could get if he came back.

37

THE INTERIOR OF the Jeep was hotter than a sauna. With John driving again, I was exiled to the back where the side-to-side motion conspired against me.

My watch was indicating 12:34 PM. At least that's what I thought it read before a huge droplet of sweat splattered on the dial, obscuring it.

I pulled myself upright, and the dazzling, brilliant sunlight hurt my eyes. But even more painful was the environment we were driving through; the countryside had been shorn clean of most of the foliage.

Interstate 55 runs just west of Lake Pontchartrain and is elevated over some of the, in my opinion, nastiest swampland in the nation. In effect, we were driving over a long interstate bridge for the entire time we were on the west coast of the lake.

"Why didn't we take the causeway over the lake?" I asked out loud.

Don finally answered, "We have no idea what shape it's in, and it's hard to make a U-turn with a trailer."

"Not if you know what you're doing," John piped up.

"Whatever."

In an effort to put the poisonous atmosphere inside the Jeep out of my mind, I squinted to the west. The trees were nearly bare, and every once in a while, you could see a decimated marina or what was left of some kind of fishing-type business. At the bigger marinas, the boats were tossed every which way, like some giant child had picked them up and dropped them.

It was frankly depressing, and this wasn't the place where the hurricane came ashore. With all the carnage, what must it be like where Ashley and May were?

The nausea came back, so I tried to redirect my mind.

"Why is it so hot?" I asked.

"Uh, it's summer, and we're down south?" Don replied.

"Seems that Don's Jeep can't handle a little heat and my light boat and trailer," John said. "I put the heat on because we were overheating. I'm sorry, but it has to be done, or we get delayed further while we pull off on the shoulder and wait for the Jeep to cool down."

"Good idea. Let's keep going," I said for lack of anything too intelligent to add.

And we did. Soon, I-55 met I-10 and John turned east. All seemed good despite the heat until we heard the siren behind us.

John and Don tensed up immediately. It didn't help my stomach any.

We pulled over on the shoulder, and John killed the motor. He even popped the hood to let in more air.

"Okay, stay calm and let me do the talking," he said.

For once, Don didn't have a snide reply.

We waited for what seemed to be an eternity when, finally, a shadow passed on my side of the Jeep—the right side. It was a Louisiana state policeman, and he bent down to talk to us right next to Don, who was so rigid that I was afraid he'd look guilty enough to get searched.

"Afternoon," the policeman said with a thick Cajun accent. "Driver's license please."

"What was I doing wrong, Officer? I didn't think I was speeding," John said as he reached for his wallet. "This Jeep is overheating, and there's no way I was speeding, sir."

The policeman said nothing but took John's license and looked around the interior of the Jeep.

Then he looked at the license for a moment, really studying it, which was a huge relief for me. If something happened to Don, now there was proof that John was down here.

"You all from Illinois?" he asked, pronouncing the silent *S*.

We all nodded, sweat dripping off us like a waterfall.

"Can I ask what you are doin' down here?"

John stepped up. "CERT. We've come down to help. This is our first deployment, sir."

The cop nodded. "I didn't realize that you folks could self-deploy," he said slowly.

"Sorry, I guess we just got overeager. We just completed the training last month, and not much really happens this time of year in Chicago," John offered.

"Hmm. Y'all got your DHS IDs?"

I was stunned. This is where it all ends. This is where we get caught and jailed, leaving Ashley and May to fend for themselves.

Now what?

"I didn't think we needed to carry them," John said. "Going to a disaster area and all, I was afraid that we'd lose them, and besides, there's a record of us at the DHS, right? Like I said, this is our first deployment, sir."

"We really aren't organized so much yet," Don offered, his mouth obviously dry and voice cracking.

The cop nodded but watched Don closely. Don smiled briefly, then resumed his deer-in-the-headlights stare straight ahead. The trooper took John's license back to his car, and we were left alone with our fears.

"We're dead," Don spit out.

"Relax, cowboy. Nothing is set in stone. You're looking at a gifted salesman. Just don't blow it, and for Christ's sake, *relax*," John hissed.

How the hell could I relax? John had a gun in that damned yellow toolbox, and even worse, Don had one in his pocket. And *it* was loaded.

To top it off, we were absolutely lying about CERT. He was going to check us out, and he wasn't going to find anything that supported our lies.

"This was a bad idea. We are impersonating first responders! We could go to jail," I pined.

John sighed. "Will you two just relax?"

"How the hell can I relax, John? You know damned well I can't relax! My daughter and aunt are stuck down there, we won't be able to get to them now, we're going to have a record, and—"

But I caught myself before I blurted out what John had planned for Don. That kind of agitated discussion would not sit well with the cop when he came back.

"And what?" Don asked.

Shit. Even John turned around to face me, with a menacing look on his face.

"Ashley! How the hell are we going to save her now?" was all I could manage.

Don was about to say something, but the cop came back and handed John's license to him. "You folks need to be more organized. They may not let you in unless they do a background check, but I hear that the coms may be out. You have a fifty-fifty chance of joining the team. Sorry about that, that you came all this way, but that's the way it works. Head up I-10 here till you see the tents. That's the staging area. They set it up quick, I'll give them that. But this is just the start, so good luck."

"Thank you, Officer," John said, relief in his voice.

The cop looked back at the boat. "Good thing you brought that. The city is flooding as we speak. It's only gonna get worse. Stay safe."

And he was gone.

"Fifty-fifty chance, huh? Great," I said when I was sure the cop was gone.

John started the engine. "Better than nothing," he said.

Then Don spoke quietly, "We can always pretend the Jeep overheated and put in early. We can just turn off and probe our way east until we find someplace we can launch, and then we don't have to answer to anybody."

The idea was stunningly brilliant. John, of course, shrugged and snorted.

"Sure. Let's just risk rocks, the prop hitting something, and being labeled as looters. You know they *shoot* looters, right?"

Poor choice of words, I thought.

38

"He's still behind us."

I clandestinely turned around and pretended to reach for something in the back. Over the top of the boat, I could see the light bar on the state police car.

"What's the plan?" I asked.

"Wing it," John said gruffly.

"Swell." I made my living developing plans. *Winging it* is not in my vocabulary.

I turned around and tried to get comfortable. It was an impossible task. We were more than just paranoid, and that would most likely lead to some sort of mistake, setting off the lights on top of the police car and our eventual failure. Just like my marriage.

It was funny; when I found out I was pregnant and told Don, he insisted we get married. After how John treated me by sleeping with everything that moved, Don's proposal seemed heroic.

It had been a long time since a guy had tried to be my hero. With my Catholic upbringing, abortion wasn't an option. So I said yes. Hell, he even had a job lined up before graduation, so the decision was easy.

It was more than John was going to do. So Don stood by our mistake turned blessing, and John went off to find riches and show me how much of a fool I was to keep the baby and marry Don.

But Don had been a great father and the most patient person I knew until he started having issues at work. But he never complained about Ashley's occasional bad decisions, at least in front of her.

So was it *my* fault we were crashing?

What had I done? How had I shut him down? And more importantly, can I fix it?

My musing was interrupted by a whoop of the siren next to us. The state trooper had pulled alongside of the Jeep, and he waved in an odd way. He flashed his hand with the fingers and thumb three times.

I realized he was telling us fifteen miles ahead.

John nodded and waved, and then the cop slowed and pulled into one of those paved spots in the middle of the interstate to turn around. We all collectively breathed a sigh of relief.

"We should listen to the radio and see if we can get some information on the flooding," Don suggested, reaching for the knob.

He tried a lot of FM stations, but there wasn't much broadcasting going on. Then Don flipped to the AM band.

Don managed to find a station that was broadcasting advisories on how to contact rescue teams and other civil defense stuff. It was unbelievably frustrating; there wasn't any information at all about the situation in the city.

"Try some more stations," I pleaded.

But to my amazement, Don turned the radio off.

"What are you doing? I want to find out what's happening," I asked.

"Look, Brenda, the airport is near here. I think we ought to check there first," he said.

Even John looked at him strangely.

"And why do you want to do that?" John asked.

"Because if we don't have to go into the city, then we reduce our risk. If they have some sort of shelter there, then we can search for her, and if she's there, then no harm, no foul."

John shook his head, but I had to admit, it made sense.

"It's worth a try," I said.

"And I think it's a waste of time," John snapped.

It was an odd way to reply. Why would he not want to try this first? Was he that intent to get Don into the ruins of the city so he could off my husband?

"But, John, why do you want to risk your boat when we might not have to?" I prodded him.

"Do you really think your daughter with your aunt were able to get to the airport, even if there is a shelter there, this quickly? With the city flooding?"

Well, John had a point too. But why not check here first? It seemed logical.

"I feel we should try the airport first. If they don't have a shelter set up there, then I think we can just go back to the original plan."

"Except that cop could have radioed ahead for them to expect us. If we go to the airport and look for someone, even *if* they set up a shelter there, right where they are going to have a lot of air operations which are dangerous, we will not only delay our arrival at the staging area, but we also show up at the airport we'll tip our hand to even *more* people that we're not CERT."

"Good point. Forget I said anything," Don finally said.

I was conflicted. John's argument made sense too. If Ashley and May had to hunker down in the assisted-living center during the storm, how would they make it to the airport, clear across town with the city flooding?

But I knew damn well why John was so adamant about *his* plan; if we found Ashley and May at the airport, he couldn't have Don killed in a place that would naturally cover up the murder.

Too quickly, we sped past the exit to the airport. I glanced to the south toward it, as if I could actually see a shelter if it were there but admittedly saw nothing.

Passing the airport filled me with dread for more than one reason.

39

Zanetti knew what VT was going to ask before he opened his mouth.

It was the same thing he'd been asking for the last twenty miles: call Katsarus and find out where they are and when we should meet them. If anything, VT was predictable.

"Look, I'm not going to ask again. Call Katsarus and coordinate," VT demanded, turning both air-conditioning vents toward him and smashing the MAX AC button.

"For the last time, VT, the cell service is down."

"Prove it."

Zanetti would have rolled his eyes, but he didn't want to take them off the road. Not used to towing a trailer, the last thing they needed was to wreck with a FEMA-owned boat, trailer, and government-issued Chevy truck.

Instead, he dug out his phone and handed it to VT. "I'm driving this missile. See if you can get a signal."

VT snapped the phone from Zanetti's hand. "I get five bars. So much for your downed network theory."

"Go ahead and call him. It's the last number I received." Zanetti didn't mention the voice mail Katsarus had left for them.

But now, considering they were about to get deep into this mission, maybe he should.

VT selected the number and dialed. After a few seconds, he frowned. "Fast busy signal."

"Proves my point."

VT tossed the phone in the center console's cup holder. Zanetti winced.

"That's an expensive phone, VT. If that's totaled, I'll have to expense that."

"You do that."

Okay, it was time to come clean. Mentioning Katsarus's voice mail would have an added benefit: it would change the subject.

"By the way, I didn't mention this because I knew what your answer was going to be. We eliminate everyone, so when I got Katsarus's voice mail, I ignored it."

VT turned to him slowly. "And when were you going to tell me?"

"Right now, as a matter of fact."

"So what the fuck did he say?"

Zanetti squeezed the wheel and shifted his weight in the seat. "He wanted to call the whole thing off."

There was a long, awkward silence. Zanetti started twisting his hands on the wheel. He knew the volcano was about to blow, and he was directly in the path of Mount VT.

Mr. Taccone Sr. gave him great latitude for this trip, but Zanetti was pretty sure that that didn't include offing his son.

"He called it *off*, and you *didn't* tell me?"

Zanetti cleared his throat because he wanted to remain calm and not end VT right here, right now. It was going to be a struggle.

"Would it have changed your mind?"

VT turned away. "No."

"Then less for you to worry about, right?"

More silence. In another mile or so, VT spoke softly, but very specifically.

"Next time, you will let *me* be the judge of what to worry about or not, *Capisce?*"

"Yeah."

VT turned back to him. "Please tell me you took care of Baxter."

"You'll never hear from him again." Zanetti never could lie convincingly, so he chose his words carefully. Problem was, VT knew that too.

"So he's dead, right?"

Zanetti turned to his boss, but only for as long as he dared. "If you don't trust me, why don't you do something about it?"

VT turned away again. It was another half hour before he spoke once more.

"How many witnesses are we going to deal with at this assisted-living center?"

Zanetti shrugged. "How the hell should I know? I'm not wild about this. We can't go killing everybody there."

"Then why did you even bring this whole thing up to me in the first place?"

There it was. VT's excuse to his old man for the mess they were about to step in. And he was the floor mat.

Well, not this time.

"These people are elderly. They probably won't even remember what we look like."

"No loose ends, Zanetti. I'm not willing to take the chance."

"Do you really think it's a good idea to leave a whole fucking old folks home riddled with bodies full of bullet holes?"

He let that sink in.

"Then we'll burn them out."

They were mobsters, Zanetti wouldn't even try to deny that, except to the police and certain lawyers. But that didn't mean they were heartless bastards ether. Heartless was bad for business, in most cases.

He said nothing and let VT stew in anticipation.

And while his boss was stewing, Zanetti made a promise to himself at that exact moment.

He made the promise that he would find an opportunity during *this trip* to end his boss and the risks he introduced to the business.

Cross his heart and hope to die.

40

"So now what, Columbus?"

I sighed as loudly as I could to send a message. John's taunts were getting old and obnoxious. But before I could say anything, Don had to open his mouth.

"Well, John, I have no idea. How's that? Why don't you use some of those outdoorsy skills and help us figure this out?"

We were driving around on the side streets of an industrial development, somewhere east of the airport, I was sure.

In the end, we had voted on checking the airport. Those two voted against stopping at the airport and I won. After all, it was my rescue mission, and besides, crying seems to be kryptonite to men.

"Well, you've been down here before, Don. I would have *expected* you to know where you're going."

"I haven't been *here* before, John. What do you want me to do?"

"I want you to think. Have you ever *thought* before?"

"Stop it, you two! This isn't helpful," I screamed.

"Well, then, Brenda, it's one thirty-three. I'd hate to run out of daylight before we can get to that home your aunt lives in," John chided me.

"Just keep heading west. We should find some sort of way in. There has to be!"

John fell silent as he guided the Jeep and trailer westward. Knowing John, he was suffering a slow burn, and that worried me.

I had no idea what exactly he was capable of, but I got the feeling it wasn't going to be nice when he finally exploded.

"How much farther am I supposed to go?"

"Until we see the airport," Don added quickly.

"I ask," John went on as if he were indignant about being interrupted, "because we only have a third of a tank left."

"What? Of gas?" Don asked, as surprised as I was.

"No, dilithium crystals."

"How did we let it go so far down?" I asked, hoping to cut off any snide comment by Don.

"Well, seems as though there wasn't a lot of gas stations on that long-ass bridge we were on before we hit I-10. Now I hope there's something for us on the way back before Don's pushing."

"Like hell," Don snapped.

"Don, he was being facetious," I replied quickly.

"Like hell," John added.

Just then we passed underneath what looked like a connecting bridge to I-10 just to our north, and there it was—a runway to our left.

"That's it! We're here," I yelled.

John immediately took his foot off the accelerator, and since we were traveling on a split highway, he took the next break in the median to turn around.

"Turn right at the next opportunity," Don said defiantly.

"Ya think?"

I kept craning my neck, looking for any signs of a large group of survivors, but that might have been a lost cause. They wouldn't keep them outside in this heat, would they?

We turned south and traveled the complete length of the runway to our right. "There's got to be some way in," John said, annoyed.

"Just keep going. There's bound to be a way in," I asked him.

When we came to a large intersection, with two turn lanes to the right, John asked, "What do you want me to do?"

"Um, I *think* you ought to turn right," Don replied.

With an annoyed look, John took the exit and we stayed to the right.

"Aw hell, this is the main entrance," John exclaimed as we slid underneath the airport direction signs.

We were immediately stopped by armed guards who had blocked the entrance way with several Humvees. They looked like National Guardsmen.

Cautiously, John slowed and lowered his window. "Is this where the CERT team is staging? We heard near the shelter here at the airport."

I have to admit, he had just asked about all the things that were important to me, except for the part about assuring me that he wouldn't blow Don away.

The guardsman that was holding out his hand to stop us glanced at all of us, quickly through the window, and suddenly, we were being surrounded by three others with what looked like M4s, pointed down, fingers resting on the trigger guards.

I gulped.

Everyone was tense, everyone, except John. He nonchalantly hung his right hand on the steering wheel and leaned his elbow on the windowsill.

"Sir, there is no shelter here. This is an operational area. Civilians aren't allowed."

"Oh, well, where are the CERT teams staging then?"

The guardsman did another once-over of us, then answered, "I don't know, sir, but you can't come in here."

"Okay, um, can I turn around here?"

I wanted John to just shut the hell up and leave; if he pushed it, we were probably going to get searched.

"Tell them to try I-10. I heard there's some FEMA activity on one of the bridges there. They're launching boats from an exit ramp or something," one of the others on the opposite side of the Jeep called out.

"Sounds good. Can I just turn around here or what?" John asked again politely.

The guard stepped away and spoke into a microphone on his shoulder connected to a radio on his belt. I heard the response but couldn't make out the words. After it stopped, he waved us through the Humvees and gave us a final warning.

"You can drive through and come out the terminal exit ramp, but don't stop. They're pretty serious about that," he said, patting his gun.

John nodded. I wasn't breathing normally again until we were past the terminal building and out on the street, traveling in the opposite direction back to where we came from.

At least I knew that Ashley and May weren't here. That only left the rest of this damned city and Don's fate to discover.

41

I-10 CUTS THROUGH the northern part of greater metropolitan New Orleans. It occasionally passes over a few bridges, routing us over railroad tracks, business highways, and the occasional canal.

As I watched the scenery pass by my window on the right side of the back seat, I was amazed to see the sun reflected off water in the streets toward the south and some more on the north.

"It's like the city's turned into the American Venice," I said blithely.

"More like the American Atlantis," Don replied.

I know it was just a flippant comment, not designed to add stress or be sarcastic, but nevertheless, it didn't make me feel any better about Ashley and May's situation. Then I thought about my own flippant comment yesterday.

I guess flippant comments shouldn't be so flippant.

"So we better get our story straight," I said, trying to shake the gnawing feeling in my gut about my daughter and aunt.

"What's to get straight? We've used it all before," Don replied.

"But not where they're going to ask us for our IDs before we actually do something," I said.

"Relax. You worry too much," Don huffed.

"Of course I do! That's *our* daughter in there, without power, maybe standing in floodwater, and my aunt who is disabled! How the hell do you expect me to feel, Don? Maybe if you felt this way about us, Ashley and me, you'd have worked harder at keeping those jobs you lost!"

I regretted it even before I finished the sentence, but I had built up way too much momentum to stop before I did any damage.

"I'm…I'm here, aren't I?" was the only thing Don could stammer. I had embarrassed him deeply, and he was having a hard time recovering. It wasn't fair, but then again, it wasn't fair to put me through all this and not help at all.

"So is John and he isn't even related." That was about the dumbest thing I could have said, but I was in pure reaction mode and couldn't stop. I knew the real reason John was here, and it wasn't to help.

But I seemed to need to hurt Don. I had to make him *feel* something. And I was going to blow any chance of fixing us.

And I didn't care. When do you stop the losses and just get on with your life? I was in the process of writing him off, writing off our relationship, friendship, history, and future.

I was apparently okay with that. More or less.

But what I wasn't okay with was what John was going to have done to Don. I needed to stop it, and I needed to figure out how I could be better than I ever thought I could be—stronger, smarter, and more capable.

But I wasn't starting from a position of strength.

So I did what I always did. I changed the subject even though I knew I was leaving egos bruised and injured in my path.

"I think we should just stop and look for a place to launch the boat. What difference does it make where we start? Why do we have to explain ourselves to anyone?" I asked.

"Because they can arrest us if they think we're looters," John said.

"What would we be doing to give off that impression?" I asked. "Just by boating around the flooded streets of New Orleans, looking for stranded loved ones? Pretty thin evidence. It's not like we're armed or anything."

Don was not saying a thing. He didn't react to my comments. He didn't even try to one-up John. He just sat there, arms folded, staring straight ahead as we headed eastward on I-10, east of the airport.

John didn't react either, but I expected as much from him. So much for my taunt. It bought me nothing.

"The government can do whatever it wants if they declare Martial Law. They can create curfews, force people to go somewhere or to stay put. And they can shoot on sight."

"Thanks for being so positive, John," I mumbled.

"I *am* positive these things can happen. So it's better to just slide in on their terms and go about our business."

"And here I thought you were an independent kind of man," I taunted.

"I am. It's just that I want to stay out of prison."

"Look," I said, turning up the heat, "there's a canal we're going to cross. Let's just put in there and be done with it."

"How do we get out of the canal and into the city then?"

We barreled over the short bridge in literally seconds. I even think John sped up just to eliminate the option of launching here. Why, I couldn't say, but I was suspicious of all his actions now.

"What are we going to do if they won't let us in, John? What then? If they let us go, if they let us turn around, we'll have to find a way in on our own anyway. Why not just get ahead of the game?" I asked and turned to Don because I really needed him to help me, and besides, it was his idea, "Am I right?"

Don didn't even flinch.

"All right, Brenda, all right. Looks like the floodwater is deep enough under this bridge. I'll back down the entrance ramp on the other side and we'll launch, but I'm not going to be responsible for anything that happens to your Jeep while we're away from it."

"Too late," Don said. "We're here."

42

As we crested the highest point on the bridge, we found many police and official vehicles and a single E-Z UP tent over some people sitting, standing, and working at a table. Lined up on the interstate entrance ramp were a few boats on trailers attached to various SUVs sporting different agency badging. The boats were all different too; some of them the inflatable type, being launched on the very same entrance ramp John had wanted to use.

John slowed the Jeep before we came up to the first car, lights flashing, and some sort of officer standing outside of it, holding up his hand for us to stop.

"Afternoon, Officer. Is this where the CERT groups are staging?"

The officer didn't give us the detailed once-over that the National Guardsman had at the airport. He just waved us through, telling us to see the ramp coordinator about launch sequence.

"Well, that was a lot easier than I thought it would have been," John remarked, slowly stepping on the gas to make the Jeep roll up toward the other tents at the top of the bridge.

"We're not in the water yet," Don warned.

"Have faith, Donny-boy, we're nearly there now. We've gotten this far."

I wish I could have believed John, but I knew Don was right. We weren't on our way yet, and if we had stopped and launched in that canal, we could have avoided all this.

"What happens if we pull the CERT thing, and they find out we're lying?" I asked. "You think they're just going to let us go?"

"It's a chance we're going to have to take," John said.

"Yeah, well, I'm not lovin' it," I said to no one in particular.

As we approached, one of the officials looked up and started jogging toward us. I couldn't help but to notice he was wearing a gun on his belt. Apparently so did Don.

"That's a nasty-looking gun he's got there."

John sorted. "That's a puny gun. It's a Glock, most likely a nine millimeter in caliber. It's used by people who squat to pee."

"So," I said, "you're saying you wouldn't mind being shot by it?"

John glanced at me via the rearview mirror, but before he could reply, the official was at his window.

"Afternoon, what agency are you with?"

The man was young, muscular, and wore khaki shorts with a polo shirt that was embroidered with the FEMA patch. Good-looking and sunburned despite wearing a yellow boonie hat that was also labeled with the FEMA patch, he had an all-business expression.

It was do-or-die time.

John cleared his throat. "We're with CERT. We're looking for the staging area for the CERT groups."

"There's no CERT teams here. If you're here to help, pull over behind that trailer with the police boat, and we'll get you staged to go in. You can prepare your craft there and wait. One of you will have to register your group with control, under that tent."

"I'll go register," I said, glancing at John's reflection in the mirror. He raised his eyebrow but said nothing until we had pulled away from the official.

"That's not a good idea, Brenda. I'm a salesman by trade. It would be better—"

"Okay, then either Don or I will prepare the boat and back it down if they clear us while you go bullshit the authorities," I spit out.

"I, uh, see your point."

As soon as John stopped the Jeep behind the other boat, I opened the door and slipped out, not even waiting for either of them to say or do anything.

The tent didn't seem too far away, but the sun was hot and the concrete of the bridge radiated so much heat that if I looked across the floodwater to the top of the next I-10 bridge, I could see heat waves in the air.

The shade of the tent did little to protect anyone from the misery.

"Agency?"

One of the officials sitting behind a folding table was looking up at me, and he seemed overworked. This was it, I had a choice to make and I had to make if fast.

"CERT," I replied.

"ID?"

Shit. "Yes, well, this is our first deployment. We've just completed our training, and well, we don't have many checklist yet—"

"Look, lady, we're a little busy here. This has been one cluster fuck from the beginning. Do you have your ID badges or not?"

"Not here," I stammered.

"Then I can't let you go in."

43

"What do you mean, you can't let me in? My husband and I came all this way from Chicago with a friend who is donating the use of his boat, and you're going to turn us away?"

I was shaking mad, and it probably came out in my voice. And I probably spoke a bit louder than I should have.

One of the other officials came over, a tall, older man with gray hair and looking very fit.

"What's the problem?" he asked the guy sitting behind the table.

The official looked up at the tall guy from his seat. "This woman is claiming to be CERT and wants to help, but she has no DHS badges. She says they have a boat and her husband and friend came with. I told her I can't let her in."

"We came down from Chicago last night," I repeated, as if that would make any difference at all.

The older official thought for a moment. "It has to do with liability, ma'am. If you have a badge, we know they've done a background check on you."

"If we were looters or something, do you think we would have checked in with you?" I was hoping that logic would win the day.

But the older man frowned sadly and shook his head. "It's the rules, ma'am. I'm really sorry."

I was about to throw a fit when yet another man, a shorter one with a shaved head, wearing bib overalls and a white short-sleeved T-shirt, stepped over to the table.

"Hey, y'all, I heard what you was sayin', but, Ted, c'mon, we could use the help. This has been one cluster fu—oh, excuse me, ma'am, but it's been a mess from the start. If you want, I'll go with 'em an' mentor 'em."

I frankly didn't know what to do. The last thing I wanted was someone going with us. But we'd never get to launch from a safe ramp if I didn't play along. Then again, it wasn't the *last* thing I wanted to do; the *last* thing would be to sneak around and damage John's boat trying to get in to find Ashley and May. We'd end the trip when we were so close, and we'd be liable for John's boat. Like we could afford that now.

"Billy, I can't lose you here. We got so much to organize."

"Ted, they came all the way from Chicago just to help out. It don't make no sense to turn 'em away."

Ted pulled Billy away and had a serious conversation with him. I couldn't make out what they were saying exactly, but in the end, Ted nodded.

"Okay," Ted said, stepping back toward the table. "You're in. Billy's going to go with you and help you. Next time, remember the badges, okay?"

I nodded vigorously. Ted stepped away, and the other official asked to see my license, and I provided it. He said he'd need to copy the information on everyone else in my party, and I nodded.

Billy came around the table and held out his hand. "Name's Billy Bob Lee. You can just call me Billy."

"Billy Bob? I'm Brenda Meyers. My husband is Don. He's the thin guy over at the green Jeep Cherokee, and the other person is our neighbor John Katsarus." I wondered how happy John was going to be when he learned that he'd have to show his license, providing mounting proof he was down here with us. Maybe this was a good thing.

It might be enough to prevent a murder.

Now if I could only figure out how we could convince Bill Bob here to help us or how to get rid of him—without being shot as looters.

Billy looked at his watch. "It's just before two, we'd better get movin'."

Yes, we'd better, but to where and how much of a detriment were you going to be, I wondered as I smiled weakly.

44

My watch showed 2:28 PM when Don and John came back from showing their licenses to the FEMA official who copied down all our information.

"I'm surprised they didn't want our social security numbers," Don said.

John was not happy with Billy coming along. It was only a matter of time before the volcano blew.

"So, Billy Bob, that's kind of an unusual name for someone from the south," John said sarcastically.

To Billy's credit, he smiled and turned to John. "Well, actually, my full name is Dr. William Robert Lee, after the general. My daddy descends from his line, I figure."

This stunned everyone, but it proved that Billy Bob could hold his own. This was going to be a valuable skill with our group.

We started loading up the boat according to John's instructions—placing the heavier stuff in front to equalize the trim. Billy Bob and I were to sit on the raised floor of the boat in the bow; John called it a casting deck, and the heaviest bags were to go on the bottom of the boat just aft of the casting deck. That's boat speak for behind. Yep, learned that from another of John's lectures.

He and Don were going to sit on the bench behind the center steering console.

I noticed Don eyeing the water with some nervousness.

"Don, are you afraid of the water?" Billy asked.

"No, I'm afraid of drowning or being eaten by something in the water."

"Well, your friend here has one of the best boats ever made," Billy said, patting the side of John's boat. "It's a Boston Whaler. I got one myself. They don't sink."

"I've heard *that* before, Mr. Lee. They said that about the *Titanic*."

"Aw, the *Titanic* didn't have foam floatation like this here boat. Why, you can cut 'em in half and they won't sink. They did that on a commercial long time ago."

"Billy, I appreciate your concern for my husband's phobia, but he'll never feel safe around water. He had some kind of thing happen to him in a neighbor's pool a long time ago."

"Yeah," Don said, handing me a bag to put in the boat. "I nearly drowned as they tried to teach me to swim. Damn teacher just threw me in. Seem she thought that kids will naturally try to survive. I naturally sank."

"At least you didn't get eaten by something," Billy said with a huge grin.

Don just stared at Billy for a few seconds, then turned away. I decided, at that moment, I really liked Billy.

John was doing something at the rear of the boat with a wrench, and I hoped that Don wouldn't see it, thinking he was making a repair. But Don noticed and asked John what was wrong with the boat.

"He's putting the drain plug in," Billy offered as he tossed a bag up in the boat.

"You seem to know a lot about boats, Billy," I said.

"Ma'am, we're in *Nawlins*. Everybody drinks and fishes around here."

I chuckled, and it felt good. Maybe having Billy with was a *good* thing. He seemed to be a personable guy and maybe he'd consider helping us. I'd even offer to volunteer after we got May and Ashley situated just to pay him back.

Of course, nothing lasts forever. Billy noticed the yellow toolbox and grabbed it. Immediately, Don saw this and reached over, snatching it from a very surprised and confused Billy.

"I'll take that," Don said, not offering more of an explanation.

"John's father's tools," I told Billy. "He's very possessive of them."

Billy nodded, but still looked confused. Don took them and handed them to a shell-shocked John, who took the yellow toolbox and cradled it like a baby.

We loaded up the rest of the bags and supplies on the boat. Billy asked a question, though, which I was afraid would tip our hand.

"Why y'all got so much gas? Four of them five-gallon cans is a lot of gas. They'll supply all the gas you need here back at the ramp."

"Uh, we didn't know what to expect," Don said.

"Yeah, no idea what we'd be facing," John added.

"Well, y'all can leave that here to make more room," Billy suggested.

"May as well take it with us," I quickly interrupted. "That way, we don't have to keep coming back to the ramp if we don't have to," I added, and while Billy was facing me as I made my comment, John was in the background, wincing. A few seconds later, he turned to Billy. "Well, that does it. Can you back us down?"

I'm pretty sure John meant for Billy to get in the Jeep, and while we got in the boat, he would back the boat and trailer down the ramp. I was sure this was how he was planning to ditch Billy.

It wasn't a bad plan, but I had concerns about doing this right in front of every cop for miles, especially cops who had faster boats that could catch us.

I warily climbed up with the help of John and Don, then Don got in, then, lastly, John. Billy headed for the Jeep. When he was out of earshot, I turned to John, seating himself behind the steering wheel.

"Are you sure this is a smart thing to do?"

"Isn't this what you came down for?"

"I mean ditching Billy in front of all these cops! They have boats too, and they look faster than this one as loaded down as it is!"

"I'll wait until he pulls away with the Jeep."

"Hold on there, Billy!"

We all turned around to see a police officer waving Billy down. "You get in the boat, and I'll back you in."

I turned back to John. He was turning six shades of red and gripping the steering wheel so hard his knuckles turned white.

"Now what?" Don asked no one in particular.

"Now we figure out if we can ask for Billy's help," I said.

As Billy climbed in, another official ran up to us and handed Billy one of the biggest handheld radios I'd ever seen.

"You'll need this," he said to Billy. As Billy grabbed the radio from him, the official turned to us. "One last time, folks, are you sure you want to do this? We've heard stories about people being robbed and their boats seized by gangs."

"We can take care of ourselves," John said, "We've got Billy." John did little to disguise the sarcasm.

But Don and I exchanged knowing looks.

"Okay then, Billy, you're in charge. Report in every half hour, starting at the top of the hour. If we don't hear from you, we'll come looking. Stick to the plan. You know the sector," the official said, handing him a map.

"Aye, aye, sir!"

So much for getting rid of Billy or asking him to help. We were stuck.

"Now what?" I repeated Don's question.

45

Don would not sit down. I shook my head and felt bad for him; he was going through hell to save Ashley and May.

He stood behind the center console, gripping an aluminum bar that framed the plexiglass windshield as he kept glancing at the water, creeping ever closer to the boat.

As the boat hit the water, Don tensed even more, and I would have thought that impossible. His fear of the water was turning his knuckles white, and it was going to wear him out quickly. I had to say or do something, but not embarrass him in the process.

To make matters worse, the boat was a little tipsy. Not a whole lot, but as it slid off the trailer, it rocked, sending Don into a silent panic. When he glanced over at me, I tried to say something comforting.

"You know, Don, it's probably safer and more stable if you sit down."

"Oh, this rocking will quit. These are very stable boats," Billy said.

Thanks, Billy Bob, for undermining my effort. I gritted my teeth.

Don looked conflicted; he wanted to sit down, but that, of course, was nearer the water he dreaded. Finally, John, in his own gruff way, settled the matter.

"Don, if I have to swerve to avoid something, you could get tossed out of the boat. Better sit."

With a look that I can only describe as sheer terror, Don sat quickly. "Should we be wearing life jackets?" he asked.

"Don, the water isn't even over your head here," John said, snorting.

"But you have them onboard, right?" Billy asked.

"It's a legal requirement. They're in the locker under the casting deck if you want to move all that heavy stuff," John growled.

No one, including Don, moved. I guess that settled that.

The casting deck was definitely not designed to be used as a seat. There was no place to rest my back, and the pattern molded into the fiberglass was meant to ensure good footing for fisherman, not for a leisurely lounging spot. My backside started to hurt even before the motor started.

But I did notice that Don was watching John's every move. At first, I just figured it was because he wanted to distract himself from his phobia, but the keen intensity in which he was watching—studying John's moves—it looked to me like he was trying to learn. It was like he was memorizing everything: motor start, trimming the motor, and throttle operation.

Was he concerned that something was going to happen to John? Then I realized, if Don ended up defending himself, we'd still have to use the boat to get back to the Jeep.

Genius. Why didn't I think of that? And then I realized, if that were the case, maybe Don sensed something that I already feared.

As soon as the motor was down and running, John navigated away from the ramp, carefully watching the fish-finder.

"Planning on doing some fishing?" Don asked.

"Funny. This shows the depth of the water, something I'm very worried about, considering we don't know what's hidden under the water, given that these are floodwaters, and could be covering nasty things like cars, fences, and sea monsters," John said, trying to get Don worked up.

John seemed to notice Don watching him. If I missed my guess, I think it was starting to unnerve John. He looked over at Billy.

"Billy Bob, where are we supposed to go? Do we have a search area?" John asked as he alternately glanced at Don, then Billy.

Billy stood up and dug into his pocket to withdraw a map. I stood up too, and the boat bobbled just a little, and that shot Don off the bench to reassert his death grip on the aluminum frame for the windshield.

Billy unfolded the map and took a marker out of his bib overall pocket. "Here, this is our grid," he explained, pointing at a square on the map.

"How long will it take us to get to the farthest part of that grid?" John asked.

Billy sighed. "Maybe forty-five minutes."

"You want to add anything to that, Don?"

Don looked at John as if he were crazy and gripped hard on the frame. I sighed and pointed to where I was pretty sure the assisted-living center was. John frowned. It was a long way east of the farthest grid on the map, way out of the search area we were assigned.

Billy frowned too. It was as if he knew what we were thinking. "Is that where you want to go?"

I just shrugged. "I knew someone who lived here once."

Then Billy Bob settled the question once and for all whether I should ask him to help us find Ashley and May.

He spoke very slowly and deliberately. "I know you might want to help people. That's why y'all came down here. But that's out of our grid area, and the Coast Guard has that jurisdiction. They have helicopters and boats that are better suited for that area."

"Better suited, how?" John asked.

"Airboats an' such. Flat bottoms and bigger than this boat."

Don, John, and I glanced at one another. That was bad. Very bad.

But I was damned if I was going to spend my time and waste our gas piddling around on the west side. I was on a mission, a rescue mission, for our daughter and my aunt.

Suddenly, I wasn't so glad that Billy Bob was along for the ride.

46

We motor-sailed under the I-10 bridge and headed north for a block, then east. I couldn't miss John's concerned glances at the four gas cans he loaded behind the bench seat. Neither could Billy.

"Don' worry 'bout the gas none. Like I said, there'll be plenty of it on the ramp."

John scowled. Don kept glancing at the water, as if it were going to rise up and snatch him from the questionable safety of the boat. I sat down, wishing I hadn't left our hats in the Jeep.

As I sat baking in the sun, I tried to think about how I was going to get us to the east side of town with Billy in tow. The Claude Avenue Assisted-Living Center was only a few blocks away from the industrial canal, and that was a long way from here.

I wondered if the floodwaters went all the way to the canal, and if not, how the hell we were going to get to the center. John wasn't going to want to leave his boat.

And the sixty-four thousand dollar question was, how the hell we were going to get rid of Billy?

John kept glancing at me, then at Billy. The meaning was clear: what's the plan?

Well, I didn't have a plan. So while I thought about it, I figured that since Billy was setting up the radio and testing it that he might have some news about the rest of the city.

"So, Billy, what's the situation in the city?" I asked, trying not to be too specific. If he suspected I was asking about the area he saw me point to, there might be problems.

"I heard some of the guys talkin' about all the floodin'. There was a breach in the industrial canal, and the Lower Ninth Ward is floodin' pretty bad."

"Oh," I said, trying to remain calm. "What about this side of the canal? What about the French Quarter?"

Billy shook his head. "Nothing 'bout the French Quarter, an' I guess no news is good news, huh? But there's flooding around City Park 'cause of another breach, an' Metairie is flooded too. This is gonna get worse by the time we're through."

Like I needed to hear that. Well, at least we could boat nearly all the way to the center. But that was of little comfort; it meant that Ashley and May were in the middle of the flooding.

I shook my head and tried to focus on the problem of Billy.

"Hey, what's going on here?" John suddenly asked.

I glanced up to see John straining to see around the bow of his tiny boat. Turning to see, I found several people wading in the water. In fact, as I glanced around, I noticed several more groups of people wading, all heading in our direction.

When we got closer, I saw that the closest group seemed to be a family of four, an African American man wearing one of those sleeveless T-shirts. Next to him was a shorter, heavier African American woman. The man was pushing what looked like a door with two small children on it—a boy and a girl.

Nestled around the kids were miscellaneous supplies of clothing, toys, and food.

"We have to help them," I said, maternal instinct kicking in.

"No more room in the boat," Don said instantly. The very fact he said that made me want to have John toss his selfish ass out. Wait a second.

These people, bless them, were an answer to my prayer. I stood up and took command.

"John, pull up next to them carefully. They've got children on that door. Billy, get over here and help me get the children in the boat, then you should get out and stay with the man while we bring the wife and children to the ramp. Don…just sit there and hang on."

As God is my witness, I thought men were smarter. I assumed both of them would know right away what I was thinking by what I said. Boy, was I wrong.

"Brenda, there's no room," Don said.

"Brenda, I don't think this is a good—"

"Billy, you wait here with that man, and we'll come back to get you," I said before John could finish and out of earshot of the family we were approaching.

"Ms. Brenda, I need to be with you guys," Billy started.

"It's two turns, Billy. We can't fit everyone in the boat, and I need to help that woman with her kids. John needs to steer the boat, and Don is *not* going to get near the water, so please."

Billy looked unsure, but when he pulled up to the family, careful not to knock the children off the door, Billy hopped into the waist-high water after John killed the motor. After explaining to the family what we were doing, Billy helped me get the woman on board, then he and the man pushing the door lifted the two children into the boat.

When I finally got the mother calm, she realized we were her salvation, and she began to comfort the two screaming children, still reaching out for Daddy. Billy was busy explaining the plan to the father, who seemed really grateful.

Don sat there, hanging on while John sulked.

When I finally got everybody situated in the cramped boat, now lower in the water than before, which drove Don pale with fear, I turned to John, deliberately facing away from Billy in the water but next to the boat.

"Now let's get back to the ramp, help this poor woman out to dry land, then *come back and pick up Billy*."

I had emphasized the last few words while staring directly at John and winking.

You could see the light come on. Suddenly, he was really helpful.

"Right away. We don't want to leave Billy out here too long."

Don, sensing something was up, stood and held on as John started the motor again.

I turned back to Billy.

"We'll be right back," I said to a very skeptical Billy. "Start walking in that direction and we'll reach you sooner, okay?"

Billy nodded, distrust all over his face. "Look, I could get in trouble if I'm not with you. Why don't you just troll along while we walk? Maybe we could get some of this stuff in the boat?"

"Good idea," I said to John's horror, but I reached out and took some toys to quiet the kids and a few supplies, then said loudly, "We better get back to the ramp. We don't want to leave Billy in here too long."

"Uh, wait a minute…"

Billy was still trying to get us to hang with him, but John smiled, a very evil smile, and motored away from the group, gunned the motor, and spun the boat on a dime, which sent Don into near hysterics.

47

THE CHILDREN QUIETED down eventually because I had thought to take some of their stuffed animals. I could tell that John, who never had kids and was not used to them or even reasonably comfortable around them, was ready to pop a cork.

The woman, whose name I never got, was appreciative but kept fairly quiet. She'd smile and nod but kept to herself.

As soon as we motored around the corner and saw the ramp, Don seemed to relax.

John pulled up as close as he dared to the ramp without making contact on the bottom. This left about fifteen feet for the woman to wade through, and I thought that was rather mean of John but said nothing.

Three people came running down to help us, and we created a bucket brigade to get the kids to shore. One of the officials, the one that gave me such a hard time at the tent, was so kind and gentle as he escorted the mother, arm in arm, toward the ramp.

All of them marched up to the top of the ramp, leaving an SUV that had backed down a boat on a trailer at the waterline, the boat's rear floating and the bow still resting on the trailer. I turned back to John, thinking he was going to back away now, but he was staring at something on the back of the boat.

I thought it was boat envy, but when I looked, I saw two red plastic gas cans in the back by the outboard.

When I turned back to John, he put the boat in gear and nodded to Don, then toward the gas cans.

"What are you doing?" I asked.

"We're going to need all the gas we can get," he said.

I realized he was asking Don to go up to the bow and take the cans.

"That's theft! Don, you stay right there!"

Don was quite content to do just that until John goaded him. "You know, if we run out of gas, we got to get in the water and wade the rest of the way," he said to Don.

To my horror, Don sighed and said nothing as he slowly and nervously got up to walk to the bow. John pulled up as close as he could to the other boat. "Fend off the boat, will you, Brenda?"

"I will do no such thing! This is not right!"

"Look," John said, "we all know we're not coming back here. Nobody is going to miss this, and they will get more gas as much as they can use for free. Us, not so much," John hissed.

Don passed me and crawled up to the very front of our boat.

"Don? You're not going to do this, are you?"

He glanced to see if anyone was looking, and I naturally did the same. Everyone was at the top of the ramp, and no one was paying the least bit attention to us because the kids started crying again.

"Don?"

He turned to me, angry, and whispered, "What are *you* willing to do to find our daughter, Brenda?"

I was certainly learning a lot about Don on this trip.

On the other hand, I couldn't deny that John's logic was sound. Not right, certainly not honest, but sound.

Don reached up. He was unsteady, and I could tell he was scared. Normally, I would hold on to him, but there was just no way that I was going to be a part of this. If we were caught, this would be the end of our rescue!

Don looked around again, all over this time, then quickly grabbed one of the cans. It was heavy enough for him to lose his balance, and it crashed against the bow rail of John's boat.

"Damn it," John hissed. "Be careful for Christ's sake!"

Don flashed him an angry glance. John nudged the boat even closer, but I felt it touch the submerged asphalt of the interstate ramp.

John swore under his breath.

Don checked to see who was looking again, then reached for the other can. This time, I sighed and scooted over to help him, putting more weight in the bow of the boat, and we hit bottom hard.

"For the love of God," John said.

But Don and I managed to get the second can on board. "Go," Don hissed, grabbing on to the bow rail for dear life.

"Get off the fucking bow!"

Don and I each brought a can with us and set them down in the back of the boat. This brought the stern of the boat dangerously close to the waterline.

John put it in reverse, and the boat backed away from the ramp, bow high and sending a tidal wave of water over the transom, getting Don's feet wet.

"Shit!"

He stood up and resumed his panicked hold on the aluminum frame of the windshield. I moved back to sit on the casting deck, and we were off.

But I had changed. I was now a criminal. Yes, it was what I had to do to find Ashley, but I didn't have to like it.

48

My watch indicated ten minutes after three. It was getting later and later in the day, and we still hadn't made any real progress toward the assisted-living center.

I was seething at the delay and the fact that I was now a thief. This was just awful; I had never meant that the effort to rescue my family would turn into a criminal enterprise.

But like Don said, what would stop me from saving Ashley and May? I had to admit: *nothing*.

I sat in the bow of the boat, facing the center console and the two men who were having a bad influence on my life. I was avoiding eye contact with them at all costs, which was pretty easy, actually. John was watching where he was going, and Don was alternately closing his eyes and hanging on for dear life.

He had finally decided to sit down, though.

So it was back to my self-pity party. Until John swore.

"*Shit!* They made some good time," he said.

It was an odd thing to say, so I glanced at him, then turned to see where he was looking. Directly in front of us, Billy and the father of those two children were wading through waist-deep water toward the direction of the ramp.

Billy saw us immediately and waved his arms. I could tell he was relieved to see us come back.

John, on the other hand, pushed the throttle forward to its limits.

I quickly turned back to the console. "What are you doing?" I demanded.

Don's eyes were wide-open and he stood up again, against the wind.

"Making sure we don't have to hang with Billy Bob again," John screamed over the wind noise.

John altered his course slightly so we didn't run them down, but not enough. As we sped by them, they leapt to the side, the man leaving his door and remaining supplies to fend for themselves.

Our wake swamped the door, dumping all his things into the water.

I could hear Billy and him screaming at us as we sped past. I couldn't make out what they were saying exactly, but I could imagine.

"Was that necessary?" I asked John.

He just shrugged and slid the throttle back a little from full speed once the two men were out of sight. But there were other people in the water, and they were yelling at us too.

I never felt so ashamed in my life.

"That was a sick thing you did, John! Those things were all the guy could save from his house, I'll bet. Now they're all wet and ruined!"

John said nothing but just glanced at me and raised his eyebrows. Finally, he spoke as calmly as he could.

"What if Billy had a gun? He could have confiscated my boat, and then where would we be?"

I nearly came back with the fact that he had brought enough ammo to defend Fort Knox, but I managed to keep my mouth shut despite being so mad I was shaking. I tried hard not to glance at my bag with his bullets in it, lest I give away the secret.

Don turned back to watch the others in the water flip us off and curse at us. Seems that Billy and that man weren't the only ones our wake impacted.

"I feel bad too," Don said quietly, turning back to face forward and lock his hands around the aluminum bar.

"Do you?" I asked sarcastically too quickly without thinking first.

He looked at me with what I thought was a pained expression but said nothing.

"You two, you've lost your focus," John snorted. "What do you think is going on in this city? I heard that guy tell Billy Bob that people were being robbed at gunpoint for their boats. I guarantee you, I will do the same if someone else starts flagging us down. That and *more*, if you know what I mean. I don't want to be a statistic."

Don and I exchanged glances, and I knew we were both thinking the same thing—the guns.

Don looked at John. "But those people were just trying to survive," he said.

"Whatever happened to Ashley being the focus?" John asked.

"*Nothing*," I spat. "Just try not to drown anyone, okay?"

Don sat down, feeling glum.

"C'mon, Brenda, I'm here for *you* guys," John said.

"I don't like leaving those poor people in the water with God knows what in it," I said, referring to pollution and potential diseases, thinking about malfunctioning sewers and the like.

Don stood up again, quickly, looking down at the water in horror.

"Oh, take a chill pill, Don," John mocked him. "Ol' Billy Bob is from these parts. He probably wrestles 'gators for *fun* on the weekends."

"There's *alligators* in this water, you think?" Don asked, his voice an octave higher than normal.

John belly laughed. "Man, Don, don't you know *anything* about nature?"

"No," Don snapped back at him.

"This floodwater is from the Gulf of Mexico. It's basically *salt* water," John said. "Alligators can't survive in salt water," he laughed.

"Oh," Don said, obviously relieved and slowly sitting down again, but still keeping a wary eye on the waterline, only a foot or two away from the top of the boat's sides and closer than it was at the bow.

"No," John went on, "not in salt water. That would be crocodiles from the bayou," he said with a straight face.

Don took one glance at the waterline and shot up so fast, gripping the aluminum bar so hard his knuckles turned white.

I couldn't help it. It was cruel, but it was funny. And the chuckles were few and far between in the last twenty-four hours.

49

Zanetti slowed the Suburban as he neared the official on top of the bridge.

Poor bastard, he thought. The guy must be sweating bullets out in this sun, just directing traffic. He was dressed in a dark polo shirt, khaki trousers, and a beige boonie hat with a wider brim than normal.

"I'll handle this," VT said, lowering his window and scowling.

"VT, you may want to—"

"I *got* it."

Tread lightly, Zanetti was going to say, but he shut his face. When VT threw a hissy fit, you let it run its course and you do the best you can to clean up the mess. He sighed; that's what his day was going to be like.

Cleaning up untold messes seemed to be his lot in life.

VT waved the official around to his side of the vehicle. With a scowl on his face, the official made his way over to the other side of the Chevy.

Before the guy even got a chance to open his mouth, VT flashed his badge in the official's face.

"FEMA."

The official leaned over closer to the window. "Yeah, I can see that from your license plate. What do you want?"

VT snorted. "World peace. What do you think? We're launching our boat here."

Zanetti gripped the steering wheel so hard he was sure he would leave permanent imprints. This was not flying under the radar.

"Really? Get in line. You got about three other agencies ahead of you," the official said and started to walk away.

"Hey! You don't understand. We're FEMA. We're going in now."

"VT—"

VT snapped his hand up to Zanetti, who sighed with an angry exasperation.

The official stopped in his tracks and looked back at them with mouth agape.

"I don't give a *fuck* who you are. Unless you're President Bush, you are waiting your *fucking* turn," he finally said.

He turned and walked away even though VT was starting to say something.

"VT, let it go. We got the AC on and—"

But VT was having none of it. He unbuckled his seat belt and opened his door.

"Jesus, Vinnie! Think about what the *fuck* you're doin'!"

"I am, and call me that again. *Please.*"

"All I'm sayin' is we shouldn't go makin' waves!"

"Best defense is an aggressive offense. It earns respect. I don't give a shit if I piss these guys off. It's hot, I'm pissed, we have a job to do, and that's all that counts!"

Zanetti kept his cool even though he so dearly wanted to beat the shit out of Taccone. One day might just be today, he thought.

He twisted his hands on the steering wheel as he watched VT make an absolute ass out of himself. VT had walked behind the official, quickly enough to catch up to him, grab him, and spin him around.

"Fuck this guy," Zanetti muttered. He made up his mind at that moment to see Mr. Taccone Sr. and request a lateral move in the organization. He wasn't about to babysit anymore.

The official instinctively went for this holster, and no less than three other badged officials ran over to where VT had accosted the first one. No one had their weapons drawn, but their hands were on them.

"Shit. Thanks, *Vinnie*," Zanetti said, shaking his head.

He watched as VT's hands went up and he stepped back. The first official, the one that greeted them, held out his hand, and reluctantly, VT handed him the FEMA ID badge.

This needed fixing. Zanetti put the Suburban in Park, opened his door, and slid out. He made his way slowly over to the group. They had, in the meantime, turned, and everyone walked over to the main tent.

"What's goin' on?" Zanetti asked when he caught up with the group.

VT was going to answer, but the original official answered for him. "I need to see your ID. Now."

"Yeah, yeah, sure," Zanetti said as agreeably as he could, grasping the lanyard around his neck and pulled it over his head.

"Look, can I talked to you in private?" he asked the official.

The official's nostrils were flaring. He moved over exactly three steps away from where VT was seated, surrounded by the three other officials, and crossed his arms.

"Look, you got a right to be pissed," Zanetti said. "I'm pissed, and I'm sorry you got the worst end of my boss. I get it daily, so I understand. Look, he's under a ton of political pressure. This thing is a complete mess, and heads are going to roll."

The official's nostrils stopped flaring. To Zanetti, that was a good sign.

"Between you an' me, I hope one of those heads is his," Zanetti said. "That would make my job a lot easier. Look, check out our IDs, but take my apology for the disrespect he showed you. We're all on the same team, right?"

The official's jaw was working back and forth quickly. He stared at Zanetti for a moment, then glanced back at VT, then back to Zanetti.

He handed back the badges. "Keep him in check. Everybody's doing the impossible here. We don't need *assholes* like that."

Turning, he nodded to the other officials, who were probably state or local police, Zanetti guessed, and they backed away from VT.

VT looked up, frowned, and stood as Zanetti approached him.

Handing him the ID badge, all Zanetti said without looking at his boss was, "Let's go."

They got back to the Suburban, and VT slammed his door to register his disapproval. Zanetti closed his eyes tightly, counted to ten, then pulling in line as directed by the traffic cop, he said in a quiet voice, without even looking at VT, "You almost got our cover blown. Now get this straight. I work for your *father*, for this *organization*, and if you make me pull your ass out of a fire you caused *one more time*, you will *never* see me coming."

There was silence in the truck for a full minute. Zanetti knew he'd stepped so far over the line, but frankly, he didn't give a shit anymore.

This was the pivotal moment in his career. He would either win the day or he'd offer himself up to the Illinois state's attorney and hope for the best in the witness protection program.

Either way, his relationship with VT had fundamentally changed, and it could adversely impact this contract and, quite possibly, his ability to breathe.

50

"Are we there yet?"

"For the hundredth time, John, not funny anymore," I replied with a sigh.

I glanced at my watch again. Ten minutes to five. We'd been out here about two, maybe two and a half hours, and the only person who thought of bringing a hat was John.

Even though the sun was lower now, he was still wearing it. It looked strange, a boonie hat that was camouflaged as if he was some soldier in combat. But *he* wasn't sunburned.

I usually don't burn either, but I had tied a T-shirt over my head just in case. Don, on the other hand, thought he was apparently tough enough to go without any sun protection.

"Don, are you *sure* you don't want to take one of my T-shirts and tie it around your head? You're complexion is so fair and you look sunburned."

"Not now," was all he would say. Fine. I tried.

"Are we *there* yet?"

I closed my eyes tightly and tried to ignore the comment. That way, if he didn't get a response, maybe he'd quit.

"Hello?"

John never minded being called an ass, jerk, or any other name mankind has devised to describe an irritating human being, but he sure hated to be ignored.

I smiled. My silence, and Don's for that matter, must be killing him.

Don, to his credit, let go of the windshield frame and came forward, death grip on all the handholds on the way to the bow, and knelt on the casting deck.

We happened to see a lot more boats than I thought would be out here—boats of all kinds and some looked like they were from the police or government; they had archlike structures that supported lights like you'd see on squad cars. It made me think about Billy.

I tried not to think of how badly we treated him.

I moved forward, destroying John's careful trim. "Recognize anything yet?" I asked Don as John swore softly. I could feel him adjusting the trim of the boat.

"Brenda, the damn city is flooded. Landmarks are underwater and so are most of the road signs," he snapped.

"Jeez, Don! I was just asking an honest question," I blurted out without thinking about how much stress he must be under. And John's constant mocking didn't help.

"Are we there yet?"

I turned back to face the helm. "Fuck off. He's doing the best he can!"

John's face, sweaty and in shadow, turned to ice. For the first time this trip, I didn't give a damn and turned back around.

"I'll get you there, Brenda. We'll find her," Don said.

"I know," I replied, not knowing what else to say at the moment.

"Can you turn down one of these north- and south-running streets?" Don asked.

I glanced back to see John do a mock salute at Don. "Aye, aye, Captain Magellan!"

I flashed him as angry a look as my sunburned face could muster. He just shrugged and turned south on the next street. Immediately, his eyes went to the fish-finder that doubled as a depth-sounder.

He was frowning.

"What's wrong?" I asked.

"Oh, nothing. Just that it's getting shallower here. We go too far south, we'll be portaging to the Mississippi."

I ignored the nastiness and turned back to Don.

"I don't recognize a thing, Don. I hope you do."

He shrugged. "I think I do, but I'm not used to looking at second stories of buildings for landmarks. If I could just get a glimpse of a sign or something."

"Here's a thought. How 'bout looking for street addresses?"

"Always helpful as usual, John. What street are we on, by the way?" Don asked without even turning back to face John.

"You're the expert."

"Well, John, since you think you know better than I do, please, take us there. Tell me what street I'm on and we can get there faster."

Truly, I was amazed that Don was even saying anything, especially since he knew that John had a gun, but then again, so did Don, and his was loaded.

"I'm going to slow down," John announced.

"Why? How much daylight do we have left?" I asked.

"We use less fuel when we go slower, and we've already filled up once. Who knows how long Captain Columbus over there is going to keep us at sea."

Shaking my head, I untied the T-shirt from around my head and sat down near the railing. I leaned over to dip it in the water and wiped my neck and face. It had a cooling effect, but Don shook his head when he saw me doing it once.

"What?" I asked.

"You have no idea what pollutants you're putting on your face when you do that."

I closed my eyes. "Don, there are those of us who take our immune system out for a run every once in a while just to exercise it. Not everyone has your phobias."

He turned around, and under his breath, despite the sound of the outboard, I distinctly heard him say, "Bitch."

So much for teamwork.

51

ASHLEY GREW TIRED of poking her head out of May's window at every little noise. It had been hours since she had caught a glimpse of the last boat, and she was beginning to worry that she wasn't on a well-traveled path.

In other words, it was going to be hard to get to out of here.

And even is she did escape this hell, where would she go? Where were the shelters? How would she contact her parents and tell them about May?

With no working cell phone or car, she was marooned, and it was getting dark. Already, shadows were growing over the center's backyard, and even if there was a passing boat when it got darker, she'd have a hard time seeing it or making herself seen.

Then she'd have to face another night trapped here with Bruno and no excuse to stay because May was dead.

She thought about moving her stuff back into May's room, but then she'd have to leave May and the chance to catch a ride from a passing boat. It would be just her luck to have a boat pass by when she was in the dead man's room.

No, it was better to stay in this room even though May was still here, staring with sightless eyes at the ceiling. She could always come back for her things later. That is, if Bruno didn't steal them.

So she waited and hoped and prayed and kept a fitful watch.

There were plenty of helicopters passing overhead, but fat chance of flagging them down unless she went up on the roof.

Maybe she could break the mirror in the bathroom and use it as a signaling mirror. Would the sun be too low?

It was the first positive thought that had occurred to her since she found May. Even though the sun might be at a bad angle, she could try it.

Making her way to the bathroom was hard; her eyes could not avoid May's corpse on the bed. She should cover May with the blankets, but May would still be there, rotting.

It was hard not to imagine the smell that would start coming from the room, and she worried about what the other residents might do because of it. But she couldn't help them; she could barely help herself.

At least Bruno had stayed away. For that, she was thankful, and it was one less thing to worry about.

But it did convince her that he was the cause of her great-aunt's death, and that he knew it.

She stopped in mid-stride. What if she was able to escape? How would people, namely the authorities, find her?

She even thought about her bags; they were proof she was here, and she might be implicated in May's death!

Better write a note. Explain what happened. Assign blame where it belonged.

She spun around and rummaged through May's drawers until she found an envelope that had been torn open. Why would May keep an envelope?

Looking inside, she found a letter written by May's husband. It was a short letter, saying goodbye to her.

He'd died of cancer years ago when Ashley was just a little girl, but the letter was heartbreaking.

Immediately, Ashley regretted reading it. It changed her mood from hopeful to hopelessly depressed.

But she needed something to write on and something she could hide from Bruno if he searched the room after she left—if she was able to leave.

Grabbing one of May's pens from the desk, she went to the bathroom to write a note.

"To whom it may concern, my name is Ashley Meyers, and the deceased on the bed is my great-aunt. I believe she was killed—maybe by accident—by the male nurse Bruno." What was his last name again?

It didn't matter. She was sure that anyone from the authorities would know who Bruno was or, at least, be able to find out.

"And I believe he has been stealing from the residents here. I think he gave May an overdose of some medication to calm her. Please treat her body with respect. I am going to try to make it to a shelter if I can flag down a passing boat. I don't know where I'll end up, maybe the Superdome somehow. Please call my parents, Brenda and Don Meyers…"

She finished by including her home address and her parents' phone numbers. Then she looked for a place to put it where it would be easily found, but not by Bruno. Being thirsty, she naturally turned to face the tub.

And that's when it hit her; she reached over and placed the envelope between the cold water knob and the tile.

That should do it.

Just as she stood up and considered how the hell she was going to break the mirror to use a part of it for signaling without needing stitches, she heard the floor creak. She froze. May was gone, and she was supposed to be alone.

Had Bruno come back for some of May's valuables?

Carefully moving to the door of the bathroom, she peered through the space between the side of the door attached to the hinges and the doorframe.

There was Bruno, and he was touching May's head and was examining the arm where he had injected her with the drug that most likely killed her.

52

Ashley was more angry than scared. "Looking for needle marks, or just want to be sure she can't catch you stealing from her now?"

Bruno was so startled that he jumped back, dropping May's arm. "I was lookin' for her pulse," he stammered.

"Yeah, well, she doesn't have one anymore! She's dead, and *you* killed her!"

It suddenly occurred to Ashley that perhaps she was coming on too strong, what with Bruno blocking her exit to the hallway, but she was committed.

And the fact that he seemed to be defending himself and not jumping at her gave her courage.

It lasted only seconds.

Bruno's startled expression morphed into anger. He took a single step toward her, and suddenly, Ashley felt very exposed.

"I wouldn't go about accusin' people, *beb*."

It came out like a growl and was unmistakably a clear threat. Ashley started to back up. Bruno took another step.

"What you doin' here, *beb*?"

"I've *been* here all along, mourning May's death that *you caused*!" She tried to make her voice louder, but her throat was dry and suddenly raspy.

Another step. Another step back for Ashley.

"I'm truly sorry for *Defan* May, but you got it all wrong."

"That will be for a coroner to determine!"

She kept backing up, but then she was at the outside wall with nowhere else to go. Bruno smirked and started moving quickly toward her.

From outside, she could hear something, a rumbling sound that sounded like a motorcycle. It grew louder as Bruno advanced toward her, and she prayed it was a boat's motor.

"You got the *mal pris, beb*. I'm gonna *make you the misere* now!"

Ashley slid sideways toward the window nearest the bathroom. It was directly over the awning, and it was quickly becoming her only means of escape.

She gulped down a huge breath and screamed as loud as she could. It only made Bruno pause for a second, but he was nearly on her.

It was now or never.

She turned and hoisted herself up over the open windowsill but lost her balance. As she started to fall, she felt Bruno grab her feet and try to pull her back into the room. So she kicked. She kicked like her life depended on it because it probably did. And she screamed again. But the noise faded. The boat must not be coming her way.

Ashley felt her heel connect hard with Bruno, and he let go of her as he fell back into the room. His grip had been the only thing keeping her from falling out of the window.

Suddenly weightless, she flailed her arms and legs, screaming as she somersaulted all the way down. She only quit screaming when she landed painfully on top of the aluminum awning.

But that wasn't the end of her fall. She bounced and fell again, this time off the awning, facedown. She belly flopped into the water and went all the way to the bottom.

It knocked the breath out of her.

But she managed to find her feet and stood up, tripped, stumbled, and fell again, hurting her knees.

And she swallowed a lot of water.

Gagging and coughing, she tried to scream, but it came out as staccato yelps. Turning back to look up, she could see Bruno swearing at her from the window. But she also heard the sound again, very close, and despite choking, she screamed.

A boat appeared on the other side of the broken fence, a large one, and somebody in bib overalls was standing at the bow, facing toward her and motioning the person steering to stop.

The boat's motor, which was driving a large propeller in a cage behind the driver, stopped, but the boat glided past her line of sight.

"Wait," she coughed.

Struggling to breathe, she glanced up at May's window again, but Bruno was gone. Even though she was in pain, she waded toward the fence, but she heard the motor start again.

They were leaving her!

Just as she got to the partially submerged, ruined fence, the boat reappeared like an angel descending from heaven.

It pulled right up to her, going over the fence and pushing it down farther underneath the water. Then several hands were pulling her up into the boat, and she lay on the deck, coughing and crying.

"Miss, are you all right?"

She nodded between bouts of gagging and coughing. Then she remembered her back pocket. It was where she had put her cell phone.

She dug it out, and water spilled out of it. It was useless.

"What's your name, Miss?"

She looked up at the man who asked her the question. It was the man in bib overalls and a white short-sleeved T-shirt. He asked her again.

"Ashley," she said. "Ashley Meyers."

"*Meyers?*" the man in overalls asked. "Any relation to a Don and Brenda Meyers?"

Ashley was stunned. She sat up, coughing cured.

"You *know* them? They're my parents!"

"My name is Billy Lee, and yes, I know your parents. We have a lot of people looking for them. They're wanted for questioning!"

53

WE WERE GETTING close; there were lots of buildings I thought I recognized, but with the streets underwater, I couldn't be sure.

Don must have sensed it too. He was looking around excitedly and holding on less tightly to the bow rail.

We were undeniably in the neighborhood.

When we passed a half-sunken restaurant with the top half of its sign above the water, a restaurant that had delivered awful food to us at the center the first time we came down with Ashley, I knew we were only blocks away.

My heart began pounding again, and the fatigue I had been feeling melted into history. I was ready for anything. Ready and worried.

Because we were so close, I started paying attention to my surroundings more closely and, more importantly, who was in them. I counted no less than twenty other boats going in the exact opposite direction.

Did they know something we didn't? Was the east side hit harder?

John kept glancing at his watch. I had to wonder why he was so concerned with time of day. But of course, I knew damn well what concerned John about the time. He had a rendezvous to keep.

I couldn't help it; I stole a glance toward the yellow toolbox, then quickly to Don's pocket, then down the street, hoping I had gone unnoticed.

But I couldn't keep thinking about the negative possibilities; Don had a gun, and that might be enough to keep him alive or at least discourage anyone who would hurt him, but the way he talked about them, I'm pretty sure he'd never fired a gun in his life.

To take my mind off the endless what-ifs, I wondered how we were going to fit May and Ashley and at least some of their bags in this boat. Five people seemed to be pushing it, and the weight of all our bags and supplies seemed to be too much for the tiny little boat.

But I was damned if I'd question John on the subject; he'd take it as a direct assault on his manliness.

Besides, if you want to be positive and stay that way, you should start *doing* positive things. So I looked around the boat to do some dusting and cleaning and rearranging the bags and other items lying about.

"Uh, what are you doing?" John asked me.

"Making room for Ashley and Aunt May and their things," I said, not even slowing down. Out of the corner of my eye, I caught a glimpse of the yellow toolbox again.

"Just how much baggage do you think they're going to bring with?"

I stopped and straightened up, hands on my hips, and scowled at him. He was *not* going to dictate what May left behind!

"You do know that there is a limit to what this boat can carry safely, right?" John asked.

Now it was Don's turn to give some back. He turned around from his vigil at the bow and snorted.

"Relax, John. If we sink, it's not like we'll need Dr. Ballard to find your boat. It's only about waist-high here."

I nearly laughed. Okay, I know, I had been spending the better part of the day getting those two to knock it off with the nitpicking pettiness. But I was kind of proud of Don.

"The point, Don, is not to sink in the first place! It's expensive, and where will your aunt be then? Huh?"

"Oh, take it easy, John," I said. "Can't you take your own medicine? It was funny, and you deserved it. I don't care if I have to walk or if we all have to pull the boat like slaves. Aunt May and Ashley have been through a terrifying experience, and anything they want to bring along is okay with me."

I was bracing for the "my boat, my rules" lecture, but it never came. Instead, Don, who had turned back to watching where he was going, interrupted our meaningless conversation with the words I had been longing to hear.

"There it is!"

54

John swore each time every time the boat scrapped bottom. He throttled way back.

"It must not be very deep here, huh?" Don asked.

John squinted, shook his head, and then turned back to the fish-finder.

"Ya think?" he snarled.

"So we could wade from here on in, right?" Don asked excitedly.

Even I was amazed that Don would even consider this. I turned to stare at him.

"It can't be more than a foot or two deep, right?" he asked John.

"This boat draws thirty-four inches with the motor all the way down," John said slowly. "Why do you want to wade through this water with God knows what in it?"

I flashed John an angry expression. Bastard would remind Don of his phobia, right when he seemed to be getting confident. And we were slowing down even more now.

I couldn't help but to recall the phone call I overheard. It had been obvious that John was meeting someone somewhere, and my thoughts turned to some sort of meeting at the assisted-living center between John and some very nefarious people—all at Don's expense!

"Go around the front, here, take this road. Wait," Don said, standing up on the bow. He pointed excitedly at the road reappearing from the depths of the floodwaters, just to the north of the building we were going to enter.

"Nose up to the street there, John, and we can beach the boat."

"There is no way in *hell* I am going to beach my boat on asphalt so it can scrape itself raw with every little wave that hits it," John retorted, pulling the throttle all the way to idle.

But Don wasn't waiting. He simply lifted a leg over the side and hopped out, stumbling a bit, but recovering quickly, and hurriedly wading as fast as the thigh-deep water permitted.

"What the…"

I wasn't going to wait for John to figure out how he wanted to finish his sentence. I was completely amazed at Don's bravery. I guess being this close to Ashley was affecting him as much as it was me; I hopped out as quickly as Don had and hurried after him, leaving John bobbing in his boat half a block from the "shore."

He was screaming something, but frankly, over the idling outboard with the sound of a passing helicopter overhead and the sloshing water, I couldn't make out what he was saying. And I didn't care.

I caught up to Don as he was emptying out his shoes on the street, just above the waterline.

"We may have to carry May out to the boat," I said.

He nodded without even looking at me. Then as soon as he got his shoes on again, he started sprinting toward the corner of Claude Avenue.

It was hard for me to keep up. I did hear John's boat power up, and I wondered, would that be John leaving to make his *business meeting*?

Now I could openly warn Don, and if the floodwaters were ending this far north of the river, we could walk along the Mississippi all the way to the safety, meaning I could push May in her wheelchair.

That way, we weren't dependent on John and could avoid any nasty surprises he had arranged for us.

As I rounded the corner, I saw Don standing at the door of Ashley's old Plymouth Acclaim. It looked like it had weathered the storm like a champ, not a single scratch other than the ones Ashley and May had put on it.

"She's here!" I said, thinking she would never leave her car as I ran past Don to the front doors. I bounded up the two steps to the twin glass doors and pulled. They wouldn't budge.

Wasn't expecting that!

I pulled again, then pushed and pulled as violently as I could. They didn't yield.

"Locked?" I mumbled aloud.

I looked over at Don and nodded. Then I stepped back a few paces and looked up. The windows were all closed. Since I didn't see any lights on in the lobby, I assumed that the building was without power, and that meant without air-conditioning.

It would be horrible inside, especially for elderly people.

"Don, none of the windows are open. The lights aren't on. I'm worried that they don't have—"

When I glanced over at him, he was no longer standing by the car at the curb. He was *in* the car, behind the driver's seat.

My mind wouldn't process the information as presented. It made no sense. Don had already told me that Ashley's car had broken down. What the hell was he doing inside it now?

And how did he get there?

Before I could call out to him and ask, the car stumbled and coughed to a start, gobs of blue smoke billowing out the tailpipe.

After a few uneven revs of the motor, I could see the brake lights come on, and the car suddenly lurched forward!

It ran! Not very well—it sounded like the engine was running roughly and there was a lot of blue smoke—but it ran. We could use it after all! We no longer needed to worry about getting out of here or avoiding John; we could *drive* back close to the ramp and get the Jeep!

But as Don disappeared with the chugging car around the corner, this time heading toward the river instead of the floodwaters, I wondered just what the hell he was doing.

I waited. For a full few minutes, there was no sign of Don or the car. Now I was getting really worried.

So I turned back to the door and started banging on it. No one answered. I peered in and couldn't see anyone.

But I jumped when I heard the horn. I turned around, only to see Don throwing the Acclaim around the corner and aiming squarely at me.

55

I JUST STOOD there, mesmerized by the swiftly approaching car. It was hurdling right toward me, engine roaring, thick blue smoke trailing from its tailpipe.

Funny the things that go through your mind in times of extreme stress; I remember noticing that despite the car's age, how brilliantly the sun flashed off its chrome grill.

But I delayed perhaps a bit too long. Don was going to ram into me and my mind just froze until he hit the horn, loud and long. At the last minute, I jumped behind bushes that lined the ADA ramp, not particularly worried about the consequences of landing on branches or thorns or anything else that might permanently damage me.

When I landed in the thick foliage, it hurt, but at least I wasn't a hood ornament on the Plymouth.

The resulting crash was sickening, and it could be heard echoing up and down the street. It was the loudest noise in this part of the city as far as I could tell, and if that didn't bring people running, I didn't know what would.

In fact, I hoped it would bring people. More people meant more witnesses and more protection for Don. And maybe even me.

In pain and bruised, I poked my head from the bushes as the last shard of glass dropped from the doorframe.

The rear end of the Acclaim was sticking out of what was left of the main entrance. There was smoke—steam really—and a lot of green and brown fluid leaking out from under the Acclaim's carcass.

"Don?"

No answer. I pulled myself up by a sturdier branch on the bush nearest the doorway, ignoring the pain in my joints and poked my head around the wreck.

"Don?"

The Acclaim's front end was unrecognizable and the windshield was shattered with spiderweb-type fractures.

The hood was smashed and compressed like an accordion, as was the front fenders. The front tires, well, the only one I could see at the moment, was flat, and it looked like the wheel took on the shape of a Pringle potato chip.

No wonder as it had to bounce off two steps and the curb to get through the front door.

"Don! Are you all right?"

Oddly, no one came running from the street. I looked up into the lobby, and no one came to investigate.

Oh come on! That must have been the loudest sound since the storm, I'm sure, and no one was the *least bit* interested?

Maybe they were all injured or...*worse?*

"Don? Answer me, goddammit!"

I heard a groan, then some noise in the car. Squeezing past the torn-up metal frame of the doorway and the fenders and rear door of the car, I made my way to the front door on the passenger side. All the windows were smashed, and a white powdery cloud floated through the passenger compartment.

The airbags had deployed.

Don was moving. It took him a few attempts to disconnect his seat belt, but he managed to get lose. First, he tried his door, but it wouldn't open. Then he tried the door closest to me.

He was moving, so at worst, he might have been stunned.

"Don, the front fenders are pushed back into the doors. They're not going to open. You need to climb out the window."

He just looked at me, still dazed. Now that I knew he was mostly all right, I couldn't help but laugh out loud.

"What?" he said as I helped him climb out the window.

"You look like the Pillsbury Doughboy," I said. He was covered from his head to his waist with white powder from the airbags.

He must still have been in shock because he didn't answer, just nodded. But he got us in, and that took a lot of courage. I helped him down from the windowsill on top of the car door. He winced.

"Where does it hurt?" I asked.

"Sternum. Damned shoulder strap."

"You think it's broken?" I asked him, slightly worried.

"Naw, just freakin' bruised. I'll get over it."

Who *was* this man, and what had he done with my overly sensitive husband? I looked at Don in a whole new way. Well, new for this chapter in our lives. This is how he used to be and one of the things that attracted me to him—selfless behavior.

So naturally, I had to go and screw up the mood.

"You totaled her car. How are we going to afford to replace it?"

Don shook his head. "We got it for her. We'll replace it."

"Don, we took it from Aunt May when she got sick, remember? Then we handed it down to Ashley."

"Oh. Yeah."

"You *sure* you're okay?"

He nodded. "Let's go get Ashley," he said, taking ahold of me for support and what was left of the fender of the leaking, smoking wreck.

I looked up, and two curious elderly people, sweating in pajamas and terry cloth robes, were leaning on the railing of the second-floor balcony. The stairs were curved and over to the left, and that's where I led Don.

But deep inside, I was worried. No, scared. Ashley was nowhere in sight. Nowhere.

And with the crash noise, you'd think she'd come to investigate if she weren't sick, injured, or…

56

NOT SURPRISINGLY, DON was having difficulty negotiating the staircase. As we made our way slowly up the sweeping expanse of steps, I noticed he was leaning on me heavily.

I tried not to think about that. What would we do if one of us was injured badly? How would we get to a medical facility? Were there any medical facilities? How would we avoid John and his merry bunch of assassins?

Now that the car was totaled, how would we get May home without John's boat?

I forced it out of my mind by trying to replace it with the plan details. Take the stairs, one step at a time. Find Ashley and May. Get them out of here, then figure out how to get home.

As we neared the top of this flight, I happened to look up and notice several more elderly people gathering in various states of dress on the second story, as if they were waiting for us. I could only imagine the questions we were going to get.

"I don't see her, Don."

He grunted. He must be thinking the same thing I was; if these older people, with their aches and pains, could manage to investigate the crash, why wasn't Ashley among them?

"Don..."

He shook his head, painfully. "I know what you're going to say, but there is another valid reason why she's not coming down to yell at me."

"What's that?" I asked, not sure I wanted to hear the answer.

Groaning as he stepped wrong, he hesitated on the second step from the top. "She's not here. She could have evacuated."

I looked around. I hoped to God he was right, but deep down I doubted it. She would have found a way to help the others here or send someone back. That was just the way she was.

My mood grew darker.

Don seemed to know what I was thinking. "She's going to be okay. We're going to find her, and I'm starting to think we should have stopped at the Superdome first."

I don't know why, but I turned to him and asked, "Why the Superdome?"

"Don't you remember?" Don said, gingerly taking a step up to the landing, "It was on the radio. Maybe you were sleeping, but they opened the Superdome as a shelter of last resort. The guard delivered water and enough meals for fifteen thousand people for three days."

I had to admit, I had completely forgotten the information we'd heard on the night we left, which was only last night, but it seemed like a week ago already.

I nodded and looked around at the gathering circle of elderly residents. None of them looked very healthy.

One particularly sweaty man with a cane and more wrinkles than one of Don's wool suits came directly up to me. "You bring my pills?"

"Um," I said, looking over at Don for support, "no. I'm not a nurse, and we're not part of the staff here."

Don, still hanging on to me, now stood up to his full height. "Hasn't anyone come to help you, folks?"

We got more blank stares than a theater full of moviegoers watching the end of *2001: A Space Odyssey*.

"Let's go see May," I said to Don, not taking my eyes off the group that had quite literally surrounded us.

As we started off in the direction of May's room, the circle seemed to follow us. More questions about meds, the heat, and, from the more cognizant folks, when a rescue was going to take place.

But as we entered the hallway off the second-floor common area, none of the residents followed us. It was almost like a force field was preventing them from going any farther.

Don and I both turned back and watched the group as we made our way down the hall.

Why hadn't Ashley or May been in that group? Without realizing it, I had been squeezing Don's hand tighter and tighter until he put his other hand over mine.

"She had to have gotten out. Remember, we haven't heard from her since last night. That's nearly twenty-four hours, Brenda. That's a lot of time. A lot could have taken place."

"I wish I could be as confident as you, Don."

Every step down the hall was getting more and more difficult. God only knew what we would find.

"Brenda, look, she's our daughter. We use logic for a living. How could she *not* think logically?"

Don had a point. Ashley wasn't dumb. She'd managed to get into the chemistry program at Tulane. If there was a way to get to a shelter, she would have discovered it.

Suddenly, I was feeling better. Much better actually. Each step was no longer filled with dread. I knew that we'd find them—both of them—alive and well.

It was a given.

I nearly smiled. Well, I did smile at Don. He *was* trying to cheer me up. That had to be worth *something*. Maybe this trip was the best thing that could happen to us. Maybe by working together like this, for a change, we'd find a way to go on.

Yep, I was feeling really good about the future until we got to May's open door.

57

When we entered May's room, she looked like she was sleeping, but there was just something that bothered me about the picture, you know? She didn't look right; mouth agape and all, it just felt different.

So I rushed up and shook her. I spoke to her, *yelled* at her to get up, to wake up and open her eyes and answer the burning question—where was Ashley?

I'm sure my actions and intensity made Don feel more than uncomfortable before he realized what concerned me.

Aunt May would never wake up again. There was no pulse. I know, I felt for one for a full minute. Finally, I sank to my knees at her bedside, holding her cold, still hand in mine.

And I cried. No, wailed was more like it. Deep convulsive, gut-wrenching sobs of despair, ending, lost history, and lost love. My surrogate mother was in this bed—the woman who raised me when my own mother had bailed on me after my father had bailed on both of us. And I never got a chance to say goodbye.

I felt Don's hand on my shoulder. He let me just go at it for what must have been a full five minutes. My body shook so badly that I eventually fatigued and the intensity of my sobs eased, but not my grief.

"I'm sorry, Brenda. Really, I…I was never any good at this, but I'm sorry," Don kept saying every few minutes as my grief spilled over from my eyes and ran down my cheeks.

Finally, he patted my shoulder. I recognized this as a milestone moment; we needed to do something different. I remember thinking that I hadn't felt nearly enough pain for the woman who sacrificed so much for me, who, with her husband, paid for my clothes and my food, sheltered me, sent me to school—all the books they bought me, the prom and homecoming dresses, and, finally, help with college tuition. Since they had no children of their own, and I was more or less a blood relative, I was as close to a child that they were going to get.

I blabbed all this to Don, who had heard it a million times before, but he stood there behind me, hand on my shoulder, squeezing it occasionally and keeping silent, until he thought I had grieved enough.

"C'mon," he said, "let's go find Ashley."

Oh, how that hit me too. If May were dead…

I couldn't think that way. But let's face it, Ashley wasn't here, May was and she hadn't made it through the storm, what could have befallen Ashley?

But Don was right; the longer we stayed here mourning May, the longer it would be before we found our daughter and what had happened to her.

I desperately wanted to know the cause of death, especially since nothing was obvious, but that could wait. What difference did it make anyway? She was elderly and the storm intense; it could have been a stroke, a heart attack, or any number of other things that lurk in the dark shadows in the lives of the elderly.

Tears still falling from my cheeks, I kissed May's hand and placed it back at her side, then used the bed to stand up off the floor. Don helped, guiding me while I slowly rose from the lowest point in my life.

He seemed to feel it too; Don placed both his hands on my shoulders and turned me to face him. "I know you are hurting now, Brenda. I know you are. But Ashley is going to need us now more than ever. You know how she feels about death and hospitals and whatnot. I'm willing to bet she left when she figured she couldn't do anything for poor May. Now we just have to figure out where she's gone."

I just nodded. I was too weak mentally and physically to say anything. I was done.

"Go freshen up, and then we'll get started, okay?"

I looked deep into Don's eyes. I wanted to be grateful, I did. Really, I did. But I was surprised that I didn't really see anything like compassion in his eyes, just cold, uncaring logic and a deep-seated drive to move on.

May never liked him anyway, and he knew it. I guess I couldn't blame him, but this was my step-up mother figure, and I couldn't just let her passing go without a dutiful mourning, could I?

But I just nodded, sidestepped him, and headed for the bathroom.

It was dark in the bathroom, and of course, like an idiot, I tried to turn on the lights. When they didn't go on the first time, I realized how stupid and foolish I was, rolling my eyes deeply.

When I did, I noticed a piece of paper wedged in the faucet for the shower. Odd place for a piece of paper, and it was folded so neatly too.

I reached out, took it, and put it on the counter to wait until I could wash my face. I looked back at the tub, and it was full of water.

Ashley!

The fact there was water in the tub connected me to Ashley. She'd done what Don had instructed her to do. I felt closer to her just being near the tub.

Scooping up a little, I cautiously tasted it. Yep, tap water. I knelt and splashed a few handfuls on my face, and the cooling effect was relatively luxurious. I splashed more water on my neck and down my collar.

In the bedroom, I heard Don moving about. Looking for clues, I figured, or maybe trying to gather up anything we could use.

I, on the other hand, had delayed long enough. I pushed up from the tub and stood, still feeling the cooling effects of the tub water and grabbed the folded paper, which was really an envelope.

Starting to unfold it as I walked out the bathroom door into the bedroom, I was interrupted by a voice that I did not recognize.

"Who *you* be?" a deep low voice gasped, and I jumped, dropping the envelope.

58

The voice belonged to a large black man dressed in what looked like medical garb that a nurse or surgeon would be sporting. Only his was somewhat dirty looking, wrinkled, and stained, but I wouldn't want to guess with what.

He looked nearly as startled as I was.

"I'm Brenda Meyers. May here"—I nodded toward the bed in front of him—"is my aunt."

I didn't intend to, but I started watching him very closely. It was odd how his expression went from startled to fear to suspicion to something I would call amusement.

"How did you get in here?"

It was a fair question. I wasn't so sure I wanted to give him the answer. "Ramming a car through your front door" was probably not the best way to start off a conversation.

"We got a desperate call from my daughter, Ashley, who came here to check on her great-aunt. She said that the center wasn't evacuating the residents and that management had just up and left. So we drove down last night, and now I find my aunt deceased with no proper care for her remains. And I can't find my daughter either, so naturally, I'm a bit concerned. Do you know what happened to my daughter?"

His expression of amusement intensified. I was hoping to put him in his place with a strong offense, but apparently, it wasn't strong enough.

He stepped around the bed, slowly, heading toward me. He was between me and a hasty escape through the doorway to the hall. Suddenly, I didn't feel like I should be so aggressive.

And where was Don?

"My husband was just in here. Did you see where he went?"

I took a step back toward the bathroom, hoping that the door had a lock on it.

"I ain't seen nobody, lady. Was that your car come smashin' through my front door?"

I tried standing my ground, but it had little effect on him. "We had no other way to get in."

"Oh, now you gonna have to pay for that," he said, Cajun accent coming thick now.

"Yeah? Well, who's going to pay for my aunt's *death*? You should have evacuated these people!"

"You gonna have to take that up with the management, *beb*."

"I'm *not* your friend...Uh, what is your name anyway?"

He took two steps closer, almost casually, but every one of them was a definite menacing act. "Bruno."

"Bruno what?"

Suddenly, the amused expression vanished. "What you gonna do with that information?"

"Look, I've had about enough out of you! My aunt is lying there, dead instead of sitting on a bus headed north out of harm's way. That's *your* company's fault! They...*you* are responsible for this death, and who knows how many more before the authorities get here?"

He stopped short. "You brought the authorities?"

That thought had obviously scared him.

"Damn right! When we heard that this place was in chaos, we came right down and called the police too!"

It wasn't a total lie.

Bruno frowned. He was close enough now that I could smell him, and he reeked of booze, not a great mix considering the situation I found myself in.

STORM SURGE

"Now I want to know what caused my aunt's death," I said as forcefully and as confidently as I could.

Had my voice cracked? Was it shaking?

Bruno finally backed off and looked at May, shrugging his shoulders. I bristled at the sign of disrespect.

"I dunno. You gonna have to take that up with the coroner," he said, turning toward May.

I took a huge silent breath to calm my nerves. It would appear that the showdown was over. If there ever was one, but something told me that Bruno would have tried to do something before he found out the "authorities were on their way."

The trick was to get out of here before he realized it wasn't true.

"Don't think for a minute that I won't pursue this in court," I said, trying to keep up appearances. "Now I want to know if you saw my daughter, Ashley." I went on to describe her, but something tells me he didn't need a description.

"Yeah, I might've seen her. There was a girl come here looked like that. Talked to May, she did. Then she left with some folks in a boat after the storm. I figure that girl no good, I do."

I knew he was lying, and now a new fear swept over me. He wanted me to believe she'd left. By the aggressiveness earlier, I was sure he had done something to Ashley or at least tried to and was holding her somewhere in the building.

Or worse!

"When did she go? That makes no sense. She doesn't know anyone here but her roommate and friends from college!"

It was my turn to step toward him aggressively. He, unlike me, stood his ground, turning to face me.

"Look, my husband has a gun, and he has no problem using it. What have you done to my daughter?"

"I ain't done nothin' to no one, lady."

His eyes darted toward May on the bed. It was a clear indication he had something to do with her death.

"I'm warning you, Bruno, my husband has a temper and he has a gun with lots of ammo! You better not be lying to me!"

"What the hell's going on here?"

John's voice made me jump, and Bruno spun around to see John walking through the door, eyes on Bruno, hand on his pocket where I had noticed the outline of the big gun from the yellow toolbox.

59

I tried not to be obvious by studying John's face, but I'm sure he noticed my wide eyes and furrowed brow. It all spelled *worried*. While John gave no indication he had heard anything, I knew just how good a poker face he possessed. It was a sure bet that he heard me telling Bruno about Don having a gun. Then again, he'd have known that once he opened the yellow toolbox to grab the gun he was carrying, right?

So he must also have known his gun had no bullets. Why wasn't he screaming about it? Maybe he'd gone through our bags, found the bullets in my duffel, and reloaded. If he had, I could be sure that I had a target painted on my back now too.

So I watched John's every movement, and when he stepped into the room, I made my break as casually as I could. With a quick sidestep around Bruno, I headed straight for the door.

But Bruno called out to me. "Ma'am, you dropped this."

I turned, remembering the folded envelope I had found. *Seriously?*

Not really caring about the envelope but worried what John might think it odd if I didn't retrieve it and decide that this was a good time to reenact the O.K. Corral, I stepped a few paces closer to Bruno, reaching out for the envelope.

I pocketed the folded paper and scooted back a few steps before I turned my back to retry my escape.

As I did, I glanced at John. He was staring at me intensely. He must know. He *had* to know. What was I going to say to him?

How about where the *hell* was my husband? And why didn't John tell us he was bringing not one but *two* weapons along?

I was ready. I was ready to turn it back on him if he said anything. But he let me pass without trying to stop me. Even so, his eyes followed my every movement.

It was creepy. I swallowed hard and turned to look out through the doorway. It was hard to do; I just turned my back on the two of the three people in the whole world I trusted the least.

But if Don were lying dead somewhere, it would be my fault—completely and utterly my burden.

So I was ready to die. I expected it, even. I wondered what the impact of the bullet would feel like or how badly would it hurt. Would it happen so fast, causing my death so quickly that I wouldn't even feel it?

I tensed, waiting for the bullet. But the strain finally got to me, and I bolted. I ran for all I was worth through the door and down the hall toward the second floor landing and the open expense of that second-floor lobby with all those witnesses.

John couldn't shoot *every one* of those people, so there was a limited amount of safety in being around the elderly residents of the center.

"Brenda! Wait! Where are you going?"

I could hear John yelling behind me, and it sounded like he was running too. I didn't stop or even glance back.

"Brenda? Where are you *going?*"

I ran at top speed toward the group of elderly people still at the top of the stairs.

But I could hear John's running footsteps now too. Had I just involved these innocent people? What was John planning?

The more I thought about it, the more I realized that Don could, at this very minute, be dead. He hadn't come to investigate the yelling or the noise I was making as I thundered down the hallway.

Surely, he would have heard *something* if he was still alive.

The thought slowed me. I'd lost him. His death was *my* fault, his blood on *my* hands. I would never be able to live with myself.

How was I going to face Ashley if I ever saw her again?

I made it to the group of about six or seven residents and just blurted out, "Has anyone seen my husband? The man I came up the stairs with?"

All I got were blank stares. Exasperated, I took a deep breath to ask the question again, louder so they could hear me, but it was too late.

I felt a hand on my shoulder, and it spun me around to face a very angry John Katsarus.

"What are you *doing*?" he asked.

But before I could answer or explain about the guns or accuse him of murdering my husband, I heard a scream from the hallway I had just come out of.

"Brenda! Come here! I found something," Don yelled.

60

THE FLOOD OF relief that Don's voice brought was indescribable. And it sounded like he was excited about something. He'd found a clue, I was sure of it.

It was easy to do an end run around John; he was looking back toward the end of the hallway where Don's voice had come from. I was around John and running toward the sound of Don's voice before he realized what was happening.

But as I ran, I heard him running behind me too. It had a heck of a motivational effect, and I doubled my speed.

"Don? Where are you?" I yelled.

He appeared soon after I called out, poking his head out of a room on the opposite side of the floor from May's door, waving and then ducking back in the room again. Bruno poked his head out of May's room and saw my running toward him. The look on Bruno's face was sheer annoyance.

Everything else forgotten, I ran right past Bruno and struggled to come to a halt at the door slightly down the way from May's.

"What did you find?" I asked Don as I stumbled through the doorway, breathless and heart pounding. I was so eager to hear what he found that I completely forgot to warn him about John's gun.

"Look," he said, pointing to the bed.

Duffel bags and a backpack, but not just any luggage; it was Ashley's.

"We know she was here, Don," I said, not really wanting to crush his mood. "Where is she now?"

"Or what happened to her?" John said behind me. I spun around and saw John standing in the doorway, behind Bruno who had come in from the hall. John's arms were folded across his chest. At least he hadn't drawn the gun.

And it seemed he wasn't about to let Bruno out of the room.

I'm guessing his confidence meant that he had found the bullets in my bag and reloaded, making him eminently dangerous.

Bruno turned to look at John, then back to us.

"This the girl you were askin' about? This is where I let her stay overnight. This the one I told ya went with the folks in the boat."

"That's not something she would have done if she didn't know them," I said.

Bruno shrugged. "Well, surprise, that's what she done."

"She wouldn't do that," Don said, stepping toward Bruno, past me, "unless she had to, like…to get away from something or someone. So help me, whoever you are, if you did anything to her, I'll fucking *kill* you!"

Everything happened in slow motion. I watched with fascination as Don whipped out the gun he had been hiding and pointed it directly at Bruno's face. Bruno froze and stared directly at the hole at the end of the barrel of Don's gun.

In the meantime, John had unfolded his arms, swore, and reached for his gun, stepping back into the hall. Since I was standing just inside the doorway, a little off to the side, all I saw was the barrel of John's big gun, and it didn't seem to be pointing at Bruno.

Bruno started backing up, and when his head hit the barrel of John's gun, he freaked.

I was thinking that, perhaps, I had better step in before things got really out of control, but really, what could I do? There was a better than even chance I would get shot. Don wasn't a skilled marksman; in fact, he hated guns, and John most likely wanted Don and I both dead.

But Don was *my husband*, right or wrong. When I started to move forward, Don seemed to realize that John's massive "I'm compensating for something" gun was aimed at him and not Bruno. I could see him shift aim quickly as he held the gun awkwardly in front of him.

Why John didn't shoot him, I simply couldn't figure out, but gun barrels were flying all over the place, and right smack in the middle of any potential crossfire was Bruno.

"Drop it, Meyers! You don't know what you're doing!"

Don just squinted at John. "Like hell! Why did you bring these things in the first place, Katsarus?"

It was now or never. I took a deep breath and walked right into the line of fire. Immediately, both barrels got raised toward the ceiling, and John started swearing at me.

"For Christ's sake, Brenda! You want to get shot?"

I turned to him and, putting my hands on my hips, asked, "Who would be doing the shooting, John? You *both* are being incredibly *stupid*!" I pivoted and faced Don, then John behind Bruno.

"You both are so hung up about one-upping each other that you've forgotten why we came down here in the first place! To rescue Ashley!"

Bruno was nodding his head vigorously. He was clearly scared. "An' I tol' ya that she ain't here no more! She lit outta hear with them folk in the airboat that came by. She was tryin' to shout at them, and she leaned out the window too far and fell out!"

"Fell out?" My voice pitch and volume clearly registered my alarm.

"She landed on the patio awnin' an' then in the water. She be okay though. She waded out to the boat an' they helped her up out the water. I think they was from the police or somethin'."

"Why?" Don asked, gun now pointed at Bruno's head.

"That big ol' airboat, she had a bunch of lights up on top, like a cop car."

"We need to get back to the ramp then," Don said, lowering his gun and putting it back in his pocket.

"Wait, you're just going to *believe* this guy?" John said, incredulous and clearly angry.

I turned to John and tried to show him how determined I was.

"Yes. It makes perfect sense. And Ashley was always a klutz. We need to go."

"Wait," Bruno said, grabbing my arm. "Take me with you! I can't handle it here no more. I can point out that boat you lookin', for an' I can help guide you back to where you need to go."

John was shaking his head. He pulled his gun up and pointed it directly at Bruno. "No, no, no," he said.

61

"Well? Why *not*, John?" I tried to get in his face, but Bruno was in the way.

"May's dead, and your daughter is nowhere in sight after being here for sure. And you're going to just believe this guy? How do you know he didn't overpower Ashley and he's got her hidden somewhere here?"

Don had been pointing his gun at John. He gestured with it as he pointed to different people, and I clenched my fists as the barrel swung past my head.

"We're taking this guy with us back to the ramp. Now get out of the way, Katsarus," he growled, if you could call a shaky voice growling.

But to his credit, he hadn't shot anyone accidently yet, and I guess even I would be shaky being forced to do what Don was doing.

Still, I backed out of the exact line of fire to the side of the doorway. John pointed his gun directly at Don so quickly that I didn't even realize it was happening until after the gun was aimed. Bruno, who was in the middle, was wide-eyed and stammering.

"I-I-I'll let you two settle this," he was trying to say as he ducked out of the way. But he couldn't get past John, so he moved over by me.

It wasn't a comfortable place to be.

"Drop it, Meyers! I mean it! I don't know how you got into my stuff, but I mean to take that back!"

"Father's *tools*, huh? You lied about these guns, Katsarus! There is no *fucking* way I'm giving you all the firepower!"

"John," I snapped, trying to distract him. "Why *would* you lie about taking guns along on this trip?" I shouted, hoping that he wouldn't bring up our conversation back home in front of Don.

"They gonna blow each other away," Bruno whispered to me. I wasn't listening. I was waiting to hear John's excuse.

"I carry guns wherever I go. Answer me truthfully, would you have freaked out if I had told you the truth?"

I had to give John credit; on the face of it, his response made sense. Enough sense for someone like Don, perhaps, but given the context from my perspective and our conversation not twenty-four hours ago, I knew it had to be a lie. But all this was wasting time.

"God damn you *both*! God *damn* you! If you want to kill each other, there's nothing I can do to stop you. But I'm going to count to three, then Bruno and I are going to walk out of here, hot-wire John's boat, and try and find Ashley. You two can either disarm and come with or kill each other."

Bruno looked at me as if I were crazy. "Take it or leave it," I told him.

With a quick glance at the guns, then me, Bruno closed his eyes and nodded.

"One."

"You're making a big mistake, Brenda! You haven't searched this place yet," John hissed, but I could tell by his tone that he was starting to waver.

"Two."

"I'm keeping this gun, Katsarus. You lied about having them. I have to wonder why you brought them and lied about them," Don said.

"I already *told* you!"

I took a deep breath. "Three!"

Slowly, I moved around the doorframe and came face-to-face with John and his cannon.

"Step aside, John."

"I want that gun back!"

The dam finally burst. The rage I felt at this *absurd* situation and the delay it was causing erupted.

I stuck my finger out and started to jab it at John.

"Considering our conversation yesterday, I *don't trust your answers*, John! Now you either shoot me now and take a bullet from Don or you let me by so I can find my daughter!"

"Yeah, wait, *what* conversation?" Don asked behind me. I turned.

"None of your damn business, Don! And do you really think you can outshoot a hunter like John? Put the gun down before you hurt someone!"

Don's expression turned to absolute rage, but he wavered. "I'll put this gun away when he does."

I turned back to John and raised my eyebrow, saying nothing.

"That's my gun, and I want it back now," John said, not budging.

I got directly in the line of fire, put my hands on my hips, and let him have it.

"And you fucking *lied* about it! I don't even think you have bullets in that thing unless you went rummaging through my bag!"

"Well, funny you should say that, Brenda, because after I saw the Bible, that's *exactly* what I did."

A feeling of intense cold washed down my neck. But I stood my ground. You had to play out a bluff confidently with John, or he'd call you on it.

"Then shoot me, John. By the time you get done pulling the trigger, Don would have put a bullet in your head or close to it. From this distance, even *he* can't miss. Now *get the fuck out of my way!*"

It took maybe ten long seconds, but John's face turned every shade of red from beet to purple.

I looked at both of them. "Both of you. Put your guns down now!"

To my utter surprise, John pointed his gun at the floor.

I turned to Don. "Put the fucking gun down before you screw up our lives, Don!"

Don looked at me as if he were going to shoot me, then to John, then Bruno, then slowly, reluctantly, pointed the gun at the floor.

"Can we go now?" I asked calmly, expecting John to step aside sheepishly.

"No," John said again.

62

Everyone stared at John in disbelief. He calmly pocketed the big howitzer of a handgun and shrugged.

"You realize that I've got you covered, right?" Don smirked.

I could have killed Don myself for real this time. There was absolutely no reason to push things. I guess with all the hassle John had given him on the way down, I couldn't blame him too much, but this wasn't exactly a good time for payback.

John looked like he was going to rip someone's head off. "You're making a huge mistake. You should search this place first. You don't even know where she could have gone. And I can't believe you're going to believe *this* guy," he repeated, nodding his head toward Bruno.

"So far as we know, he hasn't lied to us yet," Don said. "Unlike *you*."

John looked over at me. "Well, he's right. He's got the drop on me, so I'm at your mercy. Would you have believed me about bringing them for self-defense if I had been straight with you…considering?"

Considering the conversation we had, I had to admit, John was right. But then again, that's what John was so good at doing—using a situation to his advantage and giving you enough logic that good sense guided you just where he wanted you.

But there was no way right now that Don should hear *any* of this; he still had the only ready gun, and he would blow John away at the drop of a hat. Any hat.

So I changed the subject. "Why don't you want us to leave?" I asked John.

"Because I really think she may still be here. Falling out the window, really? Without getting hurt? We're on the second floor, Brenda. How believable is *that* story?"

"He's right," Don said behind me.

Stunned, I turned around. Don shrugged. "I hate to admit it, but he's right. At least Katsarus is a known entity. This guy isn't."

"You know, I can hear y'all," Bruno said, eyes locked on the gun still in Don's hand, pointing at the floor. "Mister? If you ain't gonna shoot nobody, could you take your finger out the trigger guard?"

Don glanced down at the gun and nodded. He put it back in his pocket but kept his hand on the handle.

"So what now?" I asked Don.

"We should do a quick search," Don said, looking around and frowning.

"Every room?" I asked, incredulous.

"Only if you want to be satisfied she isn't here. You could check up on the residents too," John said.

"Since when do you care about other people, John?" I asked but probably shouldn't have. But I knew John only too well; caring for anyone other than John Katsarus was out of scope for him.

"You should know better," John said, lowering his voice now.

I opened my mouth, but nothing came out. I had pushed it, but no one who knew John like I did would blame me. I turned to Don.

"What do you think we should do, Don?" I was hoping he would change his mind and want to get out of this place, but now I wasn't sure that Ashley had actually left. What Bruno described didn't sound like her.

"Well, if that boat was an official boat, like from the Coast Guard or something, they would have gone to a shelter, right?" he asked.

I turned to Bruno without answering.

"Where's the nearest shelter, Bruno?"

He shrugged. "I do not know."

I turned to Don. "Okay, shoot him."

Everyone was taken by surprise, and Bruno finally became very talkative, helpful even.

"Look, I'll guide you, I'll go with you, but I really don't know where the nearest shelter might be! You *gotta* believe me!"

He went on and on, and by the fear in his voice, I would tend to believe him. So where did that leave us? Staying here and waiting for something or someone to give John an advantage, or believing John and trying to rule out his theory that Bruno is a lying kidnapper?

"Relax," I heard Don say as I started pacing up and down the hallway. "We're not going to shoot you."

"Oh, Jesus, thank you," Bruno sighed.

"Yet."

Bruno became silent. I looked over at Don, and he shrugged.

"How long can it take?" he asked me directly. "The first floor is mostly offices and some of it is under a few inches of water. That will be quick to check. After this floor, that leaves just two more floors and there's four of us."

None of the choices I was given were ideal, but John was correct; I would never forgive myself if she were here and I charged on without satisfying any nagging doubt.

We had to search the place.

"Okay, let's search this place," I said as I turned to face the rest of them. "But we split up. Bruno, you go with Dirty Harry here, and I'll go with John. You take the first floor and the rest of this one. We'll meet on the top floor, and if we don't find Ashley, we're heading out to find an official-looking boat or something and ask them where they are taking people from this area," I said with authority.

"I keep tellin' ya, she ain't *here*," Bruno insisted.

"I hope you're right, for your sake. My husband has an itchy trigger finger, and if he finds out that you were lying to us, well, I wouldn't want to be you," I said as menacingly as I could.

Then I pulled John's elbow. "C'mon, Katsarus, I want to have a little *chat* with you anyway."

63

Before we parted ways, Bruno stopped us. He was shaking his head, but he reached into his pocket and, in doing so, caused Don and John to yank out their guns, taking aim at him so fast that even I gasped.

"I-I-I have a pass key that will make it easy for ya," he said, voice shaking and moving his hand very slowly.

Crisis subsided, we split up. John followed me sullenly to the floor above. The silence was awkward, but not unwelcome after the stress of the showdown on the floor below.

Finally, we reached the third floor. We had to take the stairs at the end of the hallway as the second floor was the only story in the building to have an open staircase. I figured this was done to make the center feel more like a home than a hospital. The stairwells on the ends of the floors were enclosed for fire safety, and they went all the way to the ground floor.

Before we opened the door to the floor hallway, I stopped and turned to John.

"I mean it. I want an honest answer. Are you working with someone to kill Don?"

John stared at me as if he were sizing me up. It seemed he took a full minute of just spinning things in his head.

Finally, he broke eye contact.

"I canceled the…request."

I put my hands on my hips. "So you *did* arrange for Don's murder?"

Again, he looked like he was weighing his options before he answered me. After a few seconds of silence, I prodded.

"Well?"

"When I realized you were just venting, I decided that this wasn't a viable option. I was only really just exploring solutions for you, anyway. There isn't going to be a hit."

I always knew John associated with dangerous people. But the directness in his answers now I found...*chilling*. Chilling that someone else could actually make decisions about someone else's life like that so...*casually*, as if people were just some asset or liability or property to be acquired or disposed of.

But I didn't feel like a philosophical debate right now, especially with someone who had no moral compass. I did, however, have one final question.

"So really, why *did* you bring the guns and lie about them?"

John rolled his eyes this time. It seemed like a natural reaction, not a programmed response. I still doubted it, though; John was that good of an actor.

"I know what this looked like, and it turns out I was right. See, I really did bring them for self-defense. I heard warnings about this place. Let's just say that...*friends* told me that the cops are...shall we say a lot of 'em are...*flexible* down here. Some of 'em, anyway. Since I had no way to know that was true, I thought I'd better arm *us* just in case anything went weird."

"Okay, that's one explanation, but why did you lie about them?"

"C'mon, Brenda! Considering what we were talking about yesterday, Don dying and leaving you with the insurance benefits, the house, hell, *all* your marital assets instead of handing them over to the lawyers...do you think you'd have believed me?"

"I still don't trust you, John. Your history precedes you."

"Fine. Can we get on with the search now?"

Before I could answer, he roughly pushed past me into the hall through the fire door. By the time I was able to follow him out into the third-floor hallway, he was banging on the closest apartment door.

"Ashley? Are you in there?"

"I've got the key," I said, thrusting past him and inserting it.

He looked at me with something near disgust. "This is your show, Brenda. I'm just the workhorse."

Asshole.

I waited for an answer that wouldn't come in the minute since we banged on the door, then unlocked it and peered in.

The room was dark, and no one was around. Empty. We moved to the next room and repeated the actions with the same results.

After we had completed three more, including being invited in by a very sweaty woman who needed a walker to move around, John came up to me in the hall.

"So what's the plan?"

"What do you mean?"

"I mean if you're right and she's not here?"

I took a deep breath. I really hadn't thought about it.

"Only thing I can think of is we get back in the boat and we find a cop, or one of those volunteers and ask where people from this place might have been brought."

"You mean people like Billy Bob, the guy we left in waist-deep filth to walk all the way back to the ramp and complain about us? *Those* guys?"

"Why do you always have to put things so negatively?" I asked, starting to walk away and bang on my next door.

"Because life is negative, Brenda. Look around you. Look at all this misery."

"I refuse to believe that. That's why we'd never have worked, you and me, John. You see only the worst in people, I try to see the best."

"Obviously. That's why you're still with that loser Meyers, who can't hold a job. Tell me, you sure he's still employed? He got the time off awfully quick and without a hitch, didn't he?"

Nope. I was determined that I wasn't going to go down that long, slippery slope.

As if to stifle a comeback, I opened the next door particularly quickly.

Unfortunately, it scared the hell out of an elderly gentleman who threw a book at us.

64

As they checked the rest of the second floor, Don held back, holding on to the gun so that Bruno was intensely aware of the power that Don held over him.

They quickly settled into an uneasy rhythm; Don would wait until Bruno unlocked the door with his master key, then he followed the large man into the room. Then it was Bruno's turn to wait while Don searched the room. When they failed to find Ashley or any evidence that Ashley had been in the room, the duo proceeded on to the next room. If they walked in on anyone, apologies were made and they retreated to the hallway.

When they finished checking the floor, they headed to the main stairs. Just before they got there, Don grabbed Bruno by the shoulder.

"Wait, we need to talk."

The large man said nothing but waited expectantly near the head of the stairs with the carnage Don had caused in the lobby within sight below.

"You probably noticed that other guy, he and I don't get along too well."

"Naw, I hadn't noticed."

"He brought these guns along and lied about them. I think he was going to do something nefarious to either Brenda or me."

"Yeah, he makin' you the *misere*, that for sure."

"Yeah, whatever. So I need your help."

Bruno's face went from surprise to mistrust, then an evil sort of realization that he just may be back in the driver's seat. He folded his arms and leaned against the wall.

"You need ol' Bruno's help, do ya? Well, what's in it for me?"

"You get out of here like you wanted, you stay out of jail, and"—Don looked down at the gun he was holding—"I'll give you John's big gun."

Bruno narrowed his eyes. Don couldn't tell if the orderly believed him or not but little did he care. He fully intended to give him that big Desert Eagle .50 Action Express, just not loaded and with the bullets in a separate and loose place.

He might even give Bruno some magazines too.

"Not enough. Sorry."

"Suit yourself. You'd get to beat the snot out of someone who despises you, but in reality, I don't need you. I *could* use you, but I have a gun. I can make Katsarus dance if I wanted to. Never mind."

Don turned to proceed up the stairs, but Bruno suddenly had a change of heart.

"Well, okay, I accept your offer."

"Too late. You should have agreed the first time I presented you with the proposition. Now I simply don't trust you."

Don pushed the door to the stairway open.

"Wait, Mr. Don, I can identify that boat!"

"So can I from what you told me. Frankly, you're just going to end up on the wrong side of a lawsuit with all these people here not being cared for. Maybe even criminal charges and prison time. I think you'll say anything to get a free ride and disappear."

This time, Bruno reached out and risked being shot as he grabbed Don's arm.

"Wait, look, I'll tell you the truth," Bruno said sullenly.

Don shook his arm free and got the gun ready, just in case. "Start talking."

Bruno took a slow, deep breath and exhaled. "I've been sort of takin' things from the residents here. Things that could earn me some money on the black market."

"So? What kind of things? Did you take anything from Ashley?" Don was starting to think he knew where this was going. He was about to hear a confession from this orderly about how he hurt Ashley or, worse, because she refused to give up her cell phone or maybe some other possession.

"Look, your daughter, she did catch me going through some of May's things. But I didn't take anything, truly I didn't! But she never trusted me. I was trying to make a deal with her when she heard that boat and tried to signal the people in it but really *did* fall out the window. She really did bounce on that awning and hit the water bad. But she all right. She got up, and they helped her get up in that boat, just like I described. Now look, Mr. Don, I told you something that was the truth. You got to believe me. So please, can you help me?"

"Okay, okay. Maybe I can use you," Don said slowly, through lips pulled tight in a smirk. "So listen up. I have some things I want you to do."

65

Fifteen minutes. That's all it took us to blow through the entire third floor.

Meeting at the door to the stairwell on the west side, John and I both seemed pretty satisfied that Ashley was nowhere on this floor.

"All right. I'm convinced she's not here, John. Let's get to the closest shelter and look there."

"There's still one more floor, and then there's the roof."

It really seemed like John wanted to keep us here. "Why don't you want us to leave, John?"

"Don't you want to make sure she's not…" John's voice trailed off.

"She is *alive*, John," I said, more to myself than John.

"All right, then we'll speed things up and let Don and his playmate check the next floor," he said. "Unless that Cajun idiot overpowers *your* idiot and gets the gun. Then you can't blame me of taking Don's life."

"Y'know, you really ought to lighten up on Don," I gushed without thinking. "He's doing the best he can. He may surprise you."

"What, *Don*? Surprise *me*?" John snorted as we climbed up the stairs. "I know you only stayed with him because of Ashley. It's pretty obvious he's not in love with you anymore."

I didn't know whether to admit John might be right or slap that smirk off his face.

"I don't see where my love life is any of *your* concern, Mr. Katsarus."

He snorted again. "Last-name basis now, wow, I must have really struck a nerve. I think you know I'm right."

I stopped and grabbed his arm, bringing John to a halt and swinging him around with a surprised look on his face.

"You know *nothing* about him," I nearly growled.

"I know he's no longer interested in you. Look at the way he treats you! Why don't you just give up on that loser? I'd rather see you with someone successful and who cares about you than waste your life with him!"

I started to dig my nails into John's bicep. "You know *why* he's the way he is? Did you ever *ask*, John?"

He just blinked.

"Did you know that he saw his sister raped and murdered when he was just seven years old? His sister was only thirteen, John. *Thirteen*! Rene was only a *child*!"

I'd been keeping that piece of history buried in the back of my mind for decades. It actually felt good to release it.

"He just *watched*? Well, why didn't he protect her or go for help?" John said, shrugging as if a seven-year-old could take on a drunk, abusive father.

For several seconds, I physically couldn't speak. I knew John could be a jerk, but so *callous*?

I flung his arm down. "You're a fucking asshole. I'd rather put up with Don with all his failings and baggage than a *shit* for a human being like you," I spat as I moved past him on the stairs.

"Yeah, well, I'm the fucking asshole who cares enough about you to come along on this cluster fuck and risked my boat *and* life now that your Wyatt Earp has my gun," he called after me, but I didn't respond.

I didn't even slow down.

Neither did I wait for John. When I burst through the fourth-floor stairway entrance, I just started to open doors and yelling for Ashley. After I had checked two, John moved past me.

"I'll check out the roof to save time," he mumbled.

I shook my head to clear the cobwebs. I could have sworn he had said, "Check the roof."

"The...the *where?*"

"There's a machinery shack on top. And of course then the outside part of the roof too. She might not have come down if she got locked out somehow."

"You're thinking my daughter went out on the roof during a *hurricane?*"

"No, after. To get some air or cool off, signal a helicopter, or to get away from May...uh...sorry."

I lowered my head and shook it. This was going to be painful and a waste of time, but John would chew on my one last raw nerve about being sure we left no stone unturned.

"I'll check the roof now while they're still down a floor," John said, pushing the door to the stairwell open.

But and I hated to admit this, maybe he was right about searching everywhere we could. At least I couldn't blame myself later if...

"I'll leave them a note," I said, deliberately interrupting that awful thought.

"Yeah, you do that."

I ignored the attitude and dug around for a piece of paper. Remembering the folded paper I found in May's bathroom, I pulled it out and opened it.

The first shock was the handwriting.

It was definitely Ashley's! I read it and got the second shock.

My husband was cavorting with a common criminal, and my initial impression was correct.

The third and most vital piece of information was confirmation that Ashley was not here. I even knew where she was going, and remembering the radio broadcast from yesterday, we should have known all along.

"John," I yelled, forgetting his transgressions.

But there was no answer. I looked up, and he wasn't in the hallway.

"John!"

I started running after him toward the eastern wing of the floor.

When I got to the open lobby area of the floor, I looked around but found no stairs or exit to the roof, just the elevator door, closed and powerless.

Damn it! Just when we have to get going, I've lost John, with the keys to the boat! Now I had to spend time looking for him.

"John?"

But there was no answer. Not even an echoing of footsteps that would indicate direction. The carpeting ensured that.

I swore.

"John!"

"Over here."

John's voice startled me. It had come from what looked like wall paneling next to the elevator doors, but when I got closer, it was an obscure access door.

John popped his head out of the access door and signaled me to follow. Before I could call out to him and show him the note, his head disappeared and I heard the echoes of his footsteps on some sort of metallic stairs.

He'd found the roof access.

I swore again and followed him, not even thinking that it could be a trap, that is, until I reached the top of the access stairs and my head rose above the floor of the machinery space.

It was dark except for the light coming in from an open door to the north. I could hear John walking outside.

The room was cavernous with pumps, pipes of all sizes, and water tanks. But despite the seeming clutter, I could see that no one was living up here.

So now I had to go out on the roof to get John. Damn it!

As I stepped outside, I called to him again.

"Over here," he yelled back, and I moved over to the west side of the building, hugging the wall of the machinery room and staying well clear of the roof's edge.

I saw John looking out to the west, hands up to shield his eyes from the setting sun. Then I heard it.

It was the unmistakable sound of a loud powerful boat. I happened to catch a glimpse of it between the rows of retail and residential buildings. It was heading east, this way, and in a hurry.

My guess was that it was some sort of police boat; I managed to see a bright orange hull and a light bar atop some sort of arch across the deck.

But what I found disturbing was that John was staring at it, hard. I was about to show him the note when he spun on his heal and trotted right past me.

"We gotta go," he said urgently.

It hit me right away. He had recognized the people in that boat. I looked back; it was a block closer now. Could this be his partners coming to kill my husband?

I turned quickly and started running after John.

66

Heart racing, fatigue all but forgotten, I actually caught up to John in the fourth-floor hallway. I was going to show him the paper, but we ran into Don and the murderer Bruno.

But I didn't have time to deal with that now.

"Don, here, read this. We have to go. We have to go *now*," I shouted, handing him the note and grabbing his arm to pull with all my might.

"Wait a minute, let me read this—"

"No time! There are some people coming here to kill you. We have to go now!"

Either he didn't hear me or he ignored me or didn't believe me. Nobody was moving. Don started reading the note but didn't get past the word *Superdome* before I started pulling his arm hard!

"What the hell are you talking about, Brenda?"

Don did seem a bit overwhelmed. But there wasn't any time to explain; we had to get out of there. If we delayed any longer, by the time we made it down to the first floor, that other boat would have arrived and we'd be trapped and Don would be dead.

Maybe even me.

I glanced at John, but he was expressionless. In fact, he was already moving past our group to the stairs and shoving the door open.

I was desperate for a delay, so I turned to the one person who was uniquely gifted to put the odds in our favor.

"Bruno? You want a ride to the Superdome? Then take John out."

"I already got a ride, thanks to Mr. Don here," he said smugly.

"Not after he reads that note from our daughter."

Bruno's eyes darted to the note, then to me, then he took off after John, moving faster than I ever thought a man of his size could move.

It was the way in which Don should be moving, but no, Don had to understand every angle before making a decision. I didn't think my heart could beat this quickly.

By this time, Don had finished reading the note. He looked up at me slowly, then toward the stairwell that John and Bruno had just gone down.

"What do you mean, some people coming here to kill me? What do you mean, like end my life?"

I grabbed his arm and started pulling him toward the stairs.

"Don, I'll tell you all about it as we go. Now hurry your ass up!"

As we trotted down the stairs, I breathlessly told him everything. I told him about yesterday when I agreed to meet John because he said he had to tell me something, and I thought it was about our mortgage or insurance. I admitted that John told me he thought Don and Amy were having an affair, how I was already stressed about not hearing from Ashley and quickly made a flippant comment about killing my husband if he was having an affair, and how John took that statement seriously. I told Don about John's partners being connected and, despite me being adamant about not killing Don, how I heard John making arrangements with someone over his phone while we were refueling to meet up and how I realized he was going through with the hit on Don and, finally, about the boat I saw when John and I were on the roof.

I must have sounded like a babbling lunatic.

Don never said a word as we were huffing and puffing our way downstairs. We seemed to pick up speed the more I told him. When I was finished, I glanced at him but never stopped moving down the steps to the first floor.

"Don, I *never* meant any of this to happen. I know we haven't been getting along lately, but I hope that's only temporary! I don't want you dead even if you want to divorce me."

I never asked him about the affair; I didn't care at the moment. I needed to get Don out of here and quickly. There'd be plenty of time to discuss that possibility later when we were all together and safe.

When we got to the first floor and out to the lobby, Bruno was waiting for us, breathing very hard and leaning against the wrought iron railing on the sweeping staircase. At the bottom of the stairs lay one John Katsarus, unconscious and sprawled out.

"Is he…?" I asked.

Between gasps, Bruno merely said, "He must've tripped."

I bent down and stuck my fingers near his nose. He was breathing shallowly, but breathing.

"C'mon, we need to get out of here," I insisted.

"You bringing this guy with us?" Don asked.

"A deal's a deal," I said, squeezing past the doorframe and the wrecked Acclaim. Don shrugged and squeezed out after me. Bruno tried next but was having some difficulty because, frankly, he was so large.

"Don' leave me!"

I wanted to so very badly. Ashley seemed so sure that this man caused May's death, but she left some doubt about whether or not it was on purpose.

So I reached in, grabbed his shoulders, and pulled.

It took about a full thirty seconds to extract Bruno out of the building and past the wreckage, but eventually we were all standing in front of the Claude Avenue Assisted-Living Center.

A small success and it felt bigger than it should have until I realized something.

"John still has the boat keys."

Everyone stopped and stared at me.

"I'm the smallest," I said. "I'll go in and get them."

Painfully, I squeezed past the car again and headed straight for John's crumpled form. When I started groping around in his pockets, he groaned. I froze but, realizing that we were running out of time, went back to my search without delay.

"Hey, hurry it up! We can hear the outboards!"

I looked back toward the opening where Don's face peered at me between the car and the doorframe.

Finally, I felt a float with a chain attached and pulled. Out came the keys from John's front pocket, and I ran to the car. Don helped me squeeze through, and when we stood on the stoop, we heard the distinct sound of powerful twin outboards cut from full speed to idle just around the corner where we had bailed out of John's boat.

The assassins were already here.

67

WE WERE IN deep trouble.

But the silencing of the outboard we had been hearing was all the motivation Don needed. He took off after Bruno, and I followed quickly. We broke out into a run, and when we rounded the southeast corner of the center, there was a beach of sorts, water lapping at the street and sidewalk to the north.

Behind us, we could hear Bruno huffing, and his heavy footsteps seemed to bounce off the walls of the buildings across the street from the center.

"Where's the *boat*? How do we get to it from here?" Don asked Bruno desperately.

We both faced Bruno. "How should I know? You came with him," he said.

"Then it should be wherever John left it," I added.

"That means it's probably on the west side there, right where we heard the other boat come up," Don observed. "It's the natural place to leave a boat. It's where we got off John's boat."

We all looked back toward the west side of the building. Claude Avenue was dry, but the two intersecting streets on either side of the center were partially flooded, and that's where we figured John beached his boat, but we wouldn't know until someone actually looked for it and found it.

I handed the keys to Don. "Well, now what?"

He frowned. "I guess we get behind this corner and wait for them to go in, then sneak past the front door and take Katsarus's boat."

Bruno shook his head. "Yeah, I ain't exactly the run silent kind. We could go in there"—he pointed north to the waterline—"an' wade all the way around the building to the boat. There's a street back there, and I seen people wadin' down it all day."

Don looked at him as if he were crazy. "Isn't that street flooded? With water?"

Bruno looked at Don warily. "You were thinkin' maybe it flooded with whipped cream, do ya?"

"Don has a fear of water," I explained.

In response, Don crept around the southeast side of the building, then knelt down on his haunches behind the bushes at the corner of the structure. He waited and watched. I snuck up behind him and tapped him on the shoulder to let him know I was there.

He turned to me and put a finger over his lips. Shh.

I nodded. He looked back, then back at me.

"They're coming now, two of them with big bags. They're wearing FEMA polo shirts. You sure about this?"

"Now more than ever."

He turned back to me and hissed, "What if they *are* FEMA coming to evacuate the building?"

"You want to bet your life on that? Maybe mine as well?"

He turned to look back around the bushes without saying a word. It made me wonder what he was thinking. After all, I was the one who caused all this. So I had to put a stop to it. Somehow. Or at least keep Don alive.

The bushes shook slightly as he tensed. Then he turned back to me. "They're in. Let's wait a minute, then run past the door."

"Don, I'm not sure this is the best idea," I started.

"Especially since I don' run so good," Bruno added. He startled me. For someone who was large, he moved with unexpected stealth.

Don and I both turned and hushed him, finger across our lips. Don got up and carefully snuck around the corner using the bushes that lined the sidewalk as cover.

"C'mon," he said, waving us on without taking his eyes off the main entrance to the center.

I trotted up as silently as I could, and Bruno labored behind me. Don gave the halt sign at the end of the cover provided by the bushes. There, the long ADA wheelchair ramp began its climb to the smashed doors.

"I don't see any movement and I don't hear anything, so let's go," Don said. "Quietly and quickly, okay?"

I nodded.

Bending over to take advantage of the first floor's slight rise above the street, we hurried past the still-dripping Plymouth Acclaim and didn't slow down until we were out of sight near the west side of the building.

There, we all turned the corner, Bruno breathing hard. We found two boats; John's was beached on the grass strip between the curb and the sidewalk. Figured he'd go to extra length to protect it.

Don looked at the water and waded in ankle-deep to climb up into John's boat. I followed him closely, and Bruno splashed down behind me.

The water felt nasty, not like you'd get in a pool or even the beach at Lake Geneva back home. It wasn't cold either. Not that the temperature would stop me.

Don looked around and inserted the key. "We should ditch this key and take the FEMA boat. It's bound to be faster."

"All our bags are in John's boat," I said. "And if they really *are* FEMA, do you want boat theft on your record?"

Don frowned. "It ain't your life we're talkin' about here, Brenda."

"The hell you say." I scrambled up into the boat, but Bruno paused.

"Well, there's something we *can* do," he said. "You promise me you'll wait for me?"

"Until they come out," Don answered him.

It was enough for Bruno. He waded back over to the FEMA boat, reached in and did something I couldn't see. When he came back, he had a big grin on his face, and we helped him aboard.

Then Don did something that absolutely amazed me. He told Bruno to get the boat started and take us to the Superdome. But Bruno shook his head, and I thought, *Here we go with more demands.*

"I can't."

"Well, why not?" Don hissed.

"I need somethin' to put in the kill switch!"

I shook my head. "Yeah, I pretty much have no idea what the hell you're talking about!"

"I know what he's talking about," Don said excitedly. "That red wire thing you clip to you and put in that kill switch. If you fall overboard, it will rip that thing out of the kill switch and kill the motor. Then the boat stops."

"Exactly," Bruno said, pointing at him and smiling.

"Will any wire attachment do?" I asked.

"Pretty much. They all common."

I nodded, looked over to the FEMA boat, and jumped in the water. As soon as I did, the screaming from inside started.

"Hurry up, Brenda! I think that was John's voice," Don yelled.

I shuffled over as fast as the water would let me and leaned in. It took a few seconds, but I found what I was looking for. I had to get in their boat to get it, though.

"Hurry!"

I nodded and hopped in, struggling to get over the inflatable sides. Once there, I grabbed that red curly wire and yanked it out of the kill switch and jumped overboard, stumbling and dropping the damn thing in the water!

The voices were screaming louder, and then I heard the running feet.

Well, let me tell you, nothing is a better motivator than the promise of imminent death. I reached down and searched around for the attachment, found it, and did my best imitation of a speed boat.

When I got near enough to John's boat, I tossed the wire to Bruno, and he caught it. Don grabbed my hands as I tried to get a leg over the side of the boat.

By this time, Bruno had the motor started and was trimming the drive down.

As soon as the outboard came down, Bruno threw it in reverse, and even though I was half in the boat and half out, he backed away from the shoreline.

The prop struck the ground several times as Don managed to pull me in.

I ended up on top of Don in the bottom of the boat, but I could hear John screaming at us. His boat was vibrating badly now, from the prop damage I guessed, and Bruno ducked down behind the console.

I wondered why.

Then suddenly, I had my answer. Gunshots erupted over John's heightened screaming something about his boat.

One of the shots went through the plexiglass windshield, shattering it right over Bruno's head. At this point, Bruno stopped the rearward motion and spun the helm around, reaching over to firewall the throttle.

The bow rose out of the water, and we spun around in our own length. This, however, exposed us all to the trigger-happy hitmen on the shore.

Several hit the console above Bruno's head, and he ducked down even farther. The rear of the boat was so low in the water that the prop was striking the flooded street with every blade. Some shots even hit the fish-finder, and it exploded in a Technicolor finale.

John screamed.

With the boat shaking badly, we made it to the back street and turned west. The gunshots stopped, but John's screaming kept echoing off the low-rise buildings behind the assisted-living center.

68

When the gun shots stopped, Bruno raised his head above the console. I rolled off Don.

Despite the severe convulsions the boat was going through, I managed to get up and sit on the casting deck in the bow of the boat. I held out my hand to Don, who was still lying in the fetal position on the deck.

I had completely forgotten how banged up he was after acting like a human-battering ram in the Plymouth.

But he ignored my hand and picked himself up off the deck, hanging on to the ice cooler turned seat in front of the console.

I took a deep breath and realized that I was shaking. I wondered if Don was too. But that would make what he did even more heroic.

"Thank you, Don."

He just looked at me and cleared his throat as he got to a standing position, still holding on to the fiberglass of the shattered console's instrument panel. When he steadied himself, he moved back behind the helm and tapped Bruno's shoulder.

"I'll drive now."

"But you brought me along to show you the way," Bruno whined.

"You can do that from the other seat. Now scoot."

For half a second, Bruno looked like he might try to fight Don for the seat, but I caught him glance down at the pocket where Don was carrying the handgun. Right after he did that, Bruno moved over and let Don sit down behind the helm.

Don pushed the throttle wide-open. The boat shook so violently that I thought I was going to be tossed out into the flooded street.

"No, no, no," Bruno yelled over the wind and outboard noise. He reached over and slammed the throttle back to neutral. The boat slowed and came off plane, settling a little in the water, just enough to send Don standing.

"What the hell are you doing?" he shouted to Bruno.

But the big man shook his head. "The prop is damaged. We can't go fast."

"Then we should have taken the FEMA boat like Don wanted to," I added. This was not good; there weren't very many places to hide.

"No, ma'am, that would have gotten us arrested. Don't you worry you're *Texian* heart about them catching us in that boat. It'll be some time before they can get it started after what we did to it."

"Okay, then how long will it take us to get to the Superdome at the speed that is best for the condition of the boat?" I asked, assuming that we would actually put the boat back in gear soon.

Don and I were looking at Bruno, and the big man glanced at each of us in turn before shrugging.

"Maybe couple hours at half throttle. That's if the motor and prop last an' nothin' else *makes us the misere*," he said.

A couple of *hours*? "It'll be dark by then," I said.

"Darker than you think," Don added as he put his hand on the throttle. "There's no power in the city, remember?"

I hadn't thought about that. Complete and utter darkness could hide a lot of really bad things.

"An' all them buildings will cast early shadows," Bruno contributed.

"Then I suggest we get moving," I said.

"To the Superdome?" Don asked.

I flashed an exasperated look toward Don. "Really? You read the note, right?"

"What note?" Bruno asked, now somewhat concerned.

I turned to him slowly and very deliberately said, "The note Ashley gave us detailing where she was going to go and what happened to her at the center."

Bruno just stared at me. I couldn't read his expression, but I held his gaze until Don pushed the throttle to the halfway mark and yelled, "Hang on!"

The resultant rise in the bow broke the tension between Bruno and me, but I watched as he glanced several times at Don's gun pocket. That did not give me a warm and fuzzy about his intentions.

So I got up. "Change places with me, Bruno. It will be better for the trim."

He clearly didn't like that explanation, but neither did he have a good counter reason. He slowly got up.

"Ya think ol' Bruno is too fat, do ya?"

"No, I think I want to keep the propeller from hitting bottom again, so we don't slow down even more," I said, urging him up with my hand gesture. Reluctantly, he began to stand up.

"Oh, Brenda, I can't hear him if he's that far away. I only know that we have to go west. I don't know how to get there exactly. Let him stay," Don said.

I turned to Don, who did not return my stare. Bruno did, though, but his eyes were narrowed just a shade too much for my tastes, probably his way of laughing at me, but somehow, I got the distinct impression that if something happened, it would happen to me as well as Don.

Okay, Don, I thought. It's your funeral, and I sat back down on the casting deck and put my feet up on the built-in cooler in front of the console.

Of course, it will be my funeral too, I thought to myself as I caught Bruno looking at the gun pocket again and Don oblivious.

69

Bruno had weaved us through countless streets, and Don dutifully steered wherever Bruno pointed. Oddly, Don looked like he was having the time of his life. But he had started to glance backward to where we had come, and I guessed he was starting to worry about the powerful and, obviously, much faster boat John's hitmen were using.

This was going to get dicey when we found Ashley and went home. John was an accomplice to attempted murder, and I worried about what our possible future would look like.

No doubt, John was connected to organized crime figures. He knew both Don and me, and he knew about Ashley. So, the hitmen probably did too. It seems as though our future might include the witness protection program. And that just might force us to stay married.

But Ashley's future was screwed up as well. She could never lead a normal life now, and for that, I had John Katsarus to thank. I wished they had shot him back there at the center.

The realization that that sort of thought started this whole mess wasn't lost on me, and I shook my head in disbelief that I could have caused this whole thing.

As we continued as best we could down the street, given the vibration the boat was experiencing, I couldn't help but notice the people on roofs and wading in the water, most of the latter group heading west.

It made me feel terrible that we couldn't help them somehow.

Don kept glancing over his shoulder for longer and longer periods. Every time he did so, Bruno eyed the pocket where Don kept his gun. What made me so nervous was that the gun was in Don's right pocket, the same side Bruno was sitting.

I took the opportunity to move back by Don and stand near Bruno, who was behind the console. I wanted to be near him in case Don needed any help.

Don stood up, but as he did so, he looked back over his shoulder again, and the motion moved the steering wheel slightly. I had to grab on to what was left of the bent aluminum frame around the shattered plexiglass windshield to keep from falling over.

Don felt the boat move, and he quickly turned back to look forward and correct the course; he had aimed us at the row of low-rise buildings and houses that lined the flooded street.

He grinned sheepishly and shrugged. And he continued to smile as we shook our way down the street and headed toward the high-rise buildings of downtown New Orleans in the distance.

It was a peculiar sight; Don hated the water. He didn't even want a pool, and here he was, Captain Speed, ripping through the flooded streets like Don Johnson in that boat on *Miami Vice*.

But I thought I felt the vibration intensify.

"Do we have to keep going this fast, Don?" I yelled over the wind and rattling boat.

Don looked back behind us, which naturally made me do the same. All I could see were the angry waves and middle fingers of the several small groups of people wading westward as they had to deal with our considerable wake.

"I may be out of line here, Brenda, but I don't fancy being shot. It makes it a whole lot harder to rescue Ashley," he shouted against the wind when he turned back forward.

"Don, I don't see anyone behind us," I said, holding on to the aluminum frame to steady myself. "Bruno took us all over this stupid city, and there's no way that they could know where we are. Plus, we have a hell of a head start on them. It will take them time to fix their boat."

"Yeah, but their boat is an interceptor," Bruno shouted over the rattling.

"They'll make up the time. They have two outboards on that thing," Don said, his smile morphing into a frown.

"An' don' forget, they know where you goin'," Bruno added.

Now there was something neither Don nor I had considered. It was shockingly apparent we hadn't even taken that into account; we just stared at each other for a full minute.

"We should have shot up their boat or engines," Don said to me.

"Or both," I replied.

"Now what?" he asked.

I shook my head. I was fresh out of ideas. Fatigue was setting in and now this worry.

"We keep going. What else *can* we do? Ashley needs us, and look, there will be lots of people there, even cops or maybe you're army dudes," I said to Don. "We can expose the impostors and get them jailed."

"For Christ's sake, Brenda, don't you know they're National Guardsmen?" Don said, a wry smile crossing his lips.

Suddenly, I felt a bit better. A sense of humor instead of criticism and angst. Maybe we could fix us. It was a flash thought, but a good one.

Don turned to look over behind us again, and Bruno shifted his weight. I started to say, "Don, I think that—"

But Bruno moved much faster than I would have ever imagined. Obviously, he had been playing the unfit victim because he wasn't nearly as out of shape as he came off.

He hit Don across the back of his head. Fortunately, Don was moving at the time, but it was still enough to stun him, and Bruno managed to dig into Don's pocket and extract that stupid gun before I could even reach over and try to do something.

Don fell sideways, his head hitting the top of the boat's side, which stunned him even more. I could hear him groan.

He was out for the count.

Bruno caught me in mid-swing, and when that gun barrel swung to point directly at my face, I froze, staring at the biggest damn hole I'd seen anywhere. It was like looking down the barrel of a battleship's gun.

"Oh, we gonna have some fun now," Bruno said, reaching over to the throttle.

He never got a hold of it, though. Just as his fist got near the throttle lever, our lives were upturned again.

We hit something, and at nearly 25 mph, we hit hard.

70

When we struck, the momentum acting on my body from Don's warp speed cruise twisted me around. I was torn loose from the console and catapulted forward, toward the casting deck of the boat and over the bow rail.

I landed not in but *on* the water and must have skipped, tumbling end over end until I finally hit the asphalt of the street, just a foot or two beneath the surface.

Leaving skin and cotton thread at each of my landing sites, I finally tumbled to a stop, facedown in the water. Mind in pure panic mode, I struggled to my knees and then feet, looking back at the boat.

I didn't remember much about the flight I took, but I do remember that the engine raced, then quit.

Go figure, in a flooded city, Don would find the only dry spot in town.

I limped back to the boat. Don, being nearly unconscious, made out the best of us. He had been thrown to the bow and was staring to wake up. His muscles were relaxed when we hit, so he escaped the injuries that Bruno and I had sustained.

Plus, he was still in the fucking boat.

I looked down to inspect myself. My knees were scraped, and I was bleeding from my left knee. My palms were scraped, and my head hurt. Other than being soaking wet and standing in filthy water, I seemed to be mostly okay.

Don was oblivious and starting to sit up but was reaching for something in the bottom of the boat before I got there.

Bruno, on the other hand, was thrown into what was left of the plastic windscreen and console radios. John's prized, shattered fish-finder was bent forward, and it had blood on it. I think it broke Bruno's nose because he was bleeding from it, and it looked bent to the side.

How's that for killing two birds with one stone?

Bruno was dazed and not moving. Then I remembered he had the gun, and despite the pain, I leapt into the boat to look for it. On my way in, I accidentally kicked Don in the leg.

That brought him around. "Why'd you do that?"

"Sorry, Don, but Bruno hit you and grabbed that gun. He was going to shoot me until we hit something underneath the water."

I couldn't find the damn gun! "Don, help me here! We need to get that gun before he wakes up!"

Don was still shaken, and he shook his head. "It's not here," he said.

"Wait." And I turned my attention from the floor of the boat to him.

He had scrambled to the bow of the boat and opened a locker. Reaching inside, he picked up a coil of extra dock line.

Still obviously groggy, he never the less held up the coil of rope. "Tie him up with this until we know for sure what happened to that other gun."

Why hadn't I thought of that?

I struggled to pull both of Bruno's arms behind his back. It wasn't going to work because he was lying on his back, and there was just no way I had enough strength to turn him over. The whole operation was made more difficult because he was lying in the bottom of the boat on the side of the steering console where there wasn't much room. In fact, his body was wedged tightly in between the side of the boat and the console. I had to drag him forward just to get enough room to move his massive arms and shoulders, and the tugs nearly threw my back out.

Once I got his arms where I needed them, I tied Bruno's wrists together as tightly as I could. Frankly, I didn't care if I cut off the circulation to his hands; those hands did evil things. The world would be a safer place without them.

Don moved back to the helm and pulled the throttle to neutral. I noticed that the boat didn't rock when he moved.

"Don, are we aground?"

He looked around blinking with what I guessed was pain. "Yeah, I think so. Help me push us out to deeper water."

"Let's get this tub of lard in the bow first," I said.

We struggled to move Bruno, who was starting to stir.

Then we both got out into the water, and while I didn't like the fact that my scraped-up knees were in contact with this filth, our task had to be done.

As we shoved the boat, it scraped horribly over the road, but we finally moved it out to the middle of the street where it could float.

I was worried that some of those people we angered as we were flying by them and spraying them with our wake would catch up to us. "We should go," I said.

"What happened exactly?" Don asked.

As I got back in the boat and helped him in, I recounted everything that had happened after Bruno knocked him unconscious. "Thank God we must have gotten the boat off course and hit shallow water. I'm living on bonus time now," I added.

He nodded, unimpressed, I guess, or just totally out of it because of the punishment his head had taken. I chalked it up to Don being dazed.

"What did we hit?" he asked.

I looked around and found that I could see some roadway striping under the water which wasn't very deep. It was in the middle of the intersection we happened to be crossing.

"Just shallow water here, I guess."

Don glanced over the console instruments. "That's bad," he said when he saw the fish-finder. "We needed that to see how deep the water is."

"Yeah, well, it got shot up when those assholes Katsarus hired to kill you were firing at us. But what do you care? This is John's boat."

"So what you were trying to tell me was true?"

"Don't you remember? John and his buddies tried to kill us."

He snorted. "*That's* going to make for an awkward block party next year," he said.

I smiled for maybe a second but quickly frowned.

"Are you all right, Don?"

"Yeah, well enough, I guess. Let's crank this up and get to the Superdome as quick as possible," he said groggily.

But before he turned the key, I thought I heard something echo among the buildings. "Wait! Did you hear that?" I asked.

We paused, and the distinct sound of a high-powered boat filled the air, and it was close.

71

Bruno was now starting to stir. I didn't know which prospect was more frightening, him awake and trying to get free or that boat motor getting louder.

I glanced back in the direction in which we had come. There wasn't anything visible yet, but the sound was definitely getting louder and quickly.

"What the…?"

Don and I both glanced down at Bruno in the bow. He'd just awakened and realized he was tied up. I was thinking we should have tied him to the bow rail, just to keep him in check. His arms were big and so were his fists, and they could still do a lot of damage despite being tied together.

"What are we going to do? If that's the hitmen coming…"

My voice trailed off, and even Bruno quit his whining. "Go *up the bayou*," he yelled at Don. "The water will be deeper there because the land sinks toward the Pontchartrain!"

"He means go *north*, Don," I yelled.

Don turned the key. Nothing. My heart nearly leapt out of my chest. Meanwhile, Don was mumbling something about not seeing any swamp.

I glanced over at the houses lining both sides of the street. There weren't many places to hide. Just a block or two in the direction we had been traveling, there seemed to be a wide-open area and railroad signals traversed the width of the space. At least I assumed it was tracks. I couldn't tell because of the flood.

The wide-open space provided no place to hide.

"Don, let's go. Hurry please," I yelled.

"Which way?"

Bruno sighed. "I tol' ya, up the bayou!"

"North," I yelled.

"I will if I can get this damned motor started," Don shot back, clearly feeling the urgency.

On the forth try, the motor sputtered to life with a large cloud of blue smoke. Clearly, it had seen better days.

Don threw it in gear, and we limped forward. But Don spun the wheel to avoid the high spot in the road. Even so, I could hear and feel the bottom of the boat scrape over the ground despite the more pronounced vibration.

The motor was screaming, yet we were barely traveling faster than a person could trot. We'd done some more damage, and for the first time, I realized that we may end up walking to the Superdome, which would take even more time.

"We're not going to make it to a hiding place before that boat gets here," I warned Don.

"What do you want me to do, Brenda? I got the throttle opened up as far as it will go!"

I glanced over to Bruno, who was alternately angry at being tied up and fearful about meeting those hitmen.

"Any ideas, Commodore?" I asked.

"Jus' get us around the next corner. If they travelin' fast, they won't be looking down the cross streets, I hope."

"I hope too," I said, looking back at Don. He nodded and looked back.

If only we had the gun Don had taken from John. It might not be worth much against professionals, but at least we wouldn't be easy targets. I started to look around the boat again but realized that if the grounding sent me into the water, it probably sent the gun Bruno was holding as well and was lost until the floodwaters drained.

So I looked back behind us.

I couldn't see anything yet, and it was hard to hear the other boat over the shriek of our own outboard. So I couldn't judge where the other boat was or how fast it might be gaining on us.

"Maybe it's on a parallel street," I said.

"Yeah, maybe that's why we can't see it behind us," Don agreed.

"I don' think so," Bruno said. "If it's on the street to our south, that's Claude Avenue, and it ain't flooded, remember?"

"That doesn't make me feel any better," I snapped.

But as I turned to criticize Bruno, I saw the next street. "There! Don, turn right past that blue house," I commanded.

When we came to the intersection, Don dutifully spun the wheel and the boat lazily limped around the corner.

"This thing is steering like a supertanker," Don said.

We made it around the corner, and I scanned the area for a place to hide. I was thinking a driveway or something, but as I turned around to ask what Don was thinking, the engine quit.

The silence was shocking. The only noise in the whole world was the other outboard, and it sounded like it was nearly on top of us.

I moved forward, right up to Bruno, and yelled, "Move!"

The shock on his face was total. He scooted over, and I jumped off the bow, landing in thigh-deep water.

At least Bruno was correct about the depth getting greater.

I grabbed a bow-rail support and pulled the boat toward the curb. Even still, I wasn't moving fast enough to get out of site. The boat that had been behind us was nearly at the same intersection now, and I could hear the water being pushed aside from its wake.

"Get down," Don yelled, and he ducked behind the outboard. Bruno rolled off the casting deck and lay in the bottom of the boat.

I kept pulling.

Just then, a boat flew past the intersection, and it was the same color and looked like the same type as the one the hitmen arrived in.

But it didn't stop. It kept speeding away, the sound of its twin outboards fading with every second.

I started breathing again, but I had to wonder: was John still alive?

"I can't believe they got the boat running so fast," Don said, looking accusingly at Bruno who had just popped his head above the railing.

"They must be well prepared," Bruno said.

And that was going to be a problem.

72

We bobbed around in the water so much that it was starting to make me sick. I looked over at Don sitting beside me on the bench behind the center console. He was frowning and playing with the throttle to find just the right node point of least vibration. It wasn't working.

It hadn't been long since Don had managed to start the outboard, but it was definitely on life support.

"I don't think we're going to get very far," he said finally.

Not the best news I heard today.

"Question is, what can we do about it?" I asked.

"Well, first thing is if we have to ditch the boat, we should get back to shallower water," Don offered.

"How will that help?" I asked. "That's how we got in this mess to begin with, and besides, we have no way to know how shallow the water is with that fish-finder, depth-sounder thing shot to hell."

"Yeah, but I'd rather walk than swim, especially if we have to carry our bags."

Don had a good point. I glanced at our baggage and wondered how we were going to carry them the distance to the Superdome being racked by fatigue and hunger.

"How far are we from the Superdome?" I asked Bruno.

He looked up, sneering, and shrugged. "Three, maybe four miles," he said.

"That's a two-hour walk," Don said.

"More if we have to wade, carry this stuff, and rest," I corrected.

"Wade?"

Don's facial expression held the fear of a small child facing a trip to a dark basement.

"Go south, Don. Go south," I replied.

At the next street, he turned south and slowed down. But the vibration got even worse, so he bumped up the throttle again. "Hang on," he said. "I have no way of knowing when we're going to hit, but we will."

I sat with my arms braced against the console, ready for the impact that was sure to come. At least we weren't going nearly as fast as last time we grounded out.

"So we *are* ditching the boat?" I asked.

"No, not yet at least. I think we should pass a wrench," Bruno suggested.

"Can we fix it? What do you know about outboard motors?"

"I ain't no *Couyon*, yeah. I know somethin', *beb*," Bruno said.

My hatred for him must have shown in my expression, but little did I care. "I'm *not* untying you, Bruno. You've proven you can't be trusted."

He looked away and just shrugged.

Two blocks to the south, the vibration got a little worse. Don sped up, then slowed down, but nothing could fix the problem. Finally, Bruno sat up and got Don's attention.

"Kill the motor. I'm gonna get down the boat and take a look."

Don looked at me, bewildered. "What's he going to do to the boat?"

"Get down means get out," I said. I turned to Bruno. "We're not untying you."

Don put the boat in neutral and stopped the engine. As we drifted to a bobbing stop, Bruno scooted over and laboriously swung his massive legs over the side. He looked down, then hopped out, splashing down in thigh-high water. The boat bobbed violently such that Don stood up and grabbed hold of the rail around the console.

With his hands tied, Bruno moved around to the back of the boat. "Raise the motor," he told Don.

"How?"

"The trim button on the throttle, eh?"

I rolled my eyes. "Don, you're going to take advice from this guy who tried to kill me?"

"*Beb*, this is the only way pass a wrench for the boat," Bruno replied.

When the motor was raised, Don and I peered cautiously over the back end of the boat. Don was hanging on for dear life because the back end of the boat sunk lower in the water with the weight of both of us in the rear.

But the prop was out of the water, and it was badly mangled. The blades were twisted, and some of them had large chunks missing. All of them were bent unevenly.

"Y'all got a spare prop?" Bruno asked.

Don looked at me. It was a signal to look around. Seeing as I wasn't doing anything at the moment other than keeping a wary eye on a potential killer that had almost taken out Don and not fearing the water like my husband, I moved about the boat, searching in the various seat lockers.

But I came up empty.

"Nope," is all I said after my search when I rejoined my husband at the rear of the boat.

Don had been standing up and holding tightly to the nearby console.

But when I looked back at Bruno, I noticed he was moving his arms back and forth near the prop. He looked up at me and said, "Give me a few more seconds. I'm trying to get them bent back better so we don't shimmy so much."

So we waited while Bruno fiddled. When he finished, it took us another five minutes to get the big man back in the boat. I don't know why, but I just couldn't leave him there in the water, tied up.

After a minute of trying to catch our breath, Don put the key in the ignition and fired up the outboard again. Even before he put it in gear, it was shaking the boat.

"Yeah, that worked well," I said, angry that we wasted all this time trying to fix something that couldn't be fixed.

"It means that the prop *shaft* is bent," Bruno said. "We not even in gear yet, so it ain't the prop."

"Swell," I said. "How much longer is it going to last?"

"I ain't God, *Podna*. Ha!"

73

Zanetti swore again as he scraped his trigger finger knuckle on the cheap plastic.

He had disassembled the kill switch and spliced the wires together to bypass it. It was slow, painful work, and he was in a hurry. Not to mention that VT was seething.

Finally, he thought he had completed the work. He got up and moved past VT to hook up the battery again.

He shook his head at the battery wires. Those idiots thought that disconnecting the battery would be devastating, but their real genius was taking the kill-switch wire that connected to the helmsman. That had caused the delay more than anything.

"We're lucky they didn't do something to the engines," he said out loud.

"I'm going to kill that Cajun son of a bitch slowly," Katsarus growled.

"What makes you think we're going to give you a gun, Katsarus?" Zanetti asked.

"I don't care what it costs, I'll pay you for the hit, but I want the pleasure of ending his life as painfully as I can," Katsarus growled back toward him.

VT glanced at Zanetti and right away. He knew exactly what his boss was thinking. If Katsarus did the actual killing, any evidence would point to *him*. That was the best win-win situation that Zanetti had run across in this entire trip.

VT nodded and reached down to one of the supply cases that contained extra handguns. He took out a Kimber 1911 model that had been customized for accuracy. Standing up, he hit the eject button on the grip and caught the magazine, then proceeded to empty the bullets, except for one. Then he placed the magazine back in the gun, pocketed the bullets, and handed the gun to Katsarus.

"Why only one bullet? There are three of them," Katsarus asked.

"Because Katsarus, we don't trust you. You have to prove yourself to us."

Katsarus grasped the gun and made sure the safety was on, then placed it in his waistband. "Oh, I will, I will," he said.

Finally, Zanetti had the connection made at the battery and threw a leg over the saddle-type seat. He put the keys in and fired up both motors.

It was one of the best noises he had ever heard, outside of a suppressed HK 9 mm.

VT frowned and sat down awkwardly on one of the saddle seats behind him, and Katsarus stayed in the bow.

"Well, Johnny, you may just get your wish sooner than you think," Zanetti yelled over the noise of the twin outboards.

74

After just two minutes, the boat was shaking so badly that Don brought the throttle to idle.

"We can't go on like this. It will rattle something loose. We're walking in this…filth," he said, looking at the water that was getting very dark now as the sun was setting.

"What other options do we have, Don?" I asked, irritated. I shook my head at his ignorance. It was either continue until something did shake loose or wade to dry land, which, at this point, was a long two blocks away.

He just sat there and fumed.

"Don, we're sitting ducks here. I think this is the road that leads back to the street in back of the assisted-living center. If that wasn't Katsarus and his partners in the boat that went by, they'll probably come right through here. Let's just keep going until the motor gives up," I said, annoyed, exasperated, and a little frightened.

Don slammed the throttle full forward, and we all grabbed for something to hang on to. The boat lurched forward, and despite Bruno's weight in the bow, the nose rose high in the air and the prop hit the ground again.

"Don!"

The throttle came back and the boat settled on a more even keel, but my fillings were about shaken loose. Everything was rattling and making noise. Bruno just shook his head.

"Hell of a way to treat a decent boat," he growled.

"Talk to our complaint department," Don retorted.

The violence of the shaking was having an adverse effect on my bladder. "We're going to need to stop soon," I said.

"What for? You just told me to get the hell out of Dodge," Don said, annoyed.

"I need to use the ladies' room."

"Oh, for the love of God! You have got to have the smallest bladder in the world!"

"Walgreens comin' up on the right, just about two blocks away," Bruno said, and for the first time, I was glad he had spoken up.

"That's crazy," Don said. "Look at these shadows. You'll need a flashlight and you never know what to expect in the dark," he warned.

"Well, Don, it's off the path that I'd expect Katsarus and company to use, and I need to go. I can't help it."

Don shook his head again, slowly. "The delay will give them time to catch up. It's a bad idea."

"Then where do you want me to pee?"

"Shit. Just shit!"

Bruno sat up. "Look, I know y'all don' trust me, but we might find somethin' we can use to bend the blades back a little more. We was sort o' all right until we hit bottom again."

I looked at Don with a raised eyebrow. Bruno made sense, but I was wary.

"Don, please."

He looked back to see if any boat was following us, and I immediately turned to Bruno, just in case. The large man did nothing but just sit there, staring at me and holding his tied hands out as if to say, "What do you think I can do like this, *beb*?"

Finally, Don looked back, stood up, and scanned the route forward. He squinted, shook his head, and rolled his eyes.

"The darkness coming on might provide enough cover, but I don't like not knowing where they are," he said.

"Then let's get going," I urged him. My bladder was getting insistent.

Don put the throttle down a little more, then backed off when the boat shook more violently than it had been.

The problem, whatever it was, was getting worse. We were going to lose the boat soon, and I took my mind off my steadily more urgent biological need by sorting our bags into only the necessary items we would need to carry with us.

Soon, the boat was scraping the bottom intermittently, and Don had the good sense to trim up the motor as far as he could without getting the prop out of the water.

We were shooting up a rooster tail, though, and I worried that the water we were flinging into the air might make us more noticeable to any boat that just happened to be passing by the intersection we just left behind.

"Hold on to your pee," Don said. "We'll be beaching the boat soon, and I got to find a place to stash it out of sight while you take care of things."

I nearly smiled. That would require him to get out into the darkening water and move the boat around.

Not damned likely.

75

THE BOAT MADE it all the way to the corner of the Walgreens's property. I can't say what shape the gel coat on the bottom was in, but we managed to pull up fairly close to the northeast corner of the parking lot.

I rummaged through the lockers and couldn't find what I was looking for, but I found it in, of all things, one of John's toolboxes.

Holding the flashlight like a trophy, I tested it and was satisfied that it would do for the mission I had planned for it.

Don shook his head.

Because my need had been urgent since the accident, I hopped out before Don and started sprinting through the parking lot toward the building. Of course, Don took exception to that, which, when I think of it, is a good thing.

"Brenda! You don't know what or who is in there! Will you at least wait for me?"

I appreciated his concern, but I couldn't wait. In fact, I didn't even take the time to turn around and tell him; the need was so urgent.

I guess this is what happens to you after forty years.

As I approached the building, I could tell it had been ransacked thoroughly. It was impossible to tell whether it happened before or after the storm. The windows, large plate glass affairs, were all smashed, and shards clung to the aluminum framing, just jagged and sharp enough to really do some damage to careless flesh.

I doubted it ever flooded here, but the parking lot was filthy—mud and sand all over the place and not a single car in the lot. Some of the light posts that dotted the parking lot were bent or leaning to the southwest.

Slowing as I approached the smashed doorway of the store, I listened as best I could.

Nothing.

Taking the flashlight and turning it on, but holding it more like a club, I walked inside. Behind me, Don was yelling my name, but I really couldn't wait.

Once inside, I was immediately hit with a foul smell, something worse than I anything else I had smelled in my life. Clearly, loss of power to the freezers was allowing their contents to spoil. It was simply awful, but I needed to find the bathrooms.

They were usually in the back of the store or close to one of the corners of the back wall. I played the flashlight on the floor and the walls, looking for the bathrooms and anything that could hurt me.

Or anyone.

I got the jitters. I admit it, it was spooky in there.

The air was abnormally still and silent. Not even a dripping faucet or pipe. The shelves were nearly empty, save for a few wrappers and small miscellaneous items. But the sounds were weird and very creepy. It was as if I had gone deaf, but I knew that wasn't true because Don was still shouting my name from somewhere outside.

For an instant, I wondered if he needed my help. Had Bruno somehow gotten loose and was threatening Don?

No, that couldn't be it; I had made sure he was tied up securely, and besides, Don didn't sound all that excited. That would have been my first clue.

Finally, I saw a sign in front of a dark little hallway just past the pharmacy counter, and I made a beeline for the bathroom.

Want to know why women have strong legs? We don't trust the butt gaskets sometimes provided in each stall, and we've learned to hover of the toilet. Without adequate lighting to examine the public throne, there was no way any part of my body was going to touch the seat.

About midway thought relieving myself, I noticed two problematic things. The first was that there was no toilet paper to dab myself dry, and the second was Don had started yelling about an octave above his normal angry missives toward me.

But there was no way I was going to be able to stop.

Just as I was finishing, I heard something that nearly drained my head of blood. I heard the outboard on John's boat start up.

What the hell! Was Don leaving me? Was he still alive, or had he been assaulted by some street gang bent on stealing the boat?

I put myself back together in record time, grabbed the flashlight like a club again, and ran toward the door, fearing that I was all alone in an unfamiliar neighborhood with not-so-nice neighbors.

With only a flashlight to defend myself.

76

As I neared the front of the store, near the main door, I slowed to a cautious walk.

I knew if I had to use the flashlight to defend myself, it would break and be useless as a weapon and a light. But it would certainly discourage anyone from continuing if it connected with the right body part.

I poked my head out through the door as slowly as I could, ready to run, hit, or duck at the slightest provocation. My heart was pounding again for fear of what I may have to do or, worse, what I may find.

This trip was going to give me a heart attack. I was sure of it.

My worst fear would be the sight of Don lying facedown in the parking lot, hemorrhaging uncontrollably, and dying. What would I tell Ashley?

I closed my eyes tightly, just for a second, and said a quick prayer. 'Please, God, I've already lost my surrogate mother today, not my husband *too*!'

When I opened them, my prayers were answered. There was Don, pacing back and forth and, from the looks of it and his body language, swearing up a storm.

What I *didn't* see was John's boat, or Bruno for that matter.

I hurried out of the store and, through the parking lot, over to Don on the sidewalk.

"What happened?"

Don never stopped pacing. "Tub of lard waited until I got halfway up the parking lot, chasing you because you wouldn't wait for me, then he started the boat and sailed into the sunset. That's what happened!"

"Bruno took the boat?"

Still pacing, Don waited half a beat before answering. "No, he took the fucking bus. Do you *see* the boat around here anywhere, Brenda?"

Okay, he was really upset. But at some point, I had to stop making excuses for him. "Do you have to be so sarcastic, Don? You don't see me blaming you for leaving the keys in the ignition, do you? I know we're both at our limits. We're tired, hungry, thirsty, and worried. Plus, if that weren't enough, John and his friends are trying to kill us. So if it's all right with you, I'd like to call a truce because, for Christ's sake, Don, we have to rely on each other now more than ever!"

He waited a few seconds, then nodded, still trying to walk off the anger he was feeling. But at least he was engaged now.

"How did he get loose?" I wondered out loud more than asked.

"How the hell should I know?" Don exploded. "He probably cut the ropes if not through, enough while he was fiddling around with the damn prop. Well, I hope it breaks on him," he yelled in the direction Bruno had taken the boat.

"All our bags and supplies were in that boat," I said aloud before I could think. I hadn't meant to blame Don, but sure enough, that's how he took it.

"Do you think I *planned* this, Brenda? Do you think I purposely left the keys in the ignition and walked away because I had hoped he was going to take the boat and leave us the fuck here *stranded*? Do ya think I don't know about the fucking bags we just lost? Ya think I did that on purpose?"

I took a deep breath. "No, Don, I don't. But you have to stop accusing me of thinking the worst about you. I don't, you know. I think the way you handled the whole situation back there at the center, well, that impressed the hell out of me. Really."

He nodded again, head down mostly, and began to pace once more. "I brought that asshole on the boat, didn't I? It *is* my fault. It's always my fault."

Oh, I really didn't want to see Don break down here, not with Ashley to find and killers to escape.

"Don, I need you now. I need the Don that got behind the wheel and rammed a car through locked doors because I was melting down. I need Don the problem solver." And I lowered my voice, reached out, and grabbed his arm as he paced by. "Please?"

He paused, looked around, then nodded as he looked down again. "Okay, then since we have to walk now, I figure it will take us maybe an hour or two. Let's see if we can find something to use in the store."

I shook my head. "I was in there already, remember? It's been picked clean by a mob. I don't think there is *anything* we can use."

"There may be scissors or a break-room knife or some other silly shit we can use. You never know. And mob rule is not logical. You'd be surprised what they can miss."

I nodded. "Okay, I'm in."

We walked back to the store, and the smell affected him too. He reached for my flashlight, and I gave it to him. He swung it around.

That's when I saw the bodies and gasped. Even Don swore.

I'd never smelled rotting flesh before. I never want to again, but I'll never forget that smell.

Don panned the light around, and something grabbed his attention on the long checkout counter.

He moved over to the far cashier's station, just a few feet in from the door.

"I'm pretty sure that the cash is gone, Don," I said, but we could sure use the cash if we found some. It was a long way home, and we needed gas first thing.

If we made it back to the ramp to recover the Jeep, that is, and if we weren't arrested and prosecuted for impersonating first responders. And dumping Billy Bob.

"Brenda, I think I found something more valuable than cash," I heard Don say. He flashed the light my way, on the floor, and I used it to move over to him without stumbling on two bodies.

I gasped as one of them was a girl, about the same age as Ashley. I gasped because she was Caucasian, and for a frightening instant, Don thrust something at me, and I put out my hand by instinct. What he gave me was a cell phone.

"I think it's hers. Can you identify it?" he asked.

"What?" I looked down at the phone, and slowly, it dawned on me. The case was undeniable.

It was Ashley's.

"How…? Why would it be here?"

Don shrugged. "They must have stopped here too. She left it as a breadcrumb. Just like the note."

"What if somebody took if off her? What if…"

"I'm not going to allow myself to think like that, Brenda. She's your daughter, and she has that small bladder trait of yours. I'm guessing she persuaded whoever she was with to stop here so she could do the same thing you did."

He was right. I couldn't afford to give up because I believed she had been killed and robbed. I needed a goal. The Superdome. That was my goal.

"All right. You're right. We need to go before it gets too dark. Let's just get out of here, Don. It's just a few miles. What do we really need from here? Let's just get there, okay?"

"Yeah, okay," he said.

I turned and waited for him to come up beside me. When he did, we started moving toward the door. As we made our way toward the exit, I put Ashley's Razer phone in my pocket.

We were almost to the door when the interior of the store exploded in a hail of bullets.

77

I froze.

Don basically had to trip me to get me to duck. I ended up on the floor, and he ended up on top of me, covering me.

As bullets riddled everything in my universe, I turned my head to the side, and I was suddenly staring straight into the non-blinking, non-seeing eyes of some dead guy, who had a bullet hole smack dab in the middle of his forehead. I quickly looked away.

But away meant down the length of his torso. As my gaze reached his hands, I got a surprise. When I saw the handgun he had been grasping as he died, I flinched but, just as quickly, realized it was a blessing.

Don was shielding his face from the bits of suspended ceiling that were raining down on us from the hailstorm of bullet hits. It sounded like automatic weapons firing—machine guns—which I thought were illegal.

So the fact our assailant had them was frightening. It said a lot about their intentions.

I tapped Don several times. Four to be exact. Each time, I had to tap him repeatedly, harder and harder. Apparently, he was too busy ducking and covering until I yelled.

"Don! He's got a gun!"

Don looked down at me in fear. I guess he thought someone had broken in to the store and was approaching us from behind, but when he was where I was nodding my head, he looked and saw the gun.

Don shifted and reached over. The fact he could even touch that guy, who happened to be filthy with flies and dirty clothing, nearly made me lose what little was still in my stomach. But he was successful in grabbing the gun, and that's all that counted, I guess.

The shooting now wasn't in a steady stream of bullets; rather, it was made up of staccato bursts with brief moments of silence until another gun from another direction started in.

As Don was trying to figure out how to check the gun, I glanced around again. It seemed like nearly everyone who was lying dead on the floor had some sort of firearm. In fact, the whole store was beginning to look like a bad day at the O.K. Corral.

Given our situation, I was hoping that our luck would be different, but with Don not really knowing what the hell he was doing around guns, I began to realize the irony in our plight; we escaped the professional hitmen only to be killed by…what? A street gang? A mob of looters?

What?

When the shooting stopped for a few prolonged seconds, Don grabbed me and slid me bodily behind a shelf unit and him.

"What are you do—"

"Shh!"

Surprised by the unexpected use of authority, I shut up. When I did, I heard the running footsteps that sounded like they were coming from the front parking lot.

"Stay behind me," Don said.

I wasn't about to let him fight this alone. We had no idea how many people we were facing. Hell, it could even be Katsarus and his partners. So I looked around and grabbed two guns off the nearest bodies. There was only one more body that had a gun and one more that didn't.

That was the young woman.

I showed them to Don and he whispered, "You may have to hand them to me, keep low and behind me!"

Then I heard it. The distinctive slowing of what I thought was a single pair of footsteps and crunch of glass from the front doors. Whoever it was, was nearly inside the store!

Don waited. And waited.

The footsteps were getting closer.

Finally, when I could almost hear the other person breathing, Don jumped out.

The gunshot was so loud that I couldn't hear for a long time after. Everything happened in slow motion.

Don stood, gun still extended and aimed at our unknown assailant, and he looked back at me. Don had the weirdest look on his face.

"I got 'em! I got the motherfucker!"

I stood up and went to his side. Before me was a young African American, bleeding out on the floor from a wound in his chest.

"Holy shit, you got 'em," I repeated.

"Yeah, I got 'em!"

Then Don looked around. I stayed quiet because I thought he had heard something. But soon, he relaxed.

"I think we're the only people alive in this place," he said.

"You got him! How did you do that?"

Don looked back down at the newly deceased male. "Adrenaline, I guess. Luck maybe. But I did it!"

"Well, I can hardly hear you, but good shootin', Tex! Now we better get outta Dodge before they show up with reinforcements."

"Yeah, I just want to grab his gun. We better get out of here."

Just as we picked up the guns and were headed out the door, I heard it, and considering my hearing after the gunfight, it had to be loud.

"To the people in the store, we know you in there 'cause my homey didn't come out. If you come out now, we kill ya quick. If you make us come in again, we kill you *real* slow!"

78

Shaking, I turned to face Don.

"What the hell do they want with *us*? We haven't done anything to anybody. You think that's John's guys?"

He shrugged, then shook his head. "If it were John, that's who we would be hearing from. Maybe a case of mistaken identity?"

"Does it matter?" I asked, thinking that we were targets anyway.

"What do we do?" Don asked.

"I was hoping you had some ideas."

"We need to find out how many of them we're facing. This gun looks like it can take out a whole army," he said, placing the sling of the black rifle around his shoulder and neck. He let it hang down his front, and despite the darkness, I could clearly read Military Armament Corporation on the side of the boxlike main part of the gun.

Don bent down and searched the body of the person he had just shot and pulled two long boxlike structures from the kid's belt. I recognized them as ammunition magazines, and he stuffed them into his own belt before grabbing my arm and pulling me toward the back of the store.

"This still doesn't make any sense. Maybe we should shout out to them and find out why they want to kill us," I suggested.

"Yeah, you go ahead and give them all the time they need to set up and storm us. I'm going to take a look out back."

So much for diplomacy.

He started out for the back of the store. I followed him to the back wall, where he searched momentarily for the back exit. We found a hallway leading away from the main store itself, and inside the short hall on both the right and left walls were two archways, one with a large steel door.

The archway with the door lead to a machinery room, with pumps and the circuit panel and what I guessed were some kind of water tanks, and we could see all this through the small rectangular glass window in each of the doors.

On the other side of the hallway was a large open area that seemed to serve as the employee break room; it contained tables, chairs, and a counter with coffee machine, a microwave, and sink, along with a refrigerator. Beyond that was some sort of metallic ladder that rose to the two-story-high ceiling.

Don and I looked at it for a second. Then Don got an idea.

"That ladder probably leads to the roof. That might be not only a good hiding place but also a great vantage point for scoping out the opposition."

"Going outside? That's a *good* idea?" I asked.

"If we stay low," he said, as if it should be obvious to me.

"I'd rather just get out of here before we're trapped like rats," I added. The thought sent chills down my spine.

Don must have agreed because he shrugged and stepped back out into the hallway with me.

At the end of the hall was the back wall of the building. The hallway ended at a steel door with a frosted glass window that was fairly small in size, and you could see the chicken wire embedded in the frosted glass.

A dim light shone through the small window; it was still light outside, but getting darker.

Thing was, what light there was showed shadows moving on the other side of the door. When two silhouettes paused just on the other side of the window and the doorknob started jiggling, Don and I knew we were a mere inches away from death.

We both had the same idea at the same time and leapt in unison into the break room. The room had no windows, and since the power was out, we spent some time dodging tables and chairs that were moved or shoved every which way. Some of the chairs were lying backward on the tile flooring, and I had to hop over a few of them just to keep up with Don.

We arrived at the ladder just in time. Behind me, in the hallway, I could hear the door squeak open.

I froze, but I could hear Don softly climbing the ladder, the machine gun dangling from the strap around his neck.

It didn't take much convincing at all to get me climbing. I left the guns I had been carrying on the floor, quietly, because I couldn't climb with them.

It was a surprisingly long way up. Around the top portion of the ladder, a round sort of cage was welded to the ladder; I surmised it was to protect the climber from falling. All it did was prevent me from climbing up the other side of the latter to the same height as Don.

Instead, I was trapped below him, exposed to the view of anyone who ventured inside the room, or hallway for that matter, while Don felt around for the latch of the trap door to the roof.

The back door opened, and it was a great deal lighter in the room. When I looked back, the whole hallway was bathed in it, which meant whoever was coming in was silhouetted and at a bit of a cover disadvantage. It didn't make me feel any more secure, though.

The door hit the wall and as I watched, cringing against the ladder, two young men quietly moved cautiously past the break room. Clearly, they were intent on searching the main store because, I guessed, that's where they thought we were.

They moved right past us, exposed as we were.

"Hurry," I hissed up at Don.

Finally, Don must have found the latch because he started moving up the ladder and the trap door started opening, held in one hand by Don, as he desperately grasped the ladder with the other hand with each rung.

After two of the most intense minutes of my life outside of childbirth, we scrambled out on the roof.

Outside, the sunset over the roof stung, and I squinted. Don carefully pushed me aside, and he quietly closed the trap door, swinging it shut.

We'd made it!

But the pain, fatigue, and fear started working against me, and I got dizzy. Even Don was starting to reach out in case I fell, but before that happened, our tormentor keyed the mic on his bullhorn again.

"You have to the count of three!"

79

Ducking down, Don guided me to sit on a vent while my head spun.

He looked at me and mouthed something. I shrugged and shook my head, which was not a brilliant idea.

I pointed to my ear.

He bent down and put his lips right up against my other ear. "Stay here. I'm going to have a look around."

I nodded, but again, not the best idea to move my head quickly in any direction. Dizzy, nauseous, any movement sent me dry heaving, and I gripped the edge of the vent hard enough to dent it. Closing my eyes wasn't an option either because it only got worse without proof the world was standing still.

Then suddenly, I was alone. Don wasn't next to me anymore, and I had to refocus on what he had said.

He was going to have a look around.

What? Don?

It wasn't in his nature. Who the hell was this person I was consorting with? He certainly wasn't my husband who whined and complained about his bosses and how unfair life was to him.

Despite my nausea, I twisted around slowly and found Don doing a belly crawl toward the edge of the roof at the front of the store, the gun riding on his back.

As I watched and recovered, Don peered over the edge at all four sides of the roof. By the time he made his way back to me, somewhat in the middle but near the back of the store, I felt well enough to stand, but Don pushed me back down as I started to rise.

"You want that guy to see you and shoot?"

I looked in the direction Don was nodding his head. It was the front of the store, where the bullhorn announcements were coming from.

"Only one guy?" I asked.

Don looked that way, then turned to me and nodded. "Yeah. Nobody else. I guess those two in the store are the only ones left."

At least it wasn't John's professional hitmen. Some consolation.

"Then we can just wait up here until they're gone," I reasoned.

"Yeah, about that," Don started, sighing heavily, "that will waste time. I can take care of those two morons quickly, but I need you to do something for me."

"What?"

"Stay here and don't move. I don't care how long it takes. Can you do that for me?"

"I don't know. What if it's an hour?"

"If it's an hour, then you have to promise me that you close the hatch and wait until you can flag down a helicopter and get to the Superdome, okay?"

The nausea came back with a vengeance. I knew what that option meant.

But before I could answer, he moved away, walking tall this time, to the front of the store. To say I was scared was an understatement.

Was he *trying* to get shot?

But before I could ask him, he brought the machine gun up to his shoulder and waited, took a breath, then squeezed off a round.

When Don pumped the air with his left fist, I figured he had hit his target, which was completely amazing to me.

Then it hit me: Don had just *shot* someone. Again. Oh sure, the guy with the bullhorn had been threatening us, but it wasn't like he was holding a gun to our heads just this moment. And he'd shot someone else in the store. He'd ended two lives today. My Don.

He sauntered back to me. "One down, two to go."

"What? Don, you just shot someone. You just ended a life! You...you just *murdered* that guy!"

He knelt down. "Brenda, these people would kill us for our wallets. They are animals. It isn't murder. It's a kill. That's all. Just a kill."

My mouth must have been hanging open. "Don't look so surprised, Brenda. She's my daughter too, and we really fucked up this trip."

Then without waiting for a reply, he moved over to the hatch and slowly opened it.

He mouthed he could hear someone moving around. "I need a distraction," he said lowly and began looking around for something on the roof.

Feeling helpless, I looked around too. When I shifted my weight, I felt Ashley's phone in my back pocket.

"Don," I hissed.

When he looked up at me, I dug the phone out of my pocket. "Use this," I said, handing him the phone.

He looked at me if I was crazy. "It's fried. See the water still behind the display?"

Don turned it over and nodded. A final look at me and I nodded. "What are you going to do?" I asked.

"Just you see."

He opened the hatch and looked down into the abyss. Then Don moved slightly, then again, adjusting his position. He took careful aim and tossed the phone as far as he could into the room. I thought I heard it hit something, and when it did, all hell broke loose.

Gunfire erupted and I heard someone scream. Then it was over, and silence filled the store once more.

As for Don, before I could stop him, he swung the machine gun around his shoulder, threw a leg over the opening, and was gone, leaving me alone on the roof.

80

Who *was* this man?

The Don I knew, even before the layoffs zapped his confidence, would never have gone all Rambo in front of me. But there he was, down in the depths of hell with some very dangerous people, bent on his destruction, kicking butt. I had no idea who this man was anymore. But I was beginning to like it.

Unfortunately, I was also beginning to worry. There was a very real chance that Don would be snuffed out before he could complete his metamorphosis. The thought drove me to action.

But I had no idea just what exactly I could do to help.

What if he got, God forbid, killed? What should I do then? I'd be trapped up here, with no weapons, no way down but past the guys with guns. Unless, of course, I could flag down a helicopter, but that would mean they'd actually have to fly over here, and I hadn't seen one in a while. I just might have to spend the night up on this roof, hoping that the bad guys didn't pop up through the hatch and find me.

I looked around the area. There wasn't much I could use as a weapon. So naturally, my stomach started gurgling again, and for a single, stupid second, I was afraid that the people downstairs would hear me.

How stupid could I get? Stupid and selfish, really.

Don was down there, doing God knows what, and here I was worrying about myself!

There *had* to be something I could do. Maybe a distraction or something? I got up and hunched over and walked to the front edge of the store, carefully peeking over the edge.

The person with the bullhorn was lying in the parking lot, half on dry asphalt, half in the water, and bleeding profusely. I mean there was a *lot* of blood.

Seems that Deadeye Don had nailed him in the head.

The blood pooled on the pavement, but some of it made its way into the water, drifting like an oil slick away from the store.

The thought made me pause. Who would have guessed on our wedding day, me pregnant in front of the Justice of the Peace in DuPage County, that nearly twenty-two years later, the man whose ring I accepted would become a cold, calculating killer?

Well, that's not exactly true; all these killings were in self-defense. They weren't murders.

I closed my eyes tightly to clear the thoughts, then opened them quickly to scan the rest of the parking lot. Nothing moved. There wasn't another soul for as far as I could see.

I cautiously made my way around the building, hoping to find someone on the ground that wasn't hostile toward Don or me and signal them to get help. But there wasn't a soul. Not one person.

Not even a stray dog or cat.

Even the Mississippi River looked lifeless, what I could see of it from here. I waited for five full minutes, staring at the short lengths of it that I could see between the buildings. Nothing moved on the water.

Never had I felt so alone. So absolutely powerless, helpless, and alone.

I glanced at my watch. It seemed about five minutes, but it had been fifteen since Don had gone down into the store. *Fifteen minutes!*

Don was gone for far too long. I just had to find out what the hell was going on down there. I had heard nothing! No shouts, no gunshots, nothing.

Trembling, I made my way over to the hatch. I took a deep breath, let it out, reached down to pull the hatch open, and started down the ladder as quietly as I could.

When I finally reached the main floor, I held my breath and paused. Still holding onto the ladder, I heard nothing. Not a single sound.

But then again, with all the gunplay, my hearing was shot for a while. I began to grin at the unintended pun, but quickly stifled it. Don could be…well, Don could be dead, and here I was, cracking jokes.

The guns I had left were nowhere in sight. Should that concern me?

I started shaking again. It wouldn't stop until I shook my head violently enough for it to hurt.

Finding the strength to move away from the ladder, I made my way slowly into the hallway.

It was dark. I wished I had the flashlight, but frankly I had no idea where I'd put it. Didn't I give it to Don?

Stepping toward the main store area, I realize how stupid this was with my hearing handicap. But Don was out there somewhere. I had to find him.

I *had* to know.

Once in the store area itself, it wasn't much brighter. The damned shelving units were higher than my head, and I couldn't see around them. So I had a relatively narrow viewing range.

But I couldn't miss the bodies.

When I came around to where that poor young woman was, I gulped. I tried not to look, but I couldn't help it.

Immediately, I wished I hadn't.

Her head was literally caved in by the impact of a bullet. I could feel the bile trying to make its way up from my stomach, but I fought it with every ounce of willpower I had.

It wasn't much.

Where the *hell* was Don? Why wasn't he making any noise?

I was about to call out to him when I felt a hand grab me from behind and cover my mouth.

81

For a confused moment, I thought it was Don grabbing me to tell me to be quiet. No such luck.

The person behind me was male, probably young and smelled of sweat and booze. The grip tightened so hard that it hurt and all I could do was make high-pitched humming noises in complete and thorough desperation.

I struggled as hard as I could, given the fatigue, and I thought I did a pretty fair job considering what stress and fear can add to your abilities. But it was nowhere near enough to break free.

Then I felt the cold hardness of metal against my temple and knew instantly that it was the barrel of a gun and a large one at that.

"Yoo-hoo, Mr. Asshole, I got somethin' that belongs to you!"

Whoever it was that was holding me used a sarcastically sing-song voice that, despite the ringing in my ears, I could hear only too well. I was right; it was a young and very strong male holding on to me.

"Come out, come out wherever you are!"

But Don wasn't answering. That meant one of two things: he was waiting for just the right moment or he was injured or dead.

Since we were stumbling around among the bodies and shelves in the store, I was trying to stay positive and think that Don was carefully and silently positioning himself to strike at the proper moment.

"Yo! Asshole! I got your woman! Show yourself!"

He was gradually dragging me to the front of the store where there was more light because of the big broken windows. This was problematic for him because I was fighting him as best I could every inch of the way.

But then we'd be in a more lit-up area of the store and more visible to Don. Hopefully, that was Don's plan, wherever the hell he was!

When the guy holding on to me stumbled over a body, I nearly got away. I was kicking and twisting as hard as I could, and my hands were grabbing his wrists. I tried to dig my nails into the soft skin of his arms, but it wasn't having an effect.

The booze he had consumed, I guessed.

As he sidestepped that body that had given him such grief, I caught a glimpse of the shirt on the form.

My heart stopped. It was Don's shirt!

Emotion is a funny thing. It can be a hindrance or a boost. Now concern turning into grief welled up from somewhere deep down in me, and I felt a surge of renewed energy to put up a worthy fight.

I raised my right leg and kicked at his knee with all the might I had left. It was enough; his leg buckled, and he relaxed his grip on me just enough for me to use gravity to my advantage, and I sank to the floor by Don's head, facedown in the filth.

And I wailed.

82

IN THE BACK of my mind, I was quite aware that I had pissed off my assailant who was now struggling to regain his balance and most likely in severe pain.

I didn't care. Don was dead. Nothing else mattered.

I flashed on Ashley for a moment, but if she were at the Superdome, she'd eventually be all right—most likely if the hitmen would leave her alone. But then again, Ashley would own the house, and that would make her a target.

Perhaps I should have been a little more concerned about my predicament.

In a rare moment of clear thinking, my eyes darted over Don's body. Where was his gun? I could use that against this gangbanger, and while I'm no Annie Oakley, if I went down, I would go down fighting.

And there was always the possibility that I could take this fool down.

But Don's arms were under his chest. I wondered if that's where he had been shot or stabbed and if he had died grabbing at the wound, desperately trying to stop the bleeding.

I reached out and tried to roll him over just as I heard the creep behind me take a step toward me. He must have regained his composure and was now swearing at me.

"Bitch! You gonna pay for that!"

With all my might, I tried to shove Don's shoulder aside so I could grab his gun, hopefully still under him.

At that moment, I learned two things. First, yes indeed, the gun was under his chest. The second was that Don was not dead.

Don had been lying there, pretending to be dead, until just the right moment. This was that moment.

He made an amazing push up, coming up with the little machine gun and tucking his knees under him. Once in a kneeling position, he began bringing the gun he had to bear. It was faster than I'd ever seen him move before.

I was so startled I fell backward, toward the guy behind me; in fact, my head bounced off his shoes.

Don pointed the gun at him, pulled the trigger, and held it there until the gun quit firing.

If I had hearing issues before, they were ten times worse now. Plus, the muzzle blast was blinding, and I felt the heat from the barrel.

The creep kicked me in the shoulders as he fell backward, his own gun firing at the ceiling.

Then there was silence. And I either landed in a puddle or I wet myself.

83

It had been a puddle.

In fact, the floor was about half an inch deep with water at this part of the store. At least I hoped it was water and not something more organic.

The ringing in my ears was all-consuming. It was as if someone had turned down the volume of all the other sounds and amped up the ringing in life's great audio equalizer.

I wasn't complaining, but really, it had been a hell of a day.

First Ashley, then May, then the hitmen, then Don's death and resurrection; it was all too much, and I just lay there in the cold liquid on the floor, stunned.

Then suddenly, Don was standing over me, extending his hand.

When I didn't move, he yelled a quick, "Brenda, are you all right?"

His voice was the sweetest thing I heard so far today. What I could hear of it.

He sounded far away, and the sensory illusion baffled my brain enough to keep me from moving. Don was right there, yet he was yelling and I could barely hear him, or see him for that matter.

But he reached down and basically lifted me to my feet. As soon as I was stable, I hit him—hard.

"What the hell were you thinking, scaring me like that? What kind of an asshole pretends to be dead, then scares the living shit of his wife by jumping out at her?"

His voice was so low I could barely hear it. "Um…one that saved your life?"

I turned and nearly vomited. The boy—yes, boy—that had been holding me and threatened my life lay in nearly two pieces on the floor. From his stomach up, it looked like he was ripped in two.

I'd never seen such utter devastation on another human being before and quickly turned back to bury my head in Don's chest despite the dry heaves.

Don endured it for a moment, then tapped my shoulders.

"Come on. We need to have a look around to see if there's anything left in here that we could use," he said loudly and deliberately.

"Like a barf bag?" I asked meekly.

Don snorted.

"Do you mind if I take a minute?" I asked, leaning against one of the empty shelving units.

"Look, you stay here. There's no one left. I'll take a quick look around and see if I can find anything we can use. I'm not hopeful though."

I nodded and he moved away, starting his treasure hunt. By the time he got back, I had recovered enough to manage on my own, without needing a sturdy commercial-sized shelving unit to support me.

And just as we figured, Don came back empty-handed.

"Couldn't find anything to use?" I asked, pushing off the shelves to stand.

He shook his head, frowning. "We're going to have to start walking. It's getting dark, and with this bunch"—he nodded toward the bodies—"who knows what we're going to face by the time we get to the Superdome."

"At least you have the guns," I said.

His frown deepened.

"Well, yeah, about that," he said. "These bozos emptied their magazines on each other. I checked. And, uh…I used the last ammo I had wasting that thug."

"So we are unarmed?"

Don tossed the gun away, and it hit the floor with a hollow metallic clack.

"Yep," he said. "Whatever we face, we face with our wits and without weapons."

84

It was on. The long walk. The quest. The hike.

And it sucked.

We figured it was going to be about a few miles to walk. We hadn't figured on the floodwaters.

The flooding was inconsistent, to say the least. One block we were on dry, solid ground, the next we were wading through knee-high water. That made the going tougher than I thought I could manage, but somehow, Don kept me going, which was really, *really* extraordinary, considering his phobia. It seemed nonexistent now. We made several detours a block or so long to avoid the water, and when we couldn't, he just marched through it like it wasn't there. Not even a pause or a comment or a wary glance.

Don had turned into the Terminator. Nothing was going to stop him. What a change from Sunday! He was fearless, determined, and driven.

I have to admit, it was kind of nice.

For the most part, we were alone, but every once in a while, we'd catch sight of other people, mostly in small groups, that I figured were family or something similar. We were all headed the same way, but when they stopped to rest, Don and I kept charging ahead, damn the water.

In fact, I had a hard time keeping up with him. He was so charged up that he was traveling at warp speed.

I guess he wanted to get there. Probably a good idea. Who knows what freaks and looters were lurking in the depths of the city, just waiting for unarmed, tired, and worn-out "tourists" like us?

Thoughts like that kept me moving when I really just wanted to collapse on the nearest stoop and watch the world go by because God knows I wouldn't be able to *hear* it.

But I simply couldn't. If Don was fighting his phobias silently, I had to at least keep up. I wasn't going to let him down nor would I let anything get in *my* way when it came to finding and saving Ashley.

It was sort of uplifting in a way. It kept me going, this drive of Don's. It was an inspiration.

So we marched on, with me giving it all I had and not complaining. I kept telling myself to ignore the fatigue and the pain because every step was getting me closer to Ashley. I hadn't considered just how we were going to find her at the Superdome, but that was a negative thought chain, and I pushed it out of my mind. I couldn't think about the possibility of meeting John and his partners and what they might do to all of us. I couldn't afford to think that way; I might just give up.

That's how close I was to the edge.

So I concentrated on how we'd get back to the Jeep, on the ride back to Chicago, and what we would need on the way. And how we would deal with John after we got home.

They were positive thoughts and they kept me going. Mostly, they kept my mind off the pain in my leg muscles and lower back.

So there I was, trailing Don by a few steps, thinking happy, rosy thoughts when Don stopped short and put out his arms, a clear signal for me to halt.

"What's up?"

Don shook his head and hands; be quiet.

I moved up behind him and whispered in his ear, "What did you see?"

He pointed across the intersection we were approaching. I peered over his left shoulder and saw a heavyset man running from our right to left, across the street, as best he could in the thigh-deep water.

The man was wearing a Hawaiian shirt and denim shorts, and he was obviously having difficulties getting around. Behind him, we heard shouts of several people, catcalling him and laughing.

On the right side of the street we were traveling and across the intersection was a five-story-tall apartment building. We were exposed—out in the open next to a white building. I looked up at it. It was a church and very near to us, a section jutted out from the main building.

It was the only place we could hide, and it wasn't much.

But Don turned around and grabbed me, literally carrying me over against the building. He pressed me hard up against the siding, hidden from the intersection by that four-foot-wide part of the floor plan.

"What are you doing?" I hissed.

His hearing must have been better than mine because he immediately placed a hand over my mouth and hushed me.

In seconds, I heard them too; several more people splashing through the intersection, calling out to the heavyset man we saw running.

My immediate thought was another street gang.

My eyes went wide, and Don patted my shoulder. Then he snuck a look around the edge of the building extension we were hiding behind.

I didn't have to hear what he was saying to know this was bad. The gunshot put the exclamation point on that idea.

So much for happy, rosy thoughts.

85

From our hiding place, we heard the murderous group splash around and laugh as they searched the man's body, floating now face-down in the filth.

The nausea was back, but for a different reason.

"I wish you had a gun," I said as loudly as I dared into Don's ear.

"Yeah."

To be standing there like *cowards*, hiding while the ultimate disrespect was taking place yards from where we were, was frustrating. I never felt worse about myself, except for that moment back home when I opened my mouth without thinking.

Don carefully poked his head around the corner of the building. "They're taking his wallet now."

Of course they were. I hope he didn't have anything in it they could use, but I suspected they'd try to use his credit cards if he carried them.

After a few minutes, they moved on, splashing and laughing as if it were all great fun. We waited another ten minutes, then Don gingerly stepped out from our hiding place. I followed him closely, my hands on his shoulders.

"Did you see which way they went?"

"North," he said.

"Think they're gone?"

"Yeah, but there's no guarantee that they aren't watching from some window someplace."

"Well, what should we do?"

Don shrugged, my hands lifting with his shoulders. "How should I know? I've never lived through a natural disaster, and I'm playing this by ear."

We edged closer to the intersection, but with every step, we were exposing ourselves. Out in the open, I was feeling very vulnerable. I had no clue how fast I could run if those people who killed this poor man came after us.

And I was quickly running out of strength. My legs felt like they weighed a ton, and my arms could barely swing at my side.

We waded up to the body. Don kept his distance. In the water, the man's blood could clearly be seen draining from his body.

I moved in closer.

"You know, if he had any diseases, you could contract them if that…blood touches you, Brenda."

I sidestepped the blood. "We can't just leave him here," I said.

"Why not? What could we possibly do for him now? And I really don't fancy being caught like he was. C'mon."

Just to defy Don's callousness, I moved around to the man's head, bent down, reached under his armpits, and started tugging.

"Brenda? What the *hell* are you doing?" Don half whispered, half yelled.

"Dragging him up to dry land," I said curtly. I didn't mean for it to come out that way, but I was having trouble catching my breath and moving the guy.

"That might be several blocks!"

"I mean the stoop over there."

Don looked over to the house across the street and shook his head. "You're making us a target!"

"No more than we would be anyway. We had to cross the street, Don."

"You are one crazy woman."

But he didn't help. I kind of figured he wouldn't. Don didn't normally do well with blood, body fluids, and such. I can't remember him ever changing a diaper.

Already sweaty and realizing the last time I had a shower was yesterday morning, I struggled to keep the sweat out of my eyes. Despite the pain from my scraped knee and hands after we ran John's boat aground, I managed to get the dead man over to the stoop. Getting him up the steps was a different story.

"Don, give me a hand, will you?" I asked, now bending over way too far and hurting my already tender back.

"You mean…touch him?"

"Well, you could levitate him if you want."

"Uh…really?"

"Never mind!"

I tugged and tugged, hurting my back even more. But I got him up the stairs and laid him up against the doorframe of the two-story house. Then I said a prayer, but I could hear Don fidgeting just beyond the steps.

I hurried the prayer and stepped down into the water once more.

Don was waiting for me, but I couldn't even look at him. I walked on westward, not even caring if he were following me.

86

As we walked on, it kept getting shallower. Eventually, as we made dry ground, we realized we were in the French Quarter.

That was good and bad news—good because at least we were headed in the right direction, bad because if you wanted to find an obnoxious drunk in all of New Orleans, this is where you'd find them.

I had been ignoring Don as much as I could. He was trying to make small talk while gasping for breath in the hard going, but I wouldn't answer, being still too angry at him for the disrespect he showed that poor dead man.

Finally, he fell silent and just splashed along behind me. We were both tired and slowing down. It couldn't be helped.

Eventually, we were walking on dry land. Good old dry and solid ground. Even so, my sneakers squished when I walked. The wetness of my shorts added with the fact I was covered in sweat, conspired to make me feel miserable. Every inch of me felt dirty, and I probably smelled horrible.

But that wasn't the worst of it.

As we dragged ourselves through the narrow streets of the French Quarter, I was amazed to see that most of the bars were open for business. In fact, the place just rattled with generators. But what really bothered me were the drunks.

They stumbled around and celebrated as if death and destruction was something to celebrate. This was all a joke to them, an excuse for a good time. In the middle of all this misery, these idiots felt the need to party.

And then there were the catcalls. I was amazed that despite my disheveled appearance, I was attracting catcalls and whistles from the people whose blood alcohol must have been reaching the antiseptic level.

When one of them actually stumbled up to me, I had to stop or run right into him. He stood there, swaying and asking if I wanted to party with him. Before I could do anything about it, Don came up behind me, passed me, and got right in the guy's face.

"She's busy," he snarled.

The drunk just laughed. "And about to get busier," he slurred, to the great amusement of his posse.

About three other drunken idiots surrounded us in support of their buddy. One of the asked, "What's ya gonna do about it, old man?"

"Don," I started, but it was too late.

"Who you callin' an old man, shithead?"

Okay, yeah, they were drunk. But there were *four* of them. Don didn't stand a chance, and neither did I.

I sidestepped him, but one of his buddies blocked my path. "Where ya goin', sexy?"

Don moved around me, shoving the first guy back. The first drunk stumbled, lost his fight with gravity, and went down, hitting his head on the curb, and it sounded painful. One of his buddies, the one who had called me sexy, seemed quite surprised at the turn of events, but he quickly rallied and threw a punch at Don.

Don wasn't fast enough to get out of the way, but the guy missed. Don, however, took advantage of that fact and swung at the guy's head.

And *he* missed.

But as luck would have it, Don caught the guy squarely in the throat, just about at his Adam's apple. Don grunted, obviously giving it all he had.

My second admirer went down choking and gasping for breath that wasn't coming.

This lit up the other two, but Don gave one a backhand, and he was knocked into the third, and they both went down in a tangled heap. Then Don grabbed my arm and pulled me quickly away before the others could untangle themselves.

We were half a block away when Don finally looked back. Out of my peripheral vision, I saw Don check out his handiwork, and I naturally glanced backward as well.

A police officer was bending over the second drunk—the guy that Don had throat punched—and was talking animatedly on his shoulder radio. The two dumbasses that Don bowled over were pointing at us.

"I think it's time to go," Don said, concern in his voice.

"Ya think?"

It's amazing how much energy fear gives you. We took off running as fast as we could. Not even the cop yelling *halt* could change our minds.

I looked back and the cop was getting up, talking it up on his radio, and coming after us.

"Oh shit! Don!"

He glanced back and then at me. Pulling me around a corner, he yelled, "We need to duck into someplace!"

Not his best plan, but I could hear the steps of the cop getting louder, and we were quickly running out of time to devise another.

We ducked into the nearest establishment with no lights, which turned out to be a pub.

Without even slowing down, we ran past the bar and toward the hall with the restroom sign hanging over it. At the end of the hall were the two bathrooms and the back wall of the bar, where the hallway ended at a fire door.

Running up to the door, Don stopped when he saw the sign. Alarm sounds, it read, and Don said, "Shit!"

I looked at him like the idiot he was and pushed the door open. "No power, remember?"

The light bulb went on in his head, and he followed me out to the courtyard, pushing the resistant door closed. Then we faced a backyard type of courtyard with a fence and, worse, no way out.

We were trapped.

87

There was nowhere to go. I could hear the footsteps of the police officer echoing in the hallway behind us.

This was it. We were done, and we were never going to find Ashley and save her.

I felt a squeeze on my arm, and suddenly I was being pulled sideways and thrust into a corner made up of wrought iron supports for the veranda upstairs at the rear of the building. There was a decorative half wall that made up a flower planter, and we ducked behind it, but let me tell you, it wasn't much.

To add to the danger, there was a window on the wall behind us. The shade was drawn on the inside, making a perfect reflecting surface for anyone glancing this way—from the veranda above to the concrete floor behind the planter.

Just in time, Don pressed up against me, hard, and we tried to make ourselves invisible by crouching behind the planter. But the police officer would have to be blind and stupid not to look back here.

As the officer poked his head out the doorway, I could see him in the window reflection, and that meant he could see us. I let a barely perceptible gasp escape my lips, and my eyes must have gotten wider with fear because Don, who was facing me, shook his head ever so slightly.

I got the message loud and clear. No more noises.

If the officer looked this way, there was no way he could have missed us. The wrought iron was hiding nothing, and the little decorative planter barely concealed our heads.

My eyes grew wider, and my pulse went beyond redline as I heard the radio on the officer's shoulder and heard his panting breaths. He was so, so very close that I was sure he could smell me.

I started to slink down, my back riding down the stucco wall painfully. But I was hoping that being low would provide a bit more cover.

I was wrong.

The sliding caused a slight scraping noise, and I'm sure he heard it.

Now it was Don's turn to widen his eyes. He grabbed me, and with the biggest, most smothering bear hug I had ever been given by anyone, he pulled me down on top of him.

My last glimpse of the officer's reflection proved it was only a nanosecond or two before he found us; he'd obviously heard the scraping noise and was in the process of turning his head in the direction of that noise—*our* direction. But at the precise moment we hit the ground, me on top of Don, the officer's mobile radio crackled.

I couldn't hear exactly what was said, but I could hear the officer take a step away to listen. The person on the other side of the transmission was fairly agitated, and the officer suddenly started walking away, his footsteps echoing from the doorway.

I could start breathing again.

But I held my breath until I was sure. Slowly, I raised my head and waited. And waited some more.

Finally, Don braved a question. "Is he gone?"

"I think so."

"Well, is he *there*?"

I shook my head and slowly got up. Don took my extended hand, and he stood up as well. We exchanged worried glances, then both poked our heads around the doorframe, a step away from where we were hiding.

The hallway was dark and empty. It still smelled of urine and other biologically disgusting things.

I even noticed a used condom on the floor.

"You think he went out of the bar?" Don asked.

"I don't know, Don. Your guess is as good as mine. What do you want to do?"

He bit his lip, then stepped inside. "C'mon," he said.

I followed him to the end of the hallway, where he peered around the corner into the bar. Glancing back at me, he nodded and we emerged from the hallway. Several of the drunks slumped around the bar or in the surrounding booths leered at me; I guess they saw us come in and thought were having a quickie in one of the bathrooms.

I avoided their stares.

Don asked the bartender for directions to the Superdome. The bartender scowled when it became clear we weren't going to buy anything, but he gave the street names and directions in rapid fire.

When he got them, Don dug out a $20 and tossed it on the bar, and then we were on our way.

Neither of us mentioned the last ten minutes of our lives. It was over and done with. We survived; nothing to see here. Move along.

And we did, zigzagging our way across town.

Finally, convinced that we'd lost the officer, we headed straight through the area of high-rise apartment and office towers; many of their windows were broken.

One of the name brand hotel chains' tower was missing a majority of their windows. The devastation was surrealistic. It looked like an apocalyptic movie set.

And I was fading fast. The water was nearly waist-deep, and the resistance was taking all I had. Even Don was slowing and breathing a lot harder.

"Don, you may have to go on without me," I finally had to admit.

He stopped and was breathing like he'd just run a marathon. "Not a chance. We've come this far together and we're going to get there together."

I smiled wearily but shook my head. "I can't remember when I ate last, and I have no more energy. Even the thought of saving Ashley isn't enough. I can't go on. I need rest at least."

Don shook his head again. "Alone and without a means of defending yourself. You wouldn't stand a chance out here. Look, there's a large street just ahead. I can see lights and hear some generators. Let's just get there and poke our nose around the corner to see where we are."

I nodded, breathing as hard as he was. It took about ten minutes to get to the end of the block, but we made it. We turned the corner, and there it was, our Mecca.

The Superdome.

88

Zanetti throttled the two big outboards back, and the boat's nose rose a few degrees skyward as it slowed.

In the bow, John Katsarus had been keeping a weather eye peeled for any signs of the Meyers and that very large target, Bruno. His teeth hurt from grinding, and the flesh of his palms were nearly raw from twisting and re-twisting the bowline he'd been holding on to.

But the guy that really concerned Zanetti was sitting behind him, out of his view, and was doing nothing but muttering about chasing loose ends.

"Let me take a wild guess. You two clowns are lost, right?"

Zanetti's eyes narrowed as he watched Katsarus slowly turn around, an equally volcanic expression on his face.

"Well, VT, why don't you come up here and drive and navigate?" Zanetti struggled to ask in a reasonably respectful tone.

VT shifted his weight on the saw horse-type seat and cleared his throat but didn't say a thing. That was just fine with Zanetti.

"I'm headin' back to the street we were on. The one behind that fuckin' old folk's home," Zanetti said, powering up the big twins outboards. "We've gone too far north, all the way to the interstate."

"Now you're thinkin'," VT said, and Zanetti bit his lip so hard he could taste blood. This search pattern was VT's idea!

Because of the search pattern, they'd traveled a long way, but not so far to the west. It took a full ten minutes before they got to the street Zanetti thought ran behind the assisted-living center to the east, and when they got there, he turned right.

Almost immediately, Katsarus stood up and pointed.

"What?" Zanetti asked.

"There it is! There the *fuck* it is!"

"And what the fuck would that be, Katsarus?" VT snarled, but Zanetti could plainly see what Katsarus was pointing at.

"My boat, and that big-ass dead man with it!"

Zanetti studied the area. It sure looked like the boat he'd made target practice out of, and there weren't any people around, so he nailed the throttles and VT fell off his seat.

But Zanetti wasn't able to worry about VT's humiliation; he was watching both the target boat and Katsarus carefully. This was a critical time; Katsarus wasn't a professional and was way too involved.

Zanetti expertly pulled up to the boat in question and, for good measure, decided to put the flashing lights on. White, yellow, and blue lights from the Mars Assembly on top the radar arch lit up the neighborhood. The big black man in the boat that had obviously been shot up, stood up from where he had been working on the outboard.

The look of shock and sudden fear on his face confirmed that indeed, this was the boat they had been looking for.

But he was the sole occupant.

Before they were stopped alongside, Katsarus had leapt into his boat and started for the guy who was going to defend himself. It wouldn't have been a long contest, so Zanetti and VT acted on instinct and drew their weapons. Pointing his suppressed HK at the big man, Zanetti yelled for him to freeze.

"What have you done to my boat?"

"*Oh Yi Yee, Vieux!* Shot it up y'all did!"

Katsarus anger only intensified. "Where are they?"

"Who?"

"Don and Brenda Meyers! What did you do to them?"

"Hey, I ain't done nothin' to those folks, honest! They gave me the boat and took off on foot."

"You're lying!" Katsarus took a step toward Bruno. "Where *are* they?"

"A-a-at that Walgreens back there, two blocks south! I *swear*, Mr. John!"

Zanetti hailed Katsarus. "Yo, here," he said and tossed Katsarus the Colt he had prepared, the one with only one bullet. "Maybe this will get him to tell the truth."

"Oh, I ain't lyin'. Look, look at my wrists! They tied me up! Look, when Miss Brenda went into the drugstore and Mr. Don went in, well, I took the boat. See, Mr. Don was a terrible boater. He done run over the ground an' fucked up you prop, Mr. John! I was just tryin' to fix it as best I could!"

"Where were they headed?" Zanetti asked.

"Superdome, sir."

Zanetti glanced at VT. "On foot, that will take them a couple of hours." Then to Bruno, he asked, "How long ago?"

"'Bout two hours ago. An' they was healthy too! I ain't done *nothin'* to 'em!"

Zanetti scrunched up his lips and furrowed his brow. Finally, he announced, "You know what? I believe him."

Katsarus actually agreed. "Yeah, this punk ass doesn't have it in him to murder someone, does he? He can only drug little old ladies and steal from them!" Bruno, for the first time since they had come upon him, narrowed his eyes in anger.

VT stood up. "I concur. Very well, off to the Superdome."

Bruno looked relieved. "Take me with you?" he asked.

VT spoke with authority. "Mr. Katsarus, this man is a loose end. Please eliminate this loose end."

Katsarus didn't have to be told twice before he raised the barrel of the Colt 1911M1A and thumbed the safety.

89

Ashley had to pee.

She'd consumed a lot of water in her time here. The interrogators had given her about five bottles, and she was still thirsty.

They'd questioned her for the entire time she had been at the Superdome, which was absurd given what they were accusing her parents of doing—lying to be let into the city to help her.

It wasn't like she was a dangerous criminal, worn-out, and undernourished like she was. No matter. She was done. They were either going to release her or she was going to ask for a lawyer.

Either way, she would say nothing more. Truth was, she didn't know a damn thing about her parents coming down here. What she did know she found out from that Robert Lee guy.

So when one of the officials came back with a dark blue polo shirt emblazoned with the DHS shield over the left breast and wearing khaki tactical pants with a firearm strapped on his belt, she was ready for battle.

She was *no longer* intimidated by the company uniform.

But before she could talk, he just moved around to her side and asked her to stand up. "Ma'am, you're free to go. But you should stay close because when we bring your parents in, you may want to see them, and of course, we'd like you to confirm their identity," he said.

Like hell! She wasn't about to help them make an example of her parents who had obviously come down to save *her*. It was probably cooler down on the main floor, and that's where she was going.

She nodded and asked where she could find the nearest bathroom.

"Well, you can't use the ones in the press box. That's for us. You're just a civilian," he said.

Ashley picked up on the "just a civilian" remark but, by now, had learned to choose her fights. So she kept her mouth shut and the official continued.

"You'll have to use the public washrooms, an' there's one down on the other side of the merchant hall outside. Clearly labeled and it's on the outside wall."

She nodded and turned around to leave.

"Just a minute, Miss," said the official. Ashley turned slowly, determined to give him hell if he gave her any kind of lecture about her parents.

"Just be careful," he said.

"Why would I need to be careful?" she asked cautiously.

"We kinda understaffed at the moment," the official said, letting his Cajun accent loose.

Sure that he meant well but with no clue what he really meant, she merely nodded and turned again, free at last.

After entering the wide-perimeter hallway that encircled the floor, she noticed immediately that while still hot, it had a bit fresher taste to the air. Behind her was the press box complex of offices and viewing and broadcasting boxes where she had been held for far too long.

The plan was to wait close by for her parents, probably down at the entrance, but first, relief.

The official had been correct; right across the hall was another hallway leading to the bathrooms, with the international restroom signs above the opening. There was a men's room and a ladies' room in the same hallway. She started toward the ladies' room.

Sitting next to a vendor's window on a folding chair was a young black man wearing a bright red T-shirt, who couldn't be more than sixteen. Naturally wary of him because of his riveted stare toward her, she tried to walk quickly past him.

But he stopped her before she could get into the hallway leading to both bathrooms. He jumped up and leapt right in her path.

"Y'all gots to use the shitter?" he asked menacingly.

After everything that had happened to her today, she was determined not to show fear. "Get out of my way, or I'll call the police," she said loudly.

He didn't flinch. He even smiled, an evil kind of smile, such that it was.

"I *mean* it!"

"Y'all don' understand. This here is now a pay shitter. You got to pay to use it."

"Well, I don't have any money, so how 'bout I just take a walk back to my friends in the Department of Homeland Security offices and see how they like your extortion scheme?"

The evil smile faded rapidly.

He reached out and grabbed her with both arms, quickly moving behind her. Ashley could feel his hot, putrid breath in her ear. "Then you gonna pay with the flesh," he said.

"Let go of me! You're not going to rape me! Help me! Rape!"

Screaming at the top of her lungs and fighting with renewed energy, she was dismayed that no one, absolutely no one, would budge to help her.

90

It was standing there, beckoning us. All light up and welcoming, the Superdome was truly mesmerizing.

We just stood there for what must have been ten full minutes, gaping at the lit-up structure in awe. Finally, sighing heavily, Don nudged me and said, "C'mon, it's gonna take us a while to get into this place. Standing here sweating isn't gonna get us to Ashley any faster."

I grabbed his arm with both hands and turned to him, suddenly worried. "Don, what if she isn't here? What if she's been evacuated already?"

Don scanned the upper outdoor patio, jammed with people looking like Third World refugees. He shook his head.

"I don't think they've had time to organize a mass evacuation yet, Brenda. Look at all the people who are just milling around. Can you imagine what the inside looks like?"

I could and I didn't want to.

As we walked across the street, I again asked him, "Okay, so what's the plan?"

Again, he shrugged. "Haven't got a clue. You?"

I shrugged.

"Just find a cop or a guardsman and see if they can make an announcement over the PA. Other than that, find the office or main control center and go there and ask. If the DHS gave her a ride, they ought to know where she is," I said.

"Might be better to just find the office. We could be *wanted* by FEMA after what we did to Billy Bob."

And suddenly, I knew exactly what had been bothering me all along—our dealing with Billy Bob and how that might come back to haunt us. I opened my mouth to voice my concerns to Don, but he seemed to know what I was thinking.

"Hey," he said, almost happily, "look, we can always blame it on Katsarus."

I had been emotionally drained by now. "Sure. Sounds like a plan," I numbly replied.

But what we didn't plan for was how to avoid waiting in a very long line to get in to the shelter itself. I studied the entrance and could see that the line of people seemed to have no end, starting from the south end of the building at the gate and wrapping around the mezzanine-level balcony outside and down a ramp right into the water.

As I glared at the line of people, something else caught my eye, and I grabbed Don's arm and pointed.

On the corner that faced north was another ramp and parked next to it was a boat similar to one that had been used by the hitmen.

"You think that's them?" I asked.

"Let's get a closer look," Don said.

It seemed safe enough; not that many people were milling around the north side of the complex where we were. Don and I waded up to the boat, gently bobbing and rubbing up against the cement wall of the ramp to the surrounding patio.

"What do you think?" I asked Don as he wadded around it, looking into the boat at various places.

"Hard to tell. They all look alike," he said.

But then I had an idea. I moved over to where I could see the kill switch. It was intact.

I flood of relief coursed through my veins, but before I could tell Don, a light switched on from the upper-level deck.

"You two, by the boat! What are you doing? Come up here now," a mechanized voice bellowed. My stomach knotted up immediately because it reminded me of the bullhorn that the gangbanger at the drugstore used.

We both looked up and saw two uniformed and helmeted guards, both with what I thought were machine guns strapped around their shoulders, looking down and pointing at us. One of them pointed to the ramp nearby.

At least we wouldn't have to wait in line.

But then Don opened his mouth.

"We got information that our daughter was taken here in one of these boats, sir, and we were just checking to see if we could see any evidence that she was actually here."

"Up here, *now*!" The other guardsman grabbed his rifle but did not point it at us.

"We're coming, we're coming," I yelled up.

I couldn't believe that what Don said, a perfectly logical response from a worried father, could anger anyone. These guys must be wound pretty tight.

As Don came around the back end of the boat, I just innocently mentioned to him that people seemed so jumpy lately, and before I could get to the part where I told him about how I didn't think what he said should have drawn the sort of response from the guards that it did, he interrupted me.

"I can't believe you would blame me for this asshole's shit," he hissed.

As we waded around to the ramp entrance, we continued to fight.

"Don, you didn't let me finish, that's—"

"But that's par for the course with you and me, isn't it, Brenda? All you do is criticize lately!"

I didn't know what to say. In a flash, my husband had turned into Mr. Hyde from his Dr. Jekyll. He must have reached his breaking point.

All the way up the ramp, he continued nitpicking. Finally, we reached the top and were so completely absorbed with the argument that we noticed no one else.

"Well, Don, given that fact that you went all Rambo on those gang members back at the drugstore, what, you killed four, five of them? I—"

Just as I uttered the word *killed* loudly, we were ensnared in a painful, brilliant white light that could have lit up the face of the moon.

91

Ashley was acutely aware that she was being dragged into the men's room. It reeked of urine and rotting feces, and was also hot, stuffy, and filthy, not to mention that the light was poor.

She was tripped and thrown down on the hard tile. It hurt. She kicked out and tried to roll away and get up to run, but the little kid was quick.

He was on his knees, spreading her legs and ripping at her pants. He even managed to get them unbuckled before she realized what he had done. Before she could stop him, he had lifted her hips violently and pulled down her pants to her knees.

But remembering a move she saw performed in several movies, she boxed his ears with both hands, and that seemed to produce enough pain for him to drop what he was doing, groan, and slug her hard in the stomach.

Partly because she remembered her mother admonishing her about an article she had read about rape defenses and partly because the punch had affected her bladder, she lost control.

The article had maintained that the best way to defend was merely to empty your bowels or bladder. The theory was that this would suppress or eliminate any sexual desire, and the rapist will quickly lose interest.

Well, either from the punch or active defense, it seemed to do the trick. Her assailant got a thick, hot stream of golden urine in his face.

He immediately got up, screaming something about his eyes and spitting. As he staggered toward the sinks, Ashley acted quickly. She pulled up and buckled her pants, twisted despite the pain in her gut, and pushed up off the floor.

Standing now, but dizzy, she paused only a second when she heard the rapist swear about the lack of water coming out of the faucet. When he moved over to the next one, farther from the exit door, she bolted.

As she ran, she heard his running footsteps behind her, gaining.

92

I KNEW THAT voice. I knew the name. He was a famous reporter on a famous cable news outlet. But as God is my witness, with Don and me frozen in place, I couldn't understand a word he said.

Then he thrust a microphone in my face.

Beyond the harsh glare of the brilliant white lights aimed at us, I could see a red light on top of a circular lens.

We were on TV.

Don and I aren't public speakers. That's just the way we are. Oh, we make a certain amount of presentations for work, but that's different. A worldwide audience? Not our style.

We stayed frozen.

The reporter repeated his question. "Where did you come from?"

Don said nothing. He had regressed to "deer in the headlights" status. So I leaned in slowly.

"Chicago."

"Chic…uh, okay, you came down here *why*? Why on *earth* would you travel *to* a hurricane? Are you some kind of storm chasers?"

"No."

"Well, what are you doing down here, then?"

"Rescue," I said, beyond giving complex answers or even thinking more than two syllables beyond what my mouth was handling at the time.

"So what's *your* story? Where were you when the storm came through?"

"Jeep."

"What?"

"Our Jeep," I repeated. Slowly, this was becoming easier, and more than one-word responses were beginning to form in my brain.

I could hear the frustration in the reporter's tone.

"Ma'am, what kind of hardships did you experience? Did you get any help from the government?"

"FEMA," I started.

"You got help from FEMA, how?"

"They…they tried to kill us."

"Okay, that's a wrap," the reporter said, clearly annoyed. The lights vanished, leaving us night-blind.

"C'mon Joey, let's move down to that cluster of folks down there," he said, sighing. "Lady, I hope you find your meds."

And as quickly as it started, our fifteen minutes of fame was over.

As the crew packed up, I started coming to my senses and realized we'd just blown a great opportunity to get the word out about Ashley. For that matter, it was a stellar chance to lay bare John and his partner's activities too.

"Wait," I screamed, pleaded really. "Don, give me your wallet!"

"My wallet?"

"C'mon, just do it!"

"Lady, we don't have time—"

I quickly interrupted the reporter. "You caught us off guard and I didn't know what I was saying. We've had a hell of a day, and if you want a story, I've got one for you."

Still in somewhat of a trance, Don reached back and pulled out his wallet, handing it to me as the lights went back on and the reporter appeared with that damned microphone.

I dug through Don's wallet quickly, hands shaking, until I found the picture of Ashley. With a quick side-glance to the microphone in my face, I took a deep breath and thrust the picture of Ashley in front of the camera.

"This is our daughter. We're looking for her. My husband and I came down where with a neighbor from Chicago last night to rescue my daughter, Ashley, and my aunty May from the hurricane, but we couldn't make it in time. The management at the Claude Avenue Assisted-Living Center just left the residents there. They didn't evacuate anyone but themselves, and now my aunt May is dead! We can't find our daughter, but we think she may be here please! If you can help us find Ashley…"

My voice trailed off. Lack of sleep, fatigue, emotion, and stress finally got the better of me. I broke down into sobs and could not finish the story. Don, the amazing, full-of-surprises man that he had turned out to be in this trip, stepped up.

"What my wife is saying," he began as he put his arms around my shoulder, "is that we're beat. Our neighbor, John Katsarus, was going to do away with me because he still has feelings for my wife, and he figured that a disaster area would be a perfect place for that kind of thing."

I tensed. I had never told Don this. Well, this part, anyway.

"And he hired his partners to come down and do the job, but we escaped with an orderly from that assisted-living center, and he eventually stole our boat. Some guy named Bruno. That's all I remember. Do you remember his last name, hon?"

The lights dimmed and went out. The reporter said, "That's quite a story, folks. Good luck finding your daughter."

"Wait, don't you want to report on our ordeal?" I asked, emotion drained.

"Lady, look, it sounds so…made up. Nobody's ever going to believe it. They're going to think that you just want to be on TV."

Don finally put everything into high gear. "Hold on a second. You people spend your lives sensationalizing events for ratings, and when you find an honest-to-God story that *is* sensational, you guys ignore it because it's *too* sensational?"

The reporter flashed his famous smile and moved on, not giving us the courtesy of a reply.

We were suddenly alone again in the dark.

93

Ashley knew it was only a matter of time before her assailant caught up with her. Her only hope was the few people milling around in the large perimeter corridor for vendors. They might step in to help or at least call someone.

As she approached another person who was wearing another red T-shirt, the kid chasing her shouted to stop her.

All the guy in front had to do is take a step sideways and grab her. It was very effective.

When the kid who was chasing her caught up to them, Ashley was kicking and trying to scream but for the hand across her mouth, he punched her—hard.

It took all the fight out of her. Her chaser told the person holding her to follow him. As they pulled her back toward their headquarters in the men's room, a roving cop rounded the corner and stopped short.

"What are you doing?" he bellowed.

Ashley's whole mood turned around. A cop on the beat was better than clumps of people in the hallway. And he had a sidearm.

The cop put his hand on that sidearm and moved in, pointing at the two and ordering them to take their hands off her. But something was wrong; Ashley was still restrained by the guy who grabbed her.

"I said, unhand her!"

It was then that the original banger, the one that had tried to rape her, took a large step toward the cop, who hadn't expected it. Quickly and silently, the banger swung at the officer's head.

The kid's fist connected with the cop's temple, and while it didn't take him out, it dazed the cop to a staggering waltz around to the wall. The kid stepped in and hit him again and again until, despite his feeble attempts at drawing his weapon, the cop went down, bleeding.

They dragged the cop and Ashley back to the hallway leading to the men's room. They laid him out against the wall, and the first kid started kicking the cop's limp form and wouldn't stop.

"Don' touch that gun," the other kid said.

He stopped only long enough to extract the cop's billy club from his belt, then use it to finish his task.

Ashley shut her eyes; she couldn't watch.

They both took turns at the officer's lifeless form. Ashley gagged at the sight. She'd never seen so much blood.

The two were giggling as they literally danced on top of the officer's body.

When they had had enough fun, the first one said to the one that had grabbed her, "Go get Mason. Go get everybody. We gonna have some fun with this one, too."

As the other gangbanger took off, the kid slowly approached Ashley, who was now on the floor, trying to use her back against the wall to stand up.

The kid was leering and suddenly started punching the palm of his other hand as he slowly edged toward her.

94

SUDDENLY ON OUR own again, it was time to refocus. I tapped Don on the shoulder.

"C'mon, Rambo, let's go find Ashley."

"Bastards. They make the news more than they report it."

Finally he turned to follow me. But waiting in the long line a block to the south, especially since it looked like we'd have to get down in the water again to join the long and growing line, just didn't work for me. I knew there was an opening right where we were standing, but it was heavily guarded by those uniformed National Guardsmen who yelled at us.

"Don, I can't go back down in the water again. I can't."

He nodded, looking at the line than at the guards. Then he said, "Follow me. I'm going to try something."

This did nothing for my mood, but I was ready to try anything, even one of Don's plans. As we walked toward the guards, Don leaned over to me and put an arm around my shoulder.

"Let me do the talking. Just focus on how tired and worn out you are. Can you do that for me?"

I looked at him like he'd lost his mind. But in the end, what he asked of me wouldn't be too hard.

We walked right up to the guards, who thought they were ready for us. "Sorry, folks. This entrance is for officials only."

Don went into hyper salesman. "Then talk to the news crew. They told us to wait right inside for them to come back to interview us. But my wife is at the end of her rope. She can't walk anymore or stand. She just needs to sit down while we wait. Can we use those chairs there that no one is using, or are those for officials only too?"

I even slumped over some, and Don nearly lost his balance trying to keep me from "falling." The guards exchanged worried, clueless glances, then shrugged, stepped aside, and let us by, pointing to the folding chairs.

"Thank you," Don said as he helped me limp by.

As soon as we were out of earshot, I whispered to him, "Don, that was *brilliant*! Now what?"

"We wait."

I gladly sat down in the chair, and Don sat next to me. The guards glanced at us occasionally, but I had to admit, it was pure luxury to sit, even in a steel folding chair. I must have dozed off because the next thing I knew, Don was shaking me awake.

"C'mon, they walked away."

"Who, what?"

But then I saw that the guards were gone, and Don was already on his feet, moving fast.

The adrenaline kicked in, and suddenly I was right beside him. We moved into the entrance hallway, around a few concrete walls, and then we were there.

Inside the Superdome at last.

But what we saw nipped any notion of celebration.

The noise, smell, and atmosphere were stifling. The entire football field had been taken up by rows upon rows of what could best be described as Third World refugees. I'd never seen anything like it. Not in America.

There was so much stuff on the ground that you couldn't tell what was luggage and what was garbage. And everywhere, there were people. There were people sitting on cots, sleeping on them, walking around them, just wall-to-wall people.

There were even people sitting in the stands.

"How are we ever going to find her in all this?" I asked.

Don was shaking his head. "We best find the place where they have the PA."

"My guess is the press box, then."

Don followed my gaze. "That means we climb. And heat rises."

"C'mon. We better start looking for the stairs or ramps or something," I said, definitely not looking forward to this part of the journey.

95

Zanetti throttled down and let the RIB slow to a forward drift.

There it was. The Superdome.

As they bobbed in the water a block away, Zanetti, VT, and Katsarus watched the structure, studying it. The whole outside of it was lit up like an airport runway with mega search lights, making it an imposing structure. The outdoor deck that surrounded the dome itself was jammed with people and crawling with National Guardsmen, their vehicles, and, no doubt, weapons.

Overhead, Zanetti counted at least four helicopters of various types hovering in lazy circles, waiting to swoop down to a makeshift landing zone and then fly away again, alternately ferrying VIPs and refugees to and from this base of operations.

Zanetti sucked in his breath. "I don't like it, VT. I don't like it one bit," he said.

VT was at his side instantly, his face peering down from the same level as Zanetti's. They both stared at the structure.

VT nodded. "Too many people."

"Yeah, this ain't what we expected," Zanetti added. "What do you want to do?"

VT looked at Zanetti like he ought to know better.

Zanetti sighed. "I know what the goal is. How do you want to *do* it?" he asked.

VT glanced up at Katsarus. Then he turned and dug out a magazine from one of the bags and handed it to him.

"You go in. You get them and bring them out. You fuck us, you don't come out with them, you die, got it?"

Katsarus nodded silently.

"Use this badge."

VT handed the badge to Zanetti, who passed it on to Katsarus.

Katsarus took it and closed the badge's case. Zanetti pushed the throttles forward, and in a few minutes, they were tying up next to another FEMA boat, identical to theirs.

As Katsarus hopped out, Zanetti called after him. "Good hunting."

Katsarus spit into the water as he slammed the magazine home and racked the slide. Then tucking the gun under his belt and untucking the polo shirt bearing the FEMA shield Zanetti had given him, he waded the few feet toward the ramp.

When he was sure they were out of earshot, Zanetti leaned over. "What's the plan?"

"We get everyone out here and take care of things in the dark."

"Seems too simple," Zanetti said.

"And you have a better plan?"

"Yeah, I do."

"Then please," VT said, leaning on the gunnel of the boat, "enlighten me."

Ignoring the attitude, Zanetti launched into his plan. "How eager do you think those Meyers are going to be to go with Katsarus?"

VT considered the question. "Not very," he eventually offered, scowling.

"Not likely at all. Katsarus told us that they dumped that FEMA hack just to get into the city, right? Well, we can be following up on that, investigatin' them, you know? Then when we find the Meyers, they don't know what we look like, right? They'll probably go quietly with us. And we can take care of that idiot Katsarus later. After he gets the daughter."

"Not bad, except what part of 'I want everyone dead' didn't you understand?"

"Fine, we kill the daughter too, but away from the damn dome."

VT was silent for a moment. Then he looked up. "Johnny! Wait for us. We're coming up!"

VT and Zanetti quickly gathered a few needed items, then waded around to the ramp. Midway up, they met with Katsarus.

"What's wrong?"

"Change of plans. You point them out to us, then go out to the boat and wait for us. Do nothing more," VT said as they began walking up the ramp.

As this was going on, some movement caught Zanetti's eye, and he immediately pulled down his FEMA baseball cap low over his forehead, completely blocking his face if he kept his head down.

"I don't understand," Katsarus started, but he never got to finish the sentence.

All three of them were bathed in brilliant lights, and VT, not wearing his FEMA cap, was caught like a deer in the headlights.

Katsarus twisted away, as did Zanetti. But while Zanetti sought the shadows, Katsarus ran right up to the opening and the two National Guardsmen. He flashed the badge he had been given.

"Quick! Two FEMA agents are being assaulted! Help me break it up!"

It took only a second for it to register, but when it did, the guardsmen took off on a run. Katsarus watched them and slipped away from his two partners.

Moving into the Superdome with ease, he made directly for the press box just to get the height advantage.

96

I honestly didn't know how Don was doing it. Where was he finding the energy? How could he possibly keep going despite the heat, the noise, the stifling atmosphere, but especially how was he dealing so easily with the jostling we were taking from the crowd? He was like the Terminator.

Every time he'd duck into an opening between people, we'd get separated. Then because I'd lost him, I'd start yelling out his name, but he'd always appear, waiting and frustrated, and the cycle would begin again.

Once I even took my eyes off him to glance up at the press box, I lost him again, and he was gone for three minutes.

My panic rose quickly, and I was shouting his name like some kind of madwoman. That time, he mocked me for panicking. I had to admit, I sounded pretty stupid.

We were almost there, up to the area where we might find a ramp or stairs or something, when it happened.

From out of nowhere, I got nailed so hard by someone that I was knocked on my backside. If I didn't miss my guess, I think the guy copped a pretty good feel too, and that angered me enough to power my rebound.

"Watch where you're—"

A hand was thrust in my face, a big black hand and the palm was many shades lighter. My heart stopped, and I slowly looked up.

But the face I was expecting to see wasn't there. The face I *did* see was wide-eyed, and you could tell he was a bodybuilder of some sort; it he looked nothing like Bruno.

He was also apologizing out the ying-yang.

"Ma'am, please forgive me! It's really hard for me to walk in here! Are you all right? Did I hurt you?"

I was suddenly weightless, then standing on my feet and being brushed off. The voice was intoxicating, and the strength of the man…well, I had to refocus quickly.

"Yes, thank you, I'm all right…No, really, I'm okay."

After a few minutes assuring him that I was fine, I turned to admonish Don for not helping.

But I couldn't because he wasn't there again.

"Don! Don! Don!"

It made no difference. After about five minutes of calling out his name and desperately looking around, my heart sank. This time, it was different. This time, he was really nowhere around.

We were now officially separated, and I was counting on him to be desperately looking for me as much as I was looking for him. I felt like a little lost child. We'd been together through this whole trip, but now, I was on my own.

Okay, calm down. Breathe. Don't panic!

Think!

I moved to one of the large arched openings overlooking the playing field and looked up. Halfway up to the ceiling was the distinctive line of windows that made up the press box and broadcast booth. That's where we were headed, so that's where I was going to go.

Besides, it might be easier now not having to keep up with, or find, Don with every bump and grind.

I just hoped he would be thinking along the same lines instead of staying down here, looking for me.

97

Dr. William Robert Lee, DDS, grasped the Inter-Squad Radio which was referred to by the military in their acronym addiction as an ISR. His section leaders wanted to know that he had a radio back up in case he was taken advantage of again.

Well, he'd be damned if he was going to be making any more deals with anyone he didn't know. And if he ever found one of them Meyers folks, well, he'd use that ISR to call down the authorities. They owed FEMA twenty gallons of gas!

Billy sat on the cot reserved for volunteers, such as himself, in the cordoned-off section of the main floor of the Superdome. But he couldn't relax.

It wasn't the noise or the smell or even the oppressive heat. It was the fact that these people, thousands of them, looked more like a refugee camp than the interior of a storm shelter. This just couldn't be happening, not like this, not in this country.

What a cluster fuck.

Right from the get-go, the response was so ill-conceived, ill prepared, and ill executed. What a waste of good taxpayer money.

Somebody was going to pay for this. Somebody had *better* pay for this!

Billy had promised his section chief that he would get a few hours of rest. He had promised his chief that he'd grab an MRE dinner. But as he looked around, he couldn't take food out of the mouths of the people in this shelter! Wasn't going to happen. He wasn't built like that.

Neither could he rest when people needed help. And by the way thinks looked, just making it to the Superdome wasn't the end of your troubles; it was the beginning.

On the radio, he'd heard at least five reports of violence and mayhem, mostly on the upper decks. Some gang had infiltrated the Superdome and was charging for use of the bathrooms. People were hot, tired, and they'd lost everything except what they could carry. Trying to stay cool, calm, and collected with thousands of other anxious people wasn't easy.

Overloaded shelters always seemed to be a breeding ground for violence.

He scanned the upper tiers, watching for trouble. But they weren't nearly as crowded as the main floor, and he stood up to scan his level.

And at that exact moment, his eyes landed on the well-built, sunburned man that owned the boat he was tricked out of earlier today.

It was just a glimpse, but it looked like that guy who was making fun of Don Meyers and his fear of the water. But Billy lost him in the crowd. Wanting to confront that man, Billy started to follow the object of his hatred immediately.

98

ONCE VT AND Zanetti flashed their badges, the guards pounced on the news crew. The lights went out, and while night-blind, Zanetti and VT managed to make their way toward the large open gate to the Superdome interior.

As they waited momentarily for their eyes to adjust, VT looked back at the guardsmen surrounding the news crew. VT shook his head in disgust.

"We should have confiscated that camera."

Zanetti couldn't resist tweaking his boss. "Yeah. Loose end."

VT got very quiet and stayed that way for some time.

Finally, satisfied that his eyes had sufficiently adjusted to the light inside the stadium, Zanetti asked, "Do you see Katsarus anywhere?"

"That reporter is going to have a terrible accident, Zanetti."

Yeah, Zanetti thought. *And you want me to arrange it.* Sick and tired of risking exposure for this idiot, he let that one go without comment. It would be too obvious anyway; that reporter has probably already gone to broadcast, and if anything were to happen to that reporter, suspicions would be aroused.

Nope. Zanetti was not going to go to jail for this piece of shit unless he had money up front.

"I don't see Katsarus anywhere. He's got your gun too. Talk about a loose cannon *and* loose end," Zanetti casually said.

VT looked like he was about to pop a vein. Zanetti moved a short distance away, feigning a quick visual search for Katsarus, just in case VT lost it.

"Like I said, we eliminate *everyone* associated with this contract," VT snarled. "No more fucking loose ends."

"And not to mention, you, as partner, get the full assets to his financial businesses. You may not want to sell it off, VT. Those books can hide a lot of funds, if ya know what I mean."

Suddenly, VT's expression changed. He seemed to be mulling over Zanetti's last statement and liking it as he considered the possibilities.

"Not to mention that if he is arrested before we get to him," Zanetti went on, "that he'll get caught red-handed with the gun that killed that Creole piece of shit in the bottom of his own boat. You got to love that, VT."

"I don't!" VT's expression turned angry again. "We *must* find Katsarus before the police find him. I don't want him talking at all!"

"Then we better start looking, huh?"

Zanetti turned back to the interior of the structure, smiling to himself on getting VT engaged, finally.

VT walked right past him as they moved into the interior.

"Look for the closest ramp. We're going up," VT shot over his shoulder at Zanetti.

"Why up? Better vantage point?"

"Partly. Partly because I can't stand the smell of these people," VT said.

"Then what?"

VT halted, and when Zanetti stepped up to him, he said, "Then, Tony, we kill every living thing associated with this misadventure of yours, then we go home. Then we have a little *chat* about your hairbrained idea to go on this hit."

With that, VT turned on his heel and stomped off, leaving Zanetti to bore .45 caliber holes in his head with nothing more than his eyes—for now.

99

It took forever for me to move across the hallway toward the center in search of the press box where I hoped to find Don. Along the way, I was jostled, grabbed, nearly vomited on, sweated on, pushed, and shoved, but by God, I got to the other side of the surrounding corridor.

I felt my way, literally, around the sweeping curve of the hall, past now closed vendor stands, T-shirt stores, concession stands, and as I plowed through the crowd, I felt like a salmon swimming upstream. But around the other side of the entrance, I was rewarded with a beautiful sight—a large ramp heading up to the next level.

There was just one catch; it seemed to be guarded by four mean-looking and well-armed National Guardsmen, big black rifles hanging from a sling around their necks and a finger resting near the trigger on the trigger guards.

I don't think they would have taken pity on me.

Okay, so if there is a ramp on *this* side of the field, there certainly must be on the *other* side. All I had to do was turn around and fight my way back to the southeast side of the complex. But wouldn't that be guarded as well?

But even if it were guarded, where was Don? How did he get by these guards, or…did he? I looked around more carefully this time, once again, swimming upstream—yes, in the opposite direction— toward the other ramp.

If he ran into the same problem, then he would have gone the other way too, right?

I hoped so.

Or maybe he just made a lucky guess and went around to the east-side ramp first. No, that didn't make sense, knowing Don and how tired he was, he would have gone for the shortest path.

When I got there, the ramp had a rope stretched across the width, and it wasn't lit up, but why would that stop me? Hell, in one day, I have made it through a relative's death, being shot at, being robbed, under siege, being molested by drunks, and chased by cops.

A dark ramp isn't going to stop me. Not today.

I sauntered up to the rope and looked around. Frankly, as long as I kept my chest out of public view, nobody wanted to look at a mid-forties mommy with a few extra pounds, no makeup, and hair that hadn't been washed since Sunday morning.

When I was sure no one was the least bit interested, I ducked under the rope and trotted up the ramp as fast as my fitness level would allow, which wasn't really fast, let me tell you.

Try doing swimming pool-resistance training most of the day and you'll know why.

Two flights up, I exited the ramp and made my way through the outer corridor to the west, slowly and hugging the inner wall. I did this just in case this ramp was guarded too.

But it wasn't. I rounded the corner, and while there were people walking around, there wasn't a lot of them and there weren't any guards at the ramp.

I poked my head out the archway that led to the seating area and looked for the windows of the press box. It was two levels up.

My heart sank; I wasn't as close as I had hoped. But then again, I might just be on the verge of finding Ashley, and suddenly, the adrenaline was pumping once more.

I took a quick look around, hoping to find Don. No Don, but there were a few people scattered around in the seats on this first level.

But no one who could be of any assistance.

So I ducked back into the outer corridor and made my way up the ramp. It was slow going, and the higher I climbed, the hotter and stuffier it seemed to be.

At one point, I thought I was going to pass out for lack of fresh air. But I determined that I wasn't going to let a little discomfort stop me from finding Ashley and Don. Soon, I was on the forth level, the same level as the press box and office complex. I was certain that, somehow, these two areas would lead me to Ashley.

And Don.

The fact Don was missing worried me. What if he ran into Katsarus and his partners?

I needed to rest for a moment, so I poked my head out to the seating area and picked out a nice plush seat that would normally be used to watch a Saints game and planted myself in it.

Where was Don? And where was John with his partners? I'm sure they had had plenty of time to fix their boat and get here.

But maybe they had trouble as well, but while Don and I were walking, they could still have beaten us to the Superdome.

And I'm betting that they wouldn't have been stupid enough to get their boat stolen.

I looked around the playing field and upper decks more carefully now. And I said a little prayer for Don to avoid the hitmen and for us to find Ashley and each other.

And those guards probably reported us and described us, so I assumed I had to keep a low profile. I hoped Don was doing the same.

Satisfied I could get up safely and continue, I painfully stood up and made my way through the arch into the outer corridor, intend on ignoring my aching muscles and reaching the press box to make an announcement for Ashley and maybe Don now, then tell the authorities our story and ask for police protection because of John and his partners.

And then go home.

Lost in these thoughts, I ran right into some poor man and we both nearly went down.

"My gosh, are you all r—"

But I never finished my sentence because I was looking right into the narrowing eyes of John Katsarus.

100

IT WAS USELESS; Brenda had been devoured by the crowd. After a few minutes of fruitless searching among the jostling throng, Don realized that it would be more productive to get to the press box. That was their intended destination anyway.

So he gave up his search for Brenda and headed immediately to the ramp leading to the higher levels.

Don was surprised that no one was guarding the ramp, but then again, he was on the east side of the stadium, the opposite side of the complex from the press box. He shook his head; they were assuming that the press box was where everything was being controlled. It *seemed* like a logical assumption, but everything he'd seen on this trip so far indicated anything but logic and forethought were involved.

But the objective wasn't too far out of his way. And they *did* make announcements from the press box; there'd be microphones up there somewhere, and if no one was manning the controls and if there was power to those systems, with his geek background, he was sure he could get something working.

Hopefully, Brenda was within earshot because he couldn't imagine getting a second shot at an announcement after he sent the first. Once they found someone playing with their PA system, Don was sure the management and maybe even the police or the National Guard contingent would descend upon him and drag him to the nearest Gulag.

So one announcement and he'd have to leave the press box.

On his way up, Don kept track of each level he reached. The press box was on four, he was sure of it after counting up when he and Brenda got in past those guards.

He also thought about what he was going to say. *"Ashley Meyers, Ashley Meyers, Ashley Meyers, meet your parents on level four, outside the press box."*

It was good, short, and to the point; he could get that off several times before they raided him. He was sure of that too.

And he wouldn't mention Brenda by name. It would be better for now to keep her stealthy and in the shadows. Much better for the plan.

The higher he climbed, the less fresh air there seemed to be. Despite three holes in the dome, which he noticed when he and Brenda first poked their heads out to the main floor, it was stuffy and hot and getting worse, not to mention the smell. He'd never forget that smell as long as he lived.

When he reached level four, he strolled out into the surrounding hall. There were many of the same vendor windows as was on the first level, and like those vendors, they were all closed and dark.

Making his way to where he thought the entrance to the press box or offices were, Don noticed few people milling around.

Good.

Less trouble. Less explaining. Less chance of him ending up in the pokey.

As he neared the midpoint of the hallway, though, just outside the office area, he heard what sounded like someone in trouble. Muffled screams and cries coming from the hallway on the other side of the offices. It led to the bathrooms.

Damn.

But it wasn't his problem. He was on a mission. He couldn't possibly stop unless it was…

Ashley! That sounded like *Ashley*!

He froze. The old feelings were coming back. But he just had to know.

Moving slowly and keeping to the outside wall, Don approached the opening to the hall that led to the bathrooms and listened carefully.

It was definitely someone struggling, and he'd be damned if it didn't sound like Ashley.

Bending down low, he peered around the corner.

The two things he saw appalled him. The first was a cop lying prone on the ground, bleeding and, oddly enough, his service weapon still in its belt holster. The second was some thug with his pants down to his ankles, thrusting into Ashley!

Don felt dizzy; his muscles wanted to move, but they couldn't. Rene was screaming and beating the guy on top of her.

Don's eyes started welling up with frustrated tears. As he wiped them, they darted to the cop's holster. If he crawled, he might get to the gun before he got noticed.

Shaking, he forced himself to go down on all fours and then his belly. Inch by inch, he made his way to the prone form of the cop and the holstered gun.

All the while, Rene was crying.

Don made a mental note to rack the slide. Who knew if these people carried a weapon ready to go? He prayed that when he did that and if a round ejected, that it wasn't the last round.

Slowly, as the thug started to mention his pending orgasm, Don reached the gun and carefully, slowly, quietly pulled it out of the holster. Then he stood up.

He put the gun behind his back.

"Freeze, you fucking bastard!"

The thug turned and sneered. "Fuck you," he said, eyes starting to roll into the back of his head.

The gun came out from behind Don's back.

Don walked right up to them and took careful aim.

"Get off her!" he said, voice breaking. The thug didn't look up at him, didn't even slow down. Underneath the thug, the female face of his victim slid to the side, barely out of harm's way.

Don racked the slide and pointed it at the back of his father's head. He grabbed the gun with two hands to steady himself, then squeezed the trigger as his sister screamed.

The back of the thug's head immediately erupted in an explosion of red that could only be described as a Fourth of July fireworks finally. Ashley screamed.

"That's for Rene," Don said quietly.

101

"Dad?"

Ashley's voice should have been weak and unsure. But she was scrambling to get out from under the corpse that covered her. The action wasn't consistent with Don's memory of the event nearly four decades ago, and it brought him back to reality.

Rene was long gone. Her face morphed back to Ashley's, and Don felt the pain that seemed just beyond his radar for all these years.

After she extracted herself, Ashley curled up on the floor in the fetal position, clothes torn and failing to cover her.

When his mind completely defogged, he realized that Ashley was partly naked, and he immediately looked away.

"You should, uh, get dressed."

Even to Don, it sounded callous, so he bent down and lifted her up, trying to avert his eyes. She was difficult for him to pick up as she was still feeling the aftereffects of the assault and wasn't really helping much.

When he managed to get her on her feet, he helped her pull up her pants, and she shakily buttoned her shirt using the remaining buttons.

Then she burst out crying and fell into his arms.

Recovering himself, he gently stroked her hair and hugged her gently, truly at a loss for what to do or say.

"Ashley, we should get out of here," he said as gently as he could.

"Where's Mom?" she cried into his chest.

He shrugged as they broke their embrace. "Good question. I lost her on the first level. I was looking for the press box to make an announcement to find you. Now I guess I'll have to wait for your mother. She's bound to show up at the press box. That's where we agreed to make the announcement for you over the PA system."

As he spoke, Don began to carefully wipe off the cop's gun on his shirt. He stooped when finished to place it in the cop's hand. He used his shirttail to hold the gun.

"What are you doing?" Ashley asked between sobs and sniffs.

"Look, your mother and I had to, um…bend a few rules to find you. I just don't want them to pile on any more accusations that I'd have a hard time explaining," he said.

Ashley was confused but nodded slowly. She was unsure but would trust him. He knew her only too well.

After he finished placing the gun, Don reached over and gently prodded her toward the main hallway.

"Are you all right? Can you walk?" he asked.

She nodded. "Kind of had a bad day," she sniffed, still trying to completely stop crying.

Then she stopped short, nearly pulling Don off-balance. "Oh gosh! Aunt May is…Aunt May is…"

"Dead. We know, it's all right," Don said when Ashley couldn't finish her sentence. "We went to the assisted-living center first."

She pulled away from him suddenly. "Did you find a guy named Bruno?"

"We know all about him too. He stole John Katsarus's boat, which is why it took us so long to get here."

Ashley just stood there, jaw hanging open. But Don could hear people gathering about, and he really, really didn't want to have to explain the two dead bodies.

"Look, let's go find your mother," he said, a bit less gently.

He was also trying to pick up the pace. She'd never understand the issues they had to sort out, but he'd rather not have to sort them out for the police. Not now, not here.

Still, she wasn't moving, and he had to walk back, put his arm around her shoulders, and get her walking again. "We've all had truly a life-changing experience down here, Ash. This storm has changed us. Changed us fundamentally."

She stopped and pulled away again, to Don's irritation. "You and Mom, you're not...you're not going to *divorce*, are you?"

Don looked around. Groups of people were starting to investigate the noise, so he turned around as if they were coming from the opposite direction. He turned Ashley too to complete the masquerade.

"Look, I've never lied to you. You know that, right?" he asked her.

When she nodded silently, he went on, "Well, I can honestly say I don't know. Your mom and I, we have to sort things out. And we're wiped out now from this quest. You're just going to have to give it time, like we will."

She slowly nodded acceptance, but he could tell she was skeptical. She looked back toward the cop and the thug, lying together in the bathroom hallway.

"C'mon. Let's find your mom. That's the most important thing," he said, flashing a worried glance at some people who were watching them closely.

102

My heart must have stopped a hundred times over the last twenty-four hours or so, but this time, my blood froze in my veins. Now I understood the fight-or-flight response; I was contemplating kicking him and running like hell, or maybe just running like hell.

Either way, John would probably catch up to me given my state of fitness and fatigue. And if I kicked him and hurt him, he'd just catch me angrier.

John took a moment to recover as well. At first, I could see the anger in his eyes, but then it seemed to soften a little. Maybe those old feelings for me would protect me.

Maybe not.

And then there was Don. Speaking of which, I didn't see John's partners. As I looked behind him for the hitmen, I noticed I was shaking in the heat.

"Where are your buddies, John? Hunting for Don?"

John rubbed the bridge of his nose and squinted as if trying to rid himself of a major headache.

"You better come with me, Brenda."

That was all he said, and I found it plenty threatening.

"Like hell! I'm not going *anywhere* with you. You're going to have my husband killed and probably me too now. I swear to God, you come any closer and I'll scream! And I'll be screaming your name as loud as I can!"

"Brenda, for your own good, you'd better come with me to the press box. It's where—"

But he was interrupted by what I thought was a gunshot!

I could tell John thought it was too because he involuntarily ducked and glanced in the direction of the sound.

It's what he did next that nearly made me lose control of my bowels. He whipped out a gun. This was not quite as big as the "I'm-compensating-for-something" cannon he had in his damned yellow toolbox, but one with big enough hole on the end of the barrel.

He waved it and made sure it was clear what he wanted me to do. I was to walk ahead of him in the direction he was thrusting his gun.

Everything in my body said, "Girl, you're dead if you do this," but that gunshot, it meant somebody might have just taken a bullet, and another part of me was worried sick about Don.

And now Ashley.

For a long minute, I didn't budge. Then finally, John stared back at me.

"Move," he snarled, and my body betrayed me as it automatically obeyed.

103

Ashley was slowly coming back to reality. She desperately wanted a hot shower, and now she'd not get any rest until she was sure she didn't have some disease. Still, she felt like she was in a fog or some show that she was watching. She was raw, and every step was painful.

And they needed to find the police to report this.

When her father stopped short, she nearly ran into him.

"What is it, Daddy?"

He waved his hand—shush.

Looking up, all she could see was the group of people being led by some scrawny-looking dude with a polo shirt that had a likeness of the Superdome embroidered over the breast pocket. They were jabbering away to each other, and it sounded like they were from Great Britain.

What could Dad possibly find so upsetting about these people? After all, she was just *raped*!

Then she saw them—her mother and their neighbor. Wait, their *neighbor*?

"Stay here and keep out of sight," her father said to her.

"Wait, what? Why?"

But even as the words left her mouth, she saw it—the gun.

It wasn't exactly pointing at her mother, but their neighbor, Mr. John Katsarus, was doing a lousy job of keeping it hidden. In fact, he was even gesturing with it.

The sight of Mr. Katsarus and Mom and a gun was just too much for Ashley to comprehend.

"Daddy? What's going on?"

"Just do as I told you," he said, trying to move behind some folks in the large tour group.

"Like hell! He's got a *gun*, Daddy! What's going on?"

Her father closed his eyes tightly, then just as quickly reopened them. He hissed, "Okay, you asked for it. See, your mother and Katsarus there are having an affair."

On top of everything that she'd been through today and now hearing this, Ashley's knees nearly gave out.

"It's true," Don went on. "They used to be engaged when we were all in college, your mom, Katsarus, and I. They had a falling out, and that's when I got a chance to ask her out. But they've managed to rekindle things. At least I'm sure of it. And they plan on killing me down here where the disaster could cover up any evidence."

"What?"

Ashley's head was spinning. Briefly, she entertained the thought that her father was suffering heat stroke. But the look on his face was so…so serious!

"I can't believe—" she started but Don cut her off.

"It's true. Your mother even admitted it. That's why I want to keep out of sight. I thought that she had given up on Katsarus, but it looks different now."

"Daddy, he's got a gun!"

"He's not pointing it at her. Something's up, and I want to find out what it is. Besides, he hired some of his mob buddies to help him out, and they've got to be near, so I don't want to be seen."

It was too much. Mob buddies? *Hitmen? An affair? Wanting her father dead?*

Ashley was quickly reaching emotional overload.

She couldn't help it. It was beyond her self-control limits. She called out to her mother.

"Mom? Why does Mr. Katsarus have a gun?"

The whole world of the fourth level in the Superdome exploded. It became a scene of mass panic. The Brits glanced first at the girl who had yelled gun, then to where she was looking.

When they saw the gun, pandemonium erupted. Suddenly, people were running every which way and screaming. There must have been about forty people in the tour group, and suddenly, everybody wanted to be someplace else, in a hurry.

When the crowed thinned out, Ashley was standing in the middle of the hallway, facing her mother and alleged lover with a gun, alone.

Her father was nowhere to be seen.

104

Okay, I should have been overwhelmed at seeing Ashley. Oh, she looked like hell, but so did we, and after all, finding her was the goal of the entire trip.

So I should have been overjoyed, except, with John behind me holding a gun and knowing his assassins brought him to the Superdome and they were most likely close by, well, that kicked all the joy I felt right out of me.

"Ashley! Run! Go get help!"

It was all I could think of to say. So, *so* different from what I had wanted to say to her when I found her.

But John had other ideas. That bastard trotted over and took hold of her arm to pull her toward me. He knew I wouldn't run with her under his control.

So I did the next best thing. When they got back to my side of the hallway, I started screaming and hitting, kicking, and scratching as hard as I could.

John shoved me away and down a narrow hallway which led, I guessed, to the press box. He kept shoving Ashley and me the whole length of the corridor.

"You touch her one more time you fucking asshole!"

But he shoved me through a door which swung open, and I fell into the room.

I could hear Ashley fighting with John, yelling at him to leave her mother alone and to drop the gun, and suddenly she was kicking and hitting and scratching too.

"Shut up, you two! You want to make a scene, fine, but I'm tellin' ya, it's in your best interest to shut the hell up," he snarled.

All the while, he never pointed the gun at us. He was going to let his professional partners do the dirty work. And here I thought he was a real man.

His whole life he had tried to live the macho life, so unlike Don. He even chided Don for his lack of manliness.

But in the end, he was a coward and was going to let someone else do his dirty work.

The problem now was that we were all alone, with a gunman, in a private room with no one else to help us.

105

Behind me, I could hear Ashley kicking and hitting or at least *trying* to fight John.

Bless her sweet little heart; she had plenty of fight left in her. I could only imagine what she had been through today, but she was up to the fight with all the tenacity of a cornered, wounded animal.

But her efforts were useless. John absorbed all the hits and kicks she could actually connect and slowly forced her down the four steps to the main level of the broadcast booth.

I had started to look for options like another way out. There was only one exit, and that was on the top tier of the steps we just came down and John made sure he stayed in between us and that door.

Each step was associated with a row of stadium seating although quite a bit more luxurious than your typical arena seating. Instead of velour, these were upholstered in premium leather.

Nice digs for reporters and their guests, indeed, but the knowledge didn't help us one bit.

There was a glass window on the wall next to the steps down from the vendor's hall. On the other side of the wall, I could see a room and all sorts of electrical equipment, switches, and a few microphones. Maybe it was the engineering booth for the broadcasts.

There was no way in, though. Not from this room.

Ashley had come down the steps and thrown her arms around me. Despite our desperate situation, I couldn't help myself. I did the same and I'm sure she felt my tears as they fell from my cheeks.

"Mom, don't worry! Dad's out there, and he's going for help! You should have seen the way he shot a guy who was..." I got the distinct impression that she didn't want to tell me something, but she continued. "Trying to attack me! Dad was *awesome*!"

Those last three words were meant more for John than me. But I knew what she was talking about and once again wondered and marveled at just who that man out there had become.

This trip was sure full of surprises, like my husband becoming an accomplished assassin or maybe a superhero. I guess the title depended on whose side you were on.

"I thought there would be people here. Where is everyone?" John asked no one in particular.

"What do you want with us, John? Are you going to kill *us* too?" I asked. Ashley snapped her gaze up at me.

"Ladies, please sit down. We have a few things to talk about."

I just hugged Ashley harder and did my best to ignore John.

"Ladies, I've asked you politely. We have a problem, and I need your full attention. Now if you want to live, I suggest you sit down."

I looked up and saw the anger flash in John's eyes, and by that look, I decided that we'd better sit down. Sitting would calm me a bit, and I could think.

We sat in the first row of seats, me pulling Ashley down beside me. I made sure I was between her and John. But as we occupied the chairs, we held each other's hands. I didn't want to let go of her ever again.

"I know you believe that I am trying to kill your husband."

"Well, that shoot-out at the assisted-living center pretty much clinches it, I believe," I snapped.

John paused, then took a breath and went on.

"Well, I admit it. I did. My feelings for you, Brenda, have driven me insane. I have simply never stopped loving you. There. I said it."

"So that makes it okay to kill my father?" Ashley spat.

"No. No, it doesn't," John said, his whole posture softening. "That's why I tried to call it off."

"Yeah, good job there, John. Excuse me while I feign belief, especially since you guys were shooting at us at the center," I said.

"I wasn't shooting. I didn't even have a gun."

"But you weren't exactly trying to get them to stop, were you?" I pointed out.

He took another quick, deep breath. "No. You're right. I was angry."

"Yeah, well I'd hate to see you when you get pissed then," Ashley said.

"Ashley..." I began.

But John interrupted me. "Well, okay, it doesn't matter what you two think of me. What matters is that at any minute, two very nasty and very professional killers may come through that door, and we'd better be ready for them or gone. I want you to promise me that you'll stick with me so I can protect you."

"Shooting at us is protecting us, how, John?" I asked.

"I made a *mistake*, okay? And I thought there would be more people up here so I could turn myself in. The only way we're going to survive is to kill them or join the witness protection program. Believe me, I have enough dirt on them to put them away permanently if I can just stay alive."

I don't know what it was, but despite the fact I knew John was a great salesman, I was starting to tolerate him. I could tell by Ashley's expression she wasn't, but I saw something in his eyes. Desperation? Fear? It was really unsettling.

"Ashley, see if you can call anyone on those phones. John, can you lock that door? Barricade it? I'll see if I can get anyone's attention at the window," I said, instantly going into problem-solving mode.

Ashley looked at me like I was crazy, but the do-it-now expression I flashed her got her moving. John was midway up the steps, saying that he was going to try to jam the lock, when it happened.

The door burst open, and two very angry men stepped into the room, guns drawn.

106

It was like someone flipped a switch in John, and all the faith I had put in him just moments before simply evaporated.

"I thought you were staying on the ground level to wait for me," he said to the two men, still on the stairs and obviously checking out the room.

"Yeah, well, when you pawned us off on that damned camera crew, VT here became a national TV star," the more fit, taller man said. "And we didn't like the lack of teamwork on your part, Katsarus. We figured we needed to protect our investment."

The one called VT snarled but said nothing. They both waved their pistols. I'm no expert, but they looked really military compared to John's. It didn't matter, though. John seemed glad to see them.

Of course, he could be faking it, but something told me John was playing both sides, so either way, he'd end up a winner.

Typical John.

During the pleasantries, my thoughts turned to Don. I wondered, and I worried. I hoped that Don had really done what Ashley had told me—gone for help. He should have no trouble finding either a policeman or a guardsman.

The question was, like the news crew, would the authorities find his story too far-fetched and shrug him off?

The one called VT was clearly the boss. He turned to John.

"Well, what the fuck are you waiting for, Katsarus? Go out and find Meyers."

Ashley was going to say something, but I grabbed her shoulder and squeezed hard. She got the message and said nothing. I was afraid that she was about to harp on the fact Don had gone to find help, and that tidbit of information would cause these people to finish us off sooner rather than later.

Shit! It suddenly dawned on me; we'd seen their faces! We could identify them; they *did* mean to kill us! Even if we made it out of here and got away, we would never be free from them; the rest of our lives we'd be looking over our shoulders!

Threatening me was one thing, but my baby? It was settled; I had to fight to the death—hopefully theirs, not Ashley's or mine.

I started to discreetly look around for things I could use as weapons. Whatever happened, it was up to me. I couldn't afford to wait for Don. And while he had acquitted himself well today against people who would have hurt us, half those people were drunk, and the gang outside the drugstore wasn't expecting us to be armed and employing guerrilla tactics.

These men were far more professional than the others Don had faced. I'm guessing they wouldn't make the same mistakes.

The only question was, which side would John join?

The winning side, no doubt.

So I had to make sure we were the winning side. Anything—any single object—no matter how small or insignificant that could swing the odds in our favor, that's what I desperately needed.

I noted the big base of the microphones on the table below the windows looking out on the playing field. But they were connected to cables, and it would take a moment for anyone to disconnect them to be of any use. By that time, the person trying to disconnect them would be dead.

"Look, Meyers knows what I look like. He doesn't know what you look like. It's wiser if both of you go out there and corner him," John said.

I couldn't tell what his game was, but I liked the idea of him being in here with us instead of the professional hitmen. On the other hand, it meant that Don was in grave danger if those two went looking for him.

I didn't have much time to think about it. The one called VT spoke up.

"I don't trust you, Katsarus. I think just one of us should go."

It was time for me to speak up. "Well, if you want to find my husband, just look for the squad of policemen and National Guard coming this way. He'll be leading them here," I tried to say as evenly as possible without any fear in my voice.

Everyone looked at me. If VT could spit, I think he would have, right in my face.

"I'll go. Zanetti, you stay here and watch them," he said.

He pulled his FEMA baseball cap down over his eyes and turned to take the two steps up to the door. Then he was gone. Now the odds were a little better.

"Left to face the police alone, nice of your boss to do that to you," I said.

He looked at me and squinted. I wanted to glance over at John to see if I could tell by his expression what he was thinking—what side he would choose—but I dared not take my eyes off of Zanetti.

The plan was to rush him if he lifted his gun toward me or Ashley. It was all I had. Then it was up to John to either help or…

"Thanks for caring, Mrs. Meyers. But don't worry, no matter what happens to my *boss*, I can take care of myself."

He wouldn't stop staring at me.

"What are you going to do to us?" I asked him, hoping my fear wouldn't come out in my tone.

He paid no attention. Instead, he leveled the gun at Ashley. I instinctively pulled her behind me as she yelped.

"What kind of a man shoots a girl?" I yelled.

John spoke up and Zanetti pointed his gun at him.

"You know, she's right, Zanetti. There is another way, you know."

"No, there isn't. Go ahead and make all the noise you want, by the way. This place is soundproof. That's what a broadcasting booth is," he said, and then he aimed at me.

"You know, this is a 9 mm HK. This little round will go right through you, Mrs. Meyers, and take out your daughter too."

"You bastard!" I screamed. I was darting my head and eyes around quickly now, desperate to find something, anything, that I could use.

John provided it for me.

He raised his gun and aimed it right at Zanetti. "You leave them the fuck alone, you useless shit! You move wrong. You *flinch* a muscle and I'll take you out, you son of a bitch!"

It was convincing enough for me. But unfortunately, not enough for Zanetti, who started to laugh.

"Katsarus, you stupid fuck! We only gave you one bullet! That gun is tricked out to not lock back when it's empty. Go ahead, take your best shot!"

Zanetti held his arms out wide.

"Yeah, well, funny thing about cops down here, Tony. Lots of them are open to doing business for the right price. How do you know I didn't buy a magazine from a few of them?" John asked, smiling and still aiming right at Zanetti's head.

Zanetti chuckled. "You stupid moron, Katsarus! I'm a *professional*. I do my homework. The cops down here are issued Glock 22s as their service weapon, Johnny Boy. Big ol' .40 caliber. Won't work in that .45."

John swallowed hard and squeezed the trigger.

Silence. Not even a click.

He racked the slide quickly and squeezed again, and this time there was a click, but it was obvious the gun wasn't loaded.

The look on his face matched the feeling in my stomach. Zanetti was laughing now and aiming his gun at John. But he never got a chance to fire it. Instead, John threw his gun at Zanetti, who ducked.

Unfortunately, that meant that the shot fired from the doorway, missed its mark, and just grazed Zanetti's shoulder.

But it was good enough to make him drop his HK, and it slid under the broadcast desk lining the outer wall below the plate glass windows.

My hearing gone again, I naturally looked to where the shot had been fired from. Don was at the door on the top step.

Wait…Don?

Zanetti grunted in pain but recovered quickly. He dodged a tackle by John and sprinted up the stairs, punching Don in the gut before a surprised Don could aim the gun he was carrying. But Don kept hold of the gun as Zanetti sidestepped him and ran out the door.

"Uh, thanks, Don," John nearly muttered. I knew he hated to be in Don's debt, but at least he recognized it.

Don said, "Oh, don't mention it," as he raised his gun and shot John in the belly.

107

Ashley and I both screamed at the same time. I went a little further.

"Don! What've you done?"

"I've begun solving problems, Brenda."

It was unnerving, the calm and clarity in his voice that came through despite my hearing loss. I studied the man I had hurriedly married twenty-two years ago, but the man standing on the top step and slowly starting to descend to our level was a complete stranger.

He'd shot how many people today? Five, counting the rapist attacking Ashley. And he hasn't shown any signs of being affected by it at all. For all I knew, he could have been a hitman himself.

I scrambled over to John and put his head in my hands. He was lying on the floor, on his back, the front of his shirt growing a nasty stain of red near his stomach.

Ashley came over and knelt by me, putting her hand on my shoulder.

John looked up at me and coughed. "I'm sorry, Brenda. You might not believe it, but I am. I never meant to hurt you or put you in danger. I fucked up, and I guess I'm paying the price now."

"Shh, don't talk," I said. "You're going to make it. Just hang in there. We'll get help."

I started to turn to Ashley, but Don had other ideas.

"Well, no, no one is going anywhere. You see, John, this is payback for the hell you've put me through during my marriage."

I snapped at Don. "You son of a bitch! I've *never* been unfaithful to you! John and I ended our relationship that night two decades ago, and that was it!"

Very quietly and while he took another step down, still holding his gun out, Don nodded.

"Oh, I know," he said. "That's not what I meant. Tell me, Brenda, have you ever noticed anything about Ashley's eyes?"

My throat constricted. Where was he going with this?

"Are you *insane*? What the hell are you babbling about, Don?"

He looked directly at Ashley. "You know, your mother and I had to get married, right?"

"Jesus, Don! Have you gone mad?" I screamed.

Ashley glanced at me for reassurance. Her breaths were coming in short, audible gasps. She was afraid, and I couldn't blame her.

"Don, John is badly hurt. He needs a doctor. Do you understand? You understand, right, Don?"

He didn't even look at me.

"You see, Ashley, your mother slept with me the night she discovered this pathetic ape in bed with her college roommate," Don spoke as he took another step down and nearer to us.

John winced.

"Don, Ashley is going to go get help. You don't want to become a murderer, do you? It was just a badly aimed shot, understand?" I tried to convince Don we wouldn't turn him in if he just let Ashley go and get help.

He was having none of it.

"And she got pregnant. Well, just my luck, right?" Don said, nearly laughing.

"Don, this isn't the place or time—"

But he cut me off. "Oh yes, now is the place *and* time, Brenda. Do you remember how jaundiced Ashley was when she was born?"

Ashley stiffened. I turned to her and said, "You're okay. It's more normal than you think." Then I flashed as threatening an expression to Don as I could muster.

"What does this have to do with anything, Don?"

"Everyone has to know. It's time. Well, the nurse showed me the stats. You never knew it, but I have type O. So does your mother," he said, turning to me. "Our child could only have type O."

Ashley looked at Don. "But I have type A," she said haltingly.

"Yes, I know," Don said.

"I have type AB," John gasped, suddenly looking at Ashley in amazement.

Ashley stood up, horrified. She looked at me, then to John, then back at me. Now she was livid.

"So you *did* have an affair!"

My head was spinning. It was so long ago. I mean, I was *engaged* to John! I found him cheating, and Don had always been hanging around, you know? I knew he wanted to ask me out, but he never approached me even though we had two classes together. I was so hurt and mad that I went right to his dorm room, and he took me in that night and…Well, one thing led to another. Two months later, just a few weeks before graduation, I found out I was pregnant. John and I had always been so careful, so naturally, Don and I figured…

"No, Ashley, they didn't. John Katsarus is your father. It seems I was able to sleep with your mother on the first date not because she was easy but because she was vulnerable. Little did I know, until you were born, that you were actually a gift to your mother from her former fiancé."

108

I was trembling with so many different emotions—rage, regret, fear.

"You knew this the whole time and you never thought to tell me?" I yelled.

Don grinned and shrugged. "I didn't want you to go back to John," he said. "That would have been not only bad for you, but John would have won."

Ever get so mad that your vision throbs?

"You *fucking asshole*! This was about *winning*? I thought you were a decent man, Meyers!" I nearly spit the name out.

John reached over and took my hand. He was struggling to sit up.

There was no stopping it. The fatigue, rage, and everything else just came out as a steady flow of tears. John reached up and tried to wipe them away, but the storm surge of emotions couldn't be stopped.

"Things would have been different if I only knew, Brenda. Please…believe me…"

I tried to get him to rest, but he painfully struggled up to a kneeling position and paused, trying to catch his breath.

He looked at Don. "So what's the plan, Don? What's next?"

I wasn't ready to change the subject, but I had to wonder why John was so calm. What was he up to? I was afraid to find out. I could bet that it meant the end for John, probably me, and maybe, just maybe, Ashley. Don had just stated that he had no physical ties to the child who called him dad her entire life.

Well, I wasn't about to let that happen.

"Ah," Don said, sighing and shrugging, "the plan is I live happily ever after with Amy, our financial troubles a thing of the past. We'll sell your businesses, John, and maybe sail away to Tahiti."

"And what about us, Don?" I asked.

"Well, you don't."

"You'll never get away with it. You're not *man* enough," John coughed, pushing off me slightly.

"You know, that's funny, John. I've killed five people today, maybe a sixth from a throat punch. You see, I confess. I've been misrepresenting my distaste for guns, Brenda. Instead of working late, I've been renting all sorts of handguns at the gun shop's range on the outskirts of town. They have great marksmanship classes. I have to admit, guns are sort of addicting. They can solve a lot of problems."

"You're just full of surprises this trip, aren't you, Donny Boy?" John grunted as he got to his knees. He must have been in incredible pain, yet he was so focused that he resisted my attempts to pull him back down because of his bleeding.

"Yeah. I was just waiting for the proper moment to take you two out. Thank God for hurricanes though, right?" Don chuckled. "Sorry, Ashley. I didn't plan this sort of end for you. You were supposed to be the grieving daughter. We'd become estranged after I left with Amy, but at least you would have been alive. This sort of works out a little better, though. Kind of puts the exclamation point on closure, with all of you gone. I never have to look over my shoulder again," Don said, smiling and shrugging as if he were just observing a stain on the floor.

"Well, Donny Boy, there are three of us and only one puny little you. You can't shoot us all at once," John said, painfully and heroically getting to his feet.

I stood too, ready to leap at Don, and continue to pummel him no matter if I was the one he shot or not.

I wasn't going to let the father of my child do this alone.

"No, I can't, but I don't have to," Don said, taking aim at Ashley.

John deliberately fell toward Ashley, pushing her down and under the broadcasting desk.

"So touching, a father protecting his daughter," Don said, now aiming at me instead of Ashley and John in a heap. John had pushed a wheeled broadcaster's chair in front of Ashley.

I was ready. "Go ahead, asshole. You haven't been able to stop us yet. You were never much of a father or provider. Go ahead and show Ashley who you really are," I screamed.

"Um, Brenda, she's not my daughter, remember?"

Don raised his arms and paused. I guess he was a bit unnerved by my resolve—my fearlessness in the face of death. Behind me, I could hear John moving, but I didn't dare look in that direction because I didn't want Don to notice him.

"Go ahead, Don, if you can," I taunted him.

"Oh, I can, Brenda. Time to die," he said, squinting an eye and taking aim for my head.

"Not so fast," VT's voice rang out from the top of the steps.

109

Don spun around to face VT. They both had their guns trained on each other.

I glanced at John. He was on the move, motioning to Ashley to stay down. He glanced at me and put his finger across his lips, then hunched down and, as quietly as a stalking panther, moved toward Don.

"Drop it, shithead," Don yelled.

Very calmly, very quietly, VT squinted. "Um, no," he said lowly.

"I've already killed five people today," Don insisted.

"Good for you," VT deadpanned. "You're now up to the rank of amateur."

John was moving a step closer, but teetering. If I moved to help steady him, I'm sure it would draw the wrong kind of attention to him.

So I waited impatiently.

I did, however, notice that John had Zanetti's gun behind his back. I glanced at Ashley, who was numb with fear, her lower lip trembling as if she were freezing. I couldn't risk going over to comfort her, so I just did the best I could. I winked at her.

I'm sure she thought I'd lost my mind.

"I mean it," Don was saying.

"Yes, VT, he does, I'm afraid," John said and kicked out, sweeping Don's legs out from under him. As Don went down, John took aim at VT and pulled the trigger.

But he was falling too, and the shot went through VT's upper arm, forcing him to drop the gun.

On the way down, John drew another bead on VT, but the mobster turned and ducked out of the door at the top of the steps, yelling back over his shoulder, "This isn't over!"

John fell against me, and we both sank down to the hard, cold lower step. He looked up at me and grinned, a sad sort of grin.

"Well, it is for me. Brenda, I am…so…sorry for…everything. You are and always have been the…love…of…my life."

"Shh," I told him. "Ashley! Go run for help! Hurry!"

She took off like a frightened rabbit, leaping up the stairs.

"Hang on, John! Please stay with me. Look at me. Look at me, damn it! You're going to be okay!"

But John coughed up some blood. Despite that, he struggled to speak.

"You'll never…know how sorry…I…love…"

And like that, his life ebbed away, right in my arms.

I never got a chance to thank him or even tell him I loved him.

110

I started dry heaving. The pain was that gut-wrenching.

"Noooo!" I wailed.

"Touching. Very touching."

I froze, but not out of fear—out of sheer anger.

Don had struggled to his feet by now and was taking aim at me. But he just couldn't resist rubbing it in one last time, child that he was.

"I have to go and shoot Ashley now in public. So I'm going to need a hat, and John's will do. Fitting, huh? Her father's hat will help me keep my identity secret."

John had fallen against me, and the gun he was using had ended up right in my lap. Was it a last act of love?

I'll never know. But I'll always remember it that way.

I grabbed his wrist with my left hand and the pistol in my right, quickly getting my finger inside the trigger guard, and raised the gun.

Center mass. That's the term I've heard bantered around on countless police shows and John's own advice.

Center mass.

I aimed and pulled the trigger. The noise wasn't as loud as the other guns, and I guessed that big tube on the end of the gun barrel acted like some kind of muffler; it made the shot seem so much less leathal and quiet.

But the shot went over Don's head. It sure as hell surprised him, though. His eyes were wide with shock, and he ducked then started to recover, taking aim at me once more.

I didn't wait. Correcting down, I pulled the trigger. The gun kicked like a mule.

Don's former center mass erupted in a ballet of blood and gore. He staggered back, dropping the gun. The look on his face was somewhere between shock and fear.

I squeezed again, and his chest belched more blood and tissue. I had completely lost my hearing.

"Brenda," he started to mouth as he raised his arms, reaching out to me.

I fired again, then again.

He went down, but I wasn't finished. What did John say? When in doubt, empty the magazine?

So I did. By the time I was done, Don's face was unrecognizable. It was as if I wanted to erase that image from my mind by obliterating it from the world.

When the gun would fire no more, I realized I was standing over Don's body, and I dropped my arms, the gun falling behind me near John.

I sank back to my knees, head in hands, smelling the gunpowder and sweat, mixing with my tears.

There I stayed for a moment, between John and Don, sort of where I've been my entire life. Now they were both gone.

111

"Mom! Mom! Are you all right?"

With the ringing in my ears, I could barely hear the footsteps scrambling toward me. But when a shadow eclipsed the garish fluorescent lighting from above, I lifted my gaze, looking like Tammy Faye after a prayer meeting, I was sure.

What I saw didn't help stabilize my frame of mind. Ashley was pulling, of all people, Billy Bob Lee ahead of no less than five National Guardsmen.

Then came the medics, two of them dressed in a vivid green vest with the letters EMT emblazoned across their chests and backs. One of them checked on me, then John. The other bent over Don.

"This one's gone," the EMT over John said.

"Oh yeah, this one too, what's left of him" coughed the EMT over Don.

And then Ashley was next to me on the ground, hugging me, crying with me, and we just stayed there for a moment, enjoying the fact that we were still alive.

We had made it.

We had survived Katrina when so many of the people in our lives hadn't.

"I know this is not the best time, but some people want to talk to you, Mrs. Meyers," Billy Bob was saying in my ear, his hand gently patting my shoulder.

I looked up to see VT in handcuffs, controlled from behind by the largest police officer I had ever seen. He asked Ashley, "Is this the guy?"

Ashley turned, looked, and nodded quietly. The cop dragged VT away, behind the doorframe and out into the hallway.

He kept scowling at me despite being yanked away.

I looked back at John, now being covered by the medic. I never gave Don so much as a glance.

He didn't deserve it.

112

November 2005

VT had been meticulous. No loose ends.

Thanks to his father's lawyer, he had made bail and was holding up in Vittoria, Sicily, protected from Chicago's Finest and the Feds for that matter. He was vapor.

Yes, family connections ran deep in the motherland.

He swirled his wine for the millionth time and took a sip.

This was the life. It was a well-known fact that the family takes care of its own.

He thought of Katsarus briefly. The big dumb bastard had paid the ultimate price for his stupidity. He actually *cared* for that woman.

What a fucking idiot.

Like he did every night of the week, VT sat at the same private dining table at the sidewalk café, awaiting the veal scaloppini. He never heard the car coast down the narrow street behind him, but the people around him sure noticed the black sedan, slowly moving down the tiny cobblestoned street.

As if one body, they all got up and suddenly had someplace else to be.

When the first bullet passed through his neck and wine glass, VT finally noticed. He noticed a few more places on his chest that had started erupting in bloody volcanic messes.

As he slumped over the remnants of his garlic bread appetizer, the thought occurred to him: *The family takes care of its own. No loose ends.*

113

Tony Zanetti thanked the digitized voice on the other end of the connection and closed the burner phone. He tossed it on VT's old desk and stood up. As he walked to the sliding patio doors toward the now-closed and covered-in-ground pool, he silently rehearsed how he would break the news to the don about the untimely demise of his son.

What words would make him sound as shocked as he should have been and to help him avoid a war between the Taccone family and the family he will insinuate? He would try to avoid this war, not out of guilt for falsely accusing another family but because wars were bad for business.

He stepped outside and slid the patio door closed. The cool, crisp November air got his blood flowing. It would be easier to think now. Maybe practice his performance and delivery of his lines.

It was not going to be easy to tell his new boss that his only son had been shot and killed and then try to talk the old man out of the Vendetta that was surely coming. The old man was not one to forgive, and it was going to get bloody. Both houses would be decimated, and Zanetti would then try to convince the old man that it was a rogue opportunist.

He drew in a deep breath and exhaled slowly.

As he did so, he heard the patio door slide open behind him. He turned to see the old man, Mr. Taccone, lifting his walker over the bottom-door rails with the help of two huge Sentinels.

Instantly, he was on high alert. This didn't look good.

"Tony, there you are."

Zanetti immediately moved toward the old man, hands out in a show of respect.

"I have some bad news, my friend," the old man said, his gravelly voice reverberating in Zanetti's ears.

Zanetti slowed. "Oh?"

The old man nodded, painfully, with a far-off look on his face.

"I have just received word from our overseas office. There has been a terrible, terrible tragedy."

Zanetti was almost too stiff to walk. "What kind of tragedy? Is VT all right?"

The old man paused a long time. Finally, he shook his head and lowered his eyes. "No."

Zanetti didn't know what to say. The old man knew already! How the hell did he find out so quickly?

There had to be an informant. His organization, the one he had worked so hard to take over when VT fucked up one time too many, had a fucking informant.

For the first time in his life, Zanetti was scared.

The old man finally leaned on the handlebars of his walker. He slowly looked up at Zanetti with the saddest expression Zanetti had ever witnessed from the old man. The don's face emerged from the shadows and did not look comforting.

"How long you been working for me, Tony? Over twenty years, am I right?"

Zanetti nodded. He was too afraid to speak. He was sure his voice would crack.

"You took care of a lot of loose ends for me, Tony. A lot of loose ends."

Zanetti nodded again, stealing quick glances at the two bodyguards on either side of the old man. They were not comforting faces.

"You took care of so many loose ends. Now, Tony, I would like to take care of you."

Zanetti's knees nearly buckled at the statement. When the next one came, the two goons had to come forward to keep Zanetti from falling.

"Now," the old man said, "let's go to Romano's to talk about your future. The car's out back."

He *knew*. Zanetti didn't know *how* the old man knew, but someone had snitched. The only regret Zanetti had was that he wasn't going to live long enough to find out who it was and give them some payback.

He was about to go for his last ride.

114

I HELD ASHLEY's hand as she sobbed silently.

She was the only one crying at the double funeral despite the crowd of people in attendance.

But I was the one who should have been crying. I screwed up her life. She never knew her real father, and if she *had* known, would John have been the person that everyone knew him to be? A slimy salesman who looked out for numero uno?

I wondered. I wondered how different my life would have been as well. An entirely useless exercise, I know, but I had to keep my mind occupied or I'd go to pieces.

We sat under the canopy at the cemetery, dressed head to toe in black, shivering from the damp, cold air. What few members there were of Amy's family, business associates of John's who *weren't* criminals, a smattering of former teammates and acquaintances were occupying the front few rows of chairs under the tent.

The pastor spoke about forgiveness or something like that, but I couldn't forgive myself for Ashley not having known her real father, for all the death and loss we'd experienced in the wake of Katrina. And now, Amy and John would be buried side by side for all eternity.

Something John wouldn't have wanted, I'm sure.

In the waiting limo, Ashley told me that I shouldn't blame myself, that while I may have made a flippant remark that day before Katrina changed our lives, it was John who took it seriously, opportunistic John who started the ball rolling—a ball that, in the end, ran over him, Don, Bruno, and Amy.

After what seemed like an eternity, the service concluded, and the funeral director invited everyone to the luncheon. I didn't want to go because I didn't want to have to answer a lot of awkward questions.

So we escaped into the limo without so much as saying a private prayer over the graves. What kind of person does that make me?

But as the chauffeur held our door open, one of John's cousins ambushed us and introduced himself. He seemed interested in Ashley, and when his son came up, I realized why. His son and Ashley were about the same age.

"No, I'm transferring to New York University to finish my senior year," I heard Ashley tell them. Then it was my turn.

"Yes, I knew John in school. No, he was my insurance agent and financial advisor. No, I don't know why I was listed as a beneficiary, and I really wish he hadn't done that."

The thought crossed my mind that the guy was some sort of detective as he dug deeper into my future.

"No, I'm moving to New York to be close to Ashley. I've got a new job there."

Finally, he handed me his card, and I had been right. He was an investigator for one of the major insurance companies John had brokered for.

Figures.

As a beneficiary of John's, I was probably a suspect in his death or maybe insurance fraud. John had a hell of an estate to give away.

I didn't want the money John had left me anyway; it was probably dirty. But if he had been laundering money for his partners, he'd covered his tracks well. I now owned a combination of securities and insurance payouts. All told, it came to low six-figure cash and with the house, well, $750,000 would eliminate all my debt and give Ashley the ability to pay off her student loans.

But after that, I intended to donate the rest of John's money to some charity that I could choose later after this guy cleared me of any wrongdoing, which he would eventually end up doing, of course.

With his card in my purse, I climbed into the limo after Ashley, and we put the cemetery, and metaphorically John, behind us.

As we were driven to our Chicago suburban home for one of the last times, I realized that I was so thankful that Ashley and I were going to be in the same city. See, turns out that when the truth came out about John, Don, and our situation and when they found Amy's and then May's body, everything changed.

We were no longer looters or charlatans, but heroes of some sort. Turns out that Billy Bob Lee's sister is the chief information officer of a large investment bank in New York, and she was looking for a chief technology officer.

A few phone calls and an in-person interview on Wall Street later, I had a new job.

Ashley turned to me. "Are you disappointed about giving up your dream of your own consulting business, Mom?"

"Where did that come from, honey?"

Ashley shrugged. "You look really distant."

"I was just thinking that I have never lived in New York, and… well, about all the memories I have of Chicago."

"It's going to be hard on you, isn't it?" she asked, snuggling close.

I shook my head quickly. "Not with you there. We're going to be just fine."

Ashley was obviously starting to feel it all now. She stared out the window at the buildings sliding by.

"How can you be so sure, Mom? Our whole life was, well, I dunno…"

As her voice trailed off, I reached for her hand and squeezed it.

"Now don't you start that, young lady. You'll be graduating in a year with your whole life ahead of you. And look, the equity position I'm taking in my new company means our financial troubles are *over* for good! I mean, really," I said to her, smiling.

She tried to smile. I put my arm around her shoulder, drawing her closer to me.

"Look, Lehman Brothers is the fourth largest investment bank in the world," I reminded her. "And I'm going to be their new chief technology officer. What could *possibly* go wrong?"

About the Author

Storm Surge is the debut thriller by John F. Banas. John read his first novel, *Andromeda Strain*, when he was just eight years old and has been hooked on thriller novels ever since. He is drawn to stories about average, everyday people who are thrust into impossible situations and called upon to reach above their skill and comfort level to survive.

John's first published work was a short story for an anthology titled *Down the Block*, a collection of tales about life in the big city.

Hard at work on his next thriller, John lives with his family in a suburb of Chicago, a city which provides endless material for his work.

CPSIA information can be obtained
at www.ICGtesting.com
Printed in the USA
JSHW012210110123
36156JS00001B/11